RENEGADE FLIGHT

ALSO BY ANDREA TANG

REBELWING

RENEGADE FLIGHT

ANDREA TANG

RAZORBILL

RAZORBILL

An imprint of Penguin Random House LLC, New York

First published in the United States of America by Razorbill,
an imprint of Penguin Random House LLC, 2021

Copyright © 2021 by Andrea Tang

LIBRARY OF CONGRESS CATALOGING-IN-PUBLICATION DATA
Names: Tang, Andrea, author.
Title: Renegade flight / Andrea Tang.
Description: New York : Razorbill, 2021. | Companion to: *Rebelwing.* |
Audience: Ages 12+. | Summary: Pilot-in-training Viola Park, a
probationary student at GAN Academy, enters a mech combat tournament
that becomes a fight for the future of Peacekeepers everywhere.
Identifiers: LCCN 2020049741 | ISBN 9781984835123 (hardcover) | ISBN
9781984835130 (trade paperback) | ISBN 9781984835147 (ebook)
Subjects: CYAC: Preparatory schools—Fiction. | Schools—Fiction. | Science fiction.
Classification: LCC PZ7.1.T3757 Rg 2021 | DDC [Fic]—dc23
LC record available at https://lccn.loc.gov/2020049741

Printed in the United States of America

1 3 5 7 9 10 8 6 4 2

Design by Jessica Jenkins.

Text set in Caslon.

For Dad, who has been my safe harbor, my mentor, and my stalwart lifelong champion. Also, more importantly, in the interest of filial piety and general parental fairness, I totally owe you a book dedication after dedicating the first one to Mom!

RENEGADE FLIGHT

THE BEGINNING OF THE END ─────── 1

The thing that pissed Vi off the most about ruining her life and dishonoring her family was the absurd amount of work she'd put into her own downfall.

Like most people who fucked themselves over, Vi had not actually woken up one morning and said to herself, "Ah, today's the day: commence Operation Fuck-Over!" She had, instead, very modestly planned on making her childhood dream come true. At no point was said childhood dream supposed to morph into a nightmare, much less one largely of her own making.

Later, much later, people would ask why she did it. Did she think she could get away with it? Did she ever wonder if she'd get caught? Did she even understand that what she did was wrong at all?

"It could have been avoided," some would cluck, or "How stupid, not to see how much trouble you'd create for yourself," or worst of all, "You should have known better." And Vi, with the benefit of hindsight, no matter how she turned the words over in her head, never came up with a satisfactory answer, except this: in the grand, toiling, earnestly misguided process of ruining her own life, she hadn't ever once considered what would happen next.

That was the thing about nightmares, after all. The worst were always the ones you never saw coming.

Dear Miss Viola Elizabeth Jiyeon Park,

It has been brought to the attention of the admissions committee of the Global Alliance of Nations Academy for Combat and Cybernetic Arts that you have been found guilty of improper tampering with the Tenth Annual Entrance Exams. Given the seriousness of this violation, you are hereby denied entry to the Academy and, furthermore, barred from additional attempts to sit any future entrance exam.

Appropriate representatives of the GAN Council and the GAN Academy, and members of the North American Barricade Coalition Board for Mech Pilot Certification, will convene in two weeks' time to determine the status of your current piloting license. Depending on the findings of our collective efforts, consequences of your misconduct may include the termination of your license.

With regards,

Karolyn Winchester, Headmaster, GAN Academy
Nolan Goldstein-Davies, Examiner
Fernando Diaz, Examiner
Jacinda Rogers, Examiner

◆

ONCE UPON A TIME, Viola Park had dreamed of ending wars and taming dragons. It wasn't such a farfetched goal, so far as childhood dreams went. After all, ending wars and taming dragons was a bit of a family business. People called the Parks a lot of things— defenders of democracy, if you loved them; Machiavellian assholes, if you hated them—but no one could deny that they were big fat overachievers when it came to warfare and politics. Theirs was an old, canny family of soldiers and politicians alike, as stalwart and seemingly indestructible as the North American cities where they'd made their home—or built their empire, depending on your perspective. Without the Parks, there would be no Global Alliance of Nations, and without the GAN, unscrupulous arms dealers— hand-selling their rogue battle bots and dangerously experimental AI—would have blown every last functioning government on Earth to smithereens by now.

Vi couldn't remember a point in her life when she couldn't name at least one family member serving in the GAN Peacekeeper Corps, and another sitting on the GAN Council. Parks protected what was theirs, whether it was a city, a continent, or the entire world. Vi's parents, both of them Peacekeeper pilots, had died for it. The aunts who'd taken her in afterward, one a GAN politician and the other a GAN mech engineer, had made it abundantly clear that it was the way of things in their clan: you lived to uphold GAN creed, or died trying. So the year Viola turned eighteen, it went without saying that she'd be sitting the entrance exams for the GAN Academy for Combat and Cybernetic Arts. She'd never really doubted she'd pass.

After all, that was the road map she'd been following her entire life, the GAN her eternal true north: attend New Columbia Prep for three years, earn straight As, turn eighteen, sit the GAN entrance exam, pass with flying colors on the first try, transfer to the Academy before senior year, graduate in another three, and go directly into a plum job among the Peacekeepers. It was easy to be certain of your destiny when no one had ever called it into question.

The Sunday morning before the exam was really when all that began to change.

Few things more obviously announced the arrival of certain individuals than the dramatic crescendo of a Tchaikovsky arrangement on the baby grand in the foyer. Vi, limbs akimbo beneath her duvet, smothered a few choice obscenities into a pillow before fumbling for her phone.

"Time," she croaked.

"It is currently eight o' clock A.M., Miss Park," replied her phone, obnoxiously crisp.

"It's Sunday," protested Vi.

"It is currently eight o'clock," agreed her phone. "A.M."

"A day of rest!"

"It is currently—"

Vi hurled the phone across her bed, along with the duvet, just as the dulcet sounds of the *Nutcracker* pas de deux swelled anew. "All right!" she yelled at the offending pianist. "You win! Goddammit! You win!"

The adagio, if anything, grew louder still, each note perfectly, delicately placed. "Fucker," muttered Vi. She threw a dressing gown over her shoulders, barely sliding into a pair of slippers, before slamming out of the bedroom. "You know one of my uncles was a former chief of intelligence for the North American Barricade Coalition, right?" she called, as she descended the swirling mahogany staircase. "If I wrote to him and promised to up my Christmas chocolates game, I bet I could have you murdered in your sleep."

"What a terrible stressor that would be for poor Jay," said the pianist over the final notes of the adagio. "Your slippers are mismatched, by the way."

"Your fault for dragging me out of bed! On a day of rest!" Vi tapped one red-slippered foot against her ankle, ignoring for the moment the hideous print of giggling cartoon dragons embroidered over the opposite foot. "I don't exactly have many of those right now, Alex. It's crunch time."

Alex played a little flourish across the keyboard. "Indeed."

"Crunch time for the GAN Academy entrance exams, I mean."

"I'm aware."

"The Academy for Combat and Cybernetic Arts!"

"I don't believe there's another GAN Academy, no."

"So why are you waking me up before noon on a Sunday!"

Alex's hands stilled, along with the music. At last, he looked up the staircase to where Vi stood. Vi, fuming at the railing in her dressing gown and hideous mismatched slippers, glared at him. They froze for a moment like that.

Then Alex burst into peals of laughter.

"Oh, fuck you very much," groused Vi. Her hair was probably a disaster. "If my idiot classmates knew what a troll you were under your whole sensitive musician act, they'd scrap all their tacky 3-D pinup posters of your stupid face faster than I can shoot a plasma rifle."

"Why on earth does a pinup poster of all things need a 3-D edition?" asked Alex. Between all his dumbass cackles, he sounded genuinely puzzled.

"I love that *that's* your takeaway question about all this. Aren't you, like, thirty now?" Vi leaned over the railing, stretching out the cracks in her spine with a wince. That's what she got for five hours of sleep after three hours of mech fighting practice. "Isn't that a little old for the whole teen heartthrob schtick?"

"I'm twenty-nine, thank you, chiquitita, and still younger than the actors they've got playing your fellow sixteen-year-olds on those wireless dramas you love so much."

"I'm eighteen!" Vi hugged her dressing gown over her chest, cheeks flaming. "And I watch those ironically!"

"I wasn't judging." Her uninvited houseguest raised his hands in surrender, a smile creasing the corners of twinkling dark eyes. "Watch anything you like, so long as you remember to practice your scales. Speaking of which, Academy exams or no, you have a piano lesson."

"Today? Now?" Vi raked a hand through her bedhead, irritation warring with a horrifyingly tender nostalgia she didn't care to examine too closely. Alex wasn't a Park by blood or marriage, but he was probably the closest thing she had to consistently present family. He'd been her music teacher since she was too small to reach the piano pedals, a tutor for hire on paper but, in reality, something halfway between doting older brother and mischievous young uncle. "How am I supposed to deal with piano scales when I still don't have a battle mech simulation picked out to perform?"

Alex shrugged. "To quote your esteemed aunt Anabel, 'That sounds like a you problem.'" He tapped his chin, contemplative. "What was it exactly she said again? Oh yes, 'Cutthroat fights between giant robots may be stupidly important to geopolitics right now, but they are no excuse to neglect culture.'" He actually did a pretty credible imitation of Aunt Anabel's voice.

Vi scowled, shifting from one foot to the other. The looming entrance exam had left a small but steadily growing knot in her belly from the day the dates were announced. The reminder of Aunt Anabel's general existence did not loosen it. "Where is she, anyway?"

"Anabel?" Alex's handsome face did something complicated. "The usual, I suppose. On top secret state business for the GAN Council."

"Surprise," muttered Vi.

"Hey, chiquitita," said Alex. His voice had gone all gentle and knowing, in that way it always did whenever Vi hit a mood. "You know Anabel loves you, right? Your aunt took you under her wing for a reason."

"Yeah." Vi stared at the dragons on the one slipper. "I needed to be someone's ward on paper, I guess, and any of my cousins would kill to be Aunt Anabel's. And I—she knows I'm a good pilot. I'd be a credit to her, as a Peacekeeper-to-be. It's a fair exchange."

Alex sighed. "One day, you and I are going to have words about what literal children do and don't owe their legal guardians."

"I'm eighteen!" protested Vi.

"Barely. And you're Anabel's niece, not a weapon or a political pawn." Alex stood and stretched his fingers. "Now, how's your Debussy piece coming along?"

"Um," said Vi.

The music teacher's brows arched. "Have you practiced this week?"

"Yes."

"How many hours?"

Vi tried, frantically, to think of a number he would buy. "Six!"

The eyebrows only climbed higher.

"Three?"

"Vi."

"Okay, so I'm lying; I practiced exactly zero hours, but could you blame me? It's crunch time for—"

"The Academy entrance exams. I'm aware." Alex gave her a long, inscrutable look. "There's more to life than mech piloting, you know. Even the chance at piloting a dragon for the Peacekeeper Corps."

Vi snorted. "Like what, becoming some bohemian singer-songwriter with a niche following of teen girls and a side hustle as a really annoying piano teacher? Is that why you quit the Peacekeeper Corps?"

She regretted the words as soon as they left her mouth. Alex's face, always so expressive, shuttered as he fell silent. He never talked about it, and the gossip columns had eventually piped down, but back in the day, Alex quitting the Peacekeepers had been a big deal. You couldn't really tell now, with his rumpled hair and big lumpy grandpa sweaters, but Vi's music teacher had been destined for greater things, once upon a time. He'd been nephew to the first Head Representative of the North American Barricade Coalition, a top-notch student at one of the best prep schools on the continent—and by all reports, the finest mech pilot of his generation. No one knew exactly why he'd thrown that all away before the age of thirty to pen semi-obscure love songs and teach music theory to teenagers, but it had been a slap in the face to the GAN. Some called it selfishness. Others called it madness.

Vi wondered, sometimes, in her more shameful moments, if Alex had quit simply because he was a coward. Then she'd remember every time he'd ever fixed her a plate of chilaquiles after a recital, or tucked her into bed when her aunts were away, or simply existed in her life, all careworn smile and dancing fingers at a piano bench, his warmth steadfast and dependable.

She always hated herself so much for thinking that Alex might deserve her disdain.

"It's not just the piano. I also teach guitar lessons sometimes," he said at last, voice mild. If she'd offended him, he gave no sign. "But since your mind is clearly more wrapped up in mechs than music for the moment, why don't we switch gears?"

Vi blinked, surprised, straightening her spine. "You want to do a round of mech sparring?" She'd never seen her music teacher in action, but she'd heard the stories, and seen some of his old combat simulation reels. She could learn a lot more from him than how to play Debussy, but he'd never once offered to train with her, and every time she'd asked, he'd always had an excuse ready. By her midteens, she'd given up on ever getting his help.

"Lord, no." The corner of Alex's mouth tipped upward. "I'm going to make hot cocoa." He laughed at the look on her face. "You're welcome to go beat up giant robots instead, of course, but there will be an extra mug of my mother's old Mexican recipe waiting on the counter." His eyebrows waggled. "With marshmallows."

"I like marshmallows," Vi allowed grudgingly. They were, at any rate, immensely preferable to Debussy. "Can I still pick your brain about the giant robots?"

She wasn't sure if she imagined the pause before his almost too-casual reply: "If you insist."

She followed him to the kitchen. "What was your exam like, when you joined the Peacekeepers?"

"What exam?" Alex chortled, as he poured milk into a saucepan. "We'd barely just figured out that sentient mechs were even possible to engineer, and all the governments of the world were in a panic over how to put the genie back in the bottle. You can't, of course. Once one engineer proves it can be done, it's not long before everyone else is doing it too, for good or ill."

Vi squinted at him, thoughtful. "Is it true that you helped fly the first sentient? The one dragon that became the prototype for the whole GAN fleet?"

The stirring paused, for just a beat. "Rebelwing. Yes." Another pause. "I wasn't the primary pilot, though."

"Prudence Wu," Vi acknowledged, very carefully. The name carried a heady sort of reverence when spoken aloud. The first of the dragon pilots. The first human who'd known how it felt to meld her own mind with a sentient's and to take flight. It didn't really matter how many other pilots would go on to do the same, and do it better: Prudence Wu would always be revered, because Prudence Wu had been first. It was kind of unfair, if you really thought about it.

A lot of the details around the Battle of Jellicoe's Giant were fuzzy. It had been a covert op, one of many in the endless North American skirmishes between the continent's fragile surviving government—the Barricade Coalition, smallest but oldest member nation of the GAN—and an encroaching megacorporation. The names of the operatives supporting Wu had been struck from public record—even Alex's. The simulation pared the battle down to its barest, most brutal bones: a weakened dragon, fending off a surprise attack from a stronger, battle-tested opponent.

But if Vi knew anything, it was tactical context, and she'd studied enough reports of the battle to read between the lines. Wu and Rebelwing had been leading a raid on a corporate compound, which had gone tits up well before Jellicoe's Giant arrived on the scene. Vi didn't know the details, but she knew there'd been an explosion, and dead operatives: good soldiers ostensibly there to support Wu. Her inexperience had gotten them killed, and forced Rebelwing into a fight she wasn't ready for.

Vi didn't think she imagined the movements of the saucepan slowing. When Alex spoke, though, his voice was light and neutral. "Why the interest in Rebelwing and her . . . pilots?"

"I'm thinking about using it. For my simulation piece."

Alex blinked. Very slowly, he looked up from the saucepan. "You mean—"

"I'm ready for the written exam," Vi blurted out, avoiding his eyes. "And I know I can nail the physical. But plenty of would-be cadets score fine on the written and physical, and still get rejected from the Academy because they fail the simulation. I can't let that happen." Of the three components of the Academy entrance exam, the simulation was notorious. Aunt Anabel called it the audition piece. Every prospective cadet picked from an inventory of approved dragon-flight simulations plucked from history. With the twitch of a button, you could sit in the cockpit of Storm's Fury—who had led a GAN squad against one of the early cyborg pirate attacks on the ports of Shanghai—or Firebird, during the defense of Paris.

Or, if you were either especially arrogant or especially nuts, you could choose to pilot Rebelwing. The first of the dragons. The one that had perished on her maiden flight into battle against Jellicoe's Giant.

"I need to make a statement with this piece," said Vi. "Any idiot with the slightest proficiency for sentient AI bonding can pilot a speed cruiser like Firebird, or a high-tech bruiser like Storm's Fury. But no one ever auditions in Rebelwing's cockpit."

"Because successfully piloting a simulation of the Battle of Jellicoe's Giant is astronomically hard."

"But not impossible," countered Vi.

"Most students who pilot the Jellicoe's Giant sim—which, mind you, is already a slim number—die," said Alex bluntly. "Only virtually, of course, but virtual reality deaths have sent plenty of cadets to the therapist's office, and for good reason."

"You and Prudence Wu both survived the real thing."

"Barely. Be careful, that's hot," warned Alex, as he passed her a steaming mug. "And you, Viola Park, are many extraordinary things, but you are not Prudence Wu." He grinned. "Nor are you me."

"Yeah, thank god for that." Vi scoffed. "Still, at least you have real skills. Wu is only lauded because she was the first pilot to bond a sentient mech, and crashed it spectacularly on her first go, I might add. What's she done since?"

"Held the GAN record for number of successfully flown covert rescue ops for the past five years," said Alex mildly. "We were all rookies once. Anyway, students avoid using the Battle of Jellicoe's Giant for the simulation piece because it's an unfair fight that forces you to showcase your weaknesses when you're meant to be showcasing your strengths. Not the best audition material. How's your cocoa?"

Vi breathed in the steam wafting from the mug, and took a sip. "Mmm." As ever, the chocolate, rich and warm and slightly spiced, was just sweet enough for Vi's taste. "Better than your pep-talking skills, at any rate. I know that the Battle of Jellicoe's Giant is rigged against Rebelwing's pilot. But what if I evened the odds?"

Alex's brow furrowed. "Evened the odds?"

"It's not against the rules," said Vi, "to know how to tweak a sim."

"But it is against the rules to act on that knowledge," said Alex.

"No, it's against the rules to manipulate the final results of a simulation to pull a miracle victory out of your ass," retorted Vi. "Chill, Alex. I'm not going to hack a code to, like, magically revive my mech if I get shot down or something. Just to let me prep for the Battle of Jellicoe's Giant the way Wu should have. The way *I* would have. That means approaching Jellicoe's Giant with a plan— anticipating the problems that took Wu by surprise. Being ready for them. Being prepared, god, just being better prepared; that alone would have saved lives." Vi paused for breath. "Whatever happens after that . . . happens."

"That's a slippery slope, and you know it," said Alex. "If the board of examiners catches you, they still might—"

Vi shrugged. "So I won't get caught. No big."

"Viola." Alex's voice had taken on a teacher's warning tone. "That's not—"

"Students who get rejected from the Academy usually get

rejected on the basis of their simulation scores—not because they don't do well on the sim, but because they don't take enough risks. There's nothing about piloting the Firebirds or Storm's Furies of the world that lets you *stand out*. What if I happen to miss one of the written-exam questions? What if I'm injured in a freak accident on the physical and fuck up one of the obstacles? I'll need my audition to make up for the lost points, and putting on a competent, respectable, but frankly *boring* show in the combat sim won't give me the insurance I need." Vi's fingers tightened on the mug. "I can't take the risk of *not* taking a risk. Do you understand that? I have to get into the Academy, Alex. I have to prove I'm—it's what I've wanted since I was little. It's all I've ever wanted."

Alex was already shaking his head, as he collected empty cookware for the sink. Vi didn't know why he bothered, when the Park family manor was equipped with maids of both the organic and AI variety, but a domestic chore habit was probably the least of his eccentricities. "You don't need to pick the Academy's most tactically difficult and psychologically harrowing simulation to make your case to the examiners." The side of his mouth curled upward. It wasn't quite a grimace, but it wasn't a smile either. "Take it from someone who lived through the real thing."

That, at least, guilted Vi into shutting up for a few seconds. But only a few. "I'm not trying to discount what you survived," she said. "But what kind of Academy candidate would I be if I weren't willing to take on the stuff that scares everyone else? What kind of Peacekeeper?"

Alex sighed. "Being a Peacekeeper isn't about always flying the flashiest fight, or bonding the biggest, baddest dragon. In fact, it rarely is. It's easy to romanticize, because so much of being a Peacekeeper is about thinking—and acting—outside the box to do what might otherwise seem impossible."

"So you agree," said Vi triumphantly. "Peacekeepers have to be willing to innovate. To face their fears."

"Yes," said Alex guardedly. "But always with an eye toward the why. It's not about guts and glory for the sake of guts and glory. At the end of the day, it's about . . ." He trailed off, twisting a dish towel between his hands.

"What?"

"Protecting people," said Alex. "When no one else can."

The back of Vi's throat knotted up. Laypeople and netizens had a nickname for Peacekeepers, sometimes spoken with awe, sometimes spoken with ironic derision, depending on your political feelings about the GAN, but either way, it stuck: the knights of the Alliance. Vi had always found it kind of hokey, but she got why the name caught on. Plain old fighter mech pilots were a dime a dozen these days, but the blueprints for building dragons had always remained exclusive to the GAN's engineers. Only those who could bond sentient mechs could become Peacekeepers— and only Peacekeepers could fly dragons. The chosen steeds of the GAN's mighty, painstakingly assembled fighting force, tasked with protecting the world from its own worst nature.

No matter what the cost.

With an effort, Vi swallowed the knot. "Is that what you did when you threw your lot in with Prudence Wu all those years ago?"

Alex's head bowed. It shaded his face for a moment, hiding his expression. "It's what we tried to do."

Vi didn't miss the pronoun shift. *We*, not *I*. It annoyed her, probably a little irrationally. Prudence Wu had always been larger than life: the girl who'd been a hero at seventeen, the girl who'd first flown a dragon, the girl who'd stopped a war. So much was said about Prudence Wu—or speculated, or rumored, or mythologized—that it was difficult to imagine her as an actual flesh-and-blood human being. Even Vi, with all her family's connections to the GAN's knights, had never really met the woman, recluse that Wu was. It cemented the first of the dragon pilots in Vi's head less as a person and more as a concept, like one of those propaganda figures that authoritarian regimes liked trotting out to hold normal citizens to impossible standards. *Be more like Prudence Wu: work hard, be brave, do right by your government.* A measuring stick against which anyone would be found wanting.

Alex, though. Alex was real. Alex was constant. And Alex, for better or worse, had been a steady block in the foundations of Vi's life for as long as she could remember. She'd known, intellectually, that he had been a part of the Rebelwing mission, and must have met Wu. But something about mixing her dumb music teacher up with a person who felt as distant and fantastical as Wu in Vi's head just didn't sit right.

"Would you do things differently now?" Vi asked Alex abruptly. "If you were to fly Rebelwing again. If you got another chance."

His answering smile was wry and immediate. "I know better than to go down that road. Hindsight is always twenty-twenty. Peacekeepers have to look forward, yeah? Even the retired ones. You know what they say—pilots stop living for themselves when they step into the cockpit of a GAN dragon, and start living for the world."

Or dying for the world. Like Vi's parents had.

"I know Peacekeeper creed," said Vi, more defensively than she meant to. Her voice was a little hoarse. "Better than most." The last of the cocoa scalded her throat on the way down, but Vi swallowed it anyway. "Thanks for the chocolate. I'm going to go study."

She left Alex standing alone in the kitchen with their empty mugs, the dish towel tossed over one of his shoulders. Something unfathomable lurked behind those kind dark eyes.

Vi thought it might have been regret.

◆

IN THE SAFETY OF HER bedroom, Vi stared, for the hundredth time, at the sample simulation she'd pulled up on the 3-D holo-monitor. The pieces were simple enough: a metal beast, valiantly beating its wings despite failing fuel and dwindling plasma fire reserves. A hulking war mech several times its size, tailored for mindless destruction. The makings of a tragedy, or at least a bittersweet ending.

The thing was, Vi had a plan to turn the tide of the Battle of Jellicoe's Giant.

She'd studied it from every possible angle. Alex was right: the simulation forced you to fight at a horrific disadvantage. That Prudence Wu had taken out the real Jellicoe's Giant—that she'd survived at all—was nothing short of a minor miracle, a real David and Goliath story. Wu had lost her mech, but she'd saved the day.

Vi was going to do Prudence Wu one better.

People liked talking to Vi about her dead parents. It was a whole thing. It was always easier to call people heroes after they were already dead, and Vi's parents were no exception. Prudence Wu had been just like them—a pilot who'd been forced to make sacrifices for the sake of some amorphous greater good.

Sacrifice was a cheat, so far as Vi was concerned. Vi was better than that, and she'd prove it, for all the GAN to see. Her audition would show the truth plain and simple: that Vi wasn't some half-trained schoolgirl, like Wu had been. She was a Park. She didn't lose, and she didn't let people die. All she had to do was tweak the sim settings just a touch. Messing with the sim settings was usually a pretty big no-no—most people looking to do it were trying to rewrite the sim entirely, to get the system to do all their work for them. Vi would never dream of anything so egregious. Vi's tweak was only that: a tweak, nothing more. Just enough to equip herself with the resources Wu had been too impulsive and thoughtless to leverage.

Was it entirely legal, even so? Maybe not on a technicality, but no one ever got in trouble on technicalities, so long as the final result was worth it. And this would be worth it, to create the audition piece of a lifetime. The Academy wouldn't be able to say no, not to the girl who'd figured out how to make the Battle of Jellicoe's Giant winnable. How to save every life that had been lost that day. How to do what even the legendary Wu couldn't, and put an end to the GAN's cold, hard creed of martyred sacrifice.

Vi's fingers paused over the simulation codes. *Are you sure?* The gentle prod of doubt in her head sounded suspiciously like Alex's voice. *It's like you said. You'll score enough points on the written and physical—probably. You've been literally groomed for this all your life. You could coast through the audition on another flawless, boring little antipiracy simulation without losing another wink of sleep, and you'd still have a decent shot at getting in. Probably. Is this really worth the risk?*

Yes, Vi wanted to hiss back. *"Probably" isn't good enough. And the only way to turn "probably" into "definitely" is by delivering an extraordinary audition.*

Vi stared at the hovering figure of Wu's dragon. Rebelwing's design looked comparatively clunky now, next to the sleek new upgrades of the modern-day GAN fleet, yet the beast remained strangely lovely, all chrome-plated scales and intelligent reptilian eyes.

Vi thought of Wu's dead operatives, their names lost to history, and for one jarring moment, she was nine, and eleven, and fourteen, feasting in honor of cousins trickling their way dutifully through the Academy doors, while the ghosts of Vi's parents sat on her shoulders, half-expectant, half-accusatory.

"Yes," she whispered aloud now to Wu's doomed, beautiful, obsolete mech. "Yes, it's worth it."

It was really such a small tweak. Vi's fingers pulled the simulation codes apart like one of her piano concertos, and prepared to rewrite history.

2 —————————————— THE NEW NORMAL

Of course, all Vi's lofty imaginings—the brilliant correction of a bloody history, an ingenious way around frankly stupid exam parameters, the chance to outshine a legend—were, to put it lightly, not how the GAN wound up seeing her trespasses.

When Vi first read their letter, she thought, hilariously, that it was spam mail. What else could it be? She'd done everything her family had ever encouraged: taken a calculated risk, designed to reward her with proof of her own hard-won skill. It was what Academy students did. It was what Peacekeepers did. How could you punish someone for doing precisely what they'd been trained to?

The morning after Vi was accused of defrauding the GAN and barred entrance from the only thing in life that had ever mattered, she did the only thing her body still wanted to: she went looking for a fight.

Two, to be exact. The first was more important: a message to Aunt Anabel. Like any good Park's, Vi's first line of defense was always herself, but when push came to shove, a Park girl could always call on the resources of the family, and Anabel Park was a trump card in a stacked deck. Vi was no cheat. What happened during the exam had been a simple misunderstanding. The GAN had clearly taken one look at Vi's little tweak in the sim, and—without bothering to pay attention to context, or all the extra work Vi had done—immediately lumped her in with real cheaters, the ones who lazily manipulated the entire sim to automate their victories. Vi was nothing like those guys, and the board of examiners had obviously overreacted. If Vi herself couldn't make the GAN see that, then Aunt Anabel's notoriously silver tongue—not to mention friends on the Council—would drive the message home personally.

The second fight, Vi picked entirely for her own satisfaction. After all, convincing the GAN she wasn't a fuckup meant nothing if she couldn't back her words up with actions.

She had to show them she could still fly. Which meant proving it to herself first.

And why is that? whispered the traitorous voice in the back of her mind. *Do you doubt it now? Does some part of you think the Academy made the right choice?*

Never, Vi wanted to snarl back, even though one of her hands— clenched tight around the keys to a family-owned mech training facility—had begun to shake. She ignored it. Mouth pulled thin, she lengthened her stride, as she ducked out past the house, walking past the green manicured lawns of the estate until they melted away into skyscraping concrete and chrome. Vi's feet started up a jog, as she lost herself to the comforting chaos of meaningless urban noise. The city of New Columbia hadn't been initially designed with giant robots in mind, but after the first two times North American civil wars had nearly razed it, architects and engineers grew wise. Dragon-friendly landing pads now populated every other street corner, nearly as common as metro stops. Mech training facilities specializing in combat partnered with boutique gyms and fitness studios, catering to everyone from professional fighter pilots to dilettantes with enough money to buy the fantasy of training like a real live GAN Peacekeeper.

The Parks owned three mech training facilities, all told: one across the continent in Vancouver that taught basic combat skills to civilians who could afford the tuition; one overseas in Seoul, partnered with the local GAN consulate, exclusive to Peacekeepers stationed on the Korean peninsula; and one right here in New Columbia, partnered with both a hand-to-hand combat training hall and a weapons barrack, exclusive to family members who'd learned to bond sentients. The Peacekeeper hopefuls. The ones that had once counted Vi among their ranks.

And still did, if Vi had anything to say about it. Muscle memory straightened her spine as she swiped her key across the heavy double doors of the great dome. They slid aside with a hum. Vi's shoulders relaxed, ever so slightly. At least her damn keys still recognized her.

Now she just had to choose a mech. Swallowing, she marched down the hall, toward the stables, trying to ignore the clench of her belly. She paused at the third gate, resting her palm at the hinge. Then she steeled herself, and swiped her key a second time.

The mech waiting inside didn't have quite the stature of a GAN dragon. Her silver eyes stared out from more feline features, and her teeth were longer and sharper. Vi tried to smile at those jaws, which widened in the mechanical equivalent of a yawn. Or a display of appetite for violence. It could really go either way with the Lioness.

"Hey there, Your Majesty," said Vi. "I'm here to prove a point to . . . well, to myself, really. Want to help?" Maybe the GAN could strip her piloting license on a whim, but before they had a chance, Vi would force herself to remember what really mattered: no power on the planet could strip her cockpit skills from her.

The Lioness leaned forward, teeth still bared. For a moment, Vi held her breath. The Lioness was the favored mech for pilots-in-training who needed practice bonding a creature who really did think for herself, for better or worse. She wouldn't allow just any bond, and even if she'd allow yours, that was no guarantee that she wouldn't simply empty you out of the cockpit if she didn't like your ideas. That unpredictability, according to Vi's older cousins, was precisely what made the Lioness perfect for GAN hopefuls. You couldn't fly a dragon if you were afraid of the unknown. Before you earned your right to the sky, you had to prove your mettle on the ground.

Vi stared into those silver eyes. "You don't scare me, Your Majesty," she said.

In that moment, she even meant it.

The Lioness took her at her word, bowing her metal-maned head. Chrome retracted down the length of the mech's spine, as she offered Vi the cockpit. Vi exhaled once, quickly, and bit her lip against the absurd grin threatening to spill all over her face. The Lioness had allowed Vi the bond a hundred times before, but she'd also dumped Vi on her ass more than once. For a lion-modeled mech, she had remarkably little patience for human indulgence in pride.

Vi closed her eyes, exhaling more slowly this time, just like she'd been taught in her basics. The tenets of early training ran through her head like a prayer. Concentrate on your breathing. Calm your mind. The mech will sense your intent, so make sure you're certain of what you want.

Vi opened her eyes to the Lioness's world. Piloting a real sentient was something even audition sims couldn't quite replicate, not perfectly. Literally sharing the mind of another living, thinking creature—even an artificially created one—was a jolt of adrenaline specific to the experience of each mech, moment to moment. Staring through the view screen of the Lioness's eyes heightened the definition of the world around them both: sunlight winking off the plexiglass reinforcements on the stable gates, the great silver dome of the ceiling above, and the winding hallway leading toward the training yards.

Vi leaned forward among the shifting links of chrome that cradled her in the cockpit, waking up her muscles. She stretched her arms. Chrome claws flexed and clicked beneath the touch of her hands, responding to the steady strength of her mind. *Let's go*, she prodded the Lioness gently. The Lioness tossed her head, balking at the command more on contrary principle than genuine reluctance.

Come on, coaxed Vi. *I'll make it worth your while.*

The Lioness considered this. Vi took advantage of the moment to give the mech another mental nudge. It was just enough. As one, they began trotting toward the training yard. Vi's heartbeat fluttered gently against her ribcage. A bubble of relief she hadn't wanted to admit to ballooned to life. Of course she hadn't lost her affinity. She could still do this: meld her mind to a mech's, and make herself more than what she could be alone. Here, in the Lioness's cockpit, Vi could still find calm at the eye of a stormy world.

Before the exam, Vi had rarely gone longer than two days without piloting. Time in the cockpit had been almost as much a part of her daily routine as eating and sleeping, and the only things that kept her from training had been family events, injuries, and very occasionally,

Alex's piano recitals. In the days leading up to the exam, Vi had put more hours into the cockpit than ever. She'd only allowed herself a week off after sitting the exam, assuming her acceptance letter would send her back to the training yards, freshly motivated to kick some ass at her Academy matriculation. Now that week felt like it might as well have been a month of layoff from her usual training routine. The Lioness may have accepted her bond, but that was only half the work. How well they moved together—right now, with Vi's nerves thoroughly frayed and her temper unusually short—remained to be seen. If it had been a normal training session, Vi might have dove right into advanced simulation sparring without a care for warm-up. This time, she opted for caution, starting with the most basic training exercises. A few easy laps around the yard, picking up speed, before moving into simple combat exercises. The Lioness wasn't equipped with either flight or plasma fire like a dragon would be, so target practice wasn't a necessity, but the mech was well designed for brutish, close-quarters fights, which suited Vi's mood just fine. Vi had already queued up the hologram opponent: a big humanoid robot, with scythes in place of arms. Medium-level speed and agility. Challenging, but not too challenging.

The hologram burst to life as Vi completed the last of her warm-up routines. "All right, Your Majesty," Vi murmured aloud. "Let's see if we've still got it."

The scythes swept into her sight line before the robot did, a pale flash across the Lioness's view screen. As one, Vi and her mech ducked low, just inside the robot's guard. The Lioness's steely claws jammed themselves into the delicate cables between scythe and body. "Bye-bye," said Vi cheerfully, as one of the blades fell free. It tumbled to the floor of the training yard with a spectacular crash.

Vi grinned, the click of her teeth savage, as she wheeled the Lioness around to slip under the remaining scythe. "Oh no, you don't."

The Lioness pounced, but the robot wasn't deemed a midlevel melee opponent for nothing. This time, the mech's claws struck thin air. "Easy, easy," murmured Vi, as the Lioness tossed her head in frustration, metal haunches tensed. "Overconfidence won't do us any favors, Your Majesty."

After all, Vi had learned that particular lesson the hard way.

Her grin faltered at the thought.

The Lioness's sudden roar sent a shot of adrenaline straight through the lapse in Vi's attention. The cockpit clenched around Vi. "Shit!" Like a rubber band rebounding, her mind snapped back into the present moment, five seconds too late.

The second scythe had embedded itself in the Lioness's shoulder, the pain of it searing through both their minds. Swearing, Vi wrenched them both sideways, jerking metal plating free of the weapon, but their opponent wasn't done. The robot raised the scythe a second time.

"Dodge!" Vi screamed aloud.

Damage from a hologram wasn't real, much less permanent, but it was designed to feel that way to maximize the efficacy of training. The Lioness, now favoring a shoulder that would have been blown out by damaged wiring and loose circuits, was done taking Vi's orders. Roaring again, the mech rushed the robot. Straight toward that recovered scythe.

In that moment, Vi had, for once, no real certainty what the old Vi would have done. She might have regained control over the bond, and forced the mech to retreat, or dodge, or do pretty much anything that didn't involve being impaled a second time on the business end of a combat bot's blade. She might have counterattacked. She might have, perhaps most wisely of all, slammed the emergency hologram shutdown, and ended this whole catastrophe right then and there.

The new Vi did none of these things. The new Vi was, in fact, far too tired to give a shit. Her eyes squeezed shut. She braced for impact. At least this stupid, ill-advised exercise would be over soon, one way or another.

The impact didn't arrive. Instead, the Lioness's abrupt halt sent Vi jerking against the restraints in the cockpit. "Ow! What the hell!" With the automatic certainty of long practice, she reached for the mech's bond.

Only to find it missing. Heart climbing into her throat, Vi tried again, quieting her own mind. Nothing. She couldn't sense the Lioness at all. Frantically, Vi knocked a fist against the sides of the cockpit. "Hey! Hello?"

No response. The lights of the view screen had dimmed. The robot was gone. Someone had shut down mech and hologram alike from the outside.

Which meant Vi was no longer alone in the facility.

Pulse roaring in her ears, Vi let instinct take over. Kicking out the cockpit hatch beneath her, she fumbled her way out of the mech, into the dim-lit, metallic expanse of the training yard. She landed bent kneed on solid ground, hands up, cursing the moment she'd decided not to strap a plasma gun inside her jacket. Even one of the utility knives Aunt Anabel had gifted her for Christmas—with their comforting military-issue, razor-thin precision edges—would have lent her some sense of safety, or at least control.

Vi's life always seemed to be spinning out of control without her permission these days.

The lights flickered on. Footsteps landed behind her. Vi whirled, only to find her arm caught between chrome-plated, mechanical fingers. "Viola!"

Vi stopped struggling, and blinked into a pair of familiar, mismatched eyes. "Aunt Cat?"

The chief engineer of the GAN did not release Viola's arm. "Breathe, Viola."

Vi tugged weakly against her aunt's grip. "I am—"

"You are not. Breathe properly, girl, that's it. Inhale. Good. Yes, slowly. Now exhale."

Vi, conditioned by a lifetime under the disciplinarian thumb of steel-voiced aunties, obeyed. Slowly, her ears stopped roaring. The pounding in her veins slowed, as her heart gave up its adrenaline-fueled staccato sprint. "I'm sorry," said Vi. "I don't know why I reacted like that. I should have known it was just you."

Cat snorted. "I'm the last person in the world who will reprimand you for vigilance, Viola. Besides," she added, almost offhand, "I know an anxiety attack when I see one."

"That's not—" Vi began, defensive.

Cat lifted her other hand, the one still flesh-made, cutting off the protest. "I am not here to judge."

It probably said something unflattering about the past week of Vi's life, how surprising that was. She blinked at her aunt like an idiot. "You're not?"

"No." No sense of either comfort or pity in the word, just a statement of fact. It was how Aunt Cat had always operated. She studied Vi for a moment, that famous silver cybernetic eye of hers winking alongside the darker one, both crinkled beneath the furrow of her coppery brows. "Anabel and I have been kept busy by a greater-than-average amount of petty political nonsense at GAN headquarters. We haven't made the time to see much of you lately, and now—"

Vi aimed her face into an approximation of self-deprecation. "I'm a political disgrace?"

"I said I wasn't here to judge," said Aunt Cat. "I meant it. I am, however, here to offer some advice."

Vi snorted. "You sound like Aunt Anabel."

"I did marry her," said Aunt Cat wryly. "Which is why I also caught wind of that little note you sent her. Have you seen Anabel yet?"

"No," said Vi. Her voice was small. She hated sounding small. She cleared her throat. "I'm sure that conversation is going to be a bucket of fun."

Aunt Cat snorted. "So you already have some prediction of what it will entail."

Vi shrugged. "Aunt Anabel is predictable. At least in some ways. Mostly the terrifying ones."

Aunt Cat cracked a grin at that. "Which is why I'm here to tell you something she won't, when you do next see her."

Vi's pulse had been returning slowly to its normal speed. That little tidbit kicked it right back into gear. "Oh?" She aimed for cool voiced, and landed just short of a croak. "And what's that?"

"When it comes to dealing with all things GAN," said Aunt Cat, "check your ego at the door."

"What's that supposed to mean?"

"What it sounds like." Vi nearly crossed her eyes, as Aunt Cat tapped one no-nonsense metal finger against Vi's nose. "Forget about the Academy for the moment. Perhaps you'll remain barred from its hallowed halls. If my wife works her signature magic on the school officials, perhaps not."

Ruthlessly, Vi crushed the unexpected, desperate flutter of optimism beating against her ribcage. "I don't—"

Aunt Cat barreled right over her half-hearted protestations. "Regardless of whether you remain a civilian student at New Columbia Prep, or matriculate as a cadet at the GAN Academy, I'm going to assume my wife intends to provide you with her particular, ambiguous brand of cheerful Machiavellian wisdom. Anabel will most likely tell you—oh, let's see—to take advantage of being at a new school, where people only know your name, and may know of your shame, but don't yet know you, Viola Park, as a person. Reap the benefits of the more-or-less blank slate to charm your cohort, never deign to respond to insults or rumors, avoid encouraging negativity, and forge friendships on the basis of genuine goodwill, but choose them strategically, because they'll be your staunchest allies in the event of scandal, hardship, or general disaster. Do you disagree so far?"

Mutely, Vi shook her head.

"I thought not," said Aunt Cat smugly. "Now, sweet Alexandre, on the other hand, will tell you to care for yourself and others with a gentle hand. In the event that you do find yourself wearing a cadet's flight suit, he'll ask you to focus on cultivating truth behind the Peacekeepers' wonderfully chivalrous nonsense about protecting those who cannot protect themselves, or whatever romantic frippery all that recruitment propaganda always spouts. He'll tell you that you can't control what others do, but that you can control your own actions, and that defying cruelty with kindness is a difficult but steadfast form of strength. Also true, in your estimation?"

At Vi's slightly fishlike mouth, Aunt Cat grinned, bright toothed and wolfish. "I love my wife, and I love your ridiculous music teacher, more than almost anyone else in the world, but that also means knowing them perhaps better than they know themselves. They're both clever and wise and fundamentally good-hearted, and they both, more importantly, love you. That tells me something of what they're going to impart to you. None of their advice will be bad, per se. But those two were also born and raised behind the walls of wealthy Barricade Coalition cities, coddled by family luxury. It colors their perspective."

"And yours?" prompted Vi. For someone who'd raised her, Aunt Cat had always been impressively close-lipped about her own history. Vi only knew the bare bones: Cat had grown up under the eye of cruel-handed, profit-obsessed factory supervisors in a corporate labor camp, in the southwest of North America. It was where she'd learned her remarkable engineering skill, before her escape and defection to the democratic Barricader government, but it was also where she'd lost an eye, an arm, and a family. Aunt Anabel was the wiliest person Vi knew, and Alex perhaps the kindest, but Aunt Cat knew better than anyone how to weather the worst of life's brutalities, one after another, without either self-pity or self-deceit. How to exist amid bleakness, armed with nothing but yourself, and persist all the same.

"Don't fear your own shame," said Aunt Cat.

Vi's head snapped toward her aunt. "What?"

"Anabel thinks that shame ought to be concealed or spun into something else, and Alexandre that shame ought to be apologized or atoned for. It never occurs to either of them to simply allow shame to exist for what it is: an inevitability of the human condition." Cat's expression was terribly wry. "How do you suppose the fine, progressive, upstanding people of New Columbia, crown jewel of the North American Barricade cities, reacted to a former Incorporated engineer in their midst?" She tapped the corner of her own cybernetic eye for emphasis.

"You were a child," said Vi in heated tones, suddenly angry on her aunt's behalf. "None of what the Incorporated assholes did to North America was your fault, and you got the worst of it, besides! Alex and Aunt Anabel, they . . . they never would have held that against you." Vi couldn't imagine it. Not with the fond tilt to Alex's mouth when he talked about Cat's latest creations in the labs. Not with the way Aunt Anabel kicked off her heels to stand on tiptoe and embrace her wife, wordless, breathing her in after a long day.

"Alexandre and Anabel were two people in a city of thousands," said Aunt Cat, her voice dry. "Suffice to say that I became quite accustomed to being the object of rumor and gossip at best, and blatant harassment at worst." She spread her hands, one flesh, one metal. "Sometimes, you cannot manipulate others into forgetting the worst parts of you; nor can you bear to turn the other cheek with a smile. So you wear your shame as armor. You take the thing you hate most about yourself, the thing that attracts all the jeers and whispers and spittle from strangers in the street, and you accept it. You don't try to hide it, or deny it, or make it prettier than the ugly thing it is. You learn to talk about it—and listen to others talk about it—without flinching. And eventually, it just becomes . . . another part of you. Another thing that shaped the person you are." She flexed the shining chrome fingers of her left hand. "Once your worst shame is simply a part of you, no one can use it to hurt you except yourself."

Vi hugged her elbows, weighing her aunt's words. She tried to imagine being that brazen about the black mark on her reputation. Part of her found the whole prospect darkly, deliciously enticing. The other part of her—the bigger part of her, she had to admit—could barely breathe for panic at the thought. You couldn't equate cheating on an exam to the childhood Cat had suffered.

"I don't know if I can be like you, Auntie," she confessed finally. She'd never figured out how to be anything but honest around Aunt Cat. Cat's habitual candor demanded candor in kind. "I don't know if I'm brave enough to do what you're asking. The circumstances are too different. What happened on that exam, what I lost because of it . . . that's not some accident of birth, you know? It was my fault. It's something I did to myself, that I could have prevented with better judgment."

"Certainly," said Cat tartly. "And we can stand here in the middle of this training facility all the livelong day arguing over how many mea culpas and ritual sacrifices you'll have to make to a church or temple or voodoo shrine of your choice, before you're forgiven in the eyes of some insufferable, invisible arbiter of morality." She knocked a fist against the Lioness's hide, metal ringing against metal. "Or you can try. You can get back in the cockpit."

The side of Vi's mouth quirked despite herself. "Literally or metaphorically?"

Her aunt shrugged. "¿Por que no los dos?"

"I don't even know if I'll ever fly a dragon," Vi pointed out, unable to keep bitterness from seeping into her voice. "So what's the point of either?"

If Vi's particular brand of fatalism fazed her aunt, Cat didn't let on. "I don't think that's a question anyone but you can answer." She leaned forward, mechanical eye glinting. "Tell me something true, Viola: How do you feel about piloting? Piloting sentients, specifically?"

"I don't see what that has to do with—"

"We're getting there. Answer the question." Aunt Cat's head tilted thoughtfully. "I assume there is indeed something you love about piloting, or else why while away so many hours of your fleeting youth on it?"

"Of course I love piloting!" snapped Vi. "Being good in the cockpit is the biggest thing I've got going for me. It's why my cousins pay attention to me at family events. It's how I'm going to make a living once I'm of age. Hell, it's probably the main reason people like me at all—"

"Is piloting really the reason people like you? Or does being a good pilot simply allow you to feel superior to them? To court their admiration?"

Vi's mouth snapped shut.

"Would you still enjoy piloting if you weren't among the best? If other people doubted your talent? If you doubted your own skills— really doubted them? Would you still fly, even then?"

Aunt Cat might as well have dunked cold water over Vi's head. Her jaw worked, tongue stuck to the edges of her teeth, but an answer wouldn't come.

"All those things you listed," said Aunt Cat, "are things you love that piloting talent has gained for you. But not a single one of them had to do with flying itself." Her gaze softened. "Think on that, will you? Because I promise, even if Anabel manages to change the GAN's mind about your little admission hiccup, piloting won't be the same anymore. If you're going to find love in your heart for it, you'll have to do it for yourself, and not anyone else."

♦

EVEN NOW, AFTER YEARS as a ward of the family, Vi still found that the sound of Aunt Anabel's voice at the end of a long absence always put her heart in her throat. Her aunt sounded just like Vi's parents always had, after returning from Peacekeeper deployments. Until, of course, they stopped coming back at all.

"Here, Auntie," Vi managed to croak. "In the music room, with the piano."

Heels clicked across the marble tile of the foyer. A moment later, Anabel Park appeared. She'd styled herself simply, all things considered: the heels in question low and practical, her thick black hair gathered into a simple chignon at her nape, which disappeared into a plain, conservative navy A-line dress. She might have been any other pretty professional woman in her late twenties. Some of her fellow GAN Council members wore their power in their clothes: ostentatious suits, expensive jewelry, designer accessories with name brands emblazoned in bold lettering. Vi's aunt never bothered. She didn't need to.

Aunt Anabel's head tilted to the side, red mouth pursing as she took her niece in. Vi bore her regard silently. Between Vi's time at school or the mech training yards, and Aunt Anabel's duties at various GAN consulates, they hadn't seen each other in nearly three months.

"This," pronounced Anabel, a little wryly, "was not quite the reunion I'd imagined."

A bit of tension escaped Vi's shoulders. "That makes two of us. What did the members of the Academy board say?"

Anabel snorted. "I think you ought to take more of an interest in what I had to say. I did review the footage of your audition, Viola."

Vi raised her chin. "I can explain—"

"So can I," interrupted her aunt. "And did, in fact, with great pains. I explained that my niece is a prideful young talent who committed a foolish error in judgment—"

"It was *not*," Viola began furiously.

One of Aunt Anabel's eyebrows went up. "Did you or did you not tamper with the simulation code?"

"I—" A traitorous tendril of guilt crept through the floor of Vi's belly. Stubbornly, she shook it off. "Fine, yes, I did," she admitted, "but it wasn't *cheating*."

"Wasn't it? Tampering with simulations is against examination rules. Were you aware of this?"

"I . . . yes," Vi forced herself to say. "But that rule is in place to guard against cadet candidates who want to bypass the audition entirely without doing any real work," Vi argued heatedly. "That's not what I did. I just took a shitty sim and turned a tragedy into a happy ending. That's a lot more impressive than what most Academy students pulled off in their auditions!"

One of Aunt Anabel's eyebrows went up. "So you admit to knowingly breaking the rules, then."

"Fine, technically, yes, but—"

"You admit to selecting one of the most difficult audition scenarios available, then rewriting it to make yourself look better to the admissions committee."

"That's not—"

"Yes or no, Viola?"

Vi swallowed hard. "Yes," she said in a small voice. Her chin went up. "But only on a technicality. I didn't rewrite the sim to give myself superpowers, or make Jellicoe's Giant malfunction randomly, or any other real cop-out, the way an actual cheater would have. I just . . . fought the Battle of Jellicoe's Giant the way I would have fought it—with better preparations. Good information. A smarter strategic setup from the start. It's not like I tampered with the sim to make it *easier*. If anything, I put more effort into the tampering than most people do into just auditioning straight. I didn't think the examiners would find anything so *wrong* with that." She hated that her voice went smaller still when she added, "Is there—will I really never get another chance at the Academy?"

"Oh, don't worry about that," said her aunt. "The Park name still greases some negotiations. So we've done what all good politicians do in our enlightened, globalized day and age: we have agreed upon a compromise."

"Compromise," Vi echoed, feeling obtuse. "What compromise?"

"You'll be granted admission to the Academy," said Anabel, "as a member of the probationer class."

Ice clenched around Vi's heart. She knew about the probationer classes at the Academy. Everyone did, but no one ever talked about them except in jokes, or as the butt of someone's sense of schadenfreude. Scored at the bottom of your class during the last grading period? At least it wasn't a probie class. Peacekeeper torpedoed a mission? He must have been a probie back in his cadet days. Failed the entrance exam to the Academy entirely? Better a failure than a probie.

"No," said Vi. Her fingers dug into the sides of the piano bench, so hard she swore the wood would splinter into her nail beds. "That's not me."

Her aunt's eyebrows climbed. "Not you? Who precisely do you think you are?"

"I'm not some *probie*," spat Vi. "I'm a Park. I—"

"You're a child both too clever and too foolish to leave well enough alone, who broke the entrance exam's most fundamental principles of integrity," said Anabel. "Tampering with the audition simulation—yes, Viola, for *any purpose*, including showing off—is expressly forbidden by the examination rules. I cannot for the life of me wrap my head around why you somehow thought the board of examiners would make an exception for your own incredibly stupid overstep."

"Overstep?" Vi's eyes narrowed. "Aren't you the one always telling me that there's no reward without risk? That's how career politics work, right?" She looked away abruptly, jaw tight, and added, "Besides, prospective cadets get rejected from the Academy all the time with perfect written-exam scores and perfect physicals. Without a standout audition, the examiners have made it pretty clear they want nothing to do with you, no matter how technically sound your piloting and combat skills are. I wasn't about to let myself get rejected for mediocrity." Of course, being rejected for academic dishonesty, a lack of integrity, and general icky untrustworthiness was altogether worse, but Vi wasn't about to say that aloud.

"So that was why you did it," said Aunt Anabel. If Vi had thought her aunt sounded icy a moment before, she had nothing on the Anabel of this particular moment. The air in the room could have hit subzero from that tone alone. "For all your boasts of taking daring risks that no other cadet would chance and showing off your supposedly unmatched skills, at the end of the day, you cheated because of your own self-doubt. Because you lacked confidence in your own abilities."

Vi exhaled hard, the puff of breath sharp and painful. She'd forgotten how well Aunt Anabel could aim a verbal body blow. She opened her mouth again, to deny the accusation, to find some refutation, but the truth stained her like a bruise, aching under her ribs.

"You lacked confidence," repeated Aunt Anabel. "But you covered that with arrogance, and made a mockery of the Battle of Jellicoe's Giant in the process."

"I corrected the circumstances of the Battle of Jellicoe's Giant!" Vi hadn't noticed her voice rising, but the words practically exploded out of her, raw throated. "What's so wrong with that? I did the work, Auntie. I did the work to create a version of that fight where no one had to die! In what universe is that *cheating*? People cheat when they're *lazy*! Nothing about what I did was lazy!"

"Yes, it was!" hissed Aunt Anabel. "Do you even understand why the Battle of Jellicoe's Giant is considered the most challenging and devastating simulation to audition? Did you take the time to wonder, perhaps, why the examinations committee offers such a horrific option to its potential students? Or did you just pick it because it sounded impressive, hmm?"

"I—"

"The entire point of the Battle of Jellicoe's Giant as a simulation piece," said Aunt Anabel, "is to force a cadet to perform under the worst possible circumstances. It forces the pilot to operate from a baseline of having fucked up so badly that they are almost certainly going to die, and *keep moving*. Because mark my words, Viola, it doesn't matter how rigorously you've trained, or how high your test scores are. Every pilot fails, at some point, because that is what humans do. What matters is what you do after. *That* is the point of Jellicoe's Giant. *That* is what you—with all your arrogance, and tampering, and yes, insistence on cheating the system to show off—so intrinsically misunderstood."

Silence rang between them. Anabel didn't look angry. She didn't even look disappointed. She looked perfect, actually: poised, calm, the explanation of Vi's failure dropping from her lips as cleanly reasoned as a schoolmarm's. But then, Aunt Anabel had spent Vi's entire life looking and sounding and being perfect. Vi had never wanted anything more than to be like that, to be that brilliantly, flawlessly polished.

Aunt Anabel's perfection, in this precise moment, gutted Vi worse than any knife could have.

"Then why let me enter the Academy at all?" whispered Vi at last. Her fists clenched. "If this is the only way, I'd rather just . . . finish out the year at New Columbia Prep and matriculate to a normal university like everyone else."

Aunt Anabel's eyes narrowed. "Excuse me?"

Vi's chin lifted. "I'd rather give up my shot at becoming a Peacekeeper"—she swallowed the cold lump in her throat, and continued her declaration—"than enter the Academy as a *probie*. After what I . . . the way people will see what I did, that's as good as no chance at all."

"Curious," said her aunt. Her voice had gone soft, but somehow, it still pierced every corner of the music room. "The family expected a good many things of you, but I don't think anyone expected you to end up being a quitter."

"That's not what this is!" How could Anabel Park, of all people, fail to understand? "I didn't quit, I failed. There's no future for me now, not if I stay on Academy record as a *cheater*, if I take their pity admission offer as a . . . a probie. I'm done. The last eighteen years of my life are officially fucking pointless."

"And you're so sure of this because?"

"Probies are all criminals," hissed Vi. The cold lump in her throat had gone hot. "Or freaks. Or fuckups of some kind. They're the cadets who have something *wrong* with them, who only get admitted on a trial basis in desperate times because they can bond sentient mechs. Most of them never should have been allowed to sit the entrance exam at all. They never actually amount to anything, not when everyone knows what they are." She shook her head, so fast her vision blurred. "You know, Auntie, they—there was talk in that letter from the Council of having my license stripped. You could have let them. You should have just let them!"

"To what end?" demanded Anabel. "No one has ever said that a probie couldn't be a tremendously gifted pilot. Just one who erred in judgment. You're not the first, and you won't be the last, and regardless of the disaster that was your audition, the GAN is hungry for potential like yours."

Something clicked together in Vi's head. "So it *is* desperate times, then," she said quietly. "That's the real reason you cut the deal with Headmaster Winchester."

Silence unfolded, just for a beat, as Aunt Anabel's expression shifted, red mouth pinching thin. Then she sucked in a breath. "No one on the Council wants to talk about it openly, but the GAN fleet has lost too many numbers recently. Peacekeeper squads are stretched too thin. Commanders need fresh blood to replenish what's been lost."

Vi frowned, leaning forward. "Why?" A headline niggled at the back of her mind, left over from a social studies exam–mandated browse of news reels at the school library. "Wait, don't tell me those idiots at the *Wireless Global* are actually onto something for once. I thought they only ever published sensationalist nonsense. Modern-day urban legends. They're one step above turning into a classed-up conspiracy theorist's weekly subscription."

And in this case, they'd been harping about missing Peacekeepers. Vi had refused to give it much thought, at the time. Peacekeepers fought, and sometimes, Peacekeepers died. It was the way of the world they'd built.

The expression lingering behind Aunt Anabel's gaze, though, said far more than the schlocky, ominous headline had. "Auntie," said Vi. "What's happening to the Peacekeepers?"

"What always happens to Peacekeepers in hard times. They're dying. Or going MIA on missions, at any rate. It happened right after the creation of the GAN, with seemingly every corrupt arms dealer in the world looking to test their mettle against our Corps, and again with the advent of unregulated AI weaponry in coastal territories. The usual toll of all the world's many wars." Anabel's eyes were steely, cold chips of black beneath immaculately painted lashes. "There's something that smells different about this, though. Deliberate. Calculated. We've lost sixteen pilots so far, all in the same fashion, all during separate missions, but with far too little time in between for it to be a coincidence." She paused, as if weighing her words, then said, very carefully, "Prudence Wu was most recently announced among the missing."

The name of the real pilot behind the Battle of Jellicoe's Giant sucked all the oxygen from the room. Vi inhaled sharply. "You don't think she—"

"Got herself killed?" Anabel shook her head. "No, that's not Pru. That woman would go out with a bang, not a whimper, and something about this doesn't smell right. The GAN won't publicize her name on the lists, for fear of stirring up a panic over the disappearance of everyone's favorite folk heroine, but the Council will only be able to get away with this 'classified deep-cover mission' nonsense for so long before the public grows wise." She sighed, pinching the bridge of her nose. "The fortunate side of the whole mess is that if Prudence Wu is still alive—and I'd bet money that she is—then so, in all likelihood, are the other Peacekeepers. The less fortunate side is that someone with a grudge against the GAN is very likely systematically capturing our best pilots."

"A grudge against the GAN?" Vi felt her eyebrows climb; she forgot, for just a moment, her own crisis. "You haven't exactly narrowed down the suspects here, Auntie. You've got the usual rogues' gallery of corporate arms dealers on one hand, the anti-globalization conspiracy nuts on the other, and that's not even getting into garden-variety criminals who—"

"For a girl who thinks it would be better to give up piloting entirely than enter the GAN Academy under less-than-auspicious circumstances, you're suddenly quite the keen detective," Aunt Anabel interrupted dryly.

Uncertainty flooded Vi, sharp with the prick of wounded pride. "That doesn't mean I don't care about the GAN's knights," she mumbled. "If they're in trouble—"

"If they're in trouble, you'll be in a much better position to help as a cadet—yes, even a probie cadet—than as a civilian student feeling sorry for yourself," Anabel put in smoothly.

Vi studied her aunt for a long moment. Theirs was the sort of family that expected tremendous things of its children, yet rarely made those expectations directly known. Park children, the Park elders reasoned, ought to be clever enough to read between the lines; otherwise, what was the point?

"Auntie," said Vi, suppressing a shiver. "Are you . . . not-very-subtly encouraging me to look into the missing Peacekeepers?"

Deep amid the self-imposed mist of gloom and despair, a kindling of cautious excitement struck in the pit of Vi's belly. The GAN's knights were a political instrument like any other—albeit one with teeth, and razor-sharp, chrome-plated teeth, at that—but they were also figures shrouded in both romance and notoriety for good reason. If Vi could figure out what happened to them—hell, if she could take even some small portion of responsibility for their eventual rescue and return to the safe harbor of the Alliance— her indiscretions on the Academy entrance exam would pale in comparison. It was just the sort of redemption quest that could salvage a fall from grace as lengthy as hers. The GAN might trust her again. Her family might trust her again. And Aunt Anabel would stop looking at her with those cold, disappointed eyes.

Vi's belly ached with sudden, painful want. "I'll do it," she added, in a rush. "I . . . I'd enroll at the Academy, even as a probie, if that's what it took to find the missing pilots."

Anabel blinked slowly, then gave a short enigmatic tilt of the mouth. It was the look that Aunt Cat, in fond yet long-suffering tones, called her Cheshire cat grin. "Goodness, Viola. I'm not asking you to play Nancy Drew with giant robot dragons here. Merely providing my niece with the facts of a difficult situation, and offering some . . . guidance. What you choose to do with that guidance—up to and including any additional, well, let's call them 'projects'—is entirely your own prerogative."

"Guidance," Vi echoed wryly, looking her aunt in the eye. "From GAN councilwoman Anabel Park. Right. So you must think I'm worth something after all."

For the first time all morning, Aunt Anabel's expression crumpled into something like surprise. "Viola. You're family. Regardless of what you have or haven't done, what you will or won't do, your boneheaded skull is—and will always be—worth so much more than just *something*."

"So you'll forgive me?" Vi blurted out before she thought about it, and hated herself instantly. How pathetic she must sound, shaky voiced and desperate.

"Forgive you?" Anabel's face did that odd surprised thing again. Then she reschooled her features, with a delicate snort. "You don't need my forgiveness, niece of mine. You need to get over yourself, and understand the chance you've been given." Her hands spread. "I can't force you to accept the terms of the compromise I negotiated, and

I can hardly turn you out onto the streets for refusing a pathway to the wildly dangerous career you've dreamed of since childhood. Most guardians, I imagine, would be relieved. But I would ask that you consider what's important to you, what your options are, and make the best choice you can."

Vi swallowed. There was a life—a dull, basic kind of life, but a life relatively free from shame, at least—that she could carve out for herself at New Columbia Prep instead of the GAN Academy. After all, it was what most students did: finish all four years, then head to university. Only the real piloting diehards sat the entrance exams for the Academy, knowing that acceptance meant skipping senior year at New Columbia Prep—not to mention normal higher education prospects—in favor of three grueling years in the underbelly of the GAN's most notorious training ground. Most students of means and talent had kinder options at their fingertips. Even Vi's family probably wouldn't begrudge her, not if she made something of herself elsewhere. Every self-respecting Park had backup skills, and piloting wasn't the only one in Vi's repertoire. Aunt Anabel had seen to as much. Vi was clever enough with both words and numbers, cleverer still with weapons, and a decent musician to boot.

But it would be a life built without mechs. Without dragons. The only path into the cockpit of a Peacekeeper's dragon was one riddled now with disgrace.

Alex's voice echoed suddenly through Vi's memory, warm and wistful: *Peacekeepers protect people, when no one else can.*

No matter the cost. No matter the odds of death or disappearance. Vi stared at Aunt Anabel's carefully schooled expression, thinking of the darkness in her eyes as she'd talked about the Peacekeepers gone MIA, picked off in swathes by some faceless enemy.

Vi hung on to the edges of the piano bench, as if it might keep her rooted in this moment, on the precipice of some awful, ambiguous future. "Do you really think I can find them? The GAN's missing knights? Pilots and dragons both?"

Anabel's expression didn't change. "Do you?"

Vi rasped a laugh. "I think it would have to take something as stupidly extraordinary as finding the missing Peacekeepers to get myself back into the GAN's good graces."

"That's not what I asked."

"Wasn't it?" Vi met her aunt's eyes. "If it's what needs to be done, then I'll find a way to do it."

It was an absurd plan. There was being an overachiever, and then there was being eighteen, and trying your hand at what real grown adults who sat on a real international council for one of the most powerful political bodies in the world had, evidently, failed to do. It was almost certainly not going to work. The choice should have been an easy one.

But it wasn't really a choice. It never had been. Not when it came to flying.

Besides, if Vi wanted a real shot at counting herself among the GAN's knights, she probably owed it to her fellow pilots to figure out what, precisely, was snatching them away into the abyss. If she didn't at least try, there probably wouldn't be much of a GAN left to fly *for*.

Vi looked up. Across from her, her aunt's gaze had softened, almost imperceptibly. "I see," said Anabel. "The Academy, then."

3 ——————— A TIME FOR SOLDIERS

The first tale Vi ever heard about the Academy was a monster story, told in cheerfully ominous tones over a celebratory dinner at the Park family manor.

"Don't let those beautiful holo-brochures the GAN publishes fool you," one of Vi's aunties warned. The old woman waggled a pair of gleaming silver chopsticks at some cousin whose accomplishments had been chosen as the latest family excuse for five courses of feasting. "It may look all green manicured lawns and pretty castle turrets, but make no mistake: that fancy cadet school in Hong Kong eats its students alive. Best keep your wits about you, boy, lest you end up picking yourself out from between its teeth."

In hindsight, it probably said something weird about Vi's whole personality that she'd turned a monster story into her fondest childhood dream.

None of that prepared Vi for what greeted her the first time she stepped through those famous wrought iron gates. She'd seen them a million times, in holo-images and 3-D view screen reels, but none of that replicated the cold metal beneath her hands, or the glittering lights of the ivy-covered Academy towers swirling skyward in the shadow of Tai Mo Shan. It felt like a world insulated from the rest of the island, as if someone wanted to lock it away behind a museum wall. The city of Hong Kong proper, to Vi's jet-lagged eye, had been a blur of bright lights and skyscrapers, 3-D entertainment displays and ostentatious mech landing pads. Not unfamiliar, really, to a girl who knew Seoul almost as well as she knew New Columbia. The Academy grounds—secluded by design, and tucked away in the shade of the distant, towering Tai Mo Shan—were almost eerily quiet at this hour.

They were also surprisingly well forested. Vi wasn't sure what else she'd expected of a school built into the crook of Hong Kong's highest peak, but as she followed her app deeper and deeper into the grove, the angular gothic buildings almost vanished from view entirely, obscured by endlessly twisting branches. Vi pulled a face, trying to quell the bubble of cold in the pit of her belly, a sharp contrast to the clinging summer heat. Why the hell did a school built to train mech pilots, of all things, need to cultivate such a tremendously creepy amount of vegetation? When Vi's aunties had talked of a school that ate its students alive, she'd really assumed it was metaphorical, and overdramatized for the sake of scaring her cousins. She was going to be extremely displeased if some eldritch forest monster came rampaging out of nowhere to prove her wrong. She didn't even have a war mech or a plasma rifle at hand to even the odds.

What greeted her wasn't an eldritch forest monster. It was, to her immense surprise, a girl about her own age. She wore the plain olive regulation flight suit that marked her as one of the GAN's students, but something about the way this girl stood—hip jutted out, crimson-nailed, perfectly manicured white hand planted on her waist—made the flight suit look intentional, a designer's piece in a specially chosen ensemble, rather than something that was supposed to mark the wearer as an anonymous one of many. Eyeing Viola up and down, she cocked her head. Thick red hair tumbled over her shoulder. "Viola Park." Her accent was English, what would have been called received pronunciation once upon a time, clipped and precise as a British newscaster's.

Vi blinked to attention at the sharpness of the sound. "Yes?"

That single word had apparently been the wrong thing to say. Red's bright-green eyes slitted. It was the same minute shift in expression Vi had seen a million times from an opponent right before a mech sparring round. Red was ready for a fight. "You're a probie now, aren't you?"

Probie. Vi checked a flinch. It was going to take getting used to, hearing that word spat at her just so, and still wearing the label with a straight spine. "In the flesh. Why, are you?"

Red's nostrils flared. "You really don't remember me."

Vi didn't. She sighed, scratching the back of her neck. Her aunties had ferried her to a lot of boring parties over the years. Vi didn't make friends at those parties so much as she made acquaintances—there just never seemed to be enough time to form real bonds. It was hard enough making real friends at school, when everyone you might befriend sized you up constantly. Still, it wouldn't do for Viola Park to play the recluse either, so she'd learned to exchange niceties. The trouble with niceties was that they were like confection frosting—pretty and sweet and crowd-pleasing, but inevitably temporary, and not terribly missed once they were over and done with. This wouldn't be the first time Vi had landed in social trouble for forgetting something—or someone—she shouldn't have. "Look, I didn't hook up with you at some gala or something, did I? Because I'll admit, I mostly prefer boys, but that's not to say that I haven't—"

"No, you didn't!" snapped Red. "I'm Rosalyn Davies."

Rosalyn Davies. Vi wracked her brain, and managed to summon a faint memory of old-fashioned gala invitations printed on real paper, and digital business cards stamped with addresses in London, Hong Kong, and San Francisco. There was a Davies family, English, new monied but very good at affecting blue-blooded airs, who'd come up in the AI business—one of the few who'd managed to do it 100 percent legally, which was probably why Vi's family considered them worthy of social association. The patriarch of them all—Edmund or Edward or some such thing—had a daughter. More importantly, though, he had a company that provided what his business cards called "artificial intelligence–driven security services," which was code these days for robot bodyguards. It had made the Davies family a tidy little fortune inside a single generation.

Vi blinked. "Are you here to sell me a murder bot?"

For a split second, she thought Red—Rosalyn—might actually swing on her. It wouldn't be the first scrap Vi's mouth had gotten her into.

Then, abruptly, Rosalyn grinned. It was a wolfish expression, all teeth. An odd chill ran down Vi's spine. *The GAN Academy eats its students alive.*

"I'm not here to sell you anything," said Rosalyn. "Just to escort you to your new quarters." Her mouth twisted. "As a reward slash punishment for coming in top of my class last year, I've been tasked this year with playing liaison for the probies. Evidently, I'm meant to be a good influence."

She'd already started walking away. If she cared whether Vi followed, she didn't show it. With an eye roll, Vi hurried after. "Yeah, I can feel your altruism rubbing off on me already," she muttered.

"You don't really belong among them, you know," said Rosalyn. "The probies. Everyone knows you fucked up, of course. Still, I'm surprised the GAN would let a Park wear a probationer's badge."

"Amazingly," drawled Vi, "fuckups or lack thereof are not actually dictated by birthright."

Rosalyn made a noncommittal sound. "I really did think spending time with your class would be a punishment."

"Thanks?"

"But you might be different from the others." Rosalyn glanced over her shoulder, and with a sort of grudging speculation, said, "We could be friends."

Vi's eyebrows climbed. "After all of two minutes of unsubtly veiled insults? What kind of girl do you take me for?"

"Our families would like it," Rosalyn barreled on, almost more to herself than to Vi. Her green eyes glowed catlike beneath the moon's dim lighting. "I'm a third-year here, you know, with a glowing academic record, and an all-but-guaranteed spot waiting for me on a first-class Peacekeeper squad of my choice when I graduate. Our friendship would pave the way for a good many business opportunities. But that's not why I'm offering."

Vi wrinkled her nose. Her years at New Columbia Prep flooded through her mind, along with the vast majority of her relationships with her schoolmates. The ones who'd wanted to be rivals, and the ones who'd just wanted a way to schmooze with the Parks. So things weren't so different here at the Academy after all. She wondered which category Rosalyn fell into. Maybe both. "God forbid anyone seek friendship for nonbusiness reasons."

"You're a probie," said Rosalyn bluntly. As they walked, she eyed Vi up and down. Maybe to size her up, maybe to clock a reaction. Maybe both. When Vi refused to give her further satisfaction, she continued, "It's not exactly a secret, your little fuckup, especially with a surname like yours. Anyone willing to dig through the right gossip rags, or click on society opinion blogs, well." She shrugged. "It's a tough break. But it doesn't make you any less a Park, or me any less Edmund Davies's daughter. Probies may not make friends easily here, but you could be an exception, if people remember who else you are. And if you're hanging out with me, it'll be that much easier to jog their memories. Oh, look." She came to a halt and jerked her head toward one of the imperious gothic buildings. "Home sweet home."

Vi stared at Rosalyn for a long, incredulous moment. The turrets of the great stone dormitory spiraled like a fantasy backdrop against the outline of the other girl's blood-red hair. For the first time, it hit Vi—really hit her—how far she was from home. She'd traveled overseas before, sure, but that had always been to an uncle's estate in some secluded Korean countryside, or a cousin's fine apartment in Seoul. Traveling under the broader banner of her family, inevitably accompanied by an auntie or three, was like taking a little piece of home with her, wherever she went. Back in New Columbia—at school, in the mech training yards, even at her aunts' boring parties— Vi knew where she stood. She could read the politics of a room like the back of her hand, because four times out of five, she knew where the room's occupants came from, what they had, and what they wanted. More importantly, she knew what she had to offer. But here in this eerie fortress of a campus, sealed into the shadow of a mountain an ocean away from Vi's familiar North American sprawl of cities, Vi had no idea what she could offer anyone. You couldn't bargain if you didn't know what bargaining chips you had.

Well. Sometimes, life forced you to improvise.

"I'm a pilot with a shitty reputation, not a leper," said Vi at last. "The probationary class is in nobody's five-year plan, but you lot make it sound like a prison sentence. It's not."

Rosalyn hummed, noncommittal, propping herself up against the arched entryway. "I keep forgetting you haven't met your fellow probies yet. Or their teacher." Her expression darkened. "You haven't seen what class is like with them."

Vi tried to ignore the chill that skittered through her veins. "I guess I'll find out, won't I?"

Rosalyn chuckled. "My advice? Bring your best jailhouse shiv." She peeled herself off Vi's new dormitory door, cracking her shoulders as she went. "You look me up, Viola Park, if you decide you need better friends than the lot you've been slotted in with. I'll be waiting."

Vi had barely made it onto her designated hallway when she spotted her shadow's twin: a little taller, a little broader, maybe seven feet behind her. The wooden floorboards creaked with the tread of footsteps. A couple other shadows joined the first. Without looking over her shoulder, Vi rounded a corner. So did the shadows. The floor creaked again.

With a heavy sigh, Vi stopped walking. "Can I help you?"

"Depends," said a rough, masculine voice behind her. "You Viola Park?"

"What am I, famous now?" Vi muttered. She turned around. Sometimes, you really did just need to face your problems head-on, and by her count, she had three whole new ones. Two boys, one girl, all wearing Academy-branded flight suits, none wearing smiles.

"It's a big assessment year for us," said one of the boys. "We don't need to share a roof with a cheat. Have folks thinking we're like you."

"Thinking we might be helping you," added the girl. She advanced on Vi, boys following.

Maybe it was stupid, but Vi refused to step backward. It was the principle of the matter at this point. "Poor ethical decision-making isn't an STD, you know," she told her new friends. "It's not contagious." Her hands came up, fingers loose, empty, friendly looking. "Relax."

The first boy cocked his head. "She doesn't know, does she?"

"Know what?" asked Vi. Adrenaline-stoked sweat beaded her temples. The last thing she needed—jet-lagged, stuck in a newly unfamiliar environment, literally just looking for a bed to sleep in— was a three-on-one fight.

"Don't be stupid," snapped the other boy. "She's a Park; she's got to know."

"We don't share a hive mind, you guys," Vi pointed out, mildly offended. "What am I supposed to know, and will it get me out of this delightful little gang-up?"

"The conscription call, you idiot," hissed the girl. She got right in Vi's face, nose-to-nose. "The GAN Peacekeepers aren't an infinite resource. They need to replace the MIA knights with new ones. Which means Academy students are all going to be in the running for positions in the Corps." Her lips drew back from her teeth in disgust. "Including probies. Including *cheats*."

That couldn't be right. But even if it was, this level of aggression made no sense. Vi decided to play along. "So?" She folded her arms across her chest. Vi wasn't an idiot. She knew what it meant when multiple hostile people started stalking and backing someone into a corner. If this shit was going to turn physical, Vi might as well turn it physical on her own terms. Slowly, her hands dropped, hovering at the ready. Cocking her head, she grinned with a courage she hoped she'd faked half-convincingly. "If I'm a cheat, I shouldn't be much competition for you anyway. Or are you really that shitty at piloting?"

It worked. Maybe a little too well.

She slipped the first boy's jab. Vi's knee buried itself in his belly, which made her feel like a badass for about half a second, before the other boy got his arms around her waist. Which wouldn't have been the worst problem in the world, except that it set the girl up perfectly to clock Vi right across the jaw.

"This," gasped Vi, reeling back, "is why I always fucking hated Aunt Anabel's multiple-attacker scenario—fuck!—sims." The complaint was punctuated by a punch to the gut, courtesy of the first boy, who'd recovered from Vi's knee. Fantastic. "It plays out the same way every time. The only way a three-on-one ever goes half-decent for the one is when they've got—"

"Reinforcements?"

The new voice, North American accented, pierced through the haze of adrenaline clouding Vi's mind. Her attackers jerked around. A tall, bespectacled Black girl stood at their backs, arms folded, expression calculating. Almost no one wore glasses anymore these days, except for aesthetic statement, which made this new girl look a little like a centerfold from a period magazine about sexy librarians or something.

"Stay out of this, Rogers," snapped one of the boys. "It's none of your business."

"It is when I'm pretty sure that's my new roommate you're manhandling there," remarked the new girl—Rogers, apparently. She squinted at Vi. "Are you the chick who cheated on the entrance exam and still got admitted?"

"Present and accounted for," drawled Vi. Her jaw ached.

"My roommate, then," said Rogers, sounding resigned. She turned a speculative eye on Vi's attackers. "Look, I get that you guys are scared of probie cooties or whatever, and that it's very upsetting that a whole two of us now live in a dorm of like fifty people, but I promise that beating the new kid to a pulp—which is probably great for your ego for about five minutes—will not be great for your conscription chances."

"And what would you know about conscription chances?" The other boy sneered. "You're a probie yourself. The GAN would take any of us over you."

"True, probably," agreed Rogers. "But that hasn't stopped them from opening up conscription to the dirty little likes of me and Cheaty McCheater here, has it?"

"God, please don't let that name stick," muttered Vi.

"Which means," continued Rogers, "that the GAN won't look kindly on you beating up on potential recruits. I know you're used to being allowed to do whatever you want to probies, but times are a-changing. Really, I'm the one looking out for you here."

"Shut up," snapped the first boy, but he was starting to look uncertain, as was the girl.

"It's late," said the girl. "We'll deal with this shit later."

As one, the three of them slunk away.

Vi stared after their retreating backs, then at her rescuer. "Thanks," she said.

Rogers shook her head. "Don't."

"Really, it's lucky that you—"

"No, I'm not being polite. For real, don't." Rogers looked Vi square in the eye. She jerked her head toward the dorm room door across from both of them. "We're roommates, not friends. I saved your ass from those fuckers to prove a point. Conscription means that probies are getting integrated into the same classes as the normal students. Which means they'll be even more excited than usual to bully us like we're all in one of those old retro high school movies—unless we nip that shit right in the bud."

"Wait." Vi looked at Rogers—really looked. The other girl didn't blink. "Conscription is an actual thing?"

Rogers rolled her eyes. "Lord, no wonder you had to cheat on that test. You're kind of slow on the uptake, aren't you?"

Vi's face burned. "Whatever. GAN red tape is pretty ridiculous, and I haven't heard about this anywhere else. I bet it's bullshit."

"Bet whatever you want," retorted Rogers. She keyed the dorm room door open. The metal slid aside with a whoosh. "Just hope that you don't lose all your money before you figure out what's real and what's not around here."

♦

Global Alliance of Nations
Academy for Combat and Cybernetic Arts
Official Announcement of Conscription

URGENT NEWS

Conscription of GAN students shall be regulated as follows:

1. In light of GAN conscription needs, all eligible students of the GAN Academy shall be required to participate in bimonthly combat-assessment tourneys.

2. Combat tourneys shall consist of three phases of matchups: hand-to-hand non-mech combat, combat by non-sentient mechs, and finally, combat by sentients. Only students who pass hand-to-hand and non-sentient phases of assessment shall be selected for participation in combat by sentients. Students chosen for participation in combat by sentients shall be issued temporary keys and licenses to GAN official training sentients.

3. Final decisions regarding conscripts shall be based on the cumulative results of the tourneys and overall academic performance at the conclusion of the first semester.

4. In order to maximize the candidate pool, the GAN Academy probationary class shall, for the time being, be integrated into standard classes and treated as ordinary-status students, and be included in conscription eligibility events such as tourneys, practices, and any other events deemed necessary for assessment of fitness for combat.

Because the writers of the tragicomedy that was Vi's life apparently enjoyed tormenting her, the conscription—which would have been awesome news for a pre-exam, non-probie Vi unlikely to be attacked and murdered by her classmates—did not, in fact, turn out to be bullshit.

The announcement had puttered to life across the screen of her phone just in time to thoroughly ruin any shot she'd had at a decent night's sleep. For what felt like hours, Vi stared wide-eyed at the ceiling of the shoebox-sized dorm room. The three-phase assessment was pretty common to the world of combat mech pilots these days. Before the rise of sentients, assessment of live-combat capabilities had been a two-phase deal in any training program: hand-to-hand, then combat by mechs. Hand-to-hand to prove reflexes, physical conditioning, and plain old hardheaded ability to both take and deliver damage on the basest level; combat by mechs to translate those same skills to the cockpit. Combat by sentients had added a wrinkle to that same formula in the past decade or so. Sentients were far more efficient than the old strictly human-operated war mechs, but they also picked their own pilots. Not all good fighters could persuade a sentient to bond them—that took something else, some intangible secret sauce for which the piloting world had yet to concoct a precise recipe, but which it nevertheless found ways to harvest in the classrooms of the Academy.

Vi had it. Or at least, once upon a time, she'd had it. She'd made herself the envy of her cousins: some of them had the physical grit of a fighter but none of the finesse of a mech pilot, some the charm to bond a sentient but no stomach for a fight. Vi had fancied herself that rare triple threat: someone who could fight, someone who could fly, and someone who could stand before a creature forged from metal and plasma fire and command loyalty willfully given. Among cadet hopefuls, growing up, she'd been one of the girls to beat, and prideful of her place. Once upon a time, she'd have been champing at the bit to cut a swathe through the other competitors at an assessment like this one.

Then the exam had hit a reset button on Vi's life. She'd been so proud of her work on the Battle of Jellicoe's Giant, until Aunt Anabel had pulled back the curtain on everything Vi never wanted to admit to: *When it mattered most, you suddenly lacked confidence. And then you covered up your own insecurities with arrogance.* The sting of truth still burned under Vi's skin. Had she ever really been as good as she'd thought? In the aftermath of the exam, she'd barely managed to get the Lioness under control back at the compound in New Columbia. Could she even survive a sentient's cockpit without a total meltdown? A pilot's performance wasn't just skill—it was also mindset, and Vi wasn't sure that hers would ever be the same after she'd nearly destroyed her own life.

Now, faced with the prospect of squaring off against other hungry, ambitious young pilots—none of whom had needed to cheat their way into the Academy—Vi kind of just wanted to throw up. It wasn't the most pleasant feeling in the world to fall asleep on, which wound up setting the tone for the morning. Vi had suffered through a lot of first days of school. This one wasn't actually so different, dawning with the sudden blare of an alarm that sent Vi's headspace right back to morning classes at New Columbia Prep. She muffled an expletive in the nondescript dorm-issue pillow. Scissor-kicking the matching comforter aside, she fumbled for her phone.

"Welcome to your first full day at the GAN Academy for Combat and Cybernetic Arts," trilled the app. "You currently have eleven minutes and fifteen seconds to reach orientation for the newly enacted GAN Conscription Act for Academy Students."

Right. Just a little different after all. "Eleven minutes!" yelped Vi.

"And twelve seconds!"

Vi spared a glance for the other bed, which was already neatly made and empty. "What about my roommate?"

"Tamara Rogers departed fifteen minutes and forty-one seconds ago. She is scheduled to arrive on time."

"Yeah, unlike me!"

"You will both be attending under the newly instituted Temporary Reprieve for Probationary Students, section four-one—"

Vi's stomach interrupted with a loud growl. "No breakfast first?"

"Breakfast was served one hour, twenty minutes, and six seconds ago," the app said happily.

"Are you fucking kidding me?"

"No jokes have been programmed for this module."

Vi swore again. Lesson learned: she'd have to set an earlier alarm, now that she no longer had Alex or his Tchaikovsky ballet arrangements or that goddamn piano to summon her unwillingly into consciousness. The realization made her briefly, bizarrely tight-throated, which was mortifying in its own right. She was eighteen years old. There was no call to go crying over her childhood music teacher when she had five minutes, at best, to dress for a day that might well determine whether she'd ever have a spot among the GAN's knights.

The discovery that the uniform jacket in her closet had been emblazoned with an enormous red badge that read PROBATIONARY STATUS, however, did little to encourage any optimism toward that whole idea.

"How very *Scarlet Letter* of you," she groused at the jacket as she yanked it over her shoulders.

The Academy grounds became a different world when bathed in sunlight instead of moonlight. Trees that had adopted craggy-handed shapes in the dark were friendly and green now, the manicured lawns as elegantly inviting as the manor grounds back at home. They blurred around Vi as she pelted across the grass. Maybe the Academy didn't seem like the sort of place that ate its students alive under a blue sky, but appearances could be deceiving, and Vi hated the idea of giving it an excuse this early.

She slammed into the designated classroom "only four minutes and thirteen seconds late," according to her phone. "Sorry!" she panted. Hands on her knees as she caught her breath, she tried to get a read on the room's few occupants. First-, second-, and third-years had been mixed up and divided seemingly at random into eleven different orientation groups in separate classrooms. The ones assigned to this room had half shucked their uniform flight suits, trading the top jackets for plain white tees, but Vi still caught the emblematic dragon wings of the GAN embroidered on their hips. Those shiny little embroidered wings flashed at the corners of Vi's vision like the bright warning colors on a poisonous amphibian, or a snake's rattler: *We too are the best pilots the Academy could find. We are hungry for the same things you want, and we will fight for those limited spoils. Be wary, Viola Park.*

The first cadet to catch her eye, if he'd been taken by surprise, didn't let it show, slouching against the classroom wall and wearing an expression of wide-eyed, opaque amusement. That earned Vi's instinctive respect, though it wasn't the only reason she took a beat longer to size him up. He was good-looking—extremely so, if Vi was honest with herself—but this boy's brand of good-looking was the sort of beauty that struck its viewer askance, a strange collection of features that didn't look as though they should have fit together as well as they did. His eyes, a startlingly light shade of brown—paired with the bright, whiskey-colored riot of his hair and moon-fair skin—made him look like a candle flame in the dark, enticement and warning all at once.

He was one of the few who wasn't in a flight suit, just jeans and a plain Henley, its sleeves rolled to his elbows, but he had to be a student too, and not just because of the company he kept. Mech pilots, usually the good ones, picked up that odd habit of wearing plain clothes like armor. Aunt Anabel had once described it as "pilot vibe," the unspoken aura of a person who spent most of their waking lives in the cockpit of a manmade creature of war. Spend enough time around mechs and their fighters, and you didn't need that sort of thing spelled out: you just knew. This pretty-boy motherfucker would be a dangerous competitor to tango with. Vi took a small step back.

"Welcome!"

The artificially cheery voice automated over the speaker blasted straight through Vi's ears. The other students quieted. Near the front of the room, a 3-D view screen flared to life. Gradually, a woman's face materialized. Vi sucked in a breath. She'd seen pictures of Karolyn Winchester in ads and brochures, or on the odd news segment from the wireless: the iconic blond chignon and twinkling blue eyes. But what truly set Winchester apart was the way she seemed to fill a room, even if she wasn't physically present. Even through holo-imagery, the Headmaster's gaze felt like a focal point—or a sniper's crosshairs—zeroed in on you and only you.

"Welcome," repeated Winchester, "one and all, to a new year at the Global Alliance of Nations Academy for Cybernetic and Combat Arts. I would like to begin, first and foremost, by elaborating on the rather exciting announcement that has already sent half the student body into a rumor-mongering frenzy—impressive, by the way, considering that school has been technically in session for less than forty-eight hours." She paused. "I am speaking, of course, of the conscription notice you all received."

Conscription.

The effect of one word was immediate. A tidal wave of murmurs—some excited, some apprehensive—rippled through the little crowd of cadets.

The Headmaster spoke above the whispers. "By now, most of you have had the chance to read through the rules of GAN conscription, which have hopefully jolted you out of the dog days of summer, and into a properly academic mindset." The twinkle in her eye took the sting out of what might have been a rebuke, delivered differently. A few students laughed. "As such, I thought it best to clarify the facts.

"In that vein, I'd like to take this moment to remind you of why you're all here. It's no secret that we're facing . . . let's call it difficult times." Quiet filtered through the room at that, punctuated by a few somber whispers. Vi couldn't make out full sentences, but the words *missing* and *Peacekeepers* struck her ears more than once. Academy kids weren't dumb. They knew a euphemism when they heard it. "I would urge everyone in this room to look at current events not as a reason for fear, but as an opportunity."

More murmurs at that. A note of curiosity echoed through the crowd of cadets. A few stood on tiptoe, trying to get a better look at the view screen.

The Headmaster raised a flickering, holographic hand. "I don't mean that callously, of course. Every cadet who has ever set foot on these grounds—stood where you stand now—was chosen to attend this institution for two equally important reasons: piloting skill and moral character." Winchester allowed a moment for that to sink in. "If you are sitting here today, combatting jet lag and morning fatigue with coffee and adrenaline, then both of those characteristics apply to you, whether you believe it or not. But that also means that those are characteristics you must preserve. Just as dragon pilots who grow lazy in their practice lose combat skill and aerial sensitivity, people initially believed to be good can make . . . shall we say, less-than-morally-upright choices."

That had been an entirely too obviously targeted choice of words. Some dark impulse in Vi made her want to cast an eye around the room for other probie badges, searching for her fellow scarlet letters. Instead, she slouched, backpedaling a few steps. Maybe there was a function on the Academy app that would open up one of the pretty marble tiles in the floor of the classroom so she could fall through it and die right here.

"The GAN tries to defend innocent people in an increasingly dangerous world—a hard task in the best of times—but harder than ever with Peacekeeper Corps wearing thin. Who, with the skill to serve as a Peacekeeper, is willing to risk their necks on the front lines of our battles? Why, when they could seek safer and more lucrative work in the private sector? The answer, of course, is in the room. I see it in each of your faces."

The Headmaster's hologram gazed round the room again, with those entrancing eyes of hers. Her voice filled the space, from the tiled floor to that high arched ceiling. "We need pilots who can survive the dangers of this world, and do it for the right reasons. The Alliance did not establish this school to educate sacrificial lambs. So live smart. Learn. And listen to your moral compass. Remember that good is not simply a thing that you are. It is a thing that you do. Not just once or twice. Not as a check mark on some tally of virtuous deeds. It is a continuous choice you must make. Good is an act that, as a Peacekeeper, you must choose over and over again, when it would be so very easy to choose otherwise."

She smiled, abrupt and white toothed. "Now, without further ado, let's open the school year with some true Academy spirit—let's call it a pop quiz of sorts. Something to serve as a preview of the actual conscription, and whet your appetites for competition." She made a few tsk-tsk sounds at the predictable groans from the cadets that greeted this statement. "Oh, don't sigh and moan; it's just a little exercise to get you all warmed up. It won't affect your tournament scores, I promise. For second- and third-years, this will be a review. For first-timers, well. Consider it an opportunity to get your feet wet, so to speak." Even through the hologram projector, those blue eyes seemed to twinkle. "Simulation sparring. Non-sentient mechs—remember, it's just a pop quiz, not a tournament match. Treat it like an ordinary training exercise. You'll be pairing off with another student—each first-year assigned to a second- or third-year for safety and guidance considerations. Your partner will also be your opponent for our purposes, so don't go trying to break them in two—but don't forget to look for weaknesses to exploit. Remember, this isn't about winning—it's just about showcasing what you can do."

"Bullshit it's not about winning," muttered one of the boys sotto voce. "How the hell else do fighter pilots showcase what they can do without, you know, winning fights?" Murmurs of agreement trickled through the room.

Vi tuned them all out. The bullet-speed pounding of her heart did a pretty good job of helping her out on that front. The list of assigned partner pairs, scrolling down along the holo-projector beside the Headmaster's face, did the rest. Privately, she agreed with the other cadets. Maybe the Headmaster's so-called pop quiz wasn't an official part of conscription, but anyone who didn't believe it would play a role in their chances was kidding themselves. Competition brackets didn't just arrange themselves. Vi had no doubt that whoever did best on this quiz would get a more favorable spot in the lineup of opponents, and a closer look from the judges.

Vi needed every advantage she could get. Winning the competition—and a conscription spot—didn't just mean a place in the Corps. It meant Vi would have a front-row seat to whoever—or whatever—kept making Peacekeepers disappear. She'd have an actual fighting chance at getting to the bottom of the whole mystery.

The other names blurred out of focus, until Vi found the one she was looking for: VIOLA ELIZABETH JIYEON PARK. Heart stuck in her throat, she followed the blinking letters to the name opposite hers: NICHOLAS LEE.

Nicholas Lee. Who the hell was Nicholas Lee?

Like a link straight to Vi's brain, student ID photos flickered to life beside the names. Vi squinted. Then froze. The photo didn't really do it justice, but it was hard to mistake the whiskey-bright color of the hair and eyes brightening the screen beside NICHOLAS LEE.

The pretty-boy motherfucker was going to be Vi's first fight.

"So, how do you want to do this?"

Vi wasn't sure what she'd expected from the Headmaster's little pop quiz, but it hadn't been this. Shunted off into separate simulation rooms, leaving Vi virtually alone with a randomly assigned stranger. An improbably beautiful, randomly assigned stranger, who was currently lounging against the back wall, legs splayed and arms crossed, like he was an overpaid model posing for a holovid poster captioned BORED AND AMUSED. You'd think the two descriptors would cancel each other out, but she wasn't sure how else to classify that opaque little smile playing across Nicholas Lee's fine-featured face. He'd at least changed into a flight suit in honor of the fight about to ensue, though Vi wasn't sure why he bothered, what with virtual reality and all. Between them was a nondescript black switch—the lever to start the combat simulation, whenever both fighters were ready.

Vi tore her gaze away from the switch to blink at her new partner's question. "How do I want to do what?"

"Karolyn's simulation," he said. "Don't look so freaked," he added, not unkindly. "You'll see after you're here a little longer how shit like this usually goes. She doesn't actually expect you to do well, not on a pop quiz, and definitely not as a first-year on the first day of Academy classes. She just wants to see if you break."

Vi swallowed a note of unease. Her chin tilted upward. "And if I do?"

"That's why I'm asking how you want to do this," Nicholas Lee repeated patiently. "I'm pretty good at going along with whatever people need." He leaned forward slightly, bright eyed, a conspiratorial tilt to that little smile of his. "The beauty of a simulation is that all things are possible. We could make it look like a close fight, where you triumph at the last minute, victory from the jaws of defeat. Or one where my mech beats yours into the dust, but you refuse to quit, showing off your scrappiness. Or we could play to a close draw. Or—"

"Stop!" Vi blurted out. "I don't give a shit what it looks like. Just what it is. I don't want to win, or play to a draw, or even lose, unless it's on my own merits."

Lee's eyebrows climbed upward. "Aren't you Viola Park? Didn't you—"

"Cheat my way into the Academy, earning myself a probationary badge and the ire of my illustrious family? Yes, it's all very scandalous and tragic," snapped Vi. "The last thing I need is to add to my list of sins against the moral institution of the GAN."

"Hardly that, I'd think," mused Lee. "Listen, it's just putting on a show. Everyone does it. No one's going to expel you for doing what it takes to survive. I told you, everyone who partners with me does it."

"Everyone?" Vi scoffed. "You're really telling me you're so big and bad that no one has ever just played out a combat simulation against you straight, to see what happens?"

"Why bother?" Lee shrugged. "I might lose, it's true. Anything can happen in the cockpit, especially during a simulation. But I might also win. I'm pretty good. Given the choice between taking the gamble on a bad loss and letting me help out a bit, most of the cadets here play the smart odds."

Vi took that in for a beat. She'd met a lot of arrogant blowhards in the piloting world who might have said something similar, but that wasn't the vibe she got from Lee. She knew the look of someone spouting nonsense to bolster a fragile ego. Lee, on the other hand, simply looked like he'd misplaced his ego, along with the last two fucks he had left to give. "And you help out for what, the goodness of your heart?"

Another shrug. "It makes life easier."

"And if your partner asks for a real fight in the sim?"

"They don't."

"I do."

Vi might have been imagining things. But what she might have imagined was a flicker of interest that skittered through Nicholas Lee's dangerous, candle-bright eyes. "Sure," he said, unconcerned about this as he was about everything. "We can do that too."

In a single swift movement, he covered the distance between them. For a heart-hammering moment, Vi thought he was reaching out toward her. Her back hit the wall. Shit. She hadn't meant to do that.

It didn't matter. He didn't touch her. Instead, he reached between them and flipped the simulation start switch.

Instantly, the room plunged into darkness, in time with Vi's heart, which plummeted into her stomach. Piece by piece, she found her bearings. Automated mech controls at either hand. Mobile suit specs printed in glowing all caps across the corner of the cockpit dash. She was piloting a humanoid model in the sim. Old-school, then. Good. Fewer unknown quantities.

A view screen flickered to life before her eyes. She squinted. At first, she thought the sim might be malfunctioning. Most sims took advantage of their virtual reality algorithms to throw together elaborate environments for players to interact in: an expansive ocean coast, or a sophisticated urban dwelling, or the site of a notorious historical blowout like the Battle of Jellicoe's Giant. The view screen before her only showed the same old room she and Lee had first stepped into: the same white walls, padded floor, and nondescript black switch.

The only real difference was the battle mech that had materialized across from her. Another old-school humanoid battle bot: silver chrome armor plating, long dangling limbs. No additional weapons. No plasma fire blast capabilities. Vi began to breathe a little easier. It was just bare-bones mech sparring, like she'd done a million times before. Just a pop quiz, like a million others she'd taken in school.

The wireless comms speaker in her cockpit—Jesus, even that was old-fashioned—crackled. Lee's voice emerged, just as no-nonsense and unconcerned as before. "You ready to go?"

Vi sat back, knees braced, fingers lacing into the mech controls. "Bring it."

She didn't even register the blow. One moment, she'd been looking for a gap between their mechs to close the distance; the next, she was stumbling sideways. "Shit!" Vi's head rattled with the force of impact. Cockpit alarms went haywire as they registered damage from her opponent.

She tried to remember what her instructors—what Aunt Anabel

or Aunt Cat or even Alex—might say. Breathe easy. Breathe easy. She inhaled. Exhaled. Scanned the view screen for some sign of where Lee was going to angle his next attack from.

She took too long, time enough to register the flurry of movement from the corner of her eye, and then the weight of her own mech was tumbling out from under her. The view screen blurred as she rocked backward, her bot's own metal feet akimbo over the cockpit, as Lee's mech bore down on them both.

The speaker crackled again. "I can ease up, if you want," offered Lee.

Vi clenched her mouth shut. She wished he'd sounded smug, or condescending. She wished he'd sounded gleeful, or excited, like a predator smelling the blood in the water around a downed and shaken opponent. Instead, he sounded like he still didn't give a fuck. Like easing up on his beatdown on Vi was a favor, as simple as helping her out with a problem set or carrying a suitcase for her. It made her want to eject them both from this stupid simulation and handle business with her bare fists.

"Don't you dare," she told him through her teeth, and scissored her mech's legs out over his.

The clash of metal that accompanied the reversal rattled her down to the bones, but it worked: she'd flipped him over. A thrill of relief ran through her.

It was short-lived. Metal arms and legs clamped down around the outer frame of the cockpit. The narrow walls creaked with the pressure, buckling around Vi. In vain, Vi tried to free one of her own mech's arms, but it was trapped tight under the unforgiving chrome-reinforced grip of Lee's.

"Say when," said Lee.

"Fuck you," replied Vi. Again, she tried to slow her breathing. Just a pop quiz. Just another spar. But what her brain recognized, her body didn't. Another cockpit filled the edges of her vision, another simulation. A hulking metal giant on the horizon, chrome-scaled wings alongside her arms, and the haunting ring of a sentient's consciousness inside her head. Already, her pulse was climbing, her head light.

The pressure of Lee's mech bore down. When had Vi's mech stopped moving? Not that it mattered now. Everything seemed so futile at this point.

I should tell him to stop. Continuing is pointless. I'd be dead by now if this were a real fight between mechs.

Vi craned her neck, fumbling a hand toward the cockpit speakers, ready to declare her forfeit.

Before she could move again, the room slammed back into darkness. Then, just as suddenly, into light.

Vi's knees hit the floor of the simulation room. Gone were the battle bots, the cockpit, and the crushing power of a metal monster locked around her mech. The sim was done.

A cold bead of perspiration trickled down her spine beneath the flight suit. Slowly, over the gasps of her own labored breathing, Vi raised her gaze toward the boy on the opposite end of the room. Nicholas Lee looked back at her, his expression mild and opaque, not a single hair out of place, his breathing completely, infuriatingly relaxed. He probably hadn't even broken a sweat.

"It didn't have to be like that, you know," he said quietly.

The chilly heat of humiliation clambered up the back of Vi's neck.

Fuck you, she wanted to say. *Fuck you and your fucking condescension.*

She couldn't seem to look away from those eyes, somehow both flame bright and utterly dispassionate. "Yes, it did," she said at last, in a tone that she really hoped at least conveyed the same general energy as *fuck you*. "It really did."

The intercom crackled back on, startling them both. "All right, then," broke in the Headmaster's voice, loud and cheery. "Thank you, cadets, for your time and display of skill. That concludes our little pop quiz. You'll be receiving your scores via the Academy app within the next twenty-four hours. These will determine your placement in the bracket lineup for combat assessment tourneys."

"What?" The word erupted from Vi's throat before she had a chance to take it back. Her heart had plummeted back to the pit of her belly.

Lee was still watching her with those big, bright, passionless eyes. "I told you," he said, and maybe it was the unpleasant dump of adrenaline into her veins, or maybe just the bitter tang of disappointment in her own level of stupidity, but Vi could swear that this time, he actually sounded a little sad. "This could have gone another way."

Vi made to cover the distance between them. Jarring, without the sim's battle bots encasing their bodies, but she strode toward him anyway. To her surprise, he actually backed up a few steps, hands rising. It was practically a flinch. Not the kind of body language she would have expected from the boy who'd just beaten the ever-loving shit out of her in a combat sim, but she was too angry to care. Her hands found the lapels of his flight jacket. The rough-hewn fabric, tight in her grips, left a satisfying burn across her fingers as she yanked him around, more perfunctory than violent, toward her. "Did you know?" she demanded.

He sighed, sagging in her grip a little. Whatever momentary fear had passed through him a moment ago appeared to have fled entirely. Now he just looked bored. "Know what? You're going to have to be more specific, Park."

"Oh jeez," said Vi, "three guesses, and the first two don't count. How about the fact that this goddamn sim actually had important stakes, and wasn't just some head game the Headmaster was messing around with?"

He snorted. "Not a very effective head game if the stakes aren't important, is it?"

"So you knew."

"I guessed." His head craned forward, until he was practically nose-to-nose with her. Her breath hitched. He slouched like a rag doll against the flight jacket lapels still clutched between her fists. She could have drowned in the sheer dearth of fucks to be found in his gaze. "And so would anyone else who knows anything about Karolyn Winchester." In a truly absurd show of condescension, he patted her cheek gently with one hand, like she was a child throwing a tantrum or some shit. "Don't worry, Park. Survive the Academy long enough, and you'll know exactly when she's about to screw you over, just like the rest of us do."

Lee angled his hips slightly, bent his knees, and gave a jerk of his body. His jacket snapped free from her fingers. "My advice? Don't look at your score on this assessment as a failure. Look at it as a lesson for next time."

The words struck her harder than anything his battle mech had thrown. She blinked, but when she opened her mouth, no response emerged. Lee was already turning away from her, making for the exit.

He made no effort to hold the door open behind him. She blinked again, and mentally replayed what she'd just seen. Maybe it was her imagination. She'd have to find him again, or ask around, just to be sure. One day was hardly enough time to fully recover from jet lag, and Vi's internal clock was all kinds of messed up. She knew she could logically blame basic exhaustion—which had formed a muddy sort of cocktail with the general stress of the past hour and change— for what she saw. It had probably been a trick of the eye, played with relish by her sleep-deprived brain.

Still, Vi could swear that when Nicholas Lee had turned to leave, she had caught sight of a probie badge, the flashing scarlet letter of shame identical to hers, pinned just beneath one of his lapels.

◆

VI HAD EHPECTED TO fail the quiz. Okay, maybe not totally fail— after all, she'd put up a fight. A desperate, pathetic excuse for a fight, and probably the worst performance she'd put on in a combat sim since she was a mewling thirteen-year-old brand-new to the relentless pressure of virtual reality training exercises—but she'd put up a fight all the same. She'd get the pity points for making some half-hearted attempt at playing defense, and for at least reversing Lee's takedown for all of five seconds, but pity points didn't earn anyone a good bracket in a combat tourney. She'd be matched up against the bottom of the barrel, the lost causes, too far from the true fighter pilots to catch anyone's attention.

The Headmaster's quiz was scored on a scale of 1 to 10. In her ideal world, Vi had scored a nice, mediocre 5 at best. She could only pray to hell that reality wouldn't dock too many points off of that. You could make a comeback from a 4, or maybe even a 3. Probably.

It left her off-kilter for the rest of the day. Aside from the Headmaster's firecracker of an orientation, full-time classes hadn't even yet started in earnest, which left Vi with a good amount of free time, and an even greater amount of anxiety fodder. Back at New Columbia Prep, she would have gone out with friends to blow off steam, at least trying to celebrate the temporary reprieve from the unrelenting school timetable. Friends back home—even the ones who'd just wanted to win something from her, whether it was a favor or a victory—had possessed a certain known quantity. Vi didn't have that here.

If she hadn't chosen to enroll at the Academy—if she hadn't agreed to become a probie—Vi would have been heading off for her final year at New Columbia Prep, and applying to university. Maybe her classmates would have teased her for abandoning her grand piloting plans, or maybe they would have avoided the topic like the plague, afraid of provoking some kind of breakdown. Maybe her old training partners at all the New Columbia mech combat facilities would have drifted away from her, first gradually and politely, then more rapidly and obviously, as they had less and less to talk about, without Vi's piloting license keeping her in competition with them. Or maybe without the cutthroat pressure of tournaments and conscriptions and the ever-looming GAN Academy entrance exams, they could have become real friends in time.

She'd never know now. Strangely depressed by that, she found herself retreating to the relative safety of the dorm room, worrying and pointedly ignoring Tamara, who lounged on the opposite bunk devouring a lurid-covered romance comic on her holo-projector instead of even pretending to get a head start on the reading assignments steadily trickling onto the Academy app. Vi's roommate hadn't said a word about conscription, the Headmaster's quiz, or even the drama that had transpired the previous night. Clearly, if Tamara Rogers gave half a damn about the upcoming tourney brackets, she certainly wasn't sharing it with Vi. It actually made Vi weirdly jealous, that level of sheer nonchalance about something that seemed so monumental to everyone else. For a few minutes, Vi tried to channel that same aura of peaceful disinterest. Instead, all she found herself doing was browsing listlessly through class schedules and orientation documents without actually seeing any of them. The official tournament rules had arrived in her inbox alongside her syllabus. It was roughly what Vi had expected: three phases to showcase the three disciplines of hand-to-hand, non-sentient, and sentient combat, two matches per phase. There was something confusing in there about a subjective points-and-judgment system, which Vi mentally filed away for later study. The exact rules of mech combat tourneys changed at the last minute all the time anyway.

When the Academy app beeped her results at her, she nearly threw up without even seeing the number. When she finally convinced her fingers to click across the screen to pull it up, the world seemed to fall away from her for a moment. She was back home again, getting that first rejection letter from the Academy, staring at an accusation she couldn't believe.

This was another mistake. It had to be. But there it was, blinking at her in unmistakable neon numbering: VIOLA ELIZABETH JIYEON PARK—SCORE: 10/10.

Vi's head twisted toward the figure still huddled around the romance comic on the other bunk. "Hey, Rogers. Are there ever bugs in the scoring algorithms on the Academy app?"

Tamara didn't even bother looking up from her projector. "Pro tip: if you got a zero on the Headmaster's quiz this morning, best move probably isn't blaming the technology."

"No, I actually scored—" Vi began, then paused. A memory of New Columbia Prep seized her: class rankings, whispers of grade point averages and teachers' favorites. The way the kids at the bottom of the barrel were sneered at, but the ones at the top, or close to it, always wore targets on their backs. On a hungry, competitive field, success could be as dangerous as failure. Maybe more dangerous.

Besides, Vi wasn't altogether sure that Tamara was right about the Academy's tech being perfect. If recent experience had taught her anything, it was that nothing was entirely foolproof.

"Well, it wasn't a zero," she offered, nonchalant. Not her wittiest piece of repartee, but it seemed to satisfy Tamara, who just shrugged and returned to happily ignoring the reading list in favor of her colorful erotica.

Honestly, Vi was almost tempted to do the same. You couldn't spend all your time in constant existential crisis. She glanced toward her own holo-projector. She was debating whether to put on the fifth season of some cheesy old wireless teen drama or chance asking to borrow from Tamara's stash of comics, when a message alert bloomed at the top of her screen.

"Shit," said Vi, staring wide-eyed at the message contents.

Tamara sighed loudly. "What now, have you been disinherited by one of the many Park gazillionaires?"

"No."

"Then what?"

"She wants to see me. Right now."

"Who the fuck are you talking about?"

Vi swallowed. "The Headmaster."

♦

THE HEADMASTER'S OFFICE, according to the Academy app, sat behind the doors of a stone tower covered in a shiny, winding wreath of ivy, which fit in with the general aesthetic of the situation, while being entirely unhelpful to Vi's vague sense of foreboding. "There better be an elevator in this thing," muttered Vi, knocking at the great mahogany doors. "I refuse to climb stairs at this hour, in this modern day and age."

"Oh, there is," said an amused voice over an intercom. Vi's heart leapt into her throat. American accented, very former United States East Coast, crisp and female, same as the hologram before the quiz that morning. Karolyn Winchester herself. "Do come in, dear. I've been expecting you for some time."

"So I've been repeatedly electronically informed," said Vi faintly.

In response, the mahogany doors slid aside with an exaggerated, automated groan.

"Forgive the sound effects," continued Winchester. "We've been meaning to install renovations at the school for some time, but haven't quite gotten around to it. You wouldn't believe how much trouble it is to keep proper care of a school campus overrun by both sentient mechanical beasts and precocious human teenagers."

"Sure," Vi offered cautiously. She slid one foot gingerly inside the doorframe. Wall sconces flickered on, lighting up the floor beneath. The doors closed behind her. "Now what?"

"Wait for it. Oh, and do brace yourself along the railing. For safety purposes, you understand."

Vi cast about the enclosed space for a railing, and found a long horizontal rod of metal opposite the doors. "Why do I need to—"

The floor bucked up around her knees. Biting back a shout of surprise, Vi slid forward and slammed her palms down on the metal rod.

"Told you there was an elevator!"

"I never doubted as much," Vi managed through clattering teeth. The floor, wall sconces flickering madly around her, was speeding with rapid enthusiasm toward the ceiling. Sweat slicked her grip against the metal. The joints of her fingers creaked in protest, as she tightened them against the momentum of ascent. "What was that about safety concerns again?"

No answer. Vi couldn't decide if that was more or less comforting than anything that could have been said in the moment.

The floor jarred to a halt. Vi clung to the railing for a breath, then two. The sconces retracted, leaving her briefly in the dark.

Then one of the wall panels slid aside entirely. Vi blinked at the entrance to what looked like a suspiciously normal—if appropriately ostentatious—hallway. Plush, elaborately patterned red carpeting rolled down a well-lit corridor to an open floor plan, backlit by wide French windows. A chandelier hung at the center of the space, directly over a luxuriously carved wooden desk.

Seated at the desk was the woman from the orientation hologram. She sported a black suit, a blond chignon, and the self-satisfied grin of someone who had successfully scared the living daylights out of a stranger. "Good evening, Miss Park," she said in the same crisp

American cadence that had graced both intercom and hologram. "Thank you for answering my summons. It's good to see you in person. I've heard so much about you, both from the board of examiners and from your esteemed aunt."

Vi, heart still hammering against her ribcage, folded shaking hands behind her back, and lengthened her spine. "I'm honored, Headmaster Winchester."

The grin grew. "Karolyn is fine, dear."

Vi didn't release her hands. "Was this a test?"

Karolyn Winchester steepled ivory-pale fingers across her beautiful desk, looking amused at the question. "I run a school, Miss Park. A school that instills a very particular skill set in its students." She winked at Viola. "I think you'll find that most everything in the shadow of Tai Mo, behind the gates of the Academy, is a test of some sort. You've done well, incidentally. A few of your new schoolmates vomited on my carpet as soon as they stumbled off that lift."

"Congratulations to me, I suppose," said Vi.

The Headmaster laughed. "Oh, I like you much better than the last crop of Park cousins who turned up on the doorstep of the GAN. The lot of you are all so predictably clever and talented, sometimes you forget to have personalities. Anabel assures me that you, at least, won't disappoint in that regard." She beckoned with one heavily jeweled finger. "Come closer, dear."

The Headmaster looked different in person than she did in the hologram. Vi flashed back, bizarrely, to an old-fashioned paperbound storybook Alex had gifted her when she was a child for some birthday or another. She'd been fuzzy on the finer details, far more interested in Aunt Cat's gleefully engineered presents of automated toy soldiers and collapsible dragon models, but one illustration had imprinted itself in her memory: a witch in a tower at the heart of the woods, her hands jeweled with rings, her pale hair piled as high on her head as any queen's crown. How she'd bent people toward her own ends with the crook of one of those glittering fingers.

As she walked closer, the juxtaposition fell apart a little. Karolyn Winchester was older than Aunt Anabel or Aunt Cat, but still young, or at least young-looking, her face naturally smooth and unblemished in a way that spoke of immaculate skin care rather than expensive surgeries or an excess of makeup. Closer up, she looked less like a storybook illustration and more like a person, elegant but friendly, the mischievous edge to her smile conspiratorial rather than mean-spirited.

Vi smiled back, thin and cautious. Looks could be deceiving, and Vi hadn't forgotten the Headmaster's signature on that first rejection letter from the GAN Academy, nor the hard, unforgiving line of the bargain she'd struck with Aunt Anabel. Vi wouldn't make it through the first semester of classes—let alone get a shot at finding the missing pilots—unless she played her cards with this woman carefully. Very carefully.

"Viola Park." The Headmaster rolled Vi's name around in her mouth like she was tasting it on a sampler platter. "You're probably wondering what you're doing here. You know, I originally had a hankering to strip you of your piloting license."

Vi loosened a jaw that wanted to tighten on instinct. She refused to drop the smile. "So I remember."

If Karolyn Winchester registered the reaction, she didn't bother acknowledging it. "Never thought I'd welcome you darkening the doors of my school, girl who did what you did on that entrance exam," she mused. "But you know what your aunt's like. Don't you?"

"She did raise me. It would be hard to miss, Headmaster."

"It was an interesting line of argument." The Headmaster's blue eyes glittered over the desk like the hard gems on her fingers. "No attempt to defend what you'd done, morally. No high-handed plea for her family's honor. Just pure logic, like a mathematical equation: I need pilots, and you have the skills."

"Under probation," Vi pointed out. She was getting better at saying the word without flinching.

The Headmaster ignored the bait. "I'm going to assume that as you do not live under a rock, you've heard about our missing Peacekeeper situation." The jeweled fingers steepled. "Do you have a theory?"

The question took Vi by surprise. "You care?" she blurted out before she thought better of it, and reddened. *Calm down. Recover. So far as the Headmaster knows, you're still a disgrace, so the less attention you draw to yourself, the better. There's no way that Karolyn Winchester of all people knows about your dumb lofty goals to find her missing pilots, and if she does, she has no reason to be overinterested in one probie girl putting on airs to solve the GAN's most critical mystery.*

Not that Vi was likely to come close to solving it without a place in the Peacekeeper Corps herself.

Vi suppressed a sigh. *Nancy Drew with giant robot dragons, indeed.* "I assume you have more expert opinions at your disposal than mine," she offered instead.

"Oh, I do," said Winchester. "But as previously established, I do like to test the mettle of young people. So." Her hands spread, inviting. "Your theory. What is it?"

Vi sucked in a breath. Well, here they were. She still didn't want to draw attention to herself. It was too risky, with someone like the Headmaster—the same Headmaster who'd nearly nipped Vi's piloting career in the bud before it had a chance to even start blossoming—and if there was anything Vi had learned from her own entrance exam, it was the dark side of taking unnecessary risks. Attracting too much scrutiny from a Headmaster who'd proven herself as exacting and thoroughly unforgiving as Karolyn Winchester was the very definition of unnecessary. What to say, then?

"Aunt Anabel thinks they're still alive," she decided on at last. There. A nice, safe answer. Typical Park girl response, and Vi didn't even have to cough up a real opinion.

It was as if Karolyn Winchester read her mind. The Headmaster smiled that Cheshire cat smile again. "Ah, ah, ah. Not what I asked." She wagged a heavily jeweled finger, like Vi was a naughty kid being disciplined by the principal during recess or something. Which, considering the whole probie thing, probably wasn't far off, as a metaphor. "If I wanted to know what Anabel Park thought, I'd have asked her while she was bargaining for your admission to my school." The Headmaster leaned forward, stretching toward Vi, as if in invitation or threat. Maybe both. "Now, once more: What do *you* think?"

Vi wrestled with herself for a moment, then opted for a conservative truth: "I think maybe Aunt Anabel doesn't want to admit, even to herself, that Prudence Wu and her ilk are mortal after all." She shrugged one shoulder. "Not even Parks are immune to sentiment sometimes. Rags like the *Wireless Global* can print whatever crazy conspiracy theories they want. Sometimes Peacekeepers die."

"Like your parents did."

Something shuttered inside Vi's chest. "Excuse me?"

"Jonathan and Elizabeth Park." The Headmaster's head tilted, her expression curious. "They were your parents, no? And rather famous for their martyring, taking out an entire swarm of rogue war bots in the Pacific before their dragons were destroyed."

"I've read the obituaries," said Vi flatly.

Winchester's gem-hard gaze softened, almost imperceptibly, but it warmed her features just enough to convey genuine sympathy. "I've struck a nerve. Forgive me, Miss Park. I didn't mean to."

"Didn't you?" Vi rolled her head in the general direction of their surroundings: the creaky haunted mansion–worthy elevator, the glowing wall sconces, the Headmaster's desk at the top of a goddamn tower in the woods. "You're the one who said everything you do is a test, and so far, I've seen no evidence against that, Headmaster."

"Karolyn."

Vi flashed a thin-lipped, insincere little smile. "Karolyn."

The Headmaster sighed. One of those elegant jeweled hands had started twirling an ink pen—and of course Karolyn Winchester would keep old-school pens on her beautiful wooden desk in this day and age—with all the fidgeting abandon of a schoolgirl. It made her seem tired, distractable, a little less polished. Something petty in Vi took satisfaction at that. "For what it's worth," said Winchester, "your parents were part of why I agreed to Anabel's terms."

"Oh really?" Vi folded her arms. "How do you figure, *Karolyn*?"

"They were good, first of all," said Winchester. "Very good. And I don't just mean that in the sense of pure skill. Johnny and Liz were good *people*, the sort who always had a kind word or a favor for everyone else without ever expecting anything in return, you understand?" The blue gaze had gone distant. "They had the faces you'd think of when you wanted to believe in the core principles of why the GAN was founded: valor and nobility and the desire to protect the little people in a big, unfriendly world. In the grand scheme of things, among Peacekeepers, being a good person and not just a good pilot matters more."

Winchester pointed her pen at Vi. "I took a chance on you because I wanted—still want—to believe that your parents' kid, probie or not, might have a little of the secret sauce that made them that way."

"What, willing to fling themselves at a mission where they knew they'd be outnumbered three to one so they could go out in a blaze of glory like a couple of idiots with no sense of long-term strategy?"

The pen froze. Winchester's gaze had refocused on Vi, as if seeing her for the first time, and not just Aunt Anabel or her dead parents or any other Park. "It seems I keep striking nerves I least expect to. I had wondered how you felt about the incident. If that played into the choices you made regarding your audition on the entrance exam."

At Vi's tightly wound silence, the Headmaster continued, almost sympathetically, "I'm not without a heart, you know, Miss Park. I know it's not easy, being a probationary student here. I'd like to show you a little kindness, if I can."

Vi folded her arms. "And what would I have to do, to earn your . . . kindness?"

"Simple," said the Headmaster. "Beat Nicholas Lee."

Vi blinked. The Headmaster couldn't be serious. "And how exactly am I supposed to do that? Last I checked, there was more than one cadet competing in this tourney."

"Oh, there is," said the Headmaster cheerfully. "You're right: I can't very well give you a shot at my best cadet without making you jump through the same hoops as anyone else. You've read the rules, I trust?"

Of course she had. With the well-honed discipline of a New Columbia Prep alum, Vi rattled off from memory: "Three phases of competition: the hand-to-hand, the non-sentient-combat-engagement portions, and finally, sentient combat engagement. Each competitor gets a maximum of two matches per phase. Lose the first match, and you're shit out of luck—disqualified from the tournament entirely. Win the first match, and you'll proceed to the second. Lose the second match, and you'll enter the next phase of competition by the skin of your teeth. Win both matches, and ding ding ding, congratulations, you're almost certainly guaranteed a spot in the Peacekeeper Corps."

The Headmaster smiled. "Almost."

Vi's head tilted. "Almost?"

The Headmaster's jeweled fingers spread, imploring. "This isn't your average mech combat competition, Miss Park. We have no single elimination rules or round-robin format—not every student will face every student, and there will be no neatly designated champion and runners-up on a big shiny podium at the end of the day."

"Then what's the point?"

"The point," said Winchester, holding out one hand, "is a showcase." She grinned at the frown that unfurled across Vi's forehead. "Think about it this way. Let's say I hold a traditional tournament with a single winner, in one skill area—say, oh, non-sentient mech combat piloting. Maybe a silver medalist, maybe even a bronze. That gives me one—at best, three—combat-proven prospects to refill the ranks of a fighting force that has already hemorrhaged sixteen pilots that we know of in the past month, thanks to these mysterious and extremely inconvenient disappearances."

Winchester held out the other hand. "Now, alternatively, let's say that I hold a tournament with the format and rules I just described. Every student gets at most six matches, spread across multiple combat disciplines, all crucial to the full-formed Peacekeeper. Now I have a holistic look at multiple students, and provided they don't lose the first match of the first phase, a decent chance to check out their skills in more than one discipline against more than one opponent. Instead of one winner, I get a pool of promising performers in multiple areas to pick and choose from."

Vi's brow furrowed. "So even in a straight competition, there's no objective criteria to winning."

"No. You think there should be?" Winchester shrugged. "I'm given to understand that piloting a sentient, particularly in combat, is as much art as science. Which means that the 'winners' of this tournament—if you can call them that; personally, I'd prefer the term 'successful recruits'—are chosen on both objective and subjective grounds. True, students must achieve victory in at least one phase of the tournament in order to be considered for a Peacekeeper position, but final selection from among the victors will ultimately be up to me." The Headmaster's gaze was speculative. "It's not enough to be a proficient pilot, you know. This is the Global Alliance of Nations, and we expect more than proficiency from a Peacekeeper. We expect something special."

Vi's heart sank. It would be just like the Academy entrance exam. No matter how many points you racked up in the written and physical, the ultimate decision had still hinged on the audition piece. "What does 'something special' have to do with matching up against Nick?"

The Headmaster smiled. "Assuming you survive your first match, I can arrange for you to face Nick at least once in each phase of this tournament—or however long you last against your fellow competitors. Nicholas Lee is currently the Academy's top-ranked, best all-around fighter. It simply wouldn't be fair to treat a win against him the same way we'd treat a win against anyone else—hence, a victory against him, at any phase in the tournament, automatically earns the winner a spot in the Peacekeeper Corps."

Vi's heart stopped. "So if you ensure that I get at least one shot at Nick in each tourney phase—hand-to-hand, non-sentient, and sentient—then that means that I've got . . ."

"Potentially three chances at a winner-take-all bonus, yes." Winchester shrugged. "The second- and third-years already know, at least unofficially—it's how things have always worked with mech combat tournaments at the Academy. You can always secure an easy win by beating the top contender entering the game. That lights a fire under everyone else's ass, while painting a target on the back of the Academy's top cadet, so they don't get complacent. Usually, it's good for stoking friendly competition all around." She paused. "Interestingly, ever since Nicholas became the de facto campus ace, none of the second- or third-years have been particularly keen on challenging him—not legitimately. I've yet to see another student beat him, even in unofficial training, who didn't cajole or bribe or pay him off to deliberately take a fall."

Unwittingly, Vi's brain reran the way Nicholas Lee had felt in their last face-off. How utterly helpless she'd been beneath the coldly executed pressure of his mech. How little he'd seemed to care. She shivered. "I can guess why. Winner-take-all only works in my favor if I can actually, you know, *win* against the guy, which seems like a bad gamble, especially when he can hurt me, and hurt me bad. Can't I just take my chances matching up with whoever else makes it as far as I do in the tournament?" If she made it at all. Forcibly, she wrenched her thoughts from that general direction. *Yay, positive thinking, Vi.*

"Oh, you could," said the Headmaster, affably enough. "But you're the one with something to prove, are you not? And there's no better way to prove yourself than by beating the best, when everyone else is scared shitless of challenging him. Do that, and no one will question your right to a Peacekeeper's cockpit. No one will ever sneer at you again. No one will dare. Isn't that what you want?"

"Why does what I want matter so much to you?" asked Vi.

Winchester's fingers folded, steepling and unsteepling, casting the glitter from her rings in odd patterns across Vi's field of vision. "The students at this Academy are already the best of the best, but in order for me to truly find and shape the ideal Peacekeeper, each—like a gemstone—must be carved and polished in a manner particular to their shape. You fit a certain . . . shape, wouldn't you say? I'm just trying to figure out the right way to make you shine. And that means finding the right means of motivation."

Vi colored. "So that's why you mis-scored me on the quiz. You thought I'd be desperate enough to try beating up a boy who can't seem to be beaten."

And why not? asked a traitorous little voice inside Vi's head. *You already came here because you thought you could get to the bottom of the missing pilot case. What's one more impossible task to restore your reputation at this rate?*

Winchester winked. "With the right tool set, even boys like Nicholas Lee can be beaten. And just for the record, I didn't misscore you. Believe me, Miss Park. You're precisely where I want you."

◆

THE AIR HAD TAKEN ON an unseasonable chill by the time Vi finally made her way out of the Headmaster's tower. It bit hard into her skin, sharp and startling, after the balmy Hong Kong evening, and Vi shivered as she squinted through the wooded campus. Had it been this dark when she'd left the dorms?

She'd grown up on enough ghost stories that the hazy outline of two figures, shadowed in the crook of a tree, nearly gave her an actual heart attack. It took her a beat to make out the telltale silhouette of cadet flight suits. It took her another to recognize a shock of red hair. Rosalyn Davies.

Rosalyn's companion took longer for Vi to place, but when she did, he was unmistakable. A candle flame caught in the shape of a boy—in that moment, entwined with Rosalyn beneath the shelter of that menacing black tree, like a pair of romance novel lovers stuck on the cover of the wrong book. Rosalyn had Nicholas Lee's back pressed up against the trunk, one knee pinning him in place, which must have hurt, but he didn't seem to care, his eyes shut as she kissed her way down the pale, moonlit column of his throat.

Vi looked away abruptly, cheeks hot and heart rattling, which was a little embarrassing. Voyeurism had never been her thing, but she wasn't a prude either. It wasn't like she'd never seen people getting handsy back at New Columbia Prep—you had to blow off steam somehow, and there were worse ways to do it. Big deal.

Still, something about the way these two curled around each other made Vi feel like an intruder. She backed away as quickly and quietly as she could, onto a different route back to the dorms. Still, the image of how Nicholas Lee had looked in that moment—his flight suit shucked open at the collar, head thrown back and hair tangled between Rosalyn's hungry fingers—stuck inside Vi's head, imprinting itself over far more sensible thoughts.

Thoughts like how the hell she was supposed to kick his ass. Vi paused, considering. Once again, the look on Lee's face skittered across her mind's eye. How open and guileless and utterly at her mercy he had seemed, all to the whims of a girl. How very different he had looked in that moment, beneath her hands, than he had in a combat sim, bearing down on Vi's battle mech, practically bored with the level of sheer power he had over her.

Aunt Anabel had always said that in life, as in war or politics, you needed to take in the entire field of battle, not just a single opponent. You had to use your environment to your own advantage, and that meant seeing the whole picture: the terrain, alliances and rivalries, friends and enemies and lovers, and all the ways they intersected. Everyone had weaknesses. If you couldn't tackle a problem head-on, you had to find a way to cut an angle.

Vi bit her lip. Maybe there was something to be said for taking Rosalyn Davies up on that offer of friendship after all.

The next morning dawned with the news that two more Peacekeepers had gone missing. The alert blared to life on her phone, waking her a full hour earlier than the alarm she'd set for class. Vi swore, and nearly hurled her phone across the room before remembering two things. First, that she no longer had her own bedroom. Second, that the poor phone was merely doing what Vi had programmed it to: beeping alerts at her every time news broke regarding Peacekeeper disappearances. A terrible feeling in Vi's gut suggested that her phone would be doing a lot of beeping this year.

After sparing a cursory glance toward the other bed to make sure she hadn't woken her roommate, Vi thumbed the alert open, scanning for names. Gordon Tanaka and Suzie Abubakar. They'd vanished on a joint detail guarding a crew of volunteer food-aid workers on a trip across the Mediterranean. It was the usual story: no witnesses, no signs of a struggle, no leads on who the hell could have made two elite mech pilots—let alone their dragons—just vanish into nothing.

Vi groaned into the bedcovers. Her plan for Monday morning had not included an ongoing global catastrophe. Her morning was supposed to start with a far smaller trauma: her first real sequence of classes—including the so-called probationary students' tutorial—which sounded less like a class to Vi, and more like a recurring detention period for the Academy's resident delinquents. Vi turned one bleary eye toward the time projected up at her from her phone. She could still afford another half hour of sleep. A full hour, even, if she skipped some of the niceties of her usual morning routine. Besides, two more of the GAN's own were missing. Maybe dead. And Vi still had no idea how to begin solving the mystery of how to find them again. Surely, sleeping on the matter could only help.

She regretted this logic tremendously when she woke again what felt like hours later, this time to the chipper sounds of the Academy app on her phone announcing that "you have now slept precisely thirty-two minutes and fifteen seconds past your alarm. Would you like to snooze or reset again?"

Several expletives, the rage-fueled near-destruction of her phone, and a half-buttoned flight suit later, Vi slammed into the designated classroom. And "only four minutes and thirteen seconds late." Take that, you passive-aggressive piece of garbage machinery.

"Sorry!" Vi panted. Hands on her knees as she caught her breath, she tried to get a read on the room's few occupants.

There were only three: a boy and a girl slouching at the back with such similar facial features and body language that they had to be related, and Tamara Rogers, who barely looked conscious. The Academy app had described a roster of five probationary students: three second-years, a third-year, and Vi, the singular first-year.

"Is this the"—Vi paused to double-check her phone—"the 'probationary students' tutorial' classroom?"

Tamara, sprawled on her back across a row of three desks, peered out from behind the cover of the paperbound book that had been left open-faced on top of her face. "If by 'probationary students' tutorial,' you mean punishment class for the handpicked fuckups of the Academy, then absolutely. Welcome, Valerie."

"Viola," Vi corrected indignantly. "Seriously, dude? We're roommates."

"Okay, Victoria," agreed Tamara with a yawn. She covered her face back up.

"Forgive poor Tamara," said the boy. "She's American, and while very good at pretending to be awake, here among us probies, she normally can't be bothered until noon at the earliest."

"One P.M., preferably." Tamara's voice was muffled by the book pages. "Until then, I might as well be a mech on autopilot, and I refuse to apologize for the ruse."

"Shamelessly frankly spoken too." The boy shook his head, making faint tsk-tsk noises. "You see? American."

"Honestly, I can sympathize," admitted Vi.

"Another American?"

"A Canadian, technically," said Vi. "But born and raised in New Columbia, where Washington was."

"Ah, the crown jewel of the surviving democratic cities of poor war-torn North America." The boy clucked his tongue. "And how is the Barricade Coalition faring against its corporate aggressors? I'm amazed those great hulking walls of yours weren't torn apart by those awful flying monster mechs in your first round of Partition Wars."

Vi shrugged. "We're scrappy." She squinted at him, trying to place his accent. "You a local boy?"

"Got it in one," said the boy, jerking his head at the girl beside him. "Amadeus Huang, at your service. My sister and I are authentic Hong Kongers, born in Central." He grinned. "Though Causeway Bay is our real haunt. Or was." He waggled his fingers. "Until a bit of a scrap with a very beautiful private fleet of mechs landed us . . . well, here."

"He means he committed grand theft auto," said his sister in matter-of-fact tones. "On a privately owned war mech."

"How was I supposed to know the beaut belonged to an Australian warlord!"

"The armed guards in its immediate vicinity, presumably."

Vi's mouth twitched despite herself. "Did you aid and abet, then?" she asked Amadeus's sister.

"Oh, no," she said thoughtfully. "I killed a man. With his own mech. Completely separate crime. I'm Elsbeth Huang, by the way."

Very slowly, Vi's gaze tracked between brother and sister. With their slippery black hair, snub noses, and bright eyes, they looked more like a pair of overgrown kittens turned human than literal criminals. "I honestly can't tell if you're messing with me or not," she told them.

"Oh, they're being completely earnest," came Tamara's paper-muffled voice from the other corner. Very slowly, she rolled her way off the makeshift couch she'd created with the desks. The book slipped into her hands as she yawned, cracking her shoulders. "We're all criminals here," she said to Vi, with just a hint of a challenge in her voice.

"I'm not," protested Vi, even though protesting her own unsavory reputation was feeling more and more futile. "I just—"

"Cheated on the entrance exam?" Elsbeth piped up. "Some might say that's worse."

The force of unexpected shame rammed into Vi's gut so hard she had to bite her lip. She'd heard her own fuckup thrown in her face enough times now that she should have been used to it, but every time someone new brought it up, some piece of her twisted itself up all over again. Aunt Anabel would have had the perfect retort, something cuttingly witty that would put Elsbeth in her place without making her feel lesser, and probably win her eternal friendship and loyalty besides. Alex would have let the hurt roll off his shoulders like water, smiled, and dazzled Elsbeth so thoroughly and so genuinely with his warmth that any judgment she'd harbored would evaporate like condensation on a summer's day.

But Vi was tired, and stressed, and still not over her jet lag, and simply didn't have the energy for verbal repartee or charming kindnesses. But Aunt Cat had told Vi to wear her shame as armor. That much maybe she could manage right now. "I'm not sure where cheating on exams ranks in the grand scheme of sins, on a scale from robbing warlords to literal murder," said Vi, with a casual little roll of her shoulders, "but it sounds a lot less impressive." She jerked her chin at Tamara. "What are you in for?"

"The most stereotypically North American crime of them all," said Amadeus. "Book smuggling."

Vi stared at Tamara. "Seriously?"

"Seriously," agreed Tamara, without batting an eye. "Not everyone who grew up on the continent was a Park princess."

Black market media distribution rings—book smuggling, in common parlance—had been an underground institution across North American territories for as long as the continent had been divided between corporate rule and democracy. Incorporated law couldn't regulate literal free thought, so instead, it did the next best thing by regulating art and entertainment, which meant you had to get books and movies and music from illegal distributors if you lived outside a Barricade city.

Vi raised both hands, a placating gesture. "Callout noted. For what it's worth, my aunt Cat was from the southwest territories, born under Incorporated rule. No disrespect. It's just . . . I figured book smuggling was more of a slap-on-the-wrist kind of deal." Most of the perpetrators were schoolkids, after all. It didn't really rank on the same level as mech theft or murder. It might not even rank on the same level as exam cheating.

"Not if you run the biggest illegal library distribution network off the West Coast," said Amadeus with a grin. "Pretty impressive, all things considered."

"Getting busted was less impressive," drawled Tamara. "Should have watched my back better. Distributing books and movies in bulk is a much more restful living than bonding your brains to giant metal monsters."

"But you'll be a Peacekeeper when you graduate," said Vi.

"Whoop-dee-doo," said Tamara. "Is that supposed to excite me? Toiling away in the cockpit of a dragon to risk life and limb for the sanctity of a sprawling international organization that's done fuck-all for me, personally? I was very happy with my independent business."

"Except for the constant threat of Incorporated police squads and incarceration, presumably," said Elsbeth.

"Except for that," said Tamara companionably. "At least we've all got only one more year left in this place, thank god. If we're lucky, most of us will land desk-warmer jobs where we can do boring-ass admin for decent benefits."

Vi's eyebrows climbed. "You want to be a nine-to-five nobody?"

Tamara snorted. "Better a nine-to-five nobody than dead on a battlefield and memorialized on some ugly-ass plaque."

Something folded in on itself inside Vi's chest, as she looked around the room—really looked, this time. Three of her classmates were would-be convicted criminals: a murderer, a mech thief, and a black market baron. If they hadn't been plucked up by the Headmaster for the GAN Academy's probationary class, they'd all be in prison.

"Real talk," said Vi. "Do any of you actually want to be Peacekeepers?"

Amadeus tilted his head toward her, looking quizzical. "In the sense of 'a better career option than jailbird,' then sure."

Vi didn't know what to do with that. On a theoretical level, she understood it. If she'd been caught committing a crime—not cheating the entrance exam, but a real crime, the sort that landed you with an incarceration sentence—she'd pick the Academy over prison too, if that was an option offered to her. But the Academy, for her, had always been the subject of aspiration, the position of Peacekeeper a dream that only the worthy obtained. It was supposed to be a privilege, not a last resort of the desperate and damned.

"Where's our teacher?" she asked at last. To say nothing of the final, missing student. "Shouldn't class be starting by now?"

Tamara barked a quick laugh. "Look around, new blood. Our teacher's no different than the rest of us. Probably got assigned to babysit the probie class after drawing the short straw at a faculty meeting, and doesn't want to be here any more than we do. Why would they bother showing up on time?"

"The teacher we had for this schedule block last year arrived on time pretty regularly," mused Elsbeth. She paused. "Then again, he also just turned off the lights, put on instructional videos, and fell asleep for about eighty percent of classes. I think he's retired now."

"One time, Tamara switched out the instructional video for a racy movie from her stash," said Amadeus fondly. "He didn't even notice. Good times."

Vi frowned. "So, what, this is just a glorified homeroom period? You get your fundamentals training for the cockpit in your other coursework?"

"How on earth would that happen?" asked Amadeus. He sounded genuinely quizzical. "Up until this year's conscription was announced, probies weren't trusted to pilot alongside the regular students, presumably for fear that we'd commit some grave error and injure the real future knights of the GAN. Perfectly understandable, really. Hence the existence of this class period. Probationary students exclusively, a danger only to our own. We've always been the last resort."

Vi's brows knit together. "The what?"

"The last resort," Elsbeth cut in. "We have little value outside our mech bonding skill—which means we'll only ever see action if the real cadets somehow fail on a mass scale. We're the understudies to the understudies, and the GAN have convinced themselves that they're so perfect, they'll never truly need us in that capacity." She shrugged. "Meanwhile, we're an easy source of labor—someone needs to get stuck with the shitty, mindless, paper-pushing gigs none of the real GAN brass want to do."

The wheels in Vi's mind spun. "So you're saying that none of your teachers for this class ever . . . actually worked with you on any real piloting."

Amadeus blinked. "Lord, no."

Vi stared around at all of them, trying and probably failing to conceal her faint horror. "And you've spent . . . how many hours actually learning or practicing the principles of bonding sentient mechs in this class?"

"Zero," said Elsbeth. "That would be precisely zero hours."

Vi had studied GAN Academy curricula cover to cover before prepping for the entrance exam. Cadets on a standard track covered at least five hours of theory and five hours of practicals per week in sentient bonding, for each of the three years of study. If you couldn't demonstrate adequate skill and knowledge of sentient mechanics and behavior by the time you hit your third year, you were barred from attempting to bond even the trainee dragons, which meant you'd almost certainly wash out, with no chance at the Peacekeeper Corps—and even if you did see the inside of a cockpit, Elsbeth was right: you'd probably never see real action unless shit really went to hell. Feebly, she started to calculate how far behind three second-year students would be now, and abandoned the enterprise almost immediately, overwhelmed.

"It's not as bad as my sister makes it sound," offered Amadeus in what he probably thought was a soothing voice. "Even before the conscription call shook things up, it's not like we were totally isolated from the regular students. You pick things up your own way, as a probie."

"How?" Vi demanded, sounding hollow even to her own ears.

"Without adequate practice bonding sentients in a formal classroom setting, how in hell are you ever going to catch up to the other cadets? That's the core of what Peacekeepers *do*."

"Easy," said Amadeus. "We don't catch up. We just survive."

Which was, as if on cue, when the classroom door slid aside with a hum.

The stranger who walked through it didn't look much like a GAN pilot. She also didn't look much like a teacher. She was a stout Chinese woman of indeterminate age, casually dressed in jeans and a GAN hoodie, her hands thrust into its pockets. Her thick coil of black hair had been pinned efficiently to the nape of her neck, but a couple stray strands poked out like little devil horns over the top of her wide, smooth forehead.

"Hey there," she said, cheerfully American accented. "You must be the criminal underbelly of the student body I've heard so much about." She peered around at the four of them. "To be honest, I thought there'd be more of you."

"We're missing our glorious third-year at the moment," said Amadeus Huang, the first to recover. "You must be . . ."

"Your sifu, as it were," said the Chinese American woman, with a broad grin.

"Do you have a name?" asked Elsbeth. "Last year's teacher did."

"Last year's teacher was an ass," said the self-proclaimed sifu with a wave of her blunt-nailed hand. "Let's just stick with Sifu, shall we?"

"You don't think that's a little appropriative?" Vi asked dryly. "This isn't a wushu class, and you're . . . so very American."

"Say it like an insult, why don't you," murmured Tamara with little heat.

"Ah, a Canadian!" Sifu clapped her hands together, eyeing Vi up and down, looking delighted to be insulted by a fellow North American. "I'd been told there was at least one of you here. How splendid. You're not Viola Park, are you?"

"Unfortunately, yes," said Vi.

Sifu produced a phone and thumbed the screen. "Splendid," she repeated. Vi waited for the usual remarks about Aunt Anabel, or her cousins, or god forbid, her parents. Instead, Sifu merely said, "I can't imagine attendance will take all that long. The way protest groups go on about probies, you'd think there were a hundred of you swarming through these hallowed halls, plotting to overthrow the Headmaster. Amadeus Huang?"

"Here," said Amadeus. "If there were a hundred of us, I imagine the GAN's Peacekeeper fleet would have fewer worries about finding pilots to fill dragon cockpits."

"You're not wrong." Sifu swiped her thumb again. "Elsbeth Huang?"

"Present and accounted for," said Elsbeth. "How novel, having attendance taken."

"An ancient yet oft-neglected practice. Also, literally the only way I'm going to remember your names. Tamara Rogers?"

Tamara raised a couple fingers. She was staring at Sifu over the frames of her glasses with an expression of intent curiosity. "Have I seen you somewhere else before?"

Sifu flashed an odd little smile at her. "Not unless you've been sneaking into some truly boring-ass faculty meetings, in which case I assure you that your delinquency is misplaced. There are much more exciting forbidden meetings to sneak into at this school, if that's your inclination." The older woman's facial features pulled together strangely as she spoke. It took Vi a moment to pinpoint why: with every little twitch and shift of her expression, Sifu's face looked like it belonged to a slightly different person, the features subtly altered. Yet every time Vi looked back at her, she'd swear nothing had changed at all.

Maybe Vi was just losing her mind.

Sifu's thumb paused over the final name. That odd expression of hers twitched again. "And, last but not least, our absentee third-year student. Ah, well, a first-day case of senioritis isn't anything that can't be managed in due course. Meanwhile." She tossed the phone back into the hoodie pocket and clapped her hands together once more. "What do you say to getting up from behind those desks for a fun hands-on classroom activity?"

Amadeus's brows climbed, buoyed by obvious suspicion. "What kind of 'fun hands-on classroom activity,' precisely?"

"What the hell else would you do in an Academy classroom?" Sifu rolled her eyes, which were gleaming with excitement. Or possibly mania of some sort. "Fight."

"Fight?" Vi echoed. Her heart rate picked up a little. "You mean in another combat sim, like the one Headmaster Winchester made us deal with in that pop quiz yesterday?"

"Oh, how did everyone do on that, by the way?" Amadeus asked blithely. "I got a two out of ten, so I should be safe from this draft, don't you think?"

Aggressively, Vi ignored him, pressing forward with her line of questioning. "If it's another combat sim like that one, I don't know if it'll work out, since our numbers will be uneven once your missing student gets here, but—"

"Settle down, would you, Park girl?" interrupted Sifu. Amusement danced through those oddly forgettable eyes of hers. "I'm not putting the lot of you through another combat sim, at least not right now. You can't live your entire life in simulation, and you certainly can't fight that way. Yes, I know that combat sims have their place in training," she added, before Vi could open her mouth. "I know all the arguments, don't worry." Her head tilted. "Besides, I'd have thought you of all people would be shy of simulations."

The shame was easier to swallow this time. "I'm shy of everything at the Academy," said Vi dryly. It wasn't even really a lie. Fear was a contagion. A sim may have been the site of her first failure, but Vi's newfound sense of apprehension seemed to have no real limits. Her disastrous attempt at piloting the Lioness before she left for the Academy had scared her just as well as the Headmaster's pop quiz.

Sifu chuckled. "Fair enough. No, I thought we'd break things back down to the fundamentals. Physical hand-to-hand sparring. No mechs. No sims. Just good old-fashioned human fisticuffs. After all, that's the first hurdle you'll all be facing in the tournament. Now, who here can tell me why hand-to-hand is part of a mech combat tournament?"

Vi snorted. "I know we're all . . . *probies* here"—aha, take that, inner shame; she could name herself for what she was, after all!—"but I'd like to think that the Academy wouldn't have plucked any of us from our past lives of sin for being stupid. Physical combat training is integrated into any mech combatives curriculum. It's always been that way. Lord knows why."

Sifu's gaze sidled toward Vi, paused, and pinned her in place. It was unnerving in a completely different way from the Headmaster's. "I'm surprised that you of all people, Park girl, wouldn't have figured that much out yourself. As I recall, you're all trained from the cradle to fight both in and out of the cockpit."

"Sure," agreed Vi, a little testily, "but that doesn't mean we necessarily understand the reasons." She winced. Maybe that had been too honest.

Sifu grinned. "Fair enough. Here's another question for you, then. As someone who has frequently been in both mech spars and hand-to-hand spars, which did you prefer: being encased in a nice protective bubble of metal while your mech takes the brunt of hits for you, or being hit directly with a body shot, and no lovely protective mechanical hide to brace you from the blow?"

Vi blinked. "Is this a trick question? Neither are great, but the second one tends to hurt more. Obviously."

"Precisely," said Sifu. "Mech pilots who engage in combat are going to see their fair share of wear and tear—it's inevitable, in our trade. And it's about a hundred times easier to learn to roll with the literal punches if you've already done it outside of the cockpit."

"Outside of the cockpit, you don't have to worry about fists the size of an automated car and coated in rust-resistant chrome," Amadeus pointed out. "Or plasma fire guns. Or mech-enabled laser blades. Or a number of other problems."

"True," allowed Sifu. She was still grinning. "But you must walk before you run, my boy. Hence our return to combat fundamentals: good old-fashioned human fisticuffs. Learn them, use them, love them."

"Last one's probably a bit of a tall order for my brother," said Elsbeth without heat. She hummed. "I don't think I mind so much, though."

Vi considered what little she'd learned about Elsbeth in the past hour: that she'd killed a man, that she'd managed to do it with what amounted to his own weapon, and that she seemed not to regret it terribly. She had no idea what Elsbeth was like in a fight without a mech at her disposal, but Vi was pretty sure she didn't want to find out.

"Fine," said Vi. She really was getting better at masking a pounding heart with nonchalant tones. "Let's just get this over with. How do we determine fight order?"

"Easy," said Sifu. Seemingly from out of nowhere, she produced a metal cup. Vi peered inside. Four neatly folded strips of white paper—cheap, old-fashioned paper, the sort they used to write on in notebooks before souped-up phones and hologram projectors became the norm—lay scattered within.

"What are those?" asked Vi, who was trying very hard not to read too much into the symbology of the color white in East Asian cultures (death) or the number four (also death).

Sifu grinned. "Names. I'm a traditional sort of girl, you'll find. We're drawing lots." She rattled the cup beneath Vi's nose, like a street beggar demanding her due. "And you, Park girl, shall have the honor of going first."

MONSTERS WHO TAME MONSTERS —— 6

Vi drew Amadeus's name.

She tried not to make her immediate relief look too obvious, but Tamara and Elsbeth both seemed to catch it anyway: Tamara snorted, and Elsbeth simply cocked her head at Vi, dark eyes cool with assessment and curiosity. Vi didn't love the look. She'd seen it on the faces of far too many competitive schoolmates—and occasionally on the faces of her own cousins—whenever Vi did something a little too well. It was a hungry expression, worn by those who craved a chance to prove themselves, to test their mettle against something truly worthy. Normally, Vi took it as a compliment, and was all too happy to oblige.

Normally, the people feeding her that look weren't literal self-proclaimed murderers.

Amadeus, meanwhile, was looking at Vi exactly the same way Vi was probably looking at his sister: with an expression of poorly concealed terror. As they cleared the desks in the classroom to make space, he grew paler and paler, fidgeting with his long, lean hands. "So when, ah, Sifu said that, er, all Parks are raised from the cradle to fight both in and out of the cockpit, that meant . . . um . . ."

Vi shrugged. A tendril of pity snaked through her. "Just some basic self-defense. A bit of boxing, a bit of grappling, a few stints dealing with improvised weapons. Mostly for physical conditioning. We spent more time in the cockpit, or in combat sims."

"Improvised weapons?" Amadeus repeated, panic rising in his voice. Abruptly, he set down the chair he'd gone to stack against the wall. His fingers, indented with the grooves of the seat, twisted together.

Sifu clapped a friendly hand over his shoulders. He squeaked. "Calm down, Mr. Huang, there will be no weapons in my classroom . . . well, today, anyway," she added, looking devilishly contemplative. "Basic parameters for this exercise. It's an easy little round—just two minutes, to see what you've got. Light- to medium-contact sparring. Don't get so excited that you actually try and KO each other, you hear?"

Vi heard. Amadeus, apparently, did not. He swung in on her immediately, with a wild, panic-fueled haymaker that probably would have taken Vi's head off with sheer enthusiasm if she hadn't managed to bob under. Amadeus, not to be dissuaded, aimed at her with the other hand, just as enthusiastically.

Great. It figured that Amadeus would be the sort of person whose fear of physical confrontation manifested as sloppy but dangerously unpredictable violence. This did nothing for Vi's mood about the entire affair. Enough was enough. Vi aimed the bottom of her foot straight into his torso, and pushed, throwing just enough body weight behind it to show him she meant business. "Dude," she snapped. "Calm the hell down."

He stumbled backward, windmilling his arms and red in the face. "Is two minutes up yet?" he panted.

"It's been like twenty seconds," observed Elsbeth from the sidelines.

Tamara just shook her head slowly, eyes closed, one palm clasped against her forehead.

Vi moved to close the distance. Amadeus cowered back, scrambling. That gave her pause. She didn't like getting her ass handed to her, in the cockpit or out, but she didn't love being on this end of a mismatch either. It felt too much like bullying.

In the space of that pause, the floor nearly went out from under her. She found her feet, barely. For one bizarre, dizzying second, arms flung akimbo for balance, she wondered if it was Amadeus. If he'd been holding back on her all along, or at least gotten some lucky tackle on her.

Then the floor shook again. Amadeus screamed. This time, Vi did lose her footing. She let her momentum carry her backward, rounding her spine to lighten the impact. "What the hell was that?" she yelled.

No answers seemed forthcoming. Amadeus had hunkered down on the floor, joined by his sister, both of them wide-eyed. Tamara caught herself in a similar sprawl, ducked beneath one of the desks, swearing through clenched teeth.

"Don't move!" yelled Sifu. She braced herself along the wall, moving with surprising speed toward the door. "I'm getting help. Just hang on and keep sheltering here!"

"For how long?" yelped Amadeus, but Sifu was already out the door.

That left Vi on her own with three terrified ex-criminals she barely knew, trapped on a floor that might crumble beneath them at any moment. Academy life just got better and better.

What Vi needed was focus. She squeezed her eyes shut, trying to isolate individual sensations. The spurts of rumbling beneath the floorboards. The shouts of panic and confusion inside the classroom.

Raised voices and hurried steps out in the hallway. Something singing inside her head.

The music—more a constant hum than a real melody—drew her focus. Singing was such a stupid way to think of it, but she didn't have any other words worth using. Vi's brow furrowed, as she searched for the music's source. Sense memory filtered through her mind. It was something you learned to deal with, if you had any kind of affinity for sentients: alien sounds crashing into the privacy of your own brain. Vi, for one, was no stranger to the sensation, and this bizarre song, in that sense, was no different. Music was what Vi had heard in her head the first time she'd ever bonded a mech.

And suddenly, she was in another time and place.

The memory crept in on her like cold water filling a tub, until she was practically drowning in it. She'd only been about thirteen or so. The mech in question hadn't been a dragon, of course—dragons were reserved for Peacekeepers alone. This mech had been small, compactly built, its four-legged canine body designed to travel by land, not air. "A puppy," her cousin Albert had laughed. "To turn sentient bonding into a game for children. Let's see if you can charm the little gangaji, eh, Vi?"

Vi squatted before the strange little creature. The mech canted its chrome-plated head from side to side, examining Vi from head to toe, and she stretched out a hand. The thing about sentient mechs was that they were just that: sentient. They bore hides of chrome, cockpits where their insides should be, and in their most advanced forms, far more destructive power than any ordinarily evolved creature of nature could wield. But at the end of the day, they were still living creatures, strange and emotional and replete with all the peculiarities of consciousness.

"It's all right," said Vi, wiggling her fingers toward the mech. It was the same coaxing motion she used when trying to get Uncle Jay's cat to allow a scratch under the chin. "I just want to say hello."

The pup wandered cautiously toward her outstretched fingers, mechanical gears clicking along with every step. A low, suspicious rumble curdled the back of its throat, and the pup lunged forward abruptly. Vi checked a flinch, eyes squeezing shut for a moment, bracing for the snag of metal teeth.

Instead, a chrome snout bumped up against her fingers. Vi opened her eyes, staring. The pup's silver eyes stared back. It nudged her hand again, inspecting the skin. "I know," croaked Vi. "Soft, squishy organic flesh is pretty weird, huh?"

The pup bumped her hand again, as if in agreement. The space between them seemed to crackle for a moment, replete with some unnameable energy, like electricity on a brewing storm cloud. Then, sure enough, a ripple of something through Vi's mind, cautious but curious. Noise from another brain, like an incongruent melody from a piano that hadn't been tuned yet.

"If you give me a chance," whispered Vi, "I promise I'll give back as good as I've got." Vi stopped talking, her empty fingers frozen midair. The mech tilted its head left, then right. Then, before Vi's eyes, it lay down, exposing its back to her. Chrome rippled aside at the spine, revealing the seat and pedals of a cockpit.

"Well, I'll be damned." Her cousin whistled. "It's offering you a bond. Guess you have the knack for sentient compatibility after all, eh, Vi?"

"Obviously," said Vi. Gently, she pulled herself over the open hatch and into the seat. As chrome closed up around her and the mech's view screen filled her sight line, she grinned. "It's an act of trust."

Vi inhaled, sharp, the oxygen a knife through her lungs as the memory snapped her mind back to the present. She opened her eyes and looked, unwittingly, out the window, toward the woods. Today, the trees sat beneath a canopy of moody gray sky, as if dusk had fallen early over the Academy grounds. The sweat beading the back of her neck crawled down her skin in a cold trickle as she stared at those skies, and the darkness of the woods beneath. "We've got to figure out what's wrong," she said. "I . . . call it intuition, maybe, or a sixth sense, but I think there's something out in the forest. Something that shouldn't be there."

"Could you be any vaguer?" demanded Tamara.

"Besides, the Academy . . . staff . . . will . . . oof, handle it . . . won't they?" Amadeus pointed out, between puffs of hard-won air. He'd managed to find his feet, but remained hunched over, hands on his knees, clearly still in recovery mode. "Sifu said she was getting help."

Vi shook her head, frustrated. How to articulate what was happening in her head? Flustered, she bit her tongue before opening her mouth. "I don't know how I know, but I know what I know."

Well, that wasn't it. The thoroughly unimpressed expressions on the faces around her said as much. She tried again. "Look, you've all bonded sentients, yeah? You know how it feels, when you and the mech are feeling each other out, but you haven't been offered the bond just yet. That itch inside your brain. The feeling of something else lurking under your skin that doesn't quite belong to you, but when the bond is good and true, it's like . . . it's like it should have been there all along, like a missing piece of your mind that you've just found."

Tentative nods this time. Tamara crossed her arms, slouching backward with narrowed eyes, but she didn't interrupt, or scoff, or call Vi by some other *V* name. Vi mentally tallied the victory, and continued, "There's a sentient out there. Somewhere in the woods. I can feel them inside my head."

"Why just you?" Elsbeth didn't sound particularly accusatory, despite the question. She cocked her head, blinking a few times. "I don't hear anything. Does anyone else?"

Amadeus shook his head. Tamara shrugged, eyes narrowing further, still fixed on Vi.

"Maybe you're mistaken," offered Amadeus, tentative. "Our minds play tricks on us all sometimes, pilots more so than most people. Perhaps it's something else. The ghost of an old bond, or, or . . ."

"Your imagination?" finished Elsbeth.

"I'm not imagining things," Vi said through gritted teeth. "I know the feel of a sentient in my head when I hear one. I'm not—"

"She's right," interrupted Tamara.

Vi quit midsentence, faltering. Of all corners from which to find support, Tamara's hadn't been one she'd expected. The other girl hadn't changed position, still slouching and cross-armed, but something thoughtful lurked behind that thin-eyed gaze. "Don't give me that look; I can't hear shit either," said Tamara. "But sentients are like that sometimes. The ones I worked with in my old smuggling gig, they were all cagey as fuck—one pilot only, choosy with bond offers." She shrugged, looking away. "Maybe whatever Park is hearing is like that."

It wasn't quite a vote of confidence, but close enough. Another crash shook the floor beneath them. Someone screamed in the distance. Above it all, the odd, insistent noise in Vi's head grew louder, more insistent. It was no mistake, no fever dream. Certainty, cool and measured, bloomed under her chest, displacing the spike of panic. She knew what this was. Really, she'd known it from the moment her mind filled with the clamor of an alien song.

"I have to go," she insisted, more firmly this time.

"Go?" Amadeus's voice was incredulous. "To do what? Sifu said to wait here!"

"Indeed. Say it really is, to borrow Tamara's words, 'some cagey sentient' out there," Elsbeth said in clipped, worried tones. "It may be dangerous to engage, especially if the mech is . . . unstable."

"Park," said Tamara. Her voice was sharp. "They have a point. Not all sentient bonds are safe for the pilot, and if there's something out there, it's kicking up a hell of a fuss. How are you gonna deal with that?"

Vi didn't honestly know. "That might have to be a problem for future Vi."

"Viola," Elsbeth began. "We—" Another rumble cut her off.

That decided Vi. She still didn't know what was out there, but its intentions were pretty obviously destructive, and if she and her fellow screwups stood around arguing all day, it would be too late for everyone else. "I'm going," she announced. "You don't have to follow." Without bothering to look back, she bolted out the classroom door. The forest. She had to find her way to the forest. The song in her head practically screamed for it, shutting out the clamor of students lining the twisting hallways. Her shoulders crashed hard past theirs as she hurtled down the stairs. She ignored the bruising force of the impact. Swears and shouts followed in her wake. She ignored those too.

What she couldn't ignore was the sudden dip of shadow darkening overhead as she pelted toward the woods. As she ducked beneath the cover of trees, sunlight faded from view. The scent of rain permeated the air. Vi's shoulders hunched, bracing for the downpour. She twisted her head, squinting through the riot of tree branches overhead for sight of a storm cloud.

She couldn't find one. She jogged a few paces farther into the forest, careful to avoid tripping on the gnarled roots attempting to ensnare her feet. Every few paces, she turned, trying to find the source of that shadow. Even as she ventured deeper into the woods, the shadow persisted, far darker than the growing outline of the forest canopy overhead.

The fourth time she turned around, the shadow shifted. Vi had a moment, frozen in time, to take note of wings, unfolding bat-like across the grass. There was only one creature that created a silhouette like that.

Someone's fingers closed around Vi's elbow from behind, yanking hard enough to drag her off-balance. Vi yelled, as she collided into the grabber. "Hey! What the fu—"

Heat and light crackled across the space where her face had been a moment earlier. The white-blue edges of it hurtled spots across the field of Vi's vision. Plasma fire. The calling card of a GAN dragon.

The grabber regained their grip on Vi's flight suit sleeve, and tugged her around. Amadeus Huang, still panting hard and wide-eyed, but apparently far braver than Vi had thought, glared into Vi's eyes. "You're welcome!" he yelled. So at least one of her fellow probies had followed her after all. Vi allowed herself a moment to feel oddly touched by this, then snapped her mind back to business. The shadow had vanished, but that didn't mean the danger was past. Vi scanned the skies frantically.

The next warning was heard, rather than seen: a warning roar from a mechanical throat. Vi dodged instinctively, dragging Amadeus down with her. The plasma fire blast blew right over their heads. Amadeus wailed something that sounded suspiciously like, "My hair!"

Vi couldn't blame him. She gave her own strands a quick tug. Intact, but they smelled full of smoke, as if she'd been sitting in a Korean barbecue restaurant for hours. "We'll recover," she told Amadeus.

"From what?" he demanded.

"Mechs," said Vi, wishing she could give him a more specific answer. Wishing she had one for herself, for that matter. "Sentients. They're on the loose, but something's . . . wrong with them."

"You don't say!" yelled another voice. Tamara. Vi's roommate crouched behind a tree trunk, hands flung up around her face; Elsbeth Huang huddled nearby. "Do these things even have human pilots in the cockpit?"

"No." Elsbeth spoke up, small-voiced but certain. "These are sentients gone rogue. Acting completely independently from human influence. I've spent enough time among sentients to see the difference between the ones with pilots and the ones without."

Vi tried to shake off instinctive panic at the wrongness of it all. Sentients simply didn't attack at random like this—certainly not GAN-branded sentients. The Alliance's dragons were carefully engineered, and even more carefully bonded to the appropriate pilots. Their entire function was to serve as a check on dangerous mechs. Violent attacks like these—on unarmed students, no less—were anathema to everything they stood for. Never had there existed a more surefire safeguard against the dangers of rogue AI than a GAN dragon.

Yet here they stood, on the receiving end of what could only be the business end of a GAN dragon fleet—or, at least, a few rogue members. Unheard of. Worse, if Elsbeth was right, it begged the particularly chilling question of what had become of their former human pilots.

Vi closed her eyes. The thing in her head—that call from the woods—still hadn't quit singing.

"You guys should get out of here," she said, which instantly made Tamara's eyes narrow.

"*We* should get out of here," Tamara corrected.

Vi took quick stock of what they were dealing with: creepy forest everywhere, check; giant metal dragons attacking them from the sky, check; plasma fire falling from an already stormy-looking sky, check. She opened her mouth, searching for some argument against that very good advice that wouldn't make her sound like she'd completely lost her mind. Then she saw it: the telltale flashes of silver across the sky. Oh good. More rogue mechs. Exactly what they all needed.

Think, Viola, think. What would Aunt Anabel do?

The answer to that question was entirely unhelpful. Aunt Anabel would have been five steps ahead of this whole situation, through some kind of Anabel Park witchcraft, the secrets of which remained a mystery to Vi. Playing Aunt Anabel's game only worked if you held the same cards Aunt Anabel seemed to hold on everyone, and right now—faced with sentients gone wild, a campus full of panicked students, and a ragtag gang of fellow probationary disgraces at her back—Vi's cards weren't looking so good.

But she did have the song. There had to be a way to use that song in her head. It had to be coming from one of the sentients, and if Vi had a sentient in her head, that meant that she could bond it. And if she could bond one of the sentients, maybe she could figure out how many others were out there—and get them under control.

Vi took quick stock of her surroundings. The forest, at least, offered some insulation. The trees enclosing them kept them out of sight and partially shielded from what was happening on the campus proper. Still, no thicket of branches could block out the sounds from the rest of the school. Muted screams, punctuated by the telltale crackle of plasma fire, told Vi more than she wanted to know about what was happening beyond the woods. The trees wouldn't protect them for long. Vi had to act. It would be now or never.

"You run," she told Tamara at last. "I'm going to pilot."

"You're going to what?" squawked Amadeus.

"It's not a bad idea," mused Elsbeth. Amid the growing chaos closing in on the forest, the mild, thoughtful expression on her face was downright jarring. She locked eyes with Vi. "You do what you have to do, Viola Park. None of us are really masters of our mechs, not when it comes to sentients. All it takes is a little convincing."

Vi tried not to shiver as she turned back toward the woods. "A little convincing, huh?"

Maybe that really was the best card Vi could play.

Closing her eyes, she began to sprint, as hard as she could. Which was, to be sure, incredibly stupid on a tactical level. She probably looked ridiculous, like one of those overexaggerated action characters in holovid cartoons on the wireless. If one of the sentients dive-bombed her or breathed plasma fire all over her right now, every tutor who'd ever trained her in strategy or environmental survival or plain old-fashioned common sense would say that she deserved her own epic flaming death.

But Vi ran, all the same. And the thing in her head rewarded her.

It waited for her, ducked beneath a leafy canopy of trees. Emotions fired at odd angles inside her head: confusion, intrigue, wariness of the other mechs.

What are they? Vi tried to ask as she ran. A stitch bloomed in her side. She kept breathing, kept forcing herself to focus on that alien presence in her mind. *Are they like you? Are you like them?*

The thing didn't understand. It had always lived beneath the woods. It had no knowledge of the creatures in the sky.

Beneath the woods? Vi, frowning, slowed her pace. *What's beneath the woods?*

A strange series of images and sensations filtered through her mind. Water, above all else. Endless waves of it, crashing against some distant harbor, roaring through tunnels, constantly moving, free and aimless as a living mech with no pilot.

Something else lurked beyond the water. A light, blurred through the darkness of the water's depths, beckoning. A light beneath the water beneath the woods of the Academy. Without thinking, Vi reached for it doublehanded, greedy with curiosity.

She'd forgotten where she really was. Vi's outstretched hands slammed against a cold metal surface, ramming her back into her physical body. She opened her eyes, lifted her hands, panting hard. Grooves marked the surfaces of her palms and fingertips where she'd crashed into the metal. Her heart rattled against her ribcage.

She knew that pattern. She knew it on sight, better than she knew anything else in the entire world.

Slowly, carefully, Vi looked up and made eye contact with the creature who'd called her into the woods. Silver reptilian eyes stared unblinking at her over coils and coils of bright chrome scales.

"Dragon." The word fell unbidden off the tip of Vi's tongue. King—or queen, depending on your perspective—among sentients. The first of the mechs who'd been designed with minds of their own. The creatures that composed the backbone, shield, and sword of the GAN's Peacekeepers. Even with a childhood spent inside the cockpit—even growing up among Peacekeeper cousins and their steeds—it was hard not to be awestruck the first time you met a new dragon. They were simply in a class of their own.

This one didn't look much like Prudence Wu's famous, tragic Rebelwing. He didn't even look much like the majority of dragons in the modern-day fleet—Rebelwing had been the first prototype for what would eventually become the trademark of the Peacekeepers, but the mechs modeled after her all had some semblance of her look: metallic bat-like wings, plasma fire cartridges, aerodynamic but broad bodies. This mech's body was long and reptilian, more snakelike than anything else and, remarkably, lacked wings. Save those bright chrome scales, it could have been based on a different mobile suit model entirely.

Yet somehow, Vi knew in her bones that this was a dragon all the same, through and through. She raised her hands, and showed the dragon the imprint his scales had left across her palms. "All right now, Mr. Coils," she said. "See what you did? Now you've *got* to let me bond you."

The dragon's head canted back and forth, considering her offer for a moment. A distant roar—followed by a crash and chorus of screams—promptly interrupted this decision-making process. The mech swiveled the length of his body around Vi's, just in time for a fresh blast of plasma fire to scorch through the clearing.

The blast struck the dragon's flank, and vanished. "Shielding scales," said Vi faintly from behind the protective coils. "You must be one expensive engineering project."

The dragon—or Mr. Coils, as Vi thought of him—made a grunting sound deep in his mechanical throat, as if to demur. The scales along the ridge of his back cleared away to reveal the cockpit. The meaning was clear: they were both under attack now. Was Vi going to help him fight or not?

Vi risked a glance past Mr. Coils's flank. She still hadn't caught sight of the rogue mechs—which probably meant she was dealing with stealth mechanisms on top of everything else. She didn't even know how many there were. Or, for that matter, what Mr. Coils was capable of.

"Only one way to find out, I guess," she said aloud and, before she could think better of it, slid into the cockpit.

Sensation struck her from all angles: the sights and sounds of her immediate surroundings trebled in intensity, as her body—no, the dragon's; she had to keep that straight—lengthened, tail snapping, metallic claws flexing. Vi inhaled sharply. *Breathe, Vi, breathe.* Sensory overload wasn't so unusual in itself, not in an unfamiliar sentient's cockpit. You needed time, to get used to the new mind melding up against yours, but time was exactly what Vi didn't have. As the world sharpened around her, Vi cut an angle, as best she could, through the too-vibrant color and noise of the woods, turning her attention inward, toward the information she needed.

The vague threat of panic itched beneath her skin. Something in her own lizard hindbrain still flinched at the idea of being in the cockpit, recoiled at the sense memory of the exam. *You're going to fuck up, you're going to fuck up, you're going to—*

Stop it. She wasn't sure if the chiding came from the recesses of her own mind—Aunt Anabel or Aunt Cat or even Alex, maybe—or from the cybernetic consciousness now entwined with her own. The dragon's awareness was an expansive thing in Vi's head. A tangible reminder of the work to be done.

Vi needed a way to climb skyward. That much was obvious. The rain of plasma fire earlier had been a certain indicator of other GAN dragons, which meant Vi needed to meet them on their natural field of battle.

But how to find her route?

An answer trickled piecemeal across time and space, seeping through the walls of memory. First, this: Aunt Cat asking, what felt like a million years ago, *Is there something you truly love about piloting a sentient?*

And also this: a million more years ago, Vi's hand on the little mechanical gangaji's snout. The feeling of another mind—manmade, but an independent mind all the same—pressed against hers, like something she had always known.

And above all, this: the way it felt to trust, truly and completely—not only in a sentient, or only in herself, but in what could be achieved as a unit.

Vi reached for that old sense of trust now with mental fingers, stiff with disuse, but desperate with need. Perhaps she'd lost faith in herself when she fucked up that exam, but at the very least, maybe— just maybe—she could find it in the embrace of a pilot's faith in her sentient's bond during a time of crisis. She could do that much, for now. They both could. As one, girl and dragon breathed, a low mechanical roar that rumbled through the silver-scaled walls of the cockpit. Fear still flittered between them, pulsing through Vi's frenetic heartbeat, but she had control of it. For the moment.

We need to fly, she whispered to the dragon, deep within the bond linking their minds. *You have no wings. How do we fly?*

A sensation Vi could only describe as laughter reverberated down through her bones, as the dragon twisted that long serpentine body upward. *Just you wait, little human pilot*, he seemed to say. *We'll fly yet*.

And, well, they did.

Vi's shoulders slammed hard into the back of the cockpit, ground down by the sheer force of their ascent. Sunless gray skies, clearly on the brink of releasing rainfall, burst into view. Information catapulted through Vi's mind, stats and charts and specs, as quickly as the sentient she piloted could convey the vitals at their disposal: this dragon could fly, but not the way other dragons did. Instead, he wound his way through the air like a snake, the same way he would on land or in water. He could withstand plasma fire blasts, but didn't emit any of his own.

So what can you do instead? What weapon do we have?

Vi glanced through the view screen, taking stock of the battlefield. As if in response, two silver-scaled creatures flashed through the air, blinking in and out of the heavy-clouded darkness. Vi swallowed hard. Dragons. At least two of them. Closing in for an attack on Vi.

Time seemed to slow down. The world narrowed into the facts of the situation: Two enemies. One ally. Somewhere, in that strange foggy space where her mind met her sentient's bond, Vi found an answer.

We have this.

Vi's dragon opened his mouth wide, and lightning crackled across the sky. There was no other way to describe the bolts of white-blue heat that sliced through those storm clouds, more precise than any plasma fire blast, almost knifelike as they struck home.

One bolt crackled through the first rogue dragon, another through the second. Both dropped, screaming, winging through the clouds. Vi tamped down on an instinctive wave of horror. Whatever they'd done, whatever was wrong with them, those had been GAN dragons. She'd just shot down GAN dragons, and she didn't even fully understand how she'd done it.

Fly. We've got to follow them down.

Vi's sentient balked a little. They'd hit their targets clean, the sentient insisted. The other dragons were no longer a threat, and they had no additional allies waiting in the air. There was no need to seek further assurance.

Vi closed her eyes. *That's not why I want to follow.*

Confusion wafted from her sentient's mind. The other dragons had attacked them. Vi and her sentient were in the right. Why show them a mercy that might only endanger Vi further?

Because it's what a real Peacekeeper would do.

What felt like a sigh from her sentient. The reluctance emanating off his mind was clear as day, even as he obeyed his pilot's command: *As you wish, o strange and softhearted little human.*

RENEGADE FLIGHT

Under any other circumstances, Vi might have protested that designation. Under these circumstances, she simply exhaled with the drop in her belly, as girl and dragon plummeted into one long nosedive after their fallen enemies.

Their enemy dragons—no, not the enemy, Vi couldn't bear to think of GAN dragons as the enemy; the attacking dragons, then—still appeared functional. They'd broken their landing sufficiently to keep their bodies intact, and their silver eyes still glowed with a sentient's consciousness, as they snarled and snapped chrome-covered jaws.

Vi's sentient didn't like that. Vi's sentient wanted to finish them off, negate the threat.

For a moment, Vi was tempted. Part of that was probably the mind meld—there were all sort of stories out there about what the bond between pilots and sentients did to both personalities over time. Aggression from the sentient's personality matrix could bleed over into the pilot's behavior, and vice versa. And this kind of aggression was sensible, if cold. Vi had grown up among soldiers and politicians. The only truly safe enemy was a dead one.

But the half-broken creatures huddled on the ground hadn't started life as the enemy. And they might not have been acting alone. After all, sentients had been designed to pair with human minds.

Vi snapped on one of the speakers in her sentient's cockpit. "Scanning for human pilots. Report if present in the cockpit, please." Elsbeth had given her reassurances that Vi wouldn't find any, but it didn't hurt to be sure.

No one answered the scan. Instead, one of the broken dragons stirred, snarling. Vi's reaction was half-instinctive, half-prompted by the sentient in her head. She managed to duck the narrow little

129

whiff of plasma fire. "Shit!" She and her dragon dove back toward their target, the head of her own dragon aimed low and primed for a counterattack. She felt, rather than saw, the power of that crackling blue lightning at her fingertips, built deep into her mech's weaponry reserves. She could correct her earlier mistake. It would be so easy to neutralize that threat, here and now.

"Stop!"

A human voice. But not one that emerged from inside either of the enemy cockpits. Vi wheeled her sentient sideways, reining in his power, just barely. The lightning went dormant again.

"Don't hurt them!"

Vi squinted through the view screen lenses, scanning the grounds for the source of the pleas. It didn't take her long. She sucked in a breath, leaning back in the cockpit.

Nicholas Lee didn't sound or look much like himself through the lens of her sentient's cockpit view screen. Standing down below, between those half-broken dragons, he seemed so small. Mech pilots—the good ones—were rarely ever truly helpless, even without a sentient's formidable mechanical body to wield, but there was no other word for the way Lee looked. It was his body language as much as anything else. The way he threw his arms up instinctively, shielding himself as much as the creatures he protected.

The creatures he protected. And wasn't that laughable in and of itself? Even damaged, each of the dragons had a wingspan that easily tripled Lee's height. Either one of them could have roasted him on the spot with their final reserves of plasma fire. He had no armor of his own, save plain organic flesh and bone.

He looked small. He looked vulnerable. And yet—watching the

way the boy stood alone in defense of the mechs broken and snarling on the forest floor—Vi and her dragon alike found themselves frozen in their tracks.

Vi tapped the speakers again. "Stand," she tried, and stopped. She cleared her throat, trying to sound more authoritative than she felt. "Stand down."

"Why?" Lee's hands lowered and spread out. "I haven't done anything."

"Yeah, but your friends sure did," Vi shot back. "Sentients work with human pilots. Tell me the truth, Lee. Did you have anything to do with this?"

Vi couldn't be sure from a distance, but she thought she saw a muscle in Lee's jaw twitch. "I didn't. But I can end it. Without anyone getting hurt."

"I already have. But thanks for stealing my thunder."

"I said without anyone getting hurt." The muscle in his jaw had definitely jumped this time. His gaze blazed up at her. Candle-flame boy indeed. His hands spread wider still. "Look, if you promise not to let Stormbrewer light me up with modified plasma fire, will you give me five minutes to prove it to you?"

Vi opened her mouth. She wanted to tell him that in a real altercation with rogue AI or enemy mechs, they wouldn't have the luxury of five minutes. Instead, what came out was a horribly tentative, "Stormbrewer?"

Had he just rolled his eyes? Great, she might as well just fall through the emergency hatch in her cockpit and die. "Stormbrewer, yes," he said, with minimal patience. "The name of the ride you've commandeered there. Named for that little lightning show you two put up in the sky." He cocked his head. "Or have you not worked with modified plasma fire before?"

Vi's cheeks burned. She hadn't. She wanted suddenly, very badly, to know if *he* had worked with modified plasma fire before, and if he was any good at it. She clammed her lips shut before she could ask any of the no-doubt terribly stupid questions on the tip of her tongue. Now was not the time for a competitive jealous streak to rear its head. "Five minutes," she told him instead. "Or you'll see exactly how good I am at putting on lightning shows."

Her bluff seemed to work. The side of his mouth tilted up, as he turned away from her—bold move, if he really believed the lightning show line, but still—and stepped between the two broken GAN dragons. Mechanical growls rumbling low in their throats, they curled around him. The bright ferocity in those silver eyes dimmed a little.

"Stand down," said Lee to the dragons, in an entirely different voice from the one Vi had used on him. "Please." She blinked. That voice was gently spoken, firm, certain of itself, but the words weren't an order. They were a request. She stared down at him. Everything about him was asking, rather than telling. Lee was looking for a bond, clearly—a bond would be the only way he could communicate with one GAN dragon, let alone two—but he'd fallen back on the gentlest fundamentals of sentient piloting. Between pilot and mech, one was never master over the other. Human and mech must always be equal partners, bonded by equal agency. It was the only way their minds could truly sync.

It was one of the first things you learned as a pilot-in-training, long before you could set off with grand dreams of taming the dragons of the GAN. But that softness—that precise yet yielding nature—wasn't something she'd expected to see from a boy who fought as brutally as he did.

The thing was, he was doing a beautiful job of demonstrating precisely why it worked. Both dragons had turned their attention away from Vi, toward Lee. Aggression had faded from their own mechanical body language, as they examined this odd new human. Dimmed eyes, jaws closed, growling muted.

Vi settled back in her own cockpit, a little shocked by it all. Her sentient—Mr. Coils, no, Stormbringer or Stormbrewer or whatever pretentious name his creators had bequeathed to him—echoed her cautious restraint. Lightning still brewed between his clicking metallic claws, but he'd hold it in check. For now.

And then they heard the scream, high-pitched and mechanical, cut off by a familiar white-blue blast of plasma fire.

"Stop!" yelled Lee, two seconds too late.

Vi and her sentient hit the ground immediately. That scream hadn't belonged to Lee. It hadn't belonged to anyone or anything human. It was a sound that had crawled out of one of those half-broken dragons like creaking rust, just before a blast of plasma fire had finished it off.

A new mech lumbered onto the scene, metallic humanoid body glittering, speakers on. Raised between its arms was the wicked snout of a plasma fire rifle. The mech's spotless chrome armor looked all the brighter beside the blackened wreckage where one of the rogue dragons had once lain. "Nicholas Lee," called the new mech pilot's voice. "Stand down." She sounded far more authoritative than Vi had. Under less terrifying circumstances, Vi might have been annoyed.

Nicholas Lee did not stand down. He stood before the remaining dragon, eyes blazing. "Don't," he said. Even with the sound enhanced by Vi's cockpit controls, his voice was barely audible. A plea, whispered on the wind. "They're . . . she's incapacitated. You don't have to do this."

The plea was ultimately useless. The dragon behind him rose tottering to its feet, wings fanning out. A mechanical growl rumbled low in its throat. It took Vi half a beat to realize that it was standing to defend Lee, not to attack. It took another beat for her to pull her own mech shy of the second plasma fire blast. It erupted toward Lee, and hit the shield of the dragon's wings.

For a moment, all Vi saw was the blaze. Plasma fire, brilliantly blue and white, licking over the blackening edges of the ruined dragon's bright chrome scales, deadly and horribly, strangely beautiful, like some avant-garde piece of postapocalyptic museum art. And then that too was over.

Lee was on his hands and knees, hair hung loose over his eyes as breath exploded in and out of him. Across from him, the humanoid mech bowed low, and an escape hatch popped open with a hiss. A head of glorious red hair emerged from the cockpit.

Rosalyn Davies. She looked every inch the perfect GAN pilot—her flight suit pristine and zipped to the collar, a plasma gun holstered on one hip, her eyes glaring down her nose toward the mechs she'd just eviscerated. She tapped an earpiece just above her jaw. "Headmaster. Rogue mechs contained and eliminated. Safety established."

"Safety?" Lee had found his feet, swaying slightly. "That wasn't necessary, Ros. I had things—"

"Under control?" Rosalyn's lip curled. "Don't fool yourself like that, Nicky. You may have a way with sentients, but part of our credo at GAN is to eliminate the threat of rogue AI—even our own."

"They weren't rogue," insisted Lee. "Or they wouldn't have stayed rogue for long. I was getting through to them. They were just . . . confused. Scared." He frowned. "Something was jumbling their algorithms. We could have fixed it."

"He's right," croaked Vi. Her own mech, still tapped into her head, retracted his scales to allow her exit, and she scrambled down his hide toward the confrontation on the ground. "It was working. I saw."

"You saw." Now Rosalyn was looking down her nose at Vi. "With your vast years of expertise as a GAN Peacekeeper, you saw in a single glance what he was doing."

Vi raised her hands. "Hey, not trying to start shit here, but last I checked, you were a student too."

Rosalyn's eyes narrowed. "A very much nonprobationary student specially authorized by the Headmaster's office to act in times of crisis." Her gaze traveled toward the dragon at Vi's back, looking thoughtful. "Unlike yourself. How did you happen across Stormbrewer?"

A number of potential responses flittered through Vi's head. She opted for the simplest. "I bonded him."

"You." Rosalyn's voice was unimpressed. "A probie."

Vi shrugged. "Can't fault him for taste, I suppose. The point was, I was tapped into the bond. And Nick was making something happen with those dragons. I could tell. Stormbrewer could tell."

"Nick, hmm?" The way her tongue curled around his name was half caress, half warning. "Let me tell you something about our Nicky. He's a wild card. Thrives on chaos—it's in his blood; just ask him. He'd rather let a rabid dog go free than pick up a gun and put the animal out of its misery. Which is precisely what I did here." Rosalyn's gaze hardened, as it drifted back toward Nick.

"Sometimes, good doesn't look nice, or kind. Good is simply just."

Lee shook his head, chuckling. "Artificial life is still life. You just killed those dragons—sentient dragons—for nothing. I was getting through to them." A wild look lingered in that strange, otherworldly gaze of his. "Killing them was the wrong call, Rosalyn. You made the wrong call."

"Maybe," said Rosalyn. "But I don't think so." She still sounded so fond, so self-assured. "And even if it was, it was mine to make. You'll forgive me. You always do, once you see the whole picture."

"The whole picture, is it?" New footsteps had emerged, trampling through the woods. A moment later, Sifu appeared, tailed by a shaken-looking Amadeus. Elsbeth and Tamara trailed along, not far behind. "And is that what you see, as the Headmaster's favorite mouthpiece, Miss Davies?"

Rosalyn's cheeks flushed a shade just shy of her crimson hair. "How do you know my name?"

Sifu's answering grin stretched wide. "Oh, Miss Davies, I know everything." She sketched a mocking little curtsy toward Rosalyn. "The new probationary class instructor and supervisor, at your service. You won't remember my name, so you may simply call me Sifu."

Vi blinked. For a woman whose face had seemed, at first glance, forgettable above all else, Sifu suddenly seemed uncomfortably familiar. The wolfish tilt to her mouth triggered some memory just out of reach, formless and stuck on the outskirts of Vi's brain.

Rosalyn seemed less than impressed. "Whatever." She sniffed. "Rogue AI are a danger to us all. That's a pretty obvious picture, *Sifu*."

"Those were GAN dragons," Vi pointed out, heart hammering. She knew all about rogue AI. The technology to manufacture sentience—

free will and personalities—into mechs had blessed humanity with intelligent machines for war, transport, and even companionship. But as in fairytales and horror stories alike, every blessing could as easily turn into a curse. Minds of their own made for smarter machines, but they also made for more dangerous machines—and ones that didn't always play well with their human pilots or engineers. Sentients gone rogue formed the foundation of the worst battles GAN Peacekeepers were forced to wage, the fights against murder machines that had grown too clever for their own good.

The GAN dragons were supposed to be the antidote, not the source, of that kind of strife.

"GAN dragons are still AI, just like any other sentient." Rosalyn eyed Vi up and down, lips pursed in obvious judgment. "Slapping an Alliance manufacturing label on a mech—a sentient mech—doesn't inoculate it against the same algorithmic errors that plague all AI. That's the cost of sentience, Park. You should know it better than most."

Vi's lip jutted out. "And what's that supposed to mean?"

Rosalyn's eyebrows climbed. "Just that you're of better stock than most. I'd expect you to understand this kind of thing."

Vi could take being insulted or sneered at, but she'd be damned if she'd be condescended to in the guise of flattery. "Listen, you—"

"Ah, ah, ah!" Like a magician, Sifu materialized between them, seemingly out of nowhere. "Save it for classroom combat simulations, ladies. We've got bigger problems to manage right now."

Rosalyn rounded on Sifu. "Like dealing with how a probie got ahold of Stormbrewer in the first place?"

Sifu's eyebrows climbed. "Like dealing with the fact that a pair of

GAN dragons went this badly rogue in the first place. Where are the engineers on all this? Where is our Academy Headmaster? The members of the GAN Council?"

Rosalyn shrugged one shoulder, looking irritable. "I don't know. I just go where the Headmaster tells me. Presumably, she's elsewhere managing the fallout of this whole mess."

Sifu studied Rosalyn carefully, dark eyes narrowed. "Fallout, indeed. Very well. If we don't know where our dear Headmaster is, I don't suppose you could at least tell me where the pilots of these particular GAN dragons are at the moment, or how to get in touch with them?"

Rosalyn's expression went guarded. Her arms folded. "Why does it matter right now?"

Sifu raised her eyebrows, looking genuinely incredulous. "Why does it matter? I should think that much would be beyond obvious. The bond between a sentient and its pilot should have alerted the Peacekeepers in question to any abnormal behavior on the part of their dragon. The Peacekeepers should have been the first to pick up on something wrong." She shook her head, grimacing. "I presume they'll be . . . distressed to find their companions burned and blown to smithereens."

Rosalyn's glare faltered. "That's the thing." She jerked her head toward the smoldering remains of the dragons. "These particular dragons—their pilots were Abubakar and Tanaka."

Vi's head jerked toward Rosalyn. Why were those names so familiar?

She didn't have to wait long to find out. Rosalyn elaborated, "Those two went . . . well, they went missing about three days ago." Her voice shifted on the word *missing*, like the *M* should have been capitalized. Everyone knew what the words *missing* and *pilot* meant in combination these days.

Vi felt sick. The pilots who had vanished during the mission in the Mediterranean. She'd just read about them that morning. Of course. "I thought their dragons were missing too," she blurted out.

Everyone stared at her. Vi reddened. "I keep up with the news," she mumbled.

"Original reporting was incorrect," Rosalyn said icily. "I heard as much from the Headmaster herself. Abubakar and Tanaka were piloting the mission with backup mechs, while their usual dragons were at an Academy workshop undergoing experimental repairs. The dragons reportedly escaped the Academy workshop roughly when their pilots disappeared in the Mediterranean. The mechs' so-called abnormal behavior, as Sifu here euphemizes, was probably a reaction to the loss of those pilots." A shade of regret stole over her features, as she added, blunt voiced and forcibly businesslike, "It's horrific, really. Most of the MIA Peacekeepers, they at least go missing alongside their mechs. The forcible breaking of the bond, however it happened . . ." She trailed off.

"Fucked up the sentients," finished Sifu. "In a real bad way. No, Davies, I hear you. You don't have to sugarcoat things."

Rosalyn swallowed, visibly settling her composure, then turned her attention to Vi. Or rather, the creature looming behind Vi. "Those sentients aren't the only rogues we have to deal with."

"Mr. Coils?" The nickname burst out of Vi's mouth before she could stop herself. "He's not *rogue*. He was just in the wrong place at the wrong time!"

Sifu looked thoughtful. "While you, it would seem, found exactly the right place to be at the right time. Did you offer the bond, or did Stormbrewer?"

Vi pursed her mouth. "I like to think our affair was mutual."

Rosalyn's mouth, meanwhile, was going thinner and thinner with every minute the conversation lingered on the subject. "Stormbrewer's been under lockdown for weeks, at the same workshop where Abubakar and Tanaka's mechs were being worked on. The Headmaster kept telling the engineers they ought to keep him at GAN headquarters proper, instead of a school facility where any common cadet can stumble across him in a prank gone wrong, but you know how mech engineers are. Once they set up shop, they hate moving their work. That said, I haven't the faintest notion how this creature got loose."

"Probably right around when the rogue dragons did," said Sifu. "Lucky he was in a less-violent mood than his cohort here, hmm?" Her gaze swiveled back toward Vi. "And lucky, Miss Park, for you."

Vi swallowed, folding her hands behind her back. "He was in my head, was all. It's . . . I know a sentient's consciousness when I feel it. I took advantage of the moment." She shrugged, abruptly embarrassed and uncertain why. "It was just a stress response, I'm pretty sure."

Sifu whistled. "Hell of a stress response. First time I bonded an unfamiliar sentient under pressure, I nearly got us both killed, not to mention the fallout and paperwork to contend with after." She squinted up at the dragon. "Not bad, for a first flight with a human pilot."

That couldn't be right. Vi blinked. "What?"

"Oh, you heard me just fine." Sifu shrugged. "I take it you relied on the bond to figure out weaponry and flight capabilities. Not bad—not bad at all. Most mech pilots, even the seasoned ones, need a briefing on an unfamiliar sentient just to ease the transition. Stormbrewer must have taken to you indeed."

"How does Mr. Coils—how does Stormbrewer even fly in the first place?" Vi asked, no longer caring at all how dumb the question probably sounded. "He hasn't even got wings."

"Ah, I was wondering if you'd noticed as much." Sifu gave the mech a friendly pat on the flank, as if the dragon were a particularly spirited horse. "He's one of the latest prototypes, designed in part to test some of the hover technology that our GAN's chief engineer— whom Viola here might know as Aunt Cat—has been working on, but also for amphibious capabilities. On loan to the Academy, for the moment, for educational purposes."

"Amphibious capabilities?" Amadeus, stepping cautiously forward, looked intrigued. "You mean a mech designed to travel through water as well as land and air?"

"Ah, ah, ah." Sifu wagged a finger at him. "I've seen that gleam in the eye of a hundred ex-cons or cons-to-be. Do not jack the Chief Engineer's shiny new dragon prototype, Huang. For one thing, it'll be terrible for your grades in my course. She's loaning Stormbrewer to me as a personal favor, and I have no compunctions about taking her bad temper out on your exam marks."

"It makes a certain amount of sense," mused Elsbeth. "Hong Kong is an island city, and most GAN-friendly territories are coastal. Peacekeepers need to survive ocean dives, not just aerial dogfights."

"So Stormbrewer's a Chinese dragon." Her brother sounded delighted by this. "What a culturally diverse new addition to the GAN's terrifying weapons cache."

Nicholas Lee—who'd been crouched by the blackened ruin of the destroyed GAN dragons, hair hanging over his eyes—made a sound halfway between a snort and a mean, raspy little laugh. It startled Vi. She'd almost forgotten he was there. When he lifted his gaze, she wondered how that was even possible. Plasma fire didn't have anything on the blazing brightness of those eyes. He was pissed, clearly. "Sure, Huang," he said. "That's what we're all about, hmm? Diversifying our weapons cache."

"I always did find the Peacekeepers ironically named," mused Elsbeth, sounding dreamy. She bobbed her head toward Lee. "It's good to see you, by the way, Nick. I'd wondered what inevitable pseudo-delinquent business had distracted you from coming to class this time."

"Indeed." Slowly, Sifu's attention swiveled toward Lee. "You missed an interesting period, boyo." She jerked her head toward Vi. "And the beginning of a pretty good fight between Amadeus and our new Park girl here."

"If you could call it a fight," muttered Amadeus. He rubbed sheepishly at one of his arms. "I think I saw my life flash before my eyes."

"Did you, now," murmured Nick, following Sifu's gaze toward Vi. That blazing anger behind his eyes had cooled, chilling to an almost clinical glance of assessment. "Guess I'll have to watch my back, then."

Like a bucket of cold water, the adrenaline dump that had fueled Vi's wild ride with Stormbrewer crashed abruptly into the pure dread of reality. In the chaos of the mech fight, she'd forgotten all about the tournament. She only needed to face off against Nick once from the cockpit of a sentient. Realistically, Nick was a problem for future Vi. Present-day Vi still had her first matchup in the tournament—

and an unknown first opponent—looming ahead of her. But as she looked at Nick now—how easily he flipped from hot to cold, how cavalier he sounded—all she could think of was how unpredictable he'd be in a real showdown, especially between mechs. So much of fighting sentient to sentient depended on getting a quick, accurate reading of your opponent: understanding what they wanted, how they'd move with their mech, what they were afraid of. Nick—brutal and vulnerable at turns, but mostly just frustratingly opaque—was the very definition of a dangerous matchup. To guarantee a win against a boy like that would take strategy that extended beyond grit or mere cleverness. It would take inside knowledge that Vi didn't have, and had no clue how to obtain.

She bit her lip. The memory of that crushing simulation where they'd first met hung heavy in her mind. Even as she straightened her back, plastered nonchalance across her face, and said, as brightly as she could, "I guess you will."

Sifu coughed. "If you two are done mean-mugging each other, I could use your help getting Stormbrewer back under control. You litter of useless rascals may have homework, but let me assure you that all the homework in the world pales in comparison to the amount of paperwork I'm going to have to file about this whole mess." She pulled a long-suffering face. "As the only qualified adult present, I'm afraid it'll fall to me to translate 'wild dragons nearly torch extremely expensive training academy to the ground, before being torched themselves' into something suitable for both the Headmaster's desk and the various offices of the GAN's Safety and Emergency Management Department."

"Right," said Vi. She hadn't broken eye contact with Lee, and he hadn't broken eye contact with her. "What do you need from me?"

"For starters, as the pilot who bonded him in the first place, you might ask your new friend to hurry along back to his stabling with all the other, decidedly less-rogue dragons." Sifu paused, then, almost too casually, added, "It might also be worth asking what he saw of the other two dragons who went apeshit on the campus. Stormbrewer's a new model—we would have expected to do some troubleshooting, but those two were stalwart, old-school veterans." Her brow furrowed. "That's not even getting into the fact that they returned from mission without pilots in their cockpits, and somehow went undetected for at least forty-eight hours before going berserk. Miss Davies can say what she will about missing pilots driving their dragons into madness and unchecked violence, but something about this doesn't smell right, and the pieces aren't adding up."

Vi shook her head. "He doesn't know anything—or well, nothing useful about that." At least, she was pretty sure. The feelings and images flashing through her head from Stormbrewer had been disjointed at best. "Mostly, it was just a sense of confusion."

Sifu snorted. "He's not alone in that case. Well, it'll be a problem for the Headmaster and relevant members of the GAN Council to sort out on their own time, I suppose. Let's get Stormbrewer home for now."

Vi looked up at Stormbrewer. "You heard the lady," she said, and gave him a little mental nudge.

The dragon huffed a rusty mechanical sigh and curled himself up. *Very well*, he seemed to say. If the fight was well and truly over, he'd comply with what his human companions needed of him. It was, after all, what he had been built for. Vi's shoulders came down a little.

Strange comfort, to have a machine built to get along with human pilots actually do what it was meant to, after the events of the day. But it was comfort nonetheless.

Still, she couldn't shake the sight of the blackened ruin where the two GAN dragons—Stormbrewer's fellow sentients, once upon a time—had met their end. They'd looked like a ghastly little panel in a horror comic on one of the holo-players: ashes and twisted, ruined metal beneath the grim gray sky, and between them, Nicholas Lee, with his flame-bright eyes, crumpled like he too had been a rogue machine shot down before his time.

At best, it had been a terrible start to the school year, and optimistically, things could really only get better. At worst, though— and this was the thing that made the pit of Vi's belly drop—at worst, it felt like an omen of things to come.

7 ——————————— FULL CONTACT

The matter of those two rogue dragons continued to gnaw at Vi for days afterward. The sheer wanton destruction they'd wreaked across campus before their demise probably didn't help matters. For a solid week, it was all anyone could talk about. Who had witnessed the attacks? Who had gotten caught in the crossfire? Why had the dragons gone rogue in the first place? Thank god Rosalyn Davies had been there to save the day. No wonder she was such a favorite of the Headmaster. She was always right there in the nick of time whenever anything went awry on campus. She would make an excellent Peacekeeper one day, practically a shoo-in for the conscription.

No one had said anything about Stormbrewer, or Vi. Once upon a time, that might have annoyed her. Now she was mostly just relieved. While everyone oohed and aahed over Rosalyn's heroics, Vi could finally settle down to prepare for her first match of the tournament. The pace of life at the Academy didn't miss a beat, even for mechanical dragons gone wild. Matchup announcements would be going live in three days, and the matches themselves were scheduled one week after the announcement. One week bought Vi precious little time to study whoever her opponent was. So she shut everything that had happened out of her head: the attack, Stormbrewer's song in her head, the fight with the other dragons. There would be time enough, later, to fret over the implications of rogue dragons and their missing pilots. In this moment, Vi needed to focus on the task at hand.

Classes outside of Sifu's were, initially, a source of anxiety. Vi hadn't been certain of what to expect after that explosive first period. Three other courses demanded her attention, according to the timetable on the Academy app: first, History and International Affairs of the GAN, then Intro to Navigational Geography, then finally Sentient Engineering Fundamentals for Pilots. All were taught in mixed classes with the other cadets. And as her dorm mates had made abundantly clear Vi's first night on campus, probies weren't exactly a welcome presence in normal cadet spaces.

Marching off to her first history class made Vi's hands shake, absurdly, like a common coward's. She'd steeled herself a million different times for being mocked, gossiped about, or even just stared at, with that probie badge sitting *Scarlet Letter* bright on her flight jacket lapel. But dreaming up worst-case scenarios never seemed to measure up to a tangible reality, unfolding in the moment. The thought of getting jumped again—right now, after everything—made her want to turn tail and take the first flight home to North America.

Still, she didn't let her cowardice show, shoving her hands into jacket pockets as she loped into the designated lecture hall for History and International Affairs. No one so much as glanced at her, clustered around the desks guzzling coffee or talking among themselves, as Vi settled into a spot far from the clearly already-established groups of friends. If their teacher—a Dr. Nathaniel Kerrigan, according to her app—took note of the probie Park girl who'd entered their midst, he didn't seem to care either. A fair-headed man in a three-piece suit, he reminded Vi far more of the prep school teachers back in New Columbia than of hoodie-wearing, forest-trawling, loud-mouthed Sifu.

"Welcome to History and International Affairs of the GAN," he announced in a broad Australian accent. He was still scrolling through the lecture notes on the 3-D smartboard display at the center of the lecture hall, and hadn't so much as bothered to look up at his students. "Take your seats. Let's begin."

It wasn't a bad lecture, all considered. Kerrigan mostly covered material Vi had already picked up in Modern Politics I and II back during her first two years at New Columbia Prep, and it felt good to be ahead on at least one front. It felt even better to be invisible—just another new kid who had yet to make any friends of her own. Vi had to laugh a little at herself. The old Vi would never have dreamed of wanting to be unseen, of blending in instead of standing out.

"People rarely think of you nearly as much as you think of yourself," Aunt Anabel had told Vi once. "We humans are self-centered by nature. What you think may be terribly impressive or admirable about yourself, most people will only notice in passing. They might not even care, unless it impacts them directly, or benefits them in some way. I realize that sounds depressing, but consider the flip side: anytime you think you've embarrassed yourself horribly in public, or done something shameful or insulting, well. That thing probably registered with everyone else for all of two minutes before they moved on to thinking about their own problems."

Which was just fine by Vi. All the easier to keep her head down this way, and concentrate on avoiding trouble and preparing for her upcoming opponent. Whoever they were.

♦

EVEN AS VI MARSHALED HER focus, three days flew by far too quickly for her liking. Judging by the wary nature of her classmates, she wasn't the only one. She could hardly wander down a hallway without hearing some whisper of speculation about who would be fighting whom in the kickoff event of the tournament. Of course the whole thing had to begin with the hand-to-hand event too—the most physically demanding, intimate of the combat disciplines, and the one likeliest to result in actual injury to the pilots involved. It felt deliberate, a way of feeding further into the hungry, anxious tension thrumming perceptibly beneath the skin of the entire student body.

On the promised day, Vi walked into the probie classroom to find Tamara, Elsbeth, and Amadeus glued to their phones. Nick, per usual, hadn't yet arrived. Vi canted an eyebrow round at her classmates before clearing her throat. "What happened to not giving a shit about becoming Peacekeepers?"

Tamara batted one dismissive hand in Vi's general direction. The other continued to hungrily refresh her phone. "That's not what *I* care about. I just don't want some meathead to knock me out with their giant overenthusiastic fists. My brain is my best feature." She sighed. "Fucking hand-to-hand, man. Even if I don't win, it would be nice to have an opponent I could at least survive."

"*I* would like to win," Elsbeth piped up. A mildly disturbing gleam lurked in her eye. "I find a good fight invigorating. Especially against someone bigger and stronger."

"Sometimes I can't believe we're related," muttered Amadeus. He stared at his phone with a manic sort of fervor. "I hear there's some skinny little twelve-year-old who skipped a bunch of grades in the first-year class; maybe I'll match up with him."

"Amadeus!" chided his sister.

"What? Don't you want me to win?"

"I wouldn't underestimate the twelve-year-old," muttered Tamara.

Shaking her head, Vi took a seat opposite the three of them, and pulled out her own phone. Her heart thudded a nervous little drumbeat. Initial assigned matchups scrolled their way across the Academy app on her screen in quick succession, but Vi didn't bother reading any of them except the name beside her own. When she finally found it, a spike of adrenaline promptly crash-landed against the wall of dull surprise. She looked up from her screen at the exact same moment her opponent-to-be did.

Amadeus Huang blinked big dark eyes at her, his mouth a wide O of surprise. "Huh," he said at last. "Well, this is awkward."

♦

IN THE END, THEY RETREATED to an empty classroom to discuss the matchup in private. This clearly disappointed Elsbeth, who'd cast speculative glances back and forth between Amadeus and Vi, as if she was prepared for them to throw down right there in the scant minutes before Sifu arrived, and get the inevitable over with. Easy for Elsbeth. She and Tamara had both wound up with matchups against people they didn't even know. The two of them immediately shoved their desks together, whispering in close conference, no doubt all set to go cyber-stalk their opponents in an effort to figure out what they were dealing with.

They found a suitable room at the end of the hallway, the windows dark and shuttered. "So," Vi began, closing the door behind them, "I've read through some of the rules. Hand-to-hand combat parameters seem to vary depending on the matchups, which is sort of confusing, but I figure that when you and I fight—"

"No," Amadeus interrupted immediately.

Vi turned around in surprise. Amadeus was already leaning against the back wall, feet propped up on a desk. Every so often, his gaze darted around the room like a cornered animal's. Scoping out exits, clearly, in a bald-faced attempt to get out of the conversation, which only irritated Vi further. It wasn't like she wanted to be here either.

"No," Amadeus said again, more emphatically this time. "No, no, absolutely not."

Well, Vi wasn't having it. She folded her arms, standing before him. "What do you mean 'no'?" she demanded irritably. "We have to fight. It's in the rules."

"Au contraire," Amadeus put in delicately, "there is a work-around. I can forfeit."

"Forfeiting is for cowards and deserters," snapped Vi without thinking.

Amadeus's eyebrows arched. "And what, precisely, do you think most probationary students are? It's not as though we're put in a special class for our remarkable service to society."

"You really don't even want to try?" Irritation aside, Vi was genuinely curious. Truth be told, the matchup gave her mixed feelings. Amadeus wasn't exactly a difficult opponent when it came to hand-to-hand—she'd already gotten a taste of his aptitude, or lack thereof, for fisticuffs. Still, the old competitive flame inside her—the same parts of her that used to relish the jealousy of her classmates and take secret pride in their yearning glances at her simulation scores—had wanted a challenge of some kind from her first match in this tournament. If Vi was going to fight her way into the Peacekeeper Corps, by god, she wanted to have earned it. "Some part of you must want to test yourself," she offered. "Even against me."

"Even against you," Amadeus echoed. His answering smile was rueful. "A loaded meaning, if ever there was one. You forget, I already tested myself against you."

"That hardly counts." Vi scoffed. "It barely lasted two minutes."

"Precisely the point." The smile grew. "Two minutes was all you needed to prove you would win." His hands splayed, long and pale. "Not all skills are combative, Viola Park. And not all of us want the things you want."

"And what do you want, Amadeus?" Vi's tone was half-mocking, but genuine curiosity still colored the question. Before the Academy, this boy had been a thief. A pretty shameless thief, at that, if he went around commandeering war mechs for shits and giggles. "From what I understand, when you want things, you just take them, without much regard for consequence. Otherwise, you wouldn't be here."

His expression twitched, eyes darkening for a moment. It was maybe the closest Vi had seen him lean toward actual anger. "I do take the things I want," said Amadeus. "And I happen to want the same thing most probationary students want when they come here."

"Which is?"

"That's easy." Inscrutability lurked behind his expression. "To survive. Which is why I'll be registering an official forfeit of this match with the Headmaster. Congratulations on your victory."

♦

IT WAS, ALL IN ALL, a thoroughly anticlimactic way to win her first match of the tournament. Never had such a high-stakes victory felt so hollow. Worse, Amadeus had been the only forfeit in the first round of matchups—which meant Vi was the only victor entering her second hand-to-hand contest without real experience in the first. The stories of her fellow victors didn't help. One of the first-year boys had knocked his opponent out cold with one well-placed kick to the head. Another had simply barreled his opponent over, jumped on top of him, and rained fists down on his face until a teacher finally called him off. A girl in second year had wrestled a boy to the ground and strangled him into unconsciousness with his own arm.

And what had Vi done? Watched Amadeus file some paperwork with the Headmaster's office, and twiddled her fingers while everyone else milled about with bruised knuckles and bloody fists.

Only a day passed after victors were registered before the Headmaster posted matchups for the second fight. Vi's deal with the Headmaster sat heavy in her gut. She'd known what was coming even before she pulled up the match list on her Academy app, but no one else did. Vi saw the way the others eyed her up and snickered when they saw the name matched across hers. She could only imagine the whispers that accompanied the looks, pitched too low for her to hear. This was the girl who was going to take on Nicholas Lee? The one who'd only won her first match on a coward's technicality? Please.

Well, take on Nicholas Lee she would. Vi began plotting her avenue of attack the same way any good strategist would: by running Nicholas Lee's name through every search engine on the wireless with all the fervor of a dedicated stalker. Most aspiring combat pilots left footprints across the wireless in the form of easily accessible public record: holo-tapes of training sessions, or mech fights, or records of training certificates and piloting permits. Scraps of information, all of which could provide an opponent with some clue as to what they'd be dealing with in a field of combat.

For the next several days, between classes, Vi dug up everything she could on Nicholas Lee. Which was to say, nearly nothing at all. She was almost as impressed as she was annoyed. These days, with the capabilities of the wireless being what they were, it was near impossible to make yourself a ghost in public record, yet that was precisely what Nick had done. His was a common name, especially in Hong Kong, but even with identifiers tacked on—the Academy name, mech-fighting tournament circuits, and in one particularly desperate gambit, Rosalyn Davies's name—Vi's searches hardly yielded any results of substance.

What the searches did yield was a veritable gold mine of rumors and gossip, mostly in red-flagged threads on student forums, shut down by moderators for inappropriate conversation. Still, Vi wasn't an idiot, and she knew how to pull up wireless histories of dead threads. What she read there built a grotesque little portrait—more artfully exaggerated collage than, Vi suspected, actual resemblance to the subject. Still, there was something to be said for the Picasso canvas of prurient student interest.

One. Nicholas Lee was the only probationary student at the GAN Academy whose sins had never been made public knowledge. Criminal backgrounds and public shaming usually made short work of probie reputations—and from what Vi had observed, members of the probationary class weren't exactly shy about what they'd done to earn their badges—but Nick's records had been sealed from the moment he enrolled. Which meant that:

Two. Nick had made some kind of deal with the Headmaster. No eighteen-year-old, no matter how prodigious in the cockpit, just showed up out of nowhere on the doorstep of the GAN Academy for Combat and Cybernetic Arts without family, record of study, or social media paper trail, and stayed that way without some pretty hefty authorities on his side. Whether the deal had been Winchester's idea or Nick's, Vi had no idea, but it meant that Nick presumably had something worth hiding.

Three. Regardless of whatever softhearted mercies Nick had attempted to bestow on the rogue dragons during that confrontation in the woods, when battling his fellow cadets, he was remorseless in a fight, whether barehanded or from the cockpit. Which didn't particularly surprise Vi, given their single simulation experience. What did surprise her was the way others described him: supposedly, Nick fought with a vicious, streamlined brutality that had other cadets wondering if maybe he got off on the bloodshed for its own sake. When he'd first darkened the Academy doors, trailing after Headmaster Winchester with that telltale badge pinned to his lapel and bruises all over his knuckles, classmates had openly wondered if Nick's prodigious talent for violence had something to do with his sealed personal records. He would hardly have been the first probie who'd landed a criminal record for killing someone—Vi thought of Elsbeth Huang, and her casually delivered murder confession—but there was murder, and then there was *murder*. Theories abounded during that first year when Nick was still proving his mettle in mech sparring. The most outlandish cast him as some sort of mech-piloting super assassin, with over a hundred kills under his belt, secretly trained and programmed in a hidden mountain to be activated at the Headmaster's behest. The tamest suggested that he was simply a prodigy with an anger-management problem.

Colorful as all of that was, however, none of it gave Vi a clue about how to actually deal with him physically. There were a lot of ways to be brutal and bloodthirsty, both in and out of the cockpit. The specifics— the how—mattered. But the specifics were not something, evidently, that denizens of the wireless were especially inclined to cough up.

Which left her with one option: Vi had to find a way to cozy up to Rosalyn Davies. Fucking great. Vi wondered if Rosalyn had set an expiration date on that initial offer of friendship the night Vi arrived on the campus grounds.

It didn't take her long to find out. With one week to spare before the showdown against Nick was scheduled, Vi found her chance. Rosalyn was almost always surrounded by an entourage of people, but when she saw Vi striding toward her from across the dining hall one morning, she greeted the sight with a wide, knowing smile. A quick, sharp nod to the other cadets milling around her sent them into a faintly reluctant scatter. Vi raised her eyebrows at the sight. "Wow," she observed, drawing closer. "Do they also jump and bark on command?"

It was a risky joke to make, but it paid off this time: Rosalyn actually laughed. "It's a less impressive trick than it looks like." Her expression shuttered for a moment. "We're all friends. Kind of."

"Kind of?" Vi slipped into the pocket at Rosalyn's side. Her stomach rumbled. She hadn't eaten yet, and the trays of hot food were going fast, but she wasn't sure when she'd get another opportunity to press Rosalyn for answers.

"I've always thought of it as friendship by proxy." Rosalyn, seeming to read Vi's mind, lunged elegantly past a pair of hungry cadets to snag one tray neatly off the lunchtime conveyor belt. "Here. I hope you like carbs. It's a spaghetti-and-meatballs day."

"I like food, period," said Vi honestly. She accepted the tray. "So was that what you tried to offer me when I first stumbled onto campus, fresh from North America? Friendship by proxy?" Whatever that meant. In a school full of rogue dragons and glorified gladiator games, Vi wasn't sure anything would shock her at this point. "Cold move, Rosalyn."

"Call me Ros." Rosalyn—Ros—jerked her head toward an empty table by the wide bay windows overlooking the rolling green hills of the Academy grounds. They sat. "It's what I offered all of them," said Ros, nodding toward her posse, who were fanned out in one of the dining hall aisles, pacing between tables and chatting. Every once in a while, they eyed Vi up with curious gazes. They did a better job than most of feigning disinterest, but the darting looks toward the little table by the bay windows gave them away. "I think you'll find most friendships are transactional, at the end of the day. Oh, don't look at me like that." Ros leaned in, conspiratorial. "How many of your friends at your old school were really friends, and how many just wanted to rub elbows with you because of what you or your family could do for them?"

Vi almost flinched at being called out so frankly. What else could she have expected? Ros was no different from the crowd Vi had run with back at New Columbia Prep. They'd all been cut from a similar cloth: overachievers, by and large born to overachieving families, all of whom spoke the same language and did each other the same sorts of favors. Would they have had anything in common without those arbitrary ties of economic and genetic luck?

Ros seemed to take Vi's wary silence for assent. "See? It's nothing personal." She nudged Vi's shoulder with her own. "Now, what do you want?"

"Well," said Vi awkwardly, "I was going to say that I thought I might like to be friends after all, but that feels like a trap now."

"Really." Ros looked amused. "Why?"

Vi sighed. "For real? I'm matched up against Nicholas Lee for the second round of the hand-to-hand tournament phase." When all else failed, sometimes honesty worked wonders. It was worth a shot, at any rate. "You seem like someone who might know how to beat him."

If Ros found Vi's declaration of intent surprising, she didn't advertise it. Instead, her amusement seemed to grow. "Because I'm an accomplished cadet? Or because I sleep with him?"

Vi blinked. She hadn't expected her own honestly to be returned quite so frankly. "Do you?"

Ros grinned. It transformed her face. Suddenly, she seemed so much more accessible—affable, even—than the haughty queen bee who'd looked down her nose at Vi's probie badge. "Given the chance, wouldn't you?"

"Uh," said Vi intelligently. Honest self-examination appeared to be the order of the day. That traitorous corner of her brain steered its attention away from her high school friendships and refocused itself with uncanny glee on the matter of Nicholas Lee: the breadth of his shoulders, the angular cut of his jaw, those mesmerizing eyes of his.

The way he'd moved, even behind the armor of a mech, even in the hazy reality of a combat sim: graceful, precise, and utterly unrelenting in his aggression.

"No," she lied swiftly. "Unless pillow talk includes inside baseball on how he's so goddamn good at fighting." An idea occurred to her. "Wait, is he one of those combat pilots who're great in the cockpit, but terrible, you know, in . . ." She paused at the sight of Ros's eyebrows. "There's really no way not to make this sound like an innuendo, is there?"

Ros's grin grew wolfish. "Absolutely not." She seemed to take pity on Vi, though, waving a fork at her with a casual *no worries* motion. "It's all good. I know what you mean. Unfortunately, I can't tell you what you want to hear. Nicholas Lee is a true all-arounder—capable of fighting with sentient mechs, with non-sentient mechs, and with his own two bare hands, if necessary. He's both aggressive and extremely technical—you'll have to deal with an onslaught of physical power, but he's smart about how he doles it out, which makes him a lot trickier to handle than your average muscle-bound meathead."

"Fantastic," said Vi glumly. Of course the rumors had to be right this time. The Headmaster couldn't have given it to her that easy.

Ros rolled her eyes. "Oh, don't sound so defeated already. All good pilots—even great ones, even Nicholas Lee—have weaknesses. And weaknesses can always be exploited by an opponent in the know." Her gaze became slits of green. "After all, that's why you sought me out, right?"

Vi dropped her own fork to fold her arms. "So you do know something."

"About Nicky? Not as much as you'd think." She tapped her

temple with a finger. "About general survival, though? Plenty. Given your, shall we say, uneventful victory over Amadeus Huang, you probably haven't had a chance to examine the Headmaster's rules for victors' rounds in hand-to-hand too closely, have you?"

Vi hadn't. The desire to kick herself probably showed all over her face, because Ros grinned.

"I thought not," said Rosalyn, satisfied. "Most of it is garden variety 'state the obvious' fine print: don't poke your opponent's eyes out, don't sneak in illegal weapons, don't coat the tips of your fingernails in poison, blah blah boring blah. None of *those* rules really matter to you, not directly." Her eyes gleamed as she leaned forward. "But here's the bit that does: Did you know that for hand-to-hand matches, the contestants get to choose the format? You could box, you could wrestle . . . hell, you could have an old-school fencing match if you wanted to, so long as no mechs or firearms are involved. You just have to get your opponent to agree to the rules of engagement. You might consider picking something you're good at. Maybe a little esoteric, something that he's less likely to have spent much time training for. Preferably where you can equip yourself with a reach or leverage advantage, just as you would in a mech."

Vi frowned. "He'd never agree to that, then. Won't he just shoot the format down if he thinks I might win?"

Rosalyn's answering grin was wide and white. A chill Vi couldn't account for ran down the back of her neck. "As if Nicky has ever said no to anything. Besides, Nicholas Lee isn't the only person in this tournament you have to worry about, you know."

"Sure, but he's probably the most dangerous competitor," Vi pointed out. "Not to mention my most immediate problem."

Ros's smile faded. Vi couldn't quite describe the expression that crossed Ros's face at that pronouncement: more amusement maybe, edging into disappointment. The other girl gave a wry little shake of her coppery head. "See, that's the thing I do understand about your opponent, Park. He's formidable, yes, and probably the most generally skillful of a merry lot of highly trained and aggressive combat mech pilots, but skill isn't everything when it comes to danger. Not in a place like this." Ros leaned back, still smiling a little, an echo of that same self-assured look of satisfaction she'd turned on Nick the day she'd shot the rogue GAN dragons down. "Skill is one thing. Ambition is another. Nicholas Lee has plenty of the first, and none of the second."

Vi swallowed. A creeping sense that she'd miscalculated terribly blossomed in her belly. "What are you trying to say?"

"Oh, nothing malevolent or threatening, so there's no need to look quite so serious." Ros winked. "You truly want my advice? Worry about Nicky all you'd like. But don't forget to worry about the rest of us too."

One week wasn't much, but Vi made it work for her. By the time she was due to fight Nick, Vi had had a good long time to consider the benefits and drawbacks over the different fields of combat she could propose. Like any respectable Park, she'd studied weapons and fighting arts alongside academic curricula, mech piloting, and classical-music lessons, but unlike some of her cousins, she'd never chosen a signature style of engagement. There was cousin Richard, who'd been a boxer before the Academy, and cousin Jocelyn, who'd been a fencer, and even Aunt Anabel herself, who took a disturbing amount of delight in general close-quarters combat, but Vi had no such calling card. She'd learned to fight without a mech because it was what one did, and useful cross-training besides, but so far as she was concerned with herself, when push came to shove, Vi had only ever had the cockpit. Which meant she had no obvious way to angle for an advantage against a bloodied-up veteran of both hand-to-hand and piloting fights.

Damn the Headmaster for figuring that out so easily.

Remembering Rosalyn's advice, Vi tried studying tape of some of the other fights from the first matchups, hoping that inspiration would strike. If anything, that only made her feel worse. The movements she saw in those matches confirmed what she'd already suspected based on the rumors she'd heard: Vi might equal half or more of her fellow winners in pure skill, but she'd never faced this level of naked aggression. Rosalyn was right. There was a difference between a friendly match among cousins and a showdown with a stranger who harbored genuinely violent intentions.

In the end, Vi went with the best option in a bad situation. If she couldn't place herself at an advantage, she'd at least force Nick to fight from a disadvantage.

If that worried him even remotely, he certainly gave no indication of it when she submitted her choice of combat format for his approval. He'd barely given a passing glance at the request, shrugged, and signed off on the matchup forms. To be honest, Vi wasn't even entirely sure that he'd actually read the text she'd entered on the request ballot.

Headmaster Winchester, meanwhile, had offered Vi nothing but a sharp, catlike smile when Vi submitted their choice. "Sure, if that's what you both want," she said, with the sort of gently amused cadence that suggested that what you wanted was all wrong. "You understand the rules of engagement?"

Vi had, in fact, studied what Ros called the "state the obvious" fine print on the tournament regulations. She nodded.

"The match is six minutes long. It can be won three ways: by knockout, by forfeit on the part of one of the competitors, or by the decision of the supervising instructor. That same instructor can also declare a no-contest at will."

Vi blinked. "No-contest?"

The Headmaster had the gall to look amused. "What happened to 'I read all the rules'?"

"I did," Vi protested, a little miffed. To prove her point, she recited, "'A no-contest is to be declared strictly in circumstances under which the supervising instructor observes one or both contestants engaging in inappropriate behavior that jeopardizes the fairness and safety of the match.'" She shook her head. "That's not just plain old 'at will.' That's 'someone's hopped up on athletic uppers, and their opponent's about to get their skull bashed in.'"

Winchester laughed. "Relax, Miss Park. I'll be your supervising instructor. And under my watch, true no-contest rulings are few and far between."

Vi tilted her head, assessing. "Don't you have more important things to do? I thought the whole perk of being a headmaster was to delegate stuff like playing ref to random probies during a conscription tournament."

"Oh, I absolutely have more important things to do," said Winchester, lightly and without hesitation. "But another perk of being a headmaster is that I occasionally get to put them off in favor of doing something because I want to. And I do want to see how you perform, Miss Park." Those bright gemstone eyes gleamed in the dim lights of her tower office. "None of you, as students, enter as strangers to combat. If you wish to bash each other's heads in without calling for a forfeit, well. So far as I'm concerned, that's your prerogative. You'll face worse in the field if you make it as Peacekeepers."

It wasn't, all in all, a terribly comforting reassurance.

The Academy officials assigned them a space adjacent to the training studios where they'd first faced off in simulation. Except, of course, that there wouldn't be anything simulated in this fight—all damage would be real damage. Super fun to think about.

A blank screen took up an entire wall. Winchester, when she arrived, nodded toward the screen, still smiling that maddening little grin. "That there is a one-way window. I'll be safe and sound behind it, monitoring your progress as your referee. If I call an end to a bout—whether because one of you has tapped out, or because I've determined for my own reasons that you shouldn't continue—the screen will flare red, and you'll await further instruction." She clapped Vi on the shoulder, winking at Nick as he entered. "Just remember, I want a good, clean fight, kids," she called as she sauntered out. Practically an afterthought.

Which left Vi alone with Nick in the studio, already second-guessing her choice of sparring engagement. "Fun," she echoed dully. "So much fun."

Well, there was no helping it now. Avoiding eye contact with her dubious new opponent, she went straight for the case she'd presented earlier to the Headmaster. Time to get down to business. "You sure you know how to use rattan sticks?" Just because he'd signed off on her proposed mode of combat didn't mean he actually knew anything about it. He might have agreed on a lark. Worse, he might be the sort of arrogant that saddled him with the assumption that he was unbeatable in any discipline, regardless of how well versed he was or wasn't. Those types had a tendency to overestimate themselves and make mistakes. Which, honestly, would be awesome for Vi.

She watched Nick give a slow, wary blink at the slender wooden training weapons she'd extracted from the case. With the sort of care a musician might use to handle an instrument, he picked up the one she proffered, and gave it a few experimental spins.

"I'm sure," he said. He didn't say where he'd learned, but she believed him. He moved too fluidly for it to be a lie. "I hope you know that we don't have these," he wagged the stick at her, "in the cockpit of a mech, sentient or not."

Part of her wanted to bristle at the implied condescension. Remembering what Aunt Cat had once said about ego, she tamped it down. "Not the point, hotshot." She picked up the remaining stick and waved it at him. Time to make use of all that impressive-sounding theory that Sifu had spouted during classroom lectures. "Fighting with live sticks develops faster reflexes and coordination, which translate from our bodies to our mechs—" Experimentally, she swung the stick at a wide angle, telegraphing toward his head.

He parried, eyes widening.

Vi grinned, and pressed her advantage. "Not to mention dexterity—"

Nick didn't fall for the feint toward the other side of his head, and parried the tip of her stick as she drove it gently toward his abdomen. His expression had settled, eyes narrowed into slits of amber, giving nothing away. A fighting face. All right, then. So the game was on.

"And finally," Vi said, circling him, "the use of a physical instrument as an extension of self. Just like our mechs."

She didn't include the final reason she'd picked the sticks, which was their inherent danger. All sparring—or fights—had stakes of some sort, but weapons heightened them. In addition to the usual feet and fists, the stick presented an extra danger to watch out for. This generally encouraged a degree of caution. Even Nick might play it safe.

Vi was still congratulating herself on this strategy when Nick closed in on her with a series of heavy diagonal strikes. Her first parry barely registered; the second missed entirely, forcing her to sidestep off Nick's centerline. He followed, merciless. Wood chafed against her palm, as her grip tightened instinctively.

Okay, maybe Nick wouldn't play it safe. Maybe he'd just beat her to a pulp with prejudice. Even odds, it seemed. After all, this was a boy who'd made it clear the very first time they met that he thought of her as an amusement to be toyed with, rather than a true threat to his skill. Vi had been an idiot, obviously, to assume fighting him live, instead of in a simulated mech confrontation, would be any better. Each one of Nick's stick strikes was like a carefully contained, viciously dispensed explosion. If she kept blocking directly, her stick would splinter, then break, and then it would just be her opponent raining down rattan on her weaponless body, unless the Headmaster came to her senses— odds Vi wasn't wild about chancing.

Slowly but surely, the studio had begun to fill with the familiar scent of burning rattan, the friction of wood against wood. At this rate, she'd end up with a skull fracture before she ever bonded another dragon.

Fuck that. Grabbing both ends of her stick and engaging the momentum of her hips, she slammed his next strike aside. It gave her an opening—a barely there, momentary opening, but an opening. She slid her stick beneath his weapon arm, grabbed the other end for leverage, and twisted. Nick grunted as his weapon went flying, bouncing along the floor of the studio.

They froze for a moment like that. Chest heaving, Vi stared down the length of her own rattan stick into Nick's eyes. She had the butt of the weapon wedged against his Adam's apple, her feet locked up against his. She didn't even remember getting there.

Then he shifted his feet, and grabbed the lapels of her uniform. The floor went out from under her. She tried to get her stick up as she fell, which turned out to be a mistake. He snatched the end, and twisted it from her grip, leaving her weaponless beneath him. With a snarl, she hooked her feet behind his knees and yanked, toppling him down after her.

They were, abruptly, nose-to-nose once more. Red light bathed the points of his cheekbones. Those strange bright eyes of his had gone brighter than ever, narrowed beneath his lashes, as the screen that took up the back wall blared with color.

"Time," called a voice over the speakers. "The match is over."

Vi scrambled to her feet. "Fucking hell," she panted. "Were you trying to kill me?"

"If I was, I didn't do a very good job, did I?" His hand went to his throat, where her stick had been a moment before. She wondered if it would bruise. She couldn't decide if that would please her or not. "You could have had me, for a moment there. You hesitated, that's all." He glanced at her up through those lashes. His voice was rough. "I won't—I'm not here to insult you, Park." He gave her a humorless flash of a smile. "I know you could kill me as easily as I might kill you. I'm not arrogant enough to pretend I'd keep the upper hand if it came down to that."

He was trembling. For a moment, she thought it was a case of shakes coming down from the adrenaline high of the fight, but then she got a good look at his body language: the hunch of his shoulders, the carefully neutral set of his face, as he shook and shook. That got under Vi's skin and, bizarrely, evaporated her anger. "I wouldn't kill you," she said. "For one thing, that would break, like, basically all of the Academy rules, and being slapped with probie status has us in enough trouble already, wouldn't you say?"

He didn't respond, still looking at her and shaking.

Aunt Anabel or Aunt Cat would probably tell her that he wasn't her problem now. The bout was over. She'd come away mostly unhurt. Dealing with her opponent in the aftermath wasn't part of the job.

And yet.

"Hey." Awkwardly, hesitantly, Vi pressed the palm of her hand against his shoulder, sure to telegraph the motion so he wouldn't flinch away. "I wouldn't kill you," she repeated, more quietly this time. "I'm ambitious, but I'm not that kind of ambitious" She gave a significant pause, then added, with careful lightness, "Also, there's a witness and absolutely no way to conceal the evidence. What kind of Park would I be if I committed such a sloppy murder?"

It was an absurd thing to say. They seemed to realize it at the same moment. Slowly, Nick's shoulder unclenched itself beneath her hand, as he gave a brief snort of laughter. "Yeah, okay."

The door opened with a buzz. Vi turned, expecting the Headmaster. Both she and Nick started as Sifu entered the studio instead. The red light of the screen carved out the shadows beneath her cheekbones and darkened her gaze—an uncanny effect on such an eerily forgettable face. Amid the suddenly heavy silence, their teacher locked eyes with Vi, then shifted her attention to Nick. Her mouth was a single thin line.

When she spoke, her voice carried none of the usual joking, devil-may-care cadence that Vi had come to associate with Sifu's classes. "This bout has been called to a halt and ruled . . . a draw."

"What?" demanded Vi. "Why is that even your decision?" She craned her neck. "Where's Headmaster Winchester?"

"Attending to other business," snapped Sifu. "You shouldn't be surprised to hear that there's a great deal to manage, given the growing depletion of GAN Peacekeeper numbers. Karolyn Winchester has been called away on urgent business. The matter of this match has, as such, been delegated to me, which means I get to declare when it's over, and what the results are." She swiped a thumb over her phone screen, and made a great show of glancing at the time. "And I have declared no winners."

Vi set her jaw. She'd worked for this. She wasn't giving up that easily. "You didn't have to stop the fight. We could have kept going."

Sifu grinned. "Not according to your own rules. You specifically proposed a stick fight. Nicholas agreed. You both lost your sticks. Ergo, the fight is done. Since neither of you yielded to the other or knocked each other out, I'd say it's a draw."

Vi wanted to scream. Instead, she argued, a little petulantly, "He lost his stick *first*."

"Then dropped you on your ass before you could work up the nerve to actually land a decisive blow," countered Sifu in crisp tones.

It was like being hit with the discarded rattan. Vi flinched.

Sifu saw it, and softened a little. "Here's the deal: I have a lesson for you both," she said. "If we must proceed with this incredibly stressful and unnecessarily dangerous tournament, it's my job to make sure you're fit to compete in each match—not to mention fit to pilot a dragon, should you find yourselves selected for the dubious fortune of replacing the missing members of the GAN Corps. Today wasn't a bad showing, necessarily. But you both have a tendency to make rookie mistakes—yes, even you, Nicholas. Miss Park hesitates too much, which weakens both her offense and her defense. You hesitate too little, which puts you at a disadvantage when your opponent behaves unpredictably. And both of you let panic turn you into an easy target." She looked from Vi's face to Nick's, mouth pursed. "Be here at this exact studio tomorrow morning, at eight A.M. sharp. We're going to give the two of you a little warm-up before our usual group class with the others."

"What are we going to do here?" asked Nick. Vi snuck a glance toward him. His expression had taken on an eerie opacity, his voice practically monotone. If her glance hadn't lingered, she might have assumed he was bored. But she got a good look at his hands, and the way his fingers still shook.

"We're going to start over," said Sifu. "We're going to slow our roll and break things down. Go back to the basics."

"We both know how to fight," Nick pointed out, which was actually kind of generous of him, all things considered. It wasn't like Vi had mounted an especially impressive defense—let alone any kind of real offense—during either of their confrontations, in or out of the cockpit, in sim or in real time. "We don't need to rehash—"

"Bullshit," said Sifu crisply. "Everyone needs their basics. The two of you, most demonstrably. And I want to see a better performance in the next two phases of the Headmaster's tournament."

"You know we're technically competing against each other, right?" Vi pointed out. "Isn't it, like, a conflict of interest to train us together?"

"No." Sifu's eyes narrowed. "You're both my students. I'm your teacher. I teach. You learn."

Which was a nice, fair thing to say, except that Vi needed a tournament victory way more than Nick did. Head cocked, Vi searched Sifu's unremarkable face for any clue that she might be in on Vi's deal with the Headmaster. Sifu just looked back at her, stubborn in her assertions, arms folded, the very picture of firm yet reasonable authority.

Sifu didn't get it, not really. Sifu didn't know where Vi was coming from: how it felt to walk into Academy auditions convinced that you'd nailed your simulation with your cleverness and derring-do, only to discover just how badly you'd fucked up. Sifu didn't understand Vi's deep-rooted, thorny need to author her own redemption arc. To prove that she still had a place among the best and brightest of the GAN, that she could stand among them, that she could save the ones who could not save themselves. Without a spot in the Peacekeeper Corps—without the chance to find those missing pilots—she'd just stay a fuckup forever.

Leave your ego at the door. The ghost of Aunt Cat's advice— practical, almost clinical in its simplicity—chided Vi, lurking just beneath the surface of her resentment. Sifu might not understand or appreciate the position Vi was in, and really, maybe that was for the best. But that didn't mean Vi couldn't learn from her. That didn't mean that tomorrow had to be a waste of Vi's time. Hadn't she wanted more intel on Nick? What was this but an opportunity to collect it? She might not enjoy it. But that didn't mean she couldn't benefit from it.

Sifu and Nick were watching her now. Vi broke eye contact with them both. She felt studied, and the scrutiny made her anxious.

"I'll be here," Vi told them roughly. She left before she could give more of herself away.

◆

THE DRAW DIDN'T GO over as poorly as Vi thought it might. Draws were rare in mech tournaments, but they did happen. The Headmaster's conscription was no exception. One pair of first-year boxers had exchanged sloppily panicked, half-hearted blows until time was called, and the irritably bored Academy instructor assigned to oversee them declared "a draw that really should have been two losses." Compared to them, Nick and Vi's draw at least looked half-respectable.

Still, scrolling through the wins among the other matchups, Vi almost wanted to cry. Tamara and Elsbeth had both won—Tamara by wrestling and pinning her opponent, and Elsbeth in a fencing match decided on points. Rosalyn had won her match handily as well, knocking her opponent out with a brutal kick to the head.

One small silver lining to being summoned back to the scene of their mutual failure was that Vi could tell that Nicholas Lee was just as pissed off about it as she was. He hid it a little better, maybe—he didn't storm around or yell or curse the way a lot of dudes did. He didn't even seem to sulk, not really.

Instead, he brooded. A closely related cousin to sulking, to be sure, but differentiated by the careful set of his jaw, the listless look in his eyes, the stillness of his body language, and maybe above all else, what appeared to be a valiant attempt to look very much as though he was not brooding. Vi eyed up the slouch of his frame against the wall outside the studio and gave a heavy sigh. Brooding, it seemed, was catching.

"I really hope this exercise doesn't turn out to be completely pointless," she said at last. "The physical component of the Headmaster's tourney was a bust for us both. Why bother making us run it back when fighting each other now won't even count for our final tourney scores?"

Besides, she had the next phase of the combat assessment to concentrate on. She'd already blown one shot, which meant she only had two left. Vi didn't suffer time-wasting easily. Whatever Sifu had in store for the two of them, Vi would make it count. She had to.

Leave your ego at the door.

Easier said than done, Aunt Cat.

A door slid aside, admitting one unimpressed looking Sifu, already mid eye roll. "Oh, I don't know. Because you might actually learn something about good piloting skills, should one or both of you in fact enter the Peacekeeper Corps at some point in your desperately dramatic yet short-sighted little lives?" She sighed. "Besides, there's an important difference: this isn't a fight. You're not competing for the attentions of Karolyn Winchester this time. You're just sparring."

Vi frowned. "Doesn't that just mean we're competing for your attention instead?"

"No," said Sifu, with an abundance of patience. "It means that you, being my students, are engaging in an exercise designed—and I really can't reiterate this enough—to help you learn. Which means that both of you need to slow the hell down."

"Both of us!" Vi protested. "I'm not the one who opened the fight by swinging like an ax man on the executioner's block!"

Nick's shoulders lifted in a slight shrug, arms crossed tightly over his chest. Those pale-brown eyes were like twin suns, boring straight ahead. "She picked the weapons and set the pace. I simply followed her lead."

"More like escalated," muttered Vi. "I wasn't asking to get my head taken off, thank you all the same."

Another shrug. A hint of amusement curled around the edges of Nick's mouth. "Your head's still pretty thoroughly attached to your shoulders, so far as I can see. No harm, no foul, right?"

"Enough, both of you." Sifu massaged her temples, glancing between them like she hadn't yet decided where to concentrate the full weight of her glare. "That was the Headmaster's game, but this one is mine. And this time, instead of trying to smash each other to a bloody pulp that I'll inevitably have to clean off the studio floor, I want the two of you to engage in some good old-fashioned physical conversation. Stop thinking about winning, or proving something. Start thinking about what you can learn from each other." She snapped her fingers at the screen. The red light blinked off. "I'll leave you to it. Start again. And this time, don't disappoint me."

Vi didn't miss the way Nick's face fell at that last bit. His expression—big-eyed and tight-mouthed—twisted up something inside her chest, even as the colder, more strategic part of her filed the observation away for future reference. *Note to self: Nicholas Lee is not immune to criticism. Addendum: Nicholas Lee, despite appearances, actually gives a shit what Sifu thinks of him.*

She picked up both sticks, twirling them around in each hand, opposite one another, trying to re-loosen her wrists. Nick watched her from the corner, wary-faced. "So." She swung both sticks over her head. "Physical conversation, huh? Any idea what that means?"

"Probably only one real way to find out." Nick started toward her, then hesitated. A series of expressions warred across his face. "Listen, about that last bout, I didn't mean—"

She waved him off. "Forget it. I was baiting you. You tried to defend yourself when I went on the offense, and then you just—"

"Escalated unnecessarily?"

"Got . . . a little carried away." She paused. It wasn't like she hadn't seen that kind of reaction before, where someone instantly escalated a defense with that sort of wild abandon. Sometimes, it came from inexperience and insecurity—obviously not the case here. Other times, it came from garden-variety assholery—which, while tempting to ascribe to Nicholas Lee, also went against Vi's basic people instincts. Nick put on a solid performance of assholery from time to time, depending on who was watching, but no one who interacted with sentients with the sort of quiet care he did could claim assholery as the core of their being.

But sometimes—more often than Vi liked emotionally acknowledging—those reactions emerged when someone was used to being attacked, usually by an aggressor who had the capacity and desire to hurt them. Half-consciously, she curled her fists around the sticks. She didn't know who could have commanded that kind of power over Nick, but the thought of it made her stomach churn. She made herself look him in the eye. "Catch."

He caught the stick she tossed his way with only a faint expression of surprise.

"Let's start slow," she said, snaking her own stick out in front of her into a loose guard. "Light contact. For real, this time."

He still looked wary, but the corner of his mouth tilted upward. It highlighted a dimple she hadn't noticed before. "All right."

Their sticks knocked together. Vi breathed out slowly. He'd taken her at her word. The resistance he offered was enough to keep her adrenaline going, but the strikes were carefully doled out this time, force applied with exquisitely controlled care. The guy really did know what he was doing.

They exchanged a few more blocks and parries, ripostes snaked in with light but increasingly rapid precision. Nick's fighting style hadn't fundamentally changed much, but the tenor of it felt different now. Vi was no longer defending herself from a berserker. It was more of a dance—a dangerous one, but a dance all the same, like the Tchaikovsky pas de deux Alex had made her play on the piano time and time again. Nick, when he wasn't trying to maul you, could keep up a beautiful tempo.

She grinned. Physical conversation at its finest.

This time, when the screen flared red, they disengaged naturally. All the anxious tension from the first bout had evaporated. Vi chanced a glance toward her sparring partner, dashing sweat from her eyes with her free hand. Nick grinned right back at her, wide with delight. Wordlessly, they high-fived.

"Ahem."

As one, they spun to attention as Sifu reentered the studio. For a moment, she just stood there, arms folded, head cocked to one side. Vi felt her fingers tense around the stick again, heart rate climbing.

Abruptly, Sifu smiled. It was a small, wry expression, more a sideways pull of the mouth than anything else. "You're learning," she observed.

"We're learning something, all right," muttered Vi. "What that is? Who's to say?"

Sifu just kept smiling that odd little Cheshire cat smile. "I'll tell you what, Park girl. I'm going to ask you two questions. And if you tell the truth, both times, I'll give you the answer to *your* question, plain and simple. What do you say?"

Vi raised her eyebrows. "Is that one of the two questions, Rumpelstiltskin?"

Placidly, Sifu swatted the back of her head. "One. What was the biggest difference between the second stick fight and the first?"

"What do you mean? There was a lot." Vi began to count off her fingers. "He didn't try to murder me. I didn't feel compelled to preserve my life with a few inches of rattan. I wasn't worried about breaking my—okay, actually, mostly, it was just 'he didn't try to murder me.'" She paused, then added, a little reluctantly, "And I guess, I didn't try to murder him back. Sorry, Nick."

He waved her off, looking amused, even as Sifu said, "Question two. What was the hardest part of learning to pilot a sentient for the first time?"

Like a droid with an overactive auto-replay function, Vi's brain jolted into flashback mode. She thought of that little mechanical Jindo her cousin had introduced her to, that wary snarl full of sharpened chrome teeth. "Probably trying not to get killed, while also just . . ." She trailed off, a knot of frustration stuck in her chest. "Proving that I could fight *for* a sentient—could fight *with* them, in that cockpit—without fighting against them," she finished.

That infuriating, opaque smile Sifu had been wearing stretched wide. For a moment, that oddly forgettable face of hers looked familiar, the features carved into something distinct by the sheer glee unfolding across them. "There," she said softly. "The answer. I've fulfilled my end of the bargain."

"You said you'd answer my question."

"I said I'd give you the answer in the simplest way available, not that I'd answer it myself."

Vi's fist clenched around the stick again. "I don't—"

"You *did*," said Sifu, with just enough force behind the word to make Vi back up a little, even with the weapon in hand. "You wanted to know what the lesson behind all this was." She gestured expansively: at Nick, at the rattan sticks, at the glowing red screen backlighting them both. "And that was it."

Vi stopped short. "Wait, you're seriously implying that . . . you wanted us to treat *each other* like mechs." Sifu's lesson clicked together in her head, so abruptly that she felt absurd for not seeing it earlier. "A physical conversation. Like the physical conversation between pilots and the sentients they bond." She stopped again, laughing under her breath. Understanding dawned on her. "All this time, I've been wondering why you wanted to match us again in hand-to-hand, when the next phase of the tournament takes place in the cockpit. But you didn't want us starting the spar from the cockpit. You wanted to break down mech piloting to its bare bones first."

"And how did we do?" Vi turned at the sound of Nick's voice. She'd practically forgotten he was there, but everything about the way he held himself now made his presence known. He leaned toward Sifu, whiskey-bright gaze focused on his teacher. On anyone else, his body language might have seemed menacing. On a boy like Nick, after everything else Vi had noticed about him, she recognized supplication for what it was.

Even if she hadn't, the slight break in his voice as he spoke again gave him away. "You could have told us what you wanted."

"I could have," agreed Sifu. Her demeanor gentled a little. "Sometimes, Nicholas, you seem to want easy answers. Simple solutions. The quick fix. But that's not what—"

"I don't want any of those things," said Nick brusquely. His expression looked the way it felt when you sliced a paperbound edge of old-fashioned stationery between your fingers, the subtle flare of pain. "I just want to know what I—what we're supposed to do to make you happy."

Goddamn. Vi blinked at that rough note of earnestness in his voice. He meant it. He really, truly meant it. Vi knew irony or mockery when she heard it, especially from boys like Nick, and neither were present here. You couldn't fake this shit.

The pause that descended on the room in the wake of his bald-faced honesty took on a strange, brittle shape. Nick's shoulders pulled in on themselves, drawing his lanky, lean-muscled frame into something small. This wasn't dangerous, sure-footed Nicholas Lee, unassuming and easily bored pretty boy who'd fuck you up before you could say "boo." This wasn't even the same Nicholas Lee whose touch could gentle snarling metal dragons. This was a Nick stripped down to something ugly and undisguised, wildly uncertain of himself.

From the stricken look on Sifu's face, she saw it for what it was too. Her mouth parted, but the words didn't come in time. Nick was already halfway out of the studio. "Let me know when you're ready to deal with mechs," he offered roughly without turning around. Vi wasn't sure if he was addressing her or their teacher. She wasn't sure it mattered. Some awful, clinical part of her was still stuck on the novelty of it all: Nicholas Lee, Academy bad boy and Academy golden boy in equal measure, the smirking pilot with constant bruises on his knuckles, fleeing the scene of a fight.

A spar, whispered a voice in her head that sounded suspiciously like Alex, gentle and chiding. *You heard Sifu. You saw the difference between what she made you do and what the Headmaster asked for. What Sifu had you two doing wasn't at all a fight, by the end, not really.*

"Nick," Vi called after him, beseeching. Unsure, herself, what she wanted from him. To offer calm, or comfort, or ask why someone else's happiness—why Sifu's happiness—mattered so very much.

She called for him half a beat too late. The rattan stick clattered gently to the floor in his wake as her sparring partner slammed out of the studio.

In the brief weeklong lull between tournament phases, Vi found herself near incapable of concentrating on normal classes. Studying navigational flight routes seemed so pointless. Getting an A in Intro to Navigational Geography wouldn't bring her any closer to victory against Nick, a place in the Peacekeeper Corps, or a solution to the mystery of the GAN's missing pilots. Without a tournament match to focus on for once, Vi attacked the matter of the missing pilots with what few weapons she had: access to the wireless, an inquisitive mind, and pure stubborn obsession.

Her findings were mixed. She could track all the last known locations of the missing—that bit was public record—which gave her a starting place. What didn't help was how disparate they all were. Tanaka and Abubakar may have vanished over the Mediterranean, off the coast of Malta, but Prudence Wu had supposedly vanished near Macau, several time zones away. Another pilot and his dragon had disappeared somewhere over the South China Sea, while the rest of his squad had vanished between the Hawaiian Islands in North America. There was no rhyme or reason, no hot spot that jumped out as the biggest or most dangerous disappearance spot.

It left a frustrating taste in Vi's mouth, going into the second phase of the tournament. This phase arrived with, if possible, even more fanfare than the first. This was the first time competitors would be tested in the cockpit. The hand-to-hand phase may have gotten the bloodlust out of everyone's system, but non-sentient mechs would force cadets to show off what they could really do in a mobile suit. It was the best precursor so far to what any of them might look like behind the gears of a GAN dragon.

The matchups for the first round of the second phase blared into existence on Vi's phone on a Sunday morning. It was one of the more demeaningly stressful ways she'd been woken up. A few names jumped out at her from among her fellow probies: while Amadeus had been eliminated upon his forfeit to Vi, his sister had won one of her first-phase matches, as had Tamara. Fate—or, more likely, the Headmaster's hand—had matched the two probie girls against each other for the first match of the second phase. Curiosity tweaked Vi's belly. She spared a moment to wonder whether she'd get the chance to see them in action, before her gaze froze on her own name.

She refreshed the screen a few times, just to be sure, but the print was unmistakable. In the first match of mech fights, Viola Park was to face none other than Rosalyn Davies.

◆

ALL AT ONCE, VI'S WORLD zoomed into a singular focus. The first matches of the tournament's second phase were scheduled to begin a couple weeks from the matchup announcement, which left Vi little time to prepare.

The Academy, meanwhile, remained merciless. Evidently, attacks by rogue GAN dragons were no excuse for slacking on the pace of either the academic curriculum or the ongoing tournament. The monster Vi's aunties had described, content to swallow promising young cadets whole without remorse, was clearly alive and well. The next few weeks at the Academy melted together into some sort of violent waking dream of anxiety. Vi, with the ease of preparation and practice, adjusted to the breakneck rigor of Academy coursework. She kept her nose above water, technically, but that didn't stop her from feeling like she was drowning sometimes. Attending prep school back in New Columbia had taught her how to make clockwork of her academic brain and body: turn up to lecture, take notes, do the essays and problem sets, cram the reading the next morning, rinse and repeat. That basic muscle memory worked, to an extent, even in the hallowed halls of the GAN's training grounds, but even after one month, Vi could tell it wouldn't work forever. Material from all four of her classes—including Sifu's—only piled on higher and heavier, and between Vi's worry over freezing in the cockpit and the looming matter of disappearing pilots, it was all she could do just to keep breathing.

She barely saw Rosalyn around, and couldn't figure out if it was by the other girl's design or not. Previously, Ros had always appeared to make a point of being easy to seek out—between classes, or during mealtimes at the dining hall—but now seemed constantly thronged by other students, hurrying about here or there, too busy and distracted to catch eye contact with Vi for longer than a few seconds.

When Vi did finally run into Rosalyn on her way out of the Headmaster's tower, Ros seemed almost smug. "Well, if it isn't Viola

Park! Haven't seen your face in a . . . well, it's got to have been a couple weeks at least now, hasn't it?"

Vi took a risk, and offered a smile. "What can I say? You always seem so busy."

"I'm training a lot." Ros shrugged. "Best to keep myself sharp if I'm to face you in mech combat."

The tone was cajolingly friendly, but a piece of tension, wound tight under Vi's skin, loosened just a touch. At least one of them had finally said it aloud. Vi shrugged, opting for humility. "I wouldn't worry too much about me."

A grin flared to life across Rosalyn's face. "I would."

"How's that?" asked Vi, wary.

"I research my opponents," said Ros. "I've seen tape of some of your mech combat work, prior to the Academy." She shrugged. "You weren't bad."

Vi didn't miss the past tense. Her fingers curled against her palms, biting into the training-callused flesh there. It wasn't like she could blame Ros. It was true: Vi had been pretty damn good in the cockpit, prior to that disastrous Academy entrance exam, but what had she done since? Gotten lucky bonding an experimental dragon on the loose in the heat of the moment. Whether Vi still had the right headspace—the confidence, the self-assurance, the trust in the tools the cockpit gave her—to perform in competitive mech fights was anyone's guess.

Don't forget to worry about the rest of us too, Ros had told her, the last time they'd discussed the tournament. The warning had been clear. *Worry about me.*

It was probably the best piece of advice she'd given Vi at all.

Quietly, Vi made a mental note to take a break from homework that night to scour the wireless for whatever footage she could find of Ros's previous mech fights.

◆

THE RESULTS OF VI'S searches were not comforting.

There wasn't a ton of tape out there featuring Ros, but a few highlight reels in both 2-D and 3-D could be found here and there. Even on the grainy 2-D cams, Rosalyn cut through her opponents with a choppy aggression that made Vi wince in sympathy for the thoroughly defeated pilots. The Davies girl didn't necessarily brim with the smooth, clean movements typical of seasoned combat mech pilots, but what she lacked in technique finesse, she made up for in a very obvious desire to beat the living hell out of whatever poor soul had the misfortune of facing off against her.

It both did and didn't remind Vi of the way Nick fought. In the mech simulation, then later in hand-to-hand, he had pressed his advantages relentlessly. Still, there was a different quality to how he moved—a different quality to the energy he brought to combat as a whole, if Vi was honest in her observations. Nick's violence, when he chose to inflict it, was effortless, almost as if he were a mech or a piece of AI machinery himself, programmed on autopilot for destruction. Rosalyn, on the other hand, well. Rosalyn actually tried. She threw everything she had into a fight, ferociously and desperately. What seemed an afterthought to Nick was the core of everything Rosalyn did.

And Vi—bogged down with schoolwork, stress, and a total lack of progress on the mystery she'd once sworn she'd solve—would have to figure out how to deal with that desperate violence. Somehow.

Flying Stormbrewer should have made a difference. In a fair world, that bond—so easy, so natural—would have spelled the end of Vi's self-doubt, and the abrupt return of the pilot she'd been before her Academy entrance exam. No such luck. It was the Lioness situation all over again. Whatever grace she'd been granted that had allowed her to tame her panic the day the rogue GAN dragons had attacked campus, it was absent in every other cockpit she tried. Her movements were sloppy, uncertain, guided by fear instead of years of painstakingly honed instinct.

As weeks of class time melted into each other, a knot wedged its way under Vi's chest, growing tighter and tighter with each passing day. She was, objectively speaking, in a far better position than her probie peers. Even if she failed to defeat Nicholas Lee in the Headmaster's tourneys and lost her spot in the GAN Peacekeeper Corps, so long as she survived the next three years, the worst fate available to her would be Aunt Anabel's ferociously judgmental care, and the roof of a Park family–owned manor over her head. She'd grown up privileged, not naive. Wounded pride and family gossip was a far better alternative to prison or destitution. Yet, still, she couldn't loosen that knot around her heart.

Around the third time she failed a piloting simulation, Sifu asked to see her after class. Well, it wasn't as though Vi hadn't seen that one coming. The knot tightened harder still, which Vi honestly hadn't thought was possible. Head bowed low, she trudged up to Sifu's desk. "I can explain," she said, which was probably the worst possible opener, because of all the many things Vi knew how to do, explaining anything that had happened on campus since she'd arrived was not among them.

"Explain what, exactly?" asked Sifu. "How you bonded Stormbrewer on your first day of class? Or why every performance you've had in a mech since has been a complete disaster?"

Vi swallowed. "It's not since," she said. "It was . . . before too. Ever since the entrance exams, I haven't been piloting right. Stormbrewer was the exception, not the rule."

If any of this surprised Sifu, she didn't let it show. "Well, that certainly won't do. I hear you're scheduled to face the Davies girl next in . . . what is it, two weeks now? She's not an easy opponent to handle, even for the best of pilots."

"I know," said Vi miserably. "I've seen her on tape. She's a fucking monster. I'm going to get eliminated from the Headmaster's stupid tournament without even scoring a real win."

Sifu hummed. "Well, not necessarily."

Vi snorted. "Why, is there some secret rule set that doesn't necessitate time in the cockpit to win in the combat mech divisions? I doubt it."

"No, but you're forgetting one thing." Sifu's smile didn't quite pass muster as a grin, but the sharpness of it stuck out to Vi, against the plainness of the teacher's face. "You've got me. At the end of the day, my job is still preparing as many students as I can for eventual positions with the GAN Peacekeeper Corps. In this case, that means making sure you, at the very least, survive the remaining matches that Karolyn Winchester insists on holding."

"Why me?" Vi met the teacher's eyes, her heart a heavy drumbeat against her ribcage. "I'm not your only student, and I'm definitely not the Headmaster's only student. Yet here you are, singling me out for your assistance."

A series of emotions flickered across Sifu's face, amusement chief among them. "Is that what you think this is? That I'm playing favorites?"

"Isn't it?"

Sifu shook her head. "Contrary to popular belief, teachers are in fact capable of managing our time, and as such, paying attention to the needs of more than one student at a time. You think I haven't been coaching Tamara and Elsbeth between classes? Does that surprise you?"

It did, actually. Vi felt her own eyebrows climb. "And how's that going?" She hadn't forgotten that her classmates were matched up against each other. Probie versus probie. It was bound to be the source of some tension.

"Surprisingly well, actually," said Sifu. "I don't know if you've deigned to notice, but Tamara and Elsbeth are, in fact, friends."

A surprising stroke of hurt nipped through Vi. She frowned. "What do you mean 'deigned'?"

Sifu shook her head, one corner of her mouth turned upward. "I'm not the one setting you apart from the other students. You are. For as much as you hate yourself for those missteps on the entrance exam, some Park-bred part of you still thinks you're too good for, well, all of this." As she spoke, Sifu gestured expansively at the classroom around them: the desks and seats, the 3-D holo-projector, the now-familiar windows facing the woods where Vi had first met Stormbrewer, and the door that shut them away from the rest of the Academy. All the trappings of the probie classroom.

"Ah, ah, ah," Sifu added, as Vi opened her mouth to protest. "Before you mount some grand argument about how of course you are irrevocably changed by the mistakes that made you a probie, pride went before the fall, and you live your life in naught but quiet humility among the plebes now, yadda yadda yadda, answer me this: How much time have you actually spent with the other probies outside of mandated classroom settings? Or, in the case of Tamara, the ten minutes before you fall asleep at night?"

Indignation died on Vi's tongue. "Tamara's not exactly super warm and cuddly."

"Maybe not when you first met. You were strangers, and all she knew about you at the time was that you were a rich kid with family connections who'd tried to cheat her way into the Academy. Have you given her a chance since?"

Vi folded her arms. It probably made her look like a brat, but stubbornness had well and truly set in now. "Has she given *me* a chance?"

Exasperation warred with grudging amusement on Sifu's face. "If one person has to make the first move, it might as well be you. I thought Parks valued graciousness."

"We do," Vi conceded, more than a little grouchy about this. "But you've got to admit, the schedule around here doesn't exactly leave much time for socializing."

"No, it does not," agreed Sifu, placidly enough. "Yet you seem to make time to schmooze with Rosalyn Davies."

Vi's cheeks heated. "That wasn't—I needed her advice on how to deal with Nick." It was a weak excuse, and she knew it. What was it Ros had said? *I think you'll find most friendships are transactional, at the end of the day.* Sometimes, Vi wondered if that was the only kind of friendship she'd ever really known how to forge.

Sifu was shaking her head. "It's not always a bad thing, you know, expecting things of your friends—or giving things to them. But I think you'll find life a little easier when the exchange is organic. And easier still when you actually like them."

"I like Ros," protested Vi, in far less enthusiastic tones than she'd intended. She immediately covered a wince. *Poor performance there, Park.*

Sifu didn't even grace that with a spoken response. The look on her face said so much more.

"Okay, maybe I don't like Ros," Vi relented. "But you've got to admit, she feels . . . familiar. Everything about this place has been alien to me from the start. Maybe entering as a probie magnified that." She shrugged. "Or maybe it would have felt that way even if I'd matriculated as a normal student. But can you blame me for wanting to seek out something that feels like home, even the worst parts of home?"

"I suppose not," conceded Sifu. "But it's just a thought. This is the probationary class, and you're one of us now, for better or worse." She grinned. "Which is also why I'm here to help you."

Despite herself, Vi felt a cautious thread of hope tug at her heart. Sifu was eccentric, to be sure, but she did seem to know her shit. "Could you really do it?"

"What, get you comfortable in the cockpit of a sentient again?" Sifu smiled. "Tell me, Viola Park. Do you want a place in the Headmaster's draft?"

Did she? Once upon a time, Vi would have tripped over her own tongue saying yes. Eager to feed her ambition, eager for glory, eager to prove herself more capable of those who'd come before. So certain that she'd never, ever misstep.

Misstepping now was her greatest fear. And the Headmaster's draft—the opportunity for open assessment—exposed her to the potential for misstepping like nothing else she'd yet experienced at the Academy. The thought of it alone knotted everything inside her chest up tight.

And yet.

"Yes," whispered Vi. "I . . . god, it scares the shit out of me, but I want to do it." She swallowed. "I want to at least try. Just to know that I did. Just to know that I still can."

Sifu gave her a long, hard look, as if searching Vi's features for some secret sign of deception or uncertainty. She must have been satisfied with what she saw there, because an abrupt smile broke out across her face, startling in its enthusiasm. "Well, then," said Sifu crisply. "I suppose we'd best get you back in the cockpit."

◆

GETTING BACK INTO THE cockpit sucked.

"Goddammit!" snarled Vi for the fifth time in a single sparring session. She tore the safety helmet from her head, ignoring the wisps of hair that caught in her mouth, and flung it aside. "I've been doing this since I was a child! I don't understand why—"

The hatch popped with a hiss. Over the intercom of the training room, Sifu's voice emerged, loud and clear. "Yes, yes, you've been piloting mechs since you could toddle, you bonded your first sentient while you were barely out of your mother's womb, et cetera and so forth. None of that matters here. Do you know why?"

Vi heaved a sharp, angry sigh, pinching the bridge of her nose, but intoned dutifully, "Because the past doesn't matter in the present moment when there's an evil robot busy trying to scythe your dragon in two."

Which wasn't far off from what had gone down in training. The mech wasn't even a sentient—just a fight-hardened battle bot, designed to train pure, basic combat skills without the distraction of a psychic link. Cake for someone like Vi. Or at least cake for the old Vi. The new Vi had barely avoided getting her mech's head taken clean off by the enemy combatant conjured by Sifu's training simulation.

It was the simulation, really. Every time the sim burst back into life with its combatants and ever-shifting plane of engagement, all Vi could think about was the fateful day of that entrance exam, and what she could have done differently.

"You've got to let go, Park girl," chided Sifu. "You'll waste the rest of your life obsessing over who you used to be. Focus on who you are. Focus on who *she* could be. And preferably, make sure she's someone who can kick some evil robot ass."

Vi gave another heavy sigh. "Kicking evil robot ass. Right, then. Let's start from the top."

She tugged on the gearshift, marching her mech back to its original starting position. Humanoid mechs had started going out of style when Vi was in middle school—too clunky and inefficient, especially with the rise of speedy-wheeled variations, not to mention airborne and aquatic convertible mobile suit models. Still, there was something intrinsically satisfying about stomping around on giant legs, swinging great big robotic fists through the air—and it was an easier place to start, for someone who'd been out of the cockpit for a while, than one of the more advanced models.

The lights dimmed. Vi's belly lurched. With an effort, she inhaled through her nose and exhaled slowly, listening to the rattle of her pulse skittering against her eardrums. "Your past doesn't matter in the present moment," she muttered to herself, unsure if it was a prayer or a question. Maybe both. The answer to either still lay in the fight ahead.

Vi didn't have to wait long. A loud thump, accompanied by the telltale roar of a battle bot's machinery, cracked through the air. Vi cranked the gearshift into motion-control mode, and spun, thanking the mech engineers of the past decade for tweaking gearshift options in the war mech's cockpit to the point where motion-control sensors actually allowed mobile suits to move with your physical body.

It served her in good stead now, as the fist of her mech connected with a solid crash against the claw of her new adversary. The lights were still dim, but Vi caught a glimpse of silver scales, and pale machine-made eyes, widening over the snap of razor-carved teeth.

"Wyverns?" demanded Vi aloud. "You gave me wyverns to deal with?"

Wyverns had been the nightmares of the North American Partition Wars: great winged metal creatures that blasted plasma fire and left devastation in their wake. They were the whole reason dragons had been built in the first place.

"Not quite a wyvern," allowed Sifu over the intercom. "No wings. But a variant, yes. I thought a challenge might be good for your constitution."

Vi opened her mouth to tell Sifu precisely what she could do with her constitution, involving some definitely not-school-appropriate vocabulary, when the not-quite-wyvern snapped its jaws inches from her mech's face. Vi swore, barely swerving sideways in time. A claw swiped toward her again.

The mech's arm came up to block, but too slowly, catching the claw at a weak angle. Sparks flew over the alarming creak of a weakened gear. Metal buckled around Vi. For a simulation, the fight felt alarmingly, aggressively real. She gritted her teeth, disengaged, then drove her arm forward again, pushing the weight of her hip behind it. The mech followed suit, knocking the battle bot back a few feet. Not much space. But a better spot than they'd been in before. Vi had to give credit to whoever had engineered her mech: for an old humanoid mobile suit, it had uncannily powerful motion sensors. The mobile suit might as well have been an in-born extension of Vi's own body. She barely had to think of which way she meant to move, and the mech would already be canting in that direction. It was the closest she'd ever come to direct hand-to-hand combat from the cockpit.

This time, when her adversary attacked again, she finally got a decent look at the battle bot's true shape and size. Sifu hadn't been lying—the thing trying its very best to claw Vi's mech to pieces wasn't really a wyvern, but whoever had designed this creature had definitely been riffing off some of the more violent Partition War footage. The design was clearly reptilian, body armor scaled from the top of the bot's serpentine head down to its long metal tail, swishing back and forth like an angry house cat's. The claws curved outward from both the feet and the hands, chrome clicking across the floor of Sifu's makeshift arena as the creature prowled around Vi on its hind legs.

"I call this guy Godzilla, if you were wondering," said Sifu. She sounded weirdly fond, like she was talking about a pet or something. A really violent pet. "Made famous by old-school cinema films and video games, of course. Before I joined the Academy staff, I trained fresh Peacekeeper recruits on an ad hoc basis. This was one of the more frustrating training exercises I used to run my students through."

"Great," Vi gritted out, dodging one of Godzilla's claws yet again. She barely managed to jump over the tail that came swishing after the claw, whiplike in its ferocity.

"You should be thanking me, really. Just be glad my Godzilla isn't original flavor Godzilla-sized!"

"I can hardly contain my gratitude." Vi chucked herself forward, rolling her mech over one shoulder to evade the battle bot's attempts to take her down by the legs. "How long exactly is this sim supposed to last for?"

"Oh, you know, the usual." Vi really wished she could see what sort of facial expression lay behind the mild-mannered glee in Sifu's voice. "Until you kill Godzilla, or Godzilla fake-simulation-kills you."

"Fantastic," panted Vi. She'd managed to tangle up her mech's legs with Godzilla's, which sent the beast roaring and crashing down on top of her. The collision, knocking her spine against the wall of the cockpit, rattled her teeth as her back—and her mech's—slammed into the floor. For all the lip she'd given Sifu, she had to send a prayer to any god listening that Godzilla really wasn't any larger. She'd seen footage of what happened when you matched little war mechs up against something even half the size of a truly oversized AI bot programmed with bad intentions, and it never ended well for the little ones. Godzilla was bigger than Vi's mech—enough to matter— but not enough to make the fight totally hopeless.

Still, her adversary was fast. Vi barely got her mech's arm up in time to keep a pair of snapping metal jaws from closing over her mech's face—and her view screen. "Sorry, big guy," she managed through clenched teeth. "But I've got my eye on that Peacekeeper spot."

Her hips shot up, as she twisted the mech around to bump their attacker back a few feet, yet again. Space. They needed to buy space. As many times as it took, until Vi had herself a decent kill shot. Her mech was a pretty rudimentary one, for a war mech—no plasma fire cannons, no fancy convertible chrome-edged blades. All in all, a pretty solid argument for why purely humanoid war mechs had fallen out of favor in the weapons-market establishment.

What Vi's inconveniently humanoid mech did have, though, were big, hulking metal fists. And Godzilla's jaw may have been full of snapping, razor-edged teeth, but it was just as breakable as any other jaw when pummeled by the weight of those metal hands. Which was exactly what Vi began to do, raining down blow after blow on the battle bot. It snapped and snarled under the weight of the attack, but Vi felt—rather than saw—the moment that jaw cracked. A couple of those razor-edged teeth went flying, clattering across the floor of the simulation room.

Vi didn't quit punching. She'd gotten Godzilla into a corner of the room now. Jab cross, jab cross. Uppercut. A left hook that sent another metal tooth clattering across the floor as the battle bot roared its outrage in her face.

Godzilla tried to lash its tail and only succeeded in jamming it against the corner, where it drummed ineffectually against the wall. The battle bot was swaying back and forth now, its movements gone awkward and creaky with the telltale signs of damaged wiring. A few of the wires even protruded from between those once-intimidating chrome scales, sparking at the ends where they'd been cleaved roughly in two. Vi could see the gaps in the jaw where her mech had punched out the teeth.

Godzilla still had teeth enough, though. That great reptilian head snapped forward suddenly. Vi almost took the bait, one step into backing out of the corner and freeing up her opponent's wicked metal tail. She self-corrected with barely half a second to spare, ducking under the snap of those jaws. Metal shrieked as the battle bot's lower mandible scraped across the top of her bot's head. She ignored it, and wrapped both hands around the back of Godzilla's neck, pulling her mech in close to avoid another snap of Godzilla's remaining teeth. Then, as hard as she could, she drove one of the mech's big metal knees into the battle bot's belly, where its central wiring system lived.

Alone, that might not have been enough. Even with damaged central wiring, a good battle bot could survive on backup fuel reserves, or other tricks its engineer had built beneath the hull for precisely this purpose. But Vi's mech had been chipping away at those with its fists.

Godzilla's jaws snapped open and shut once. It tried to roar, clawing ineffectually at the air. Damaged wires sparked along the scales of its body, lighting the chrome up like a Christmas tree. Then, with a tremendous crash, it slumped to the floor, eyes dimmed.

Vi stared at the downed battle bot through the lens of her view screen, panting hard. Sweat dripped into her eyes from beneath her safety helmet, pooling in patches in her clavicles, sticking to stray strands of her hair. "I did it," she mumbled. Unclear to whom: herself, maybe; or Sifu, silent for once on the intercom; or maybe the pile of dim-eyed junk metal that had once been the closest thing to an old-school Partition War wyvern she'd seen.

"I did it," she said one more time, louder now. She pitched forward, legs shaking. Her mech sank to its knees.

The lights came back up. Godzilla's metal corpse blurred for a moment, then vanished with another blink of the lights. The simulation was done.

"Well, I'll be damned, Park girl." Sifu's voice was soft on the intercom. "So you can fight after all, it would seem." Vi wished, once again, that she could see the teacher's face, look for some hint of a microexpression in those strange, plain features that might tell Vi her future. Might tell Vi what all of this meant.

"I could have told you that," panted Vi, still on her knees in the cockpit. "Or Nick could have. The question is whether I can replicate that kind of performance over a bond with a sentient."

"See, that's the thing," said Sifu, in a different voice. One that snapped Vi's head up to attention. "Not all sentients are so obviously sentients, see. It's easy to lose sight of things, amid the rush of adrenaline, and what's going to pump more adrenaline into you than a fight with a giant killer lizard? Your brain was pretty well distracted, kid."

Vi's mouth went dry. "What are you saying?"

"I think you know," said Sifu. The lights flashed again as the intercom switched off. The door at the opposite end of the room slid open, admitting Sifu herself, her hands tucked into the cuffs of an oversized pullover. She looked more like a grad student than someone who'd just put Vi through her paces against a battle bot for the first time in months. "Come on, Park girl," she called aloud, her voice slightly muffled through the shell of Vi's mech. "You must have figured it out, somewhere along the line. There's motion-matching technology for war mech cockpits, and then there's a whole new level of connection to your mech. Surely, you must have noticed, Viola."

The motion control. The smooth, effortless way the mech had cleaved to every movement Vi made. Slowly, Vi looked around the cockpit. "That's not possible," she protested against the budding realization. "Humanoid mechs are too obsolete for engineers to bother equipping with sentient technology. I would have—" She stopped. Shut her eyes.

With creaky movements, the mech lowered itself into a seated position, knees curled into its chest. Vi's arms wrapped around her knees. "This isn't possible," she said softly. "This . . . this isn't how sentient bonds work. This isn't how I was trained."

"And I keep telling you," said Sifu, "that you've got to leave the past in the past. The Headmaster's always commissioning new blueprints for sentients. This was just one of them. And you shouldn't be surprised you managed to figure it out in the end, considering your bond with Stormbrewer."

Vi's head was still buried against her knees. It was too much, too fast. "But . . . Stormbrewer's a dragon. This was very much not a dragon."

"No," agreed Sifu. "But then, that wasn't the point, now was it?" The hatch of the cockpit popped. "Hey, you have room for one more here?"

"Not really," said Vi, which was true—humanoid mechs were generally built to accommodate exactly one human, so as not to confuse the motion-matching detectors—but she scooted aside all the same.

With a satisfied grunt, Sifu hauled herself into the cockpit, squishing her hip up next to Vi's. "They'll be dragons eventually," said Sifu. "Most experimental designs start out that way, you know. Stick the algorithm into something simple, see if it works, build from the ground up. The new model of sentient isn't such a tremendous departure from the old, but the bond is subtler—less two dogs sniffing each other's butts, and more an automatic mind meld between two entities. A seamless transition, to cut down on complications and disagreements between mech and pilot. With enough tweaking, it might even allow for ordinary pilots who handle non-sentient mechs to forge bonds with sentients where there might otherwise be none. An ambitious development, to be sure, very hush-hush." She shrugged. "Lucky for me, I got access to the early prototypes."

Vi twisted her neck to stare at her teacher. It sounded like total bullshit, except for the fact that everything Sifu had so blithely described had just taken place in this very cockpit. Vi had felt it. "You got the prototypes," she repeated slowly. "Just like that, huh? A glorified babysitter slash probation officer was granted the keys to the latest and greatest on the GAN's mech-design docket."

Sifu was busy staring at the ceiling of the cockpit, hardly bothered at all by Vi's line of questioning. "Yep."

Vi didn't let it go. "Who are you, really? Because you sure as hell aren't a run-of-the-mill Academy probie supervisor."

"I should think not. I'm rather better than the last one your poor classmates had."

"You know what I mean! Who were you before you were our teacher?"

Slowly, Sifu's head turned. Stuck in the cramped space of the cockpit, those little black eyes of hers loomed uncannily large. "A pilot," she said, her voice neutral.

Vi exhaled sharply, turning away, but didn't bother pressing the issue again. She knew when she'd lost. Still, the nonanswer soured the air between them, prickled into Vi's suspicions. No one obfuscated this insistently if they weren't hiding something. What skeletons lurked in Sifu's closet?

As if Sifu could read her mind, a hand landed on Vi's shoulder, half comfort, half admonishment. "What or who I was isn't important right now. Remember? Leave the past in the past." She paused. "Except for five minutes ago. I'd thank you to remember what happened all of five minutes ago, because it was a rather significant accomplishment for a girl who—with the exception of an adrenaline-fueled run-in with a certain rogue dragon—has been out of the cockpit for months." The hand tightened on Vi's shoulder. "Congratulations, Viola Park. You managed—without even realizing it in the moment—to bond one of the newest sentient prototypes produced by GAN engineers, then used that same sentient to win yourself a rather hefty simulation victory. You might yet survive the Headmaster's tournament."

The morning Vi was to face Rosalyn dawned with a bizarre sense of calm that settled into Vi's bones. The work she'd done with Sifu had tugged apart something inside of Vi. Her nerves still nipped at her, but they no longer felt debilitating. Whatever was going to happen was going to happen. All Vi could control at this point was how she met whatever was waiting for her.

The familiar cap of red hair was already visible from around the corner when Vi entered the designated room. As Ros turned to greet Vi, the other girl smiled, wiggling her fingers in a little wave. The expression was friendly but sharp-edged, Ros's eyes glinting beneath the unforgiving overhead lights of their chrome-coated makeshift arena. It brought Vi up short, just for a moment. Nick had been all blank-faced business. This already had a different vibe. The deadly, quiet opacity of Nick's businesslike intent on bashing her head in had, at least, been something that felt straightforward. Predictable, almost, once Vi realized what was happening.

Ros wasn't like that, though. Ros still wanted to play at being friends. It was the politic thing to do. But Vi had spent three years in prep school prior to the Academy, and knew a thing or two about rivals and frenemies. Just because someone smiled at you sweet as sugar didn't mean they would think twice about poisoning your proverbial tea. Vi may have studied tape of Rosalyn's combat performances in the cockpit, but there was watching a 3-D projection of some poor idiot getting their mech tossed headfirst across a training stadium, and then there was experiencing the force of that throw yourself. Vi swallowed. Her nerves, previously so strangely calm, nipped a little harder.

"I hear you almost took your first real tournament-match victory over Nick in the last phase," said Ros by way of conversation. Her teeth flashed. "Nicely done."

The passive-aggressive vibe wasn't lost on Vi. Operative words were key. *First real tournament match* and *almost victory* her ass. Vi returned Ros's smile. "You're too kind. I have your advice to thank for my success."

Ros's smile slipped, just a little, but Vi caught it all the same, and allowed herself a small, petty, internal fist pump. Early passive-aggressive point to Team Viola Park. Game on. "Oh, you're terribly welcome," said Ros, poisonously pleasant. "I hope you're able to continue taking it to heart now."

The mechs had already been prepped. Vi's gaze darted toward the metal machine waiting in her corner. The tournament proprietors had provided them with standard humanoid battle bots. No plasma fire cannons or animal-inspired chrome-coated fangs and claws to duke it out in here. Clearly, someone had a taste for the classics. "I do the best I can."

Strapping into the mech—even what was technically an unfamiliar one—was enough old hat to Vi that her fingers did the work on their own, setting safety buckles into place and shutting all the doors of the cockpit. There was a moment of comfort, small and familiar, in the ritual of it. Through the whole thing, she kept her gaze fixed loosely on the ceiling lights. Three hung above the mechs. Two were already on, bright white spotlights on the opposing mechs. The third would indicate the start to the match. Vi breathed out slowly, watching that light. She'd been here before. She could do this. She could—

The light flashed on. And suddenly, Rosalyn Davies was on the attack.

A single spike of fear-fueled adrenaline shot through Vi like a knife. One hard blow from one of Ros's metal fists rocked her, the cockpit thrumming with the impact. Vi exhaled, sharp, and circled out. She was still standing. Her mech was still intact. The lessons over the years in combat mech piloting flickered through her mind. Breathe, breathe, breathe.

Ros didn't take long to attack again. One of her mech's metal legs swung toward Vi with the force of a baseball bat seeking a ball. Vi got her own mech's leg up to check it, just in time, and tried countering. Ros danced out of the way. Vi struck air, swearing under her breath.

She studied Ros's mech through the view screen of her mech, careful to keep her own mech in motion to avoid further blows. She needed to figure out where she could cut an angle in on the other mech, which meant she needed to learn Ros's pattern of movement. The first thing Vi realized was that Ros hadn't changed up her game at all. It all unfolded precisely as it did on the tape Vi had seen: an immediate, aggressive offense, with little care for defending herself so long as she kept attacking.

The second thing Vi realized was that she was no longer afraid of Ros.

It seemed a small thing, but that kind of shit mattered. Sixty seconds ago, Vi been afraid of the unknown. Now, sixty seconds and a few metal blows later, Ros was a known quantity, at least in part. Vi's jaw, previously clenched tight with her own nerves, loosened as she stretched her fingers out over the mech's console. She might still lose. But she recognized that fact clinically now, as a technical possibility rather than a nightmare scenario. Whatever Ros dealt out, Vi would handle.

It turned out to be a full body tackle, mech to mech. Vi grunted with the force of the collision, as they hit the ground. Immediately, Ros scrambled for position. Chrome sparked, as her mech's arms shot in close around the head of Vi's mech, wrenching at the cockpit. Vi winced at the shriek of twisting metal, as the walls of the cockpit shuddered around her. Ros's grip was punishing, but she'd left just an inch of space between her mech and Vi's.

An inch was all Vi needed. She ducked her mech's head under the arm. Ros scrambled again, but Vi was ready this time. She kicked her mech's legs out, scissoring them with a clang against the other mech's chrome-plated body. Ros tumbled over. Vi followed the momentum, shoving herself on top and bearing down. Her mech's knees pinched over the torso of Ros's to keep the machine trapped and immobile.

Ros's mech tried to buck beneath her. Vi slammed a metal fist into its head, aiming for the cockpit. Then she followed the blow with another. And another. And another.

Long metal arms struggled to cover the mech's head against Vi's onslaught, but there was only so much Ros could do. Blow after blow landed. An ugly crunch gave way beneath one of Vi's punches as the hull of Ros's cockpit began giving way. Vi punched at it again. The chrome creaked.

The overhead lights flickered. "Halt!"

The volume on the intercom, flipped as high as it would go, sliced through the moment. Vi's hands—her mech's hands, really—stilled over Rosalyn's half-broken mech.

The directive crackled over the intercom again: "This contest has been called to a halt. Competitors, return to your places."

Cautiously, Vi's mech stood. She'd taken surprisingly little damage, given how aggressively the match had begun. The outer hull of her cockpit was probably dented in more than one spot, and when she gingerly tested the full weight of the mobile suit on its now lightly wobbly metal legs, the knees buckled a little, but nothing broke. Vi had kept her mech whole. Kept it whole, when she'd thought for sure that it would be torn to pieces in this matchup. Her heart fluttered for a beat, edging toward giddy. She hadn't seen that coming.

What she did see coming were the legs of Rosalyn's mech, whipping out to topple her. Vi tried to base the weakened legs of her own mech out in time, but Ros was faster. Swallowing a yelp, Vi pulled the legs of her mech in tight, instinctive, as its metal spine clanged against the floor of the arena. The legs shielded her, just barely, from the swing Ros's mech took at her. It lurched forward—head still partly caved in at a grotesque angle—dragging one leg, but its chrome-plated fists still working.

"What the hell!" yelled Vi.

Then, just as suddenly as Ros had attacked, the mech slumped over with a clang.

The overhead lights flared on, blinding in their sudden intensity. A door slid open with an aggressive electric buzz. The Headmaster swept through, golden hair piled high on her head like a crown, gemstone gaze blazing. Held aloft in her carefully manicured hand was a remote emergency brake.

"Now that," said Karolyn Winchester, "is quite enough of that." One red-nailed thumb slid over the edge of the brake.

The once-smooth, silvery skull of Rosalyn's battle mech slid aside with a remote-controlled crunch, revealing the cockpit, and the girl within. Ros still sat in the pilot's seat, wide-eyed and white-faced, her fingers pale-knuckled over the console. Her red hair, usually immaculate, hung in sweat-stained wisps over her clammy forehead.

Winchester looked up at her through narrowed eyes. "Miss Davies," she called. "Do you care to explain why you continued to attack after an official stop was called to this match?"

For a moment, Rosalyn didn't reply. Her chest rose and fell; her gaze darted back and forth between the Headmaster and Vi. "I don't know," she croaked. She blinked rapidly, several times. "I must have lost control of the mech."

"You lost control," the Headmaster repeated flatly.

"Must have," said Rosalyn. Her brows knit together. "My reaction time was off—I was stuck in the moment, took me an extra few seconds to process the command. Adrenaline, I guess. I tried to get back up, but the console must have misfired. Probably damage from the fight. I got knocked around pretty hard." She offered Vi a flinty smile. "You okay?"

"A-OK," said Vi.

The Headmaster kept frowning. "You normally do better than this,

Rosalyn. It's why I expect so much of you. It's not like you to lose control of a mech. This one's not even a sentient."

Had Ros just flinched? "Of course, Headmaster," the other girl said. She sounded appropriately chastened, voice tight, but her gaze hadn't strayed from Vi. "I got caught up in the moment. It's been a long time since I've piloted an unfamiliar mech, sentient or non-sentient. It won't happen again."

The Headmaster made a mildly derisive sound. "Certainly it won't in this tournament, given how resoundingly you've lost this match. It should be a relief for you, in some ways—instead of spending your time preparing a strategy for phase three, and figuring out how to manage a battle between sentients, you'll have time to review methods of control to eliminate pilot error. You of all people would know how crucial that is to the GAN's efforts. Peacekeepers cannot afford mistakes. It's a good lesson. Let the results of this match be your teacher."

Ros's mouth thinned. Her knuckles, still on the console of the mech, went whiter still. After a moment, she smiled. "Of course," she said. Her voice was different now. Honey sweet and warm. Nothing like the sour-faced, chastened girl of a moment ago. "It might even be a blessing in disguise. Useful to give even probies a bit of a go at the big leagues every once in a while."

"Indeed," said the Headmaster dryly. She glanced toward Vi. "Congratulations are in order, Miss Park."

"Yes, congratulations," echoed Ros. She extracted herself at last from the broken mech, still smiling as her feet landed on the floor. "That was well fought—very genuine, really, especially considering the lack of simulation to manipulate in your favor. You've clearly grown since your entrance exam." She walked toward Vi's mech, until she was almost nose-to-nose with the mobile suit. One hand rested against a dent in the hull. "I do hope I didn't hurt you. That bit at the end there, it really was an accident."

Vi met the other pilot's eyes, wide and bright and earnest. She had nothing substantial to back herself up beyond the thrum of self-preservative instinct in her gut. But she knew it, as certainly as she'd known anything: Ros was lying.

"No," said Vi after beat. "I'm not hurt at all."

◆

NEVER HAD VI WONDERED if it was possible to be a sore winner. Yet that was precisely how she felt now. Beating Rosalyn Davies wasn't the same thing as beating Nicholas Lee—it didn't guarantee the same pride of place at the Academy and, ultimately, the Peacekeeper Corps—but it should have been a triumph all the same. Ros was never going to be an easy opponent, and even in event of victory, she was never going to go down easy. That Vi had won—and won so definitively—should have filled her with euphoria.

And it did, sort of. An undeniable thrill had shot through Vi when she'd landed blow after blow on the head of Rosalyn's mech. That thrill had flared into giddy satisfaction the moment the halt to the match had been called. Vi had faced her fears and survived—better than survived. She'd conquered them, decisively.

So why couldn't she shake that look in Ros's eyes from memory? Why did Vi's heart still skip and shudder cold into the pit of her belly whenever her body recalled Ros's broken mech rearing forward to attack? Attack, still, after the match had ended, after its fight was long since lost?

People so often said one thing while really meaning another. Rosalyn Davies was no exception. But Vi hadn't known how to deal with the passive-aggressive niceties Ros professed while unblinking hatred stared Vi down. In the hours that followed, Vi couldn't help but wonder if the whole thing had been in her head. Maybe Ros really had lost control of the mech by accident in the heat of the moment. Maybe the spirit in which she'd intended those passive-aggressive niceties hadn't been so passive-aggressive after all. Maybe Vi was just assuming the worst because she'd been so worried about a poor outcome that her brain couldn't catch up to the notion of a good one. Maybe Vi was the one being an asshole.

Between the chaos of fighting Ros and all the brooding rumination afterward, Vi had almost forgotten about the other fights. When she finally stumbled back to her dorm room—intent on a hot shower and a multi-hour nap—she nearly walked right back out into the hallway.

Tamara Rogers, sitting on the bed opposite Vi's, was openly crying. It was hard to tell right from the get-go. Tamara, flight jacket still sitting loose on her shoulders and open at the collar, had her knees pulled up to her chest, chin down. At first glance, she might have just been brooding, or sulking, or contemplating taking a nap of her own. Only the hitch in her shoulders, and the occasional perfunctory sniffle, really gave her away.

Vi froze in the doorway, feeling like the world's biggest dumbass. Of fucking course. A complicated guilt twisted at Vi's belly. Sifu's old, frankly worded accusation danced through her head: *It wouldn't kill you to be friendlier with your fellow probies. You could make the first move, with Tamara. It would be the gracious thing to do.*

Instead, Vi had straight-up forgotten about everyone else in the tournament who wasn't herself, Nicholas Lee, or one of their opponents. Forgotten, in fact, all about her own roommate's matchup against their classmate. Sifu had pointed out that Elsbeth was Tamara's friend. It always sucked a spectacularly awkward amount, losing to someone you actually liked.

"Hey," said Vi. She tried to lean in the doorway as casually as she could, but it wound up feeling stiff and stupid. "I, uh . . . look, I'm sure it was a close match. I hear Elsbeth is a tough bitch in the cockpit. There's no shame in losing to an opponent like that, right?"

Tamara looked up at Vi, blinking big dark eyes. They were slightly bloodshot. "I won," she said. Her voice was dull.

"You . . ." Vi trailed off. Her hands knit together. "Oh."

That was the thing. As much as it sucked losing to someone you actually liked, it wasn't as if beating them felt much better. Not when the stakes mattered as much as these. Vi wracked her brain for something useful to say.

Before she could come up with anything, Tamara opened her mouth again. "You know, it's funny, Park. I didn't even really want this." She gave a watery little chuckle. "Would winning be good for me? Sure, I guess. A place in the Peacekeeper Corps, if I get it, means job security, at least. A roof over my head. A steady paycheck, so long as I don't get myself blown to bits." She stopped to wipe at her nose with the back of her flight jacket sleeve.

"I sense a 'but' coming," said Vi.

Tamara snorted into her knees. "But," she agreed, exaggerating the enunciation. "But when I got into that mech and faced El, it was . . . god, it was like everything changed." Her arms tightened around her legs, hugging them closer to her chest. "Sifu used to work with us both, you know, between classes and after normal school hours and stuff. We'd spar against each other with spare training mechs, and it was all super chill. Like a game, almost. We'd end up laughing half the time. But when the match started, and the lights went, I just . . . my whole mindset shifted."

"You wanted to win," Vi said softly.

"And so did Elsbeth," confirmed Tamara. She shook her head, tilting it backward as her eyes squeezed shut. The late afternoon sunlight beaming through the window caught on the half-dried tear tracks crossing her cheeks. "We must have sparred a dozen times over. But it's never been . . . like that. We've never gone that hard at each other. Never fought like . . . like . . ."

"Like you really wanted to hurt each other."

Tamara met Vi's gaze at last. "Yeah."

Like how Nick had been, with the rattan sticks, before he'd come to his senses. Like Ros had been a few hours ago.

But this wasn't about Nick or Ros. Cautiously, Vi took a seat at the foot of her roommate's bed. When Tamara didn't try to shove her away or yell at her to go sit on her own bed, Vi scooted a couple inches closer. "Being in competition with your friends is weird," said Vi. "I think that's part of what made it so hard sometimes to have real friends in pilot-training courses before the Academy, you know? Everyone's always eyeing each other up, trying to see who's better, who's worse, who's going to be a threat if there are only three places in a cadet class and twenty cadet hopefuls. It's a fucked-up way to relate to people you care about."

Tamara didn't say anything, but she'd turned toward Vi, just a little, apparently intent on Vi's speech. Vi sucked in a breath, abruptly self-conscious. "Look," said Vi, "I know we came to the Academy—to the probie class—from pretty different places in life—"

"No shit," said Tamara wetly.

"—and I'm not trying to, like, tell you how to feel about the Headmaster's recruitment methods or, hell, the Peacekeepers in general. It's . . . okay, maybe when we pare it down to its bare bones, a spot in the Corps is just another way to survive and make some money for you. And that's . . . I don't think there's anything wrong with that."

"No?" Tamara cast Vi an impressively deadpan sidelong stare. "How fortunate I am, to have escaped the judgment of an almighty Park family scion."

Vi tamped down an instinctive urge to snap at the other girl. Instead, she sucked in a breath. Released it, the same way she did when taking a hit in mech sparring. "Okay," she said. "I might have deserved that. I'm not . . . you don't need my approval, or anyone else's. It's not coming out right, but all I'm trying to say is that we don't have to want the same things to respect each other, and you don't have to thirst after the same shiny prize that everyone else in this tournament does for a hard loss—or a hard win—to sting."

Advice, Vi was realizing belatedly, that she could probably apply to her own match against Ros. "Maybe we don't have much in common, besides mech bonds and, like, two square feet of living space," she continued. "But with all the fucked-up shit that's been happening this school year, between the missing pilots and the rogue dragons and this crazy bloodbath of a tournament, I like to think that maybe we've at least got something to bond over."

"Trauma?" Tamara suggested dryly.

"Succinct way of putting it." Vi knocked her knee against her roommate's. "Maybe we don't have to love each other, or even particularly like each other. But maybe we can have each other's backs." She shrugged. "Or at the very least, I can have yours."

Tamara was quiet for a long moment. Then she blew her nose and said, clear-voiced and a little grudgingly, "Considering that you did sort of save us from rampaging rogue dragons attacking the campus, it does seem to be in my own self-interest to have yours too." She paused. "Unless we match up in the third phase of competition."

Vi's eyebrows climbed. That final bit might have sounded like a threat, but Vi caught the wry tilt to Tamara's mouth, the slightly mischievous gleam in her eye. Vi put a hand to her heart. "My goodness, Rogers. Was that a joke?"

"Not if I have to kick your ass, it won't be." Tamara was grinning, though. The curve of her mouth was small, but present all the same.

After the ugliness and confusion of the match against Ros, it was like a balm to Vi. She'd have to contend with the fallout of Ros's elimination from the tournament later. For the moment, this small piece of companionship with her roommate felt like its own victory.

◆

VI HADN'T CALLED HOME in nearly two months. It wasn't a deliberate snubbing of the family, by any stretch. She'd exchanged brief letters on the wireless with both her aunts and Alex, but letters were different. You could hold things back in a letter, edit the words and move sentence fragments around until the emotions behind them felt less real. Letters didn't talk back to you. Something about chatting directly to a competent adult human who'd known Vi and cared about her since she was born, and telling them how she felt about Academy life—how she really felt, like it was a freak tsunami hitting Victoria Harbour and cresting wave after wave right over Vi's head—drew her up short.

Which was why she nearly jumped out of her skin the day her phone buzzed an incoming call alert with a 3-D holo of Alex's smiling image flashing to life just above the screen.

Her thumb hit the answer button with maybe a little too much aggression. Voice-only phone calls were a bit of an old-fashioned relic, but Vi usually liked them. It could be useful, hiding your face when you spoke to someone. Easier to cover unwanted emotions.

Of course, sometimes those emotions bubbled to the surface anyway. "Hello? Alex, is that you?" Vi sounded shrill, even to herself, but couldn't spare the mental energy to give a shit. "Are Aunt Anabel and Aunt Cat okay? Why are you calling?"

The other end of the line produced a couple seconds of utter silence that spiked Vi's already panic-fueled heart rate embarrassingly high. Then soft, familiar laughter trickled over the speaker.

With an incoherent sound—half growl, half shout—that was honestly more relief than anger, Vi threw herself backward onto her dormitory bed. It wasn't especially comfortable—predictably far narrower than her bed at the Park family manor, and with a truly terrible mattress that managed to be too soft and too hard in different spots—but the gesture was still pretty satisfying. "Answer my question!" she ordered.

"I'm going to assume you mean questions, plural, and proceed accordingly," said Alex, clearly still smothering laughter. "One. Yes, it's me. Two. Both your aunts are perfectly fine. Three." A palpable moment of hesitation on the line. Then, cryptically, "There's something I wanted to tell you, before you hear about it from someone else."

And just like that, Vi's heart was in her throat again. "You're really not doing anything to reduce the ambiguity of this situation."

"Right. Sorry." She could imagine him mussing his hair with a spare hand as he paced the kitchen, or sprawled over the piano bench. "I'm, ah . . . I'm reenlisting in the GAN Peacekeeper Corps. I get my official papers in three days."

Vi's breath knotted itself up somewhere inside her diaphragm. Whatever she'd braced herself for, it hadn't been that. Three months ago, she'd have cheered him on for finally seeing the light and giving up his boring old music gig. Three months ago, she'd have had a million questions, all fueled by the excitement of her own wildly imaginative ambition. Where would he be stationed? Would he hold the same honors and rank as he had before he'd retired? What sort of missions would he be flying, and what model of dragon would be involved? Did he, an old man now pushing thirty, think he still had the same magic that had made him so famous in the cockpit back in his late teens?

Instead, what came out of her mouth was, "I thought you said flying for the GAN stopped making you happy."

It surprised her. It must have surprised him too, because there was another pause on the other end of the line. "Not exactly," said Alex. "Just that music made me . . . happier than flying or fighting did. And that was okay, for a while. But times are changing."

"What's that supposed to mean?"

"The missing—"

"Yeah, the missing pilots," said Vi. For no logical reason at all, the threat of tears suddenly pricked at her eyes. "They started going missing, what, six months ago? Seven? Definitely before I enrolled at the Academy. That hasn't changed."

Silence on the other end of the line. Vi's heartbeat crescendoed, as if to fill the gap. "Alex. That hasn't changed, has it?"

"Fifty-four."

Vi blinked. "What?"

"Peacekeepers." Alex stopped, drew a breath. "That's how many have gone missing in total since you've enrolled at the Academy. Fifty-four pilots."

A frantic bout of mental math scrambled through Vi's brain. "There were only sixteen gone at the start of the school year, and that was already news. How is this not blowing up the wireless?"

"How do you think?" Even across the cheap phone line, the exhaustion in Alex's voice was a palpable thing. "The GAN Council is keeping it quiet to avoid alarming the public, or compromising ongoing missions. Everything I'm telling you is strictly off the record. I just wanted to let you know."

"That you're singlehandedly going to replace fifty-four pilots." Vi imbued her voice with as much derision as she could muster. She was pissed, which made it easier. "Wow, Alex. I know you had a fancy reputation as a pilot back in the day, but that's a little egotistical, even for you, don't you think?"

He actually had the gall to laugh. "Well. I figured I'd try to make a dent, at least."

"I thought that's what the Headmaster's tournament was for." Vi swallowed. "So that she could recruit thirsty, ambitious young things like me. So that old-timers like you wouldn't have to . . . do this."

"Okay, one: thirty—much less twenty-nine—is not old. You've been brainwashed by all those teen wireless dramas. And two, answering a loss like this for the GAN necessitates a good deal more than the efforts of a handful of green-as-grass cadets fresh from the Academy. The Corps will need experienced pilots. Otherwise, more people will get hurt."

"Why is that your responsibility, though?" Vi blurted out. It was such a blunt, selfish thing to say, but she couldn't help it. Ever since she could remember, the GAN's Peacekeepers had always been inundated with more problems than they could realistically solve. There was always a fleet of rogue AI some hubris-ridden engineer had lost control of and accidentally set on an unsuspecting fishing village; or some warlord having a go at violent, poorly disguised neocolonialism; or arms dealers using random cities as playgrounds to test their wares. The Peacekeepers couldn't be everywhere, and couldn't save everyone. Life wasn't a superhero holo. The world still sucked. But the GAN's knights tried to make it suck a little less.

And sometimes—a great deal of the time—they died trying.

"Why is that my problem?" Now Alex really sounded surprised. "I just realized, I never confirmed. I am, in fact, talking to Miss Viola Elizabeth Jiyeon Park, correct?"

"Don't be a dick."

"Language," he chided absently. "But you are, aren't you? The same Viola Park who badgered me for years about dragons every time I tried to get her to practice a recital piece? The one who dreamed of being a high-flying hero, and used to wax poetic about the mission of the GAN as the ultimate shield protecting the people of the surviving democratic world from the nefarious dangers of unregulated war mechs and rogue AI—"

"You shouldn't have to do it!" Viola burst out. Her eyes squeezed shut. How to articulate what she wanted to say? The missing pilots were supposed to be her problem, not his. The missing pilots were the whole reason she was putting herself through the hell of this tournament. She'd plotted this year out so neatly in her head: how she would fulfill her deal with the Headmaster and emerge as a victor, Nicholas Lee's scalp tucked neatly in her belt. How she would be cautiously accepted into the Peacekeeper Corps. How she would earn the trust of her fellow pilots by getting to the bottom of the disappearances. The arc of Viola, notorious little Park-girl probie, brought full circle and purified by the sheer lengths she would go to, to make things right.

It was a crazy, extremely stressful plan, and it had absolutely no point whatsoever, if someone like Alex got stuck carrying out Vi's thankless little redemption sentence. Vi breathed out slowly, clutching the phone in one white-knuckled fist. She imagined herself, squaring off across from her music teacher, like they were about to fight or something. It was such an absurd image, but she couldn't shake it. "You . . . I didn't always get it, but I could tell, even before that whole fiasco with the entrance exam, that you actually *liked* being retired. You liked teaching music, and writing stupid love songs, and staying out of GAN politics. You shouldn't have to give that all up, just because . . . just because . . ."

"Just because other pilots are increasingly, obviously in trouble?" His voice was gentle. "Just because people are probably dying?"

"It's not fair," snapped Vi. "There are other good pilots in the world who can bond sentients!"

"Not that many." A little teasingly, "And not as good."

"Wow, okay, old man, slow your roll. It's been what, ten years since you sat in a dragon's cockpit?"

"Eight, actually."

"Oh, right, that's so much better." Fifty-four. Not even half a year, and *fifty-four* pilots gone missing. How many more disappearances—how many potential deaths—would the coming months bring? Vi swallowed that awful, hot lump in her throat, which finally let her give voice to the real fear lurking in the back of her head: "What if you die too?"

Alex gave a quiet little sigh that was almost a laugh. "Well, then," he said, in that stupid gentle way of his, "then I suppose I die."

This time, the pause on the line carried a different weight. Vi gave a sharp inhale, half-resigned to the tears pricking behind her eyes. She didn't mind crying so much these days. But when she exhaled, what came out instead of a sob was, "That is such hot bullshit, and you know it."

This time, Alex did laugh, mostly out of surprise from the tenor of it. "Excuse me?"

"You heard me." Vi's fist had clenched around the phone. Something was tearing itself out of her that couldn't be contained now. "There's protecting people, and trying to do right by the world, and putting what little goodness you can into this stupid, screwed-up world, and then there's *bullshit*. 'Guess I'll die' isn't trying to do right. It's bullshit put through a martyr-shaped cookie cutter."

"That's . . . quite the image."

"Shut up!" The tears were back. "Aren't you the one who's always preaching all that nonsense about carving out a space for your own joy? Well, why do you have to give it up now?"

"Vi, there are other things at stake beyond—"

"No! I don't accept that!" She took a breath, rubbing her palm over her eyelids, trying to calm the emotion rioting inside her chest long enough to say what she meant. "You . . . people always talk about selfishness like it's this terrible mortal sin, but why? Why shouldn't we want to live, and live goddamn happily, just because? Awful shit happens in the world all the time, and we can't stop all of it. When do we get to say no? When do we get to tap out, and say, 'I can't do the good and noble thing this time—I'm too tired and too spent; please delegate this to some other sad sucker with a hero complex'? When do we get to just . . . just be *selfish*?"

Selfishness would have saved her parents' lives. Selfishness would have kept them far from the deadly waters of the Pacific during that fateful mission, and left them laughing at wireless dramas and sharing a family dinner with their daughter instead.

Selfishness might still save Alex's, if only she could just make him understand.

"Viola. Listen to me." Alex hadn't raised his voice, but it shut Vi up all the same. That was Alex's particular gift: a gentleness that carried iron at its core. "One of the greatest strengths I've observed in you since you were a child *is* selfishness. You, Viola Park, have always been remarkably, unapologetically willing to put yourself first. And never once has that precluded your also being *kind*. And before you scoff at that, consider this: In putting yourself first, you also put the people you care for first. Your aunts, your cousins—yes, including the ones whose names you continually mix up—and, I daresay, me. Maybe you don't need to save the whole world, but you wouldn't turn your back on it either. You don't have to be a martyr to be a good person, querida."

Vi really did scoff at that. "But you do?"

"You know, I feel like I ought to be offended that you don't have more faith in the possibility that I might actually survive reenlistment. I'm not *that* old."

"Too old to be funny. I'm serious, Alex. Why are you really doing this?"

He sighed. "I'm not trying to be a martyr. Truly, I'm not. Once upon a time, probably around when I was your age, maybe I might have. But there's a bigger picture here than all that. I promise." A little wryly, he added, "And if all goes according to plan, it shouldn't—with luck—involve me dying."

Vi sucked on the back of her teeth, frustrated. "You're seriously not going to tell me what nonsense you're up to?"

"Honestly? I probably shouldn't even have told you that I'd reenlisted at all. Much like everything else to do with the MIA pilots fiasco, my reentry into the Corps was done discreetly, no news networks in the know, nothing."

"All part of your master plan, I'm guessing?"

"Ah, and now I've said too much." He sobered. "I wanted to tell you, though. Just so you wouldn't worry if I don't return your letters for a little while."

That nearly set Vi crying again. "You could have lied to me. Said you were going on some weird arty music retreat in the woods or something. That would still be on-brand."

"Fairly on-brand," he agreed, "but let's be real: you'd have seen straight through me anyway. Are you or aren't you a Park?"

Vi forced out a hoarse, watery chuckle. It sounded awful. "Well, I'm currently cyber-stalking my sparring partner slash soon-to-be mech combat rival, so I guess I must be."

"Sounds like fun. Don't give them too much trouble."

"Oh, believe me," said Vi darkly, "the trouble is all him."

"I do believe you." Alex's voice shifted again. "Listen, regardless of what happens with this enlistment, and those missing pilots, you should know that I—"

"Don't," said Vi. Her voice came out softer this time. "My parents told me they loved me before their mission too. I already knew they did. And saying it now will just feel like you're trying to say goodbye."

"All right." Alex cleared his throat. "Then regardless of what happens, you should know that I want you to keep practicing that Debussy piece."

Vi groaned. Somewhere deep inside her chest, a knot loosened itself. "You're terrible."

"I am. And so was your last run-through of that music. Play it for me properly when you come home." A smile lingered in his voice. "I'll wait."

◆

ANOTHER WEEK PASSED. Vi didn't hear from Alex again.

But somehow, somewhere between coursework and tourney prep, early in the mornings and late in the evenings, Vi began renting time on the pianos in the GAN Academy's music building.

◆

THE FINAL DAYS LEADING up to the second mech fight, if anything, saw Vi even more wrecked than the first had. For an agonizing twenty-four hours, Vi debated with herself whether or not to seek Rosalyn Davies out again.

"What, are you nuts?" Tamara scoffed. "You said it yourself. That girl hates your guts now."

"That's not true," protested Vi. They sat across from one another in the little dorm room, phones out, each scrolling through a 3-D assignment module. They still had an hour of study hall left. The scrolling made for a good show of studiousness, but Vi didn't kid herself for a second that either she or Tamara were really fooling each other. Vi couldn't seem to quit glancing at her name matched up across from Nick's on the official second-phase tournament roster. Which would be a little embarrassing, except that she'd caught Tamara pulling up extra holograms to sneak glances at wireless recordings of mech fights at least twice.

"She tried to bash your head in after time was called during the first match," Tamara pointed out unhelpfully.

"That was an accident," said Vi. "According to her."

Tamara didn't bother gracing that with a response.

Vi sighed, and turned off the 3-D holo-projector. There didn't seem to be much point in pretense now. "Look, maybe she does hate my guts. All I'm saying is that it's not a sure thing."

"She hasn't spoken to or seen you since the match."

"Which is why it's not a sure thing."

"*Park.*"

"*Rogers.*" Vi ducked the pillow Tamara threw at her. "Look, all I'm looking for is closure. Even if she doesn't want to help me—"

"—which she won't—"

"I think I should see her." Vi ignored the curdling of her belly at the thought. "Maybe she won't be champing at the bit to help out the girl that got her eliminated from the tournament, but she's still the person who knows Nicholas Lee best. Knowledge is power, right?"

Tamara snorted. "Because that was so helpful the first time you asked for her advice."

Tamara had a point, Vi had to admit. Ros's coaching hadn't exactly panned out as Vi had hoped during the first tourney. Still, you could learn as much from the gaps in a story as from the parts the teller filled in.

Which was how—despite Tamara's sidelong glances of deep judgment—Vi wound up going to see Ros the next night.

She'd barely finished knocking at Ros's dormitory room door when the chrome slid aside with a hum, revealing a curtain of red hair. Ros tossed it over her shoulder. Momentary surprise barely flickered across her features. "Let me guess," she said. "You got matched up with Nicholas Lee again, and you're looking for a way to handle him?"

"Looking for a way to win," Vi corrected, offhand. She stuck her hands in her flight suit pockets. "I'm curious what you might think."

"Curious, huh?" Ros's arms crossed, as she stepped over the threshold. "You know what I'm curious about? Why you care about the opinion of someone you beat."

Vi raised her eyebrows. "I'm sorry. Did my win somehow also knock all your knowledge of Nick's piloting style out of your head?"

The surprise lingered a little longer on Ros's face this time. Vi pressed her advantage. "Come on, Ros. You said you wanted to be my friend. Friends help each other, ideally regardless of what happens in mech competitions. And whatever you believe, I do need help. I remember how the combat sim felt the first time I met Nick."

"Oh, that?" Ros waved a dismissive hand. "That's nothing."

"Nothing?" Vi stared at the other girl, dubious. "The pressure was relentless."

"Sure," allowed Ros. "But there are ways to stave that off." Her eyes gleamed. "You just have to figure out how to get inside his head."

Something about the look in Ros's eyes gave Vi pause. That was the thing about Ros. She could play affable, while remaining surprisingly candid about what she expected of people. In Ros's worldview, Vi's former status—and family—seemed to override whatever blight probationary status had left on Vi's reputation. But sometimes, the way she lumped Vi in part and parcel with herself—as if they were both better, smarter, meaner than the people around them, unfettered by rules of fair play—sat uncomfortably in Vi's gut.

"What do you mean?" Vi asked at last. "Like, scare him or something? Fat chance of that happening. It's not like I'm much of a threat."

"Don't underestimate yourself." Vi wasn't sure she liked the way Ros preened a little when she said, "Nicky's not immune to fear, believe me."

He really wasn't, Vi remembered with a pang. She'd seen him afraid before, the last time they'd faced off. She hadn't won, but she'd seen him scared.

He was supposed to be her opponent. An obstacle to her goal. Why didn't she feel better about seeing him scared? Why did it make her gut twist?

"You should really be reaching out to him, not me," Ros continued.

"That would be the smart strategic move, with a boy like him. You might uncover something worth using. Fears. Desires. A personal history, even. I think you'll find Nicky friendlier than you think. Just try talking to him."

"Try talking to me about what?" asked Nick, sliding past in the dormitory hallway.

Vi's shoulders tensed automatically. With an effort, she forced the muscles to unclench. "How you got so good at beating the hell out of people, obviously."

A series of subtle expressions flitted across Nick's face. Rosalyn rolled her eyes with exaggerated judgment toward Vi, who shrugged, raising her eyebrows, as if to convey, *What? It's not technically a lie.* And truthfully, it wasn't. When a kid could beat the hell out of anyone, and was also clearly scared of something, the two traits were most likely linked.

"Right," said Rosalyn. "Well, given that I'm the only member of this little party who doesn't have a tournament match to prepare for, I'll leave you two to it." She slid back inside before Vi could protest. Nick followed the motion of the sliding chrome door with narrowed eyes.

"So how about it?" asked Vi, only half joking. "Care to grace a hard-luck rival with your training secrets?"

It took him a moment to turn away from that closed door. "Oh, they're the same as yours, most likely," he said. His voice was breezy. He always sounded that way when he wanted you to think he was full of shit.

Vi cocked her head. Which meant, of course, that he probably wasn't. Still, she made her own tone appropriately skeptical when she asked, "What, getting beat on by a bunch of mech-obsessed, soldierly cousins without enough bloodthirst to chase career political aspirations like the other half of the family?"

Nick looked briefly like he might laugh—with surprise, if nothing else. Genuine humor really did have a way of lighting up those strange, lovely features of his, especially when he'd been startled into it. The dimple in his cheek and the lift of his brows made him seem warmer, less like some untouchable, untraceable enigma. "I suppose it was a comparable experience," he said. He sounded like he was talking to himself as much as to her, wry-voiced and reflective. "You don't always choose your family, but you always learn from them, one way or another."

It was the biggest hint he'd ever voluntarily offered about himself. Vi spent about a millisecond feeling flattered. Then, eyebrows raised, she asked, "So what was your lesson? Professional murder?"

And just like a light switching off, the humor in Nick's features was gone. Something inside Vi's chest twinged at that, at having been the cause of dimming that brightness. "Something like that." Careful, cool neutrality flooded his expression once more. "Why? Are you really feeling that nervous about the next match?"

"You wish," retorted Vi, with a sense of bravado she wasn't entirely sure she'd carried off. The early wisps of a not-altogether-pleasant epiphany had started taking form in the pit of her belly. Her cyber-stalking had already come up with next to nothing. Mentally, she made a note to herself: she'd been scanning the wireless for the wrong search terms. Nicholas Lee had taken remarkable care to make himself—or at least, that name—a dead end.

You don't always choose your family, but you always learn from them, he'd said. Once upon a time, Nicholas Lee had belonged to a family. A family that made their living on violent things he didn't want to talk about. She'd seen what her "professional murder" joke had done to the look on his face. Vi only knew of one industry in the entire world that actually peddled professional murder, and still got away with it more often than not.

What Vi needed wasn't a name at all. What Vi needed was a very particular sort of business record.

WIRELESS TERMINAL USER: VIOLA E. J. PARK
Search Query Log

Selected Database: [all]
Search Against: [all]
"Nicholas Lee" or "Nick Lee"
["Nicholas Lee" or "Nick Lee"] and "GAN Academy"
"Nicholas Lee" and "Rosalyn Davies"
.
..
...
..
.

Selected Database: Probationary Student Enrollment Records
Search Against: Registered Arms Dealer Networks

When the search alert beeped on Vi's wireless monitor the next evening in study hall, she almost ignored it. She'd had at least five different search tabs open—each for a different research assignment she was trying with remarkable grace not to fail under the present circumstances. She had, in that particular moment, been cramming for a navigational geography quiz. One research result on the history of mechs in aerial warfare could wait an hour.

Only a cursory glance upward showed which tab had beeped. Well. Perhaps Intro to Navigational Geography could wait ten minutes.

The record that popped up on her monitor just looked like more noise at first. A few common company names that happened to match up with enrollment through the Headmaster's office. Nothing that should have stood out on its own.

What caught Vi's eye was one name, scattered across a couple corporate registries, then spotted through a few news articles and gossip blogs. *Jefferson Lynch.* She'd heard the name before, of course. Aunt Anabel had her own personal shit list of exactly his type: technically legal arms dealers who'd gotten off from repeated GAN war crimes prosecutions through loopholes and briberies that were practically open secrets to the public. Lynch had spoken out openly against the GAN on multiple occasions, railing against Peacekeepers every time they got in the way of his war profiteering.

What jumped out now were three things: First, a rumor. It started with a couple of the gossip blogs: trysts with various women, which quickly evolved into speculation over who'd wound up pregnant. One woman, a minor Hong Kong holovid model named Janet Lee, appeared more often than not on the rumor rags. Vi eyed her photo for a moment: the flawless tawny skin and high cheekbones, the way the long, graceful line of her neck disappeared into various designer cheongsam. Lee was a common enough surname, especially in Hong Kong, but that kind of beauty was rare. A business-magazine profile, dated a few years after Janet Lee's name linked itself to Jefferson Lynch's on the gossip blogs, provided something a little more official: mention of one child in Jefferson Lynch's household, gone unnamed. A boy.

Second, the lack of any mention of the child whatsoever in any Lynch puff piece dated after that single article.

And third, a meeting at the GAN headquarters, according to the Office of the Headmaster's records. That in itself shouldn't have been so remarkable, perhaps. It was part and parcel with the games a guy like Lynch would play, scheduling meetings with the GAN to look compliant with Alliance rules, even when they were anything but. Maybe especially when.

But Lynch had only met with one GAN department on the day of that visit: the Office of the Educational Provost. The same office that held the purse strings of the Academy for Combat and Cybernetic Arts.

The meeting had taken place exactly two years ago. Right when Nicholas Lee, coincidentally, would have been enrolled at the Academy as a first-year probationary student.

Vi pulled up a profile photo. Jefferson Lynch was a pleasant-looking, neat-handed white man, slight of frame, with a shock of auburn hair and smiling green eyes that invited you to confide in him. He looked more like a schoolteacher, or maybe a social worker, than someone who could command a battalion of murderous AI with the twitch of a thumb. Vi searched Lynch's features for some whisper of Nicholas Lee. The shape of the nose, maybe, or the particular tilt of his smile, but no dead ringer. If Nick was Lynch's kid, their looks alone weren't enough to tell the tale of linked genetics.

Vi scrolled through the lists upon lists—and there were many—of Lynch's alleged crimes. Illegal arms dealing. Illegal modifications to legal AI. Money laundering. Aiding and abetting of mass murder. Aiding and abetting of terrorism. Nothing that stuck, but enough to make him notorious. He was exactly the sort of white whale that the GAN authorities practically salivated over: someone openly despicable enough to have earned the hatred of most polite society, yet just out of reach of the GAN's legal arm. Still, they'd close in on him eventually, if Aunt Anabel's shit list was any indication. It was what the GAN did.

A man like that, Vi realized with a cold twist in her belly, might just also have reason to destroy the Peacekeeper Corps. Why let yourself continue being the prey when you could as easily turn hunter?

Nicholas Lee's particular set of skills had no doubt made him a useful asset to the Headmaster. How much easier would it be for a man like Lynch to pull apart the fabric of the GAN from the inside, with a boy like Nick already planted there? Vi stared at that meeting log, the records of Jefferson Lynch's child, who'd disappeared from public media as suddenly as he'd appeared. What sort of bargain might a man like Jefferson Lynch have made with Headmaster Winchester, to put his own boy right under the GAN's nose? And how could she have allowed those terms?

Vi was an old hand at piecing together a pilot's skills based on limited information. Between the secondhand accounts she'd studied and what she'd felt for herself in their encounters, she'd painted a grim picture: Nick's fights were always bloody, always brutal. That sort of painstakingly honed killer instinct had to be taught, and taught well. He'd learned those skills somewhere. Who would be a better teacher than someone like Jefferson Lynch? Lynch, who sold violence at a profit, who'd been in the GAN's crosshairs for years for the things his weapons did to people? Lynch, who'd no doubt instilled the same values in his child—a child who would be perfectly placed to serve as his father's spy behind enemy walls?

But Nick didn't just learn violence—he also learned fear, whispered a voice nagging at the back of Vi's mind. *Why so quick to assume your opponent—your opponent, yes, but still a fellow cadet here at the GAN Academy—is a willing participant in this terrible theoretical scenario you've concocted when you should have been studying plasma fire reserve equations?*

That jarred her back to reality. Whatever that meeting between Jefferson Lynch and the GAN two years ago had been about—and whether it meant anything for the missing Peacekeepers—would have to wait. Vi was already five minutes later than she meant to be for class.

It was a grim reminder that academic work—and the grueling

schoolyard life that buoyed it forward—still happened. Inside two weeks alone, Sifu must have trotted Vi through half a dozen new models of mobile suit. Vi got time in the boxy humanoid mech, but Sifu insisted that she familiarize herself with multiple makes, not just an easy favorite. Thus began a long procession of robotic wolves, birds, and even at one point, an old-school dragon.

"There really is a difference," Vi mused one day. "Between the old sentients and the new kind the Headmaster commissioned."

"Oh?" Sifu's reply over the intercom was neutral. "How do you figure?" They were back in the simulation room, Vi waiting to see what new horrors her teacher had cooked up to test out on her. Vi found herself in the cockpit of an old-fashioned dragon: the closest she'd come to piloting Rebelwing since the day of her disastrous entrance exam audition. It wasn't an easy thing. The feel of the cockpit—the span of almost-familiar wings and the panoramic display of the view screen—still raised her heart rate unpleasantly. But she could breathe through it now. That was something, at least.

"Take this guy, for instance." Vi knocked lightly on the edge of the view screen. "Bonding him was a whole-ass conversation. For the old-school sentients, offering the bond is less a feat of piloting or engineering, and more like an argument between old married people. I push you, you pull me, until we decide as two separate individuals that we're going to work together. But the new ones . . ."

Vi's nose scrunched up as she trailed off. She wasn't sure what she was getting at. If anything, she should have felt grateful to the new sentients. After all, it was a new sentient that had gotten her over her mental block in the cockpit..

"The new ones don't feel like they have their own personalities, so to speak," said Vi slowly. "That's why I couldn't even tell that I had the bond at first. It was more like they just . . . molded to mine." Which wasn't to say that piloting that mech hadn't been its own challenge, especially when she was confronted with a battle bot like Godzilla mid-simulation. And yet.

"I don't know, the bond just doesn't feel as earned," Vi admitted. "It doesn't require any of the physical conversation stuff you had me practicing in sparring, not really. What's the point of such a rigorous training program if you can skip half the steps in the process?"

"You wouldn't be the first pilot to feel that way," said Sifu. "You ought to hear the old-school brigade among the GAN Peacekeeper Corps going on about the Headmaster's so-called newfangled commission. They remember a time when bonding their first sentient was a big old song and dance, and one that a new pilot might not always survive. But fact remains that Karolyn Winchester is going to do as Karolyn Winchester does. Besides which, most of the old-school Peacekeepers are also old-school enough to recognize that with their own ranks dwindling, beggars can't be choosers. If Winchester's new model of sentients opens up more piloting opportunities to Academy students—or indeed, the global public—that means more potential Peacekeepers."

"And more potential abusers of sentient tech," pointed out Vi. "Not everyone looking to bond a sentient is interested in becoming a Peacekeeper. Some people are just greedy for power. Who's to say black market arms dealers won't be looking to rip these off the first chance they get?"

"They probably will," conceded Sifu. "Which is precisely why the newly commissioned blueprints and model mechs haven't been officially announced at press conferences yet—much less made available for display to non-GAN personnel." The tenor of her voice, even over the intercom, had gone flat and neutral. Vi perked up instinctively. Neutral tone meant there was something you were trying not to give away: a reason to feel something other than neutral. "Karolyn's no idiot. She knows to play her hand carefully. You never know who's watching these days. Tread cautiously, Vi."

◆

VI TREAD CAUTIOUSLY, all right. She hadn't forgotten being jumped on her first night on campus, and though nothing like it had happened since, she didn't much care for the possibility of a repeat performance. It probably helped that she and the other probies mostly stuck together these days, which meant Vi was rarely alone, but the closer the second match loomed, the higher Vi's shoulders went up around her neck.

Two days before the match, Rosalyn Davies invited her to lunch.

"It's probably to murder you," said Tamara predictably, as soon as Vi mentioned it.

"Ros would never murder me over lunch; she knows that would make her a social pariah in North America," replied Vi absently. "It would be nice to know what she wants, though."

"Amelioration, perhaps?" suggested Amadeus delicately. He sat beside his sister, on the far end of the probie classroom, while Vi and Tamara occupied the section nearest the door. Sifu was due to arrive in about five minutes to start class. Nick, in a truly on-brand move, was nowhere to be seen. "You said your last encounter with her was . . . less than bad."

"It was also less than good," said Vi. She frowned down at her desk. "I don't think she actually likes me. But whatever she feels toward me, it's . . . better than whatever she feels toward Nick."

"Weren't those two hooking up?" Tamara leaned forward, clearly intrigued by this notion. "What, is it trouble in paradise?"

Vi winced. "Not exactly. More like . . ." She trailed off, trying to conjure the right words to describe the incredibly weird vibe Ros and Nick's whole dynamic gave off. Her moments of fond possessiveness, coupled with evident disdain. Their body language around each other, and the way he simultaneously deferred to and shrank from her. That entire fight between them over the fateful day in the woods with the rogue dragons.

"I think I understand," Elsbeth put in. She'd been a quiet presence in the classroom since her match against Tamara, but now she spoke up with a surprising amount of intensity. Glancing around at the other probies, she stirred furiously at the coffee she'd snagged from the dining hall that morning. "The man I killed was like that with his mechs. He used to build sentients just to hurt them. He said they were experiments to do with as he wished, because they were his and wouldn't exist without him." She shrugged placidly. "Until one of them bonded me instead of him, and we killed him. Which is how I wound up here."

A tremendously awkward silence blanketed the classroom for a few seconds. Elsbeth took the time to slurp loudly on her coffee.

"Uh," said Vi. She coughed. "I don't think that's an exact analogy."

Elsbeth's head tilted as she tipped the last drops of coffee onto her tongue. "Why not?" she asked around the thermos spout.

Vi opened her mouth, full of explanations for how you couldn't just compare a teenage girl who treated her boyfriend slash boy toy questionably with an evil business tycoon who liked torturing sentient creations for shits and giggles. She didn't have time to make them. The door buzzed aside. Sifu entered, flanked by Nick. The two of them cast a curious look toward Vi, but didn't remark further.

It was an agonizing wait until the lunch bell rang. When Sifu finally released the class, Vi practically ran for the door. It wasn't that she was all that excited to see Ros—kind of the opposite, really. But seeing Ros was always preceded by such horrendous, precipitous bouts of anxiety that Vi just wanted to rip the Band-Aid off quickly. Also—according to her phone—she was already late. She broke into a light jog toward the dining hall.

As it turned out, she needn't have bothered. Ros had yet to appear. Vi, frowning, checked her phone a few times. No texts. Around the ten-minute mark, Vi actually started worrying. She grimaced. She hated being one of those people who always made mountains out of a few minutes of tardiness. Yet here she stood, ruminating over a missing guest to a lunch she didn't even really want to be at, and fishing for her phone to compose a message: *hey ros, sorry I was late, wondering if we're still cool to meet, or maybe we should just*—

"What the fuck!"

Vi's head snapped toward the sound of the exclamation. A girl's voice. She couldn't be 100 percent sure it was Rosalyn's—Vi wasn't close enough to ID the voice—but the sharp bite of anger got her attention all the same. It was coming from the edge of the wooded patch around the Headmaster's office, a few meters off from the dining hall.

"I already told you to back off." New voice. Lower-pitched, quieter.

Male, from the sound of it. Vi began sidling toward the sound of the altercation.

The girl again: "You don't get to tell me *shit*." The sharp ring of a slap turned Vi's creeping into an actual run.

"Hey!" she yelled, rounding the bend into the grove. Part of Vi—the part that always sounded like it spoke with Aunt Anabel's voice—wanted to chide herself for running toward an obvious fight with no real strategy in mind.

That part stuttered to a halt as she took in the scene before her. The girl was Rosalyn, all right. Her fingers, white-knuckled, were curled around the other combatant's shirt collar. She had him pinned against a tree.

Nick Lee. One cheek smarted bright red—no doubt, from Rosalyn's hand. Vi's attention flitted toward him instantly, and she braced for him to telegraph some retaliation. She'd been on the receiving end enough times, of parries, counterstrikes, takedowns. She knew better than most precisely what he was capable of.

He didn't pull any of that shit now. If he cared to remove himself from Rosalyn's grip at all, he did a remarkably poor job of showing it. He slumped against the tree, staring at some point past her shoulder, like he was off in his own world. Nick had at least five inches on Rosalyn, but Vi had never seen him look so small.

Rosalyn gave him a shake. "Since when the hell do you, *Nicholas Lee*, say no to anyone? Since when do you say no to me?"

"Since now, apparently." Nick's shoulders climbed toward his ears, but that stubbornly vacant expression remained on his face, as if carved into stone. "I've done a lot of shit to make you happy, Ros." His voice was soft, but surprisingly firm. "I . . . look, I don't have a lot

of rules, okay? But this is one of them. You know this is one of them."
The color of his tone shifted, and Vi thought immediately again of
Nick asking Sifu, *How do we make you happy?* "I can't—"

Rosalyn shook him again. It rattled his head, cracking the back
of his skull against tree bark. A few leaves scattered down on them.
"*Fuck* your rules, Lee. I always knew your stock, knew you'd sell your
soul to the highest bidder if they asked pretty enough, but I didn't
think you were also pathetic enough to—"

Vi didn't realize what she was doing, until she did it. One moment,
she was watching Rosalyn slam Nick's head into that tree; the next,
she was between them, her back up against Nick's chest and her hands
braced on Rosalyn's shoulders. "Hey!" She removed one hand to snap
her fingers under the other girl's nose. "Calm your shit down!"

Rosalyn's lips pulled back from her teeth. "Stay out of this, Park.
You don't know what's going on here."

"I know that whatever it is, it's not going to be solved by knocking
Nick around." Vi tried for casual practicality. "Come on, Ros. Save
that energy for school. Don't waste it on a brawl."

It was, perhaps, a poor choice of words.

"A brawl?" snarled Rosalyn. "You think that's what this is?"

"Not exactly." Vi's hands hadn't left the other girl's shoulders. In
her peripheral vision, she saw Ros's hands curl into fists. "From where
I stood, it looked like he was telling you no, and you were knocking
his head into a tree for the trouble. Most brawls are two-sided, at
least."

Rosalyn barked an incredulous little laugh. "You calling me a bully,
Park?"

"I'm not calling you anything," said Vi. At her back, Nick was utterly silent, but she could feel his heartbeat fluttering behind one of her shoulders, a drum against her skin, even through layers of clothing. "I'm telling you to back off. Please."

Rosalyn blinked those bright-green cat eyes at Vi. Normally, they reminded Vi of the Headmaster's rings, like two chips of jewelry, as bright and as likely to cut you up if approached at the wrong angle. In this moment, they were just big and wounded, full of furious offense. Slowly, her fingers unclenched from those fists. "How come you're so keen to defend him, Park?" Speculation twisted her features around. "You want to get into his pants? There are easier ways of managing that, you know."

Vi's ears burned. Her entire body felt intensely aware of the boy at her shoulder, his pulse against her back, as he hung behind in silence. The one she'd thought of as a killer. The one she thought might be a spy responsible for the missing-Peacekeeper crisis. Part of her wanted to wash her hands of this whole mess. It wasn't all that hard, if she stretched her own powers of speculation, to justify Rosalyn's behavior: that Vi didn't have the whole story, that Nick was more dangerous than he let on, that Rosalyn was probably just eliminating a threat to them all.

It would have been the easy thing to do, telling herself Rosalyn was in the right. And maybe that was what cemented Vi's decision.

Exhaling hard, Vi gave Rosalyn a gentle shove, forcing her to back up a little. It didn't buy the three of them much space, but it was better than being sandwiched in whatever fucked-up drama kept drawing Rosalyn and Nick back together. "I thought the GAN Academy was in the business of training future Peacekeepers," said Vi at last. "Protectors. Not queen-bee types who beat on people because they're angry and have an easy target at hand."

"You're shitting me." Rosalyn shoved at Vi's shoulders, but it didn't have much force behind it, and Vi's feet were planted. "You think you're doing anyone a favor by protecting *him*?"

Vi didn't move. "He told you no."

Rosalyn drew back at last, head cocked. "You really mean it." Her gaze narrowed again, assessing. That wounded look was still there, but it had iced over, turned itself sharp. "You understand what this means for you, don't you? What you're throwing away by siding with him?" She was practically nose-to-nose with Vi. "You'll never defeat a boy like that in a tournament without my help."

Vi raised her eyebrows. "So far, I haven't defeated him with it either. But I seem to recall defeating you just fine."

Ros started forward. Vi braced herself for the hit, but the boy at her shoulder beat her to the punch.

"It's the GAN's new sentient blueprints," Nick blurted out. "She wants a chance to imprint on the new fleet of mechs before the Headmaster's winning picks from the tournament take up all the open spots in the Peacekeeper Corps." The smile he turned on Vi looked almost feral, a glimpse of the boy who beat people bloody with clinical precision. "I may not be good for much," he said. "But I'm good at knowing things."

Rosalyn drew back. Vi followed the motion, sidestepping Nick as he pushed himself forward. "I can't do it," he said. "I could say yes to anything except this. It's a betrayal of the GAN. And I can't do that, not for someone who—"

"Who what?" Rosalyn's voice dropped low and dangerous. "Go on, finish that sentence, Nick."

Nick's Adam's apple bobbed, but he didn't step back or flinch away from her this time when he said, "Someone who hasn't even been able to bond a sentient in a year."

Time froze, along with Rosalyn's gaze, fixed in place on Nick. Vi remembered, with a lurch, the first time she'd ever seen Ros in a mech: an old-school battle bot, not a dragon. A non-sentient, entirely mechanical. No mind of its own.

"Why do you suppose that is, Ros?" That old, lazy cadence returned to Nick's tone as he continued speaking. The devil-may-care shield slid back into place as he slouched against the tree, but the look in his eyes didn't change, wide and wild. That was fear. Well-disguised fear, but Vi had spent enough time in close quarters with him to recognize Nick's particular brand of fear for what it was, brandished like cheap armor, daring the things he was afraid of to nestle in close. "You weren't always like this. Once upon a time, you could bond a sentient as well as any Peacekeeper. What happened? Did you get lazy? Somehow regress in combat piloting? Or was it because you became so obsessed with building yourself up that no sentient would partner with you? Maybe because, just like everyone else, you've only ever seen the bond between sentients and their pilots as—"

The blow from Rosalyn caught Nick full across the jaw, snapping his head back against the tree.

Something twisted around inside Vi at that sound, flaring outward and searing hot beneath her skin. This time, when Vi moved, she didn't stop at just putting herself between Nick and Rosalyn. As Ros's fist swung toward Nick again, the heel of Vi's palm crunched against Rosalyn's nose. The roar of Vi's own heartbeat in her ears drowned out the other girl's shout of fury and shock. Distantly, Vi registered blood on her hands as she threw the rest of her weight against Ros.

"What the fuck, Park!" Rosalyn's hands flew toward her own face, defensive, as Vi drove her backward onto the forest floor. "You're dead, you hear me? Dead!"

Vi reared back, hips angled forward over the knee she'd planted on Rosalyn's chest. Beneath her, Ros gasped through the blood bubbling from her nose. "Am I?" panted Vi. "Because from where I'm sitting right now, I think I look pretty damn alive compared to you."

"You think he'll reward you for this?" Ros demanded, fury palpable even through her nosebleed. "That he'll take a fall in your next fight, or better yet, fuck you?"

"Frankly, I don't especially care," said Vi, her tone carefully, utterly bored. She rested on her haunches, watching Rosalyn bleed. She leaned in close, looking Ros right in those furious green eyes, and added, low-voiced, "Touch Nicholas Lee like that again, and it'll be more than your nose left bleeding on the ground."

Vi stood up. Her ears were still roaring, her head and belly strangely light. A giggle threatened to escape the cavern of her chest. Punch-drunk, she thought. Literally.

Her attention turned toward Nick. He slumped against the tree, but seemed lucid still, despite the bruise blooming along the underside of his jaw. They'd matched up often enough by now that bruises weren't an alien sight on him. It hadn't awakened that searing-hot simmer inside of her until she'd seen Rosalyn leave them on his skin.

Vi bent her head, hands braced against the tops of her thighs, exhaling slowly through the sudden panic whipping itself through her heart. She'd well and truly fucked her social status now, left any semblance of even transactional friendship crumpled and bleeding and full of vengeful fury on the forest floor a couple feet away. Vi stared, for a moment, at the wild-eyed boy she'd ruined that alliance for.

Nick stared back with that whiskey-bright gaze of his, hair a riot of sun-drenched color over an extraordinary, sharp-boned face, bleached of color against the darkness of his bruises.

He might be a spy. He might even be a killer.

Vi stretched a hand out toward him. "My lunch plans just got canceled," she said. Her voice was hoarse. "You want to get cleaned up and eat something?"

His head canted to the side. In that moment, he resembled nothing so much as one of those contrary mechs he so easily gentled. A sentient, trying to get a read on a potential pilot, uncertain of whether or not they were worth allowing a bond.

"Okay," he said. His voice was hoarse too. "Yeah, okay. Let's do that."

In some ways, what happened next wasn't all that different from the Headmaster's tournament matches, or even that pop quiz on the first day of school. They'd been here before, bruised and sweating and running on nothing but adrenaline. Physical conversation wasn't new to them. The verbal kind, however, was a lot trickier.

Nick didn't say much when they sat down. They'd picked a spot at the edge of the forest, far from both the dining hall and the Headmaster's tower. Despite the talk of food, neither of them had actually bothered grabbing anything from the cafeteria.

"She wasn't always like that," said Nick abruptly. He picked at the edge of his jacket, worrying at the stray threads just beneath that ubiquitous probie badge. "I just . . . I thought you should know. That she used to be different."

Vi didn't ask who he was referring to. Her head tilted sideways, resting on one of her palms as she observed him. If she'd thought he'd looked like a candle flame in the dark the night she'd seen him kiss Rosalyn, the Nick of that moment had nothing on this one here. Daylight brightened what nightfall would have obscured, and there was a good deal more to show now. Bloodstained and fiercely bright-eyed, he was a riot of color and tightly coiled energy, just barely contained inside that bruised-up skin. This wasn't a candle flame; this was a wildfire.

"Were you always like this?" asked Vi.

He eyed her sidelong, looking startled and intrigued in equal measure by the question. "Like what?"

"The man of a million faces," said Vi. "The fighter. The mech tamer. Yet also—"

"Rosalyn's boy toy?" He gave her a ghoulish little grin. "What? It's the nicer version of what you were thinking."

"Stop," snapped Vi. "Don't do that. You're trying to give me excuses to put you down. That's not what I'm after."

He held her gaze, searching, bright and defiant and cautiously mistrustful. Looking for a sign that she was anything other than honest. Looking for a sign that she was baiting him. She let him. Choosing to trust a boy like Nicholas Lee felt objectively about eleven kinds of stupid, but she wanted—foolishly, selfishly, and oddly desperately—for him to trust her.

I don't want to hurt you, she thought. *Please, please, look at me and see that I don't want to hurt you.*

The moment passed. His shoulders slumped.

"I used to think I was in love with her," he said. There was no particular emotion to the statement. He was reciting a fact, rendered carefully neutral by the passage of time, and presumably a good amount of emotional hardening. "She made it seem inevitable, you know. I was easy pickings, and she was . . . her." He shook his head, laughter rasping from his throat as he rubbed a palm over his face. "Even if I hadn't been as desperate for a friend as I was, she would have been hard to say no to. Most probies aren't like you. Most of us come to the Academy because we've got worse choices elsewhere."

The old Vi would have flinched at that, or taken offense. The new Vi just nodded. "Ros took you under her wing when you didn't have anyone else."

"It was easy, going along with whatever she wanted, you know?" Nick gave one of those humorless, aborted laughs again. The sound lodged hard and bitter in his throat. "She makes things simple. When one person is your everything, and all they want is for you to do them small favors, you think you've won the lottery. It takes a long time for those little favors to add up, and by the time they do, you just . . . you don't know how to say no anymore." Nick gazed toward the trees, eyes narrowed against the sunlight spilling across the leaves. His expression shifted slightly, like he was caught in another world that Vi wasn't privy to. "Winchester had certain conditions inked, governing the terms of my enrollment here, you might say. For a probie, I was a pretty hot commodity, it turns out. What you called me earlier, a mech tamer?"

At Vi's nod, he continued, "Well, our beloved Headmaster noticed that skill set too." His mouth twisted. "Along with what I could do in a combat tourney. In any situation demanding violence, really. Anyway, it made me a commodity for the Academy, probie or not.

And in case you haven't noticed, Karolyn Winchester tends to reward problematic commodities in interesting ways. The existence of the entire probationary student program is a great example. And that's not even getting into what she does to bring you into the fold on a one-on-one basis."

Vi frowned. "One-on-one?"

"The Huang siblings? Amadeus has a good mechanic's mind, and Elsbeth bonds stronger than almost any other cadet at the Academy, so Winchester offered them time with state-of-the-art sentient models in exchange for their troubleshooting skills. Tamara has a shot at graduating a semester early from what she affectionately dubs 'global hellhole school' in exchange for putting GAN intel ops in touch with her barely legally permissible smuggling contacts. So, you see, everyone gets something they want, and we all get to feel special. I'm sure Karolyn offered you something too."

With a pang, Vi recalled her first night in the dimly lit tower, where the Headmaster's office sat like a witch's hut, while Karolyn Winchester tempted Vi with exchanges and stipulations and opportunities to prove herself. A chance at the Peacekeeper Corps if she showed them she was good enough to beat Nicholas Lee in a mech combat tournament. A chance at finding the other missing Peacekeepers if she survived. "And you?" Vi asked softly, half-afraid of the answer. "What were you offered as motivation for . . . cultivating your talents?"

"The most valuable prize of all," said Nick. "Secrets." His voice was wry. "I'm Winchester's champion and attack dog, but by virtue of those roles, I also get to play her confidante. It makes sense, right? You want the person engaging in beatdowns on your behalf to know what

weapons they're working with, and who they might use them against."
He shook his head. "I can't blame Ros for seeing an opportunity there
and taking advantage. She wanted access to Winchester's office.
Access to the same things I'd have, as Winchester's very violent right
hand. Meeting reports. Engineering-development records."

Vi nodded, with a lurch in her belly. "Information. Actionable
intel."

A spy after all. He'd said it himself: he was Winchester's right
hand, her attack dog and confidante in one. It put him in the perfect
position to collect.

"It really freaked Rosalyn out, when sentients stopped offering her
the bond." Nick's voice went soft. "I get that. I don't know what I'd
do if I lost—" He cut himself off, shaking his head again. "Anyway,
Ros being Ros, her way of dealing with it was to find a way to force
it, so she asked me to get her the blueprints for the new mechs the
Headmaster had commissioned. On paper, those mech blueprints
are strictly staff access only: Academy teachers, Peacekeepers, the
Headmaster, and no one else. Students aren't supposed to see them,
but Ros knew Winchester would make an exception for me, and
she wanted in on it. I guess that seemed like an opportunity. Maybe
where the old sentients had turned away from her, the new ones
would embrace her. I think maybe she just wanted to be wanted. But
you can't force something like that, regardless of the mech model. Not
when they have minds and hearts of their own."

"Why would she think the new mechs would bond her any more
easily than the old ones?" asked Vi.

"They wouldn't," said Nick bluntly. "She . . . I think she must
know that, on some level. But sometimes, desperation trumps logic.

Part of it is the why. She never understood why sentients suddenly abandoned her like that, when she'd been able to bond them easy as anything upon enrollment, just like anyone else accepted to the Academy's hallowed halls."

"But you do," said Vi. The look on Nick's face answered her question as well as anything he might have said in that moment. For a boy who wore as many masks and donned as many roles as he did, when struck off guard by emotion, he did a terrible job of hiding it.

"Ros isn't a bad person," said Nick. "I can tell you think I'm just some half-smitten idiot making excuses for her, but she's not, and I say that as someone whose life would be a lot easier if I could turn her into the villain of my story." He huffed a wry little laugh at himself before sobering. "It's more like . . . somewhere along the line, she lost sight of what she came here for, and the sentients she used to bond all figured out she'd lost the mojo. Remember, a sentient mech's personality matrix is at least partially the creation of its engineer, all of whom are GAN employed. No GAN-created dragon wants to bond someone whose wants and motives fundamentally fail to align with GAN values."

"And Rosalyn's don't, I take it?"

"They used to," said Nick. Wistfulness clung to his voice, made its way across the planes of his face. "Once upon a time, she wanted to be a real Peacekeeper, uphold the idealism of the GAN, bought into the best version of what the knights of the Alliance stood for, hook, line, and sinker. A bit like you."

"Gee," deadpanned Vi. "Thanks."

"That wasn't an insult," said Nick. "Believe it or not, I liked that version of Rosalyn. Thought it was naive, maybe, the sort of thing the privileged daughter of a rich, big-shot political family would think"—Vi snorted, more to cover self-consciousness than anything else—"but I liked that she believed in something . . . good. That she cared about something other than herself, or seemed to, anyway. It made me think that maybe she could care about . . ." He trailed off, mouth twisting. "It's not important. The point is, you can't get through the Academy on highbrow beliefs alone, or any idiot could ace the entrance exams and survive the Headmaster's curriculum without breaking a sweat. Rosalyn's a lot of things, but she's no idiot. She figured out that much pretty quick—that she'd need a game plan if she wanted to be someone at the Academy, and eventually, someone in the GAN's Peacekeeper Corps. Hers was collecting people she considered useful." He shrugged. "I suppose I should consider myself flattered."

Vi barked a laugh. "Well. I guess that makes two of us. She gave me a whole speech once on transactional friendships. Not that either of us ever got much out of ours—if you could even really call it a friendship. I haven't even beaten you in a tournament match yet."

She had her head turned away from him. Her heart was still rattling around in her ears when a hand—palm open, warm and gentle—landed carefully over the back of her neck.

"Good luck," said Nick. His voice was strangely rough, like he'd wanted to say something else, but couldn't find the right words. "At the next tourney, I mean."

Vi's eyes fluttered shut. It wasn't like they hadn't touched each other before, but that had been in training, with sticks or fists or feet. Touch that delivered comfort—touch that opened itself to vulnerability—felt inherently different and alien, coming from Nick of all people.

Her head listed toward his. The grip on the back of her neck tightened marginally, fingers climbing toward her hairline. Their foreheads bumped together. Vi's breath caught in the back of her throat, as sudden heat bloomed beneath her skin. They were on that precipice again, staring down a fall into the unknown from the top of a cliff. How many times had she faced off against him at this kind of proximity without looking over the edge? How many times had he thought of this? How many times had she thought of the same thing, if she was honest—really, truly honest—with herself?

Slowly, careful to telegraph the motion so he could turn away if he wanted to, Vi raised the tips of her fingers until they were cradling the underside of Nick's jaw. His breath hitched a little, but he didn't pull back. Gently, Vi tilted his head, and leaned forward to press her mouth against his cheek, near his ear. "You too," she managed hoarsely. "May the best pilot win."

Then, before she could do something truly stupid, she pulled back from him and walked away.

That confrontation with Nick stuck with Vi, rattling around in her head in training, all the way up to the promised morning of their match.

It felt different from facing Rosalyn. Facing Rosalyn had been accompanied by its own brand of stress. It hadn't just been about the very real possibility of Vi getting her ass kicked by a viciously competitive opponent. It had also been Vi's way back into the cockpit, her first time really discovering for herself whether she could still be the pilot she'd thought she was before slapping on a probie badge.

Vi knew she could handle the cockpit now. That wasn't the problem. The problem was Nick himself. This match felt, more than anything else, like a rehash of the first time Vi had faced Nick during the Headmaster's pop quiz at the beginning of the school year, truth be told. The same trickle of anxiety down her spine, possibly to be confused with sweat dripping down the back of her flight suit. The spike of adrenaline in her gut, as her hands curled and uncurled, replaced in her mind's eye by great chrome fists. She had no doubt that Nicholas Lee—whoever he was, wherever he'd come from— would give her, once more, one hell of a fight.

The only real difference was that this time, no part of the conflict would be simulated. There would be no opportunities for do-overs, no resets, and all of the damage would be real. Simulations had their place, but you had to do the real thing if you ever wanted to figure out how to handle real consequences. And pilots—particularly the dragon pilots of the GAN—always had to deal with consequences, for good or for ill.

Déjà vu struck her as Vi shook off the shiver that threatened to trickle down her spine, and pulled on her flight jacket. Her phone pinged. Vi glanced down, heart climbing into her throat as she read the notification from the Academy app she'd been expecting for the last couple hours: Park, Viola J. E. to report to Examination Hall C for Preliminary Mech Warm-Ups. Assigned Mobile Suit: 2EB31A.

She sucked in a breath. Showtime. No turning back now.

Examination Hall C sat opposite Vi's dorm on the other end of campus, inside a building that looked like a Victorian manor from the outside, and an amusement park fun house from the inside. That was the particular flavor of the examination halls, all majestic polish, and the flavor of old world, history-soaked prestige, painting over the cutting edge of all things new.

But what greeted Vi upon her arrival in Examination Hall C was nothing new to Vi. She half expected a 3-D sim projector screen: the mechs that had been prepared for the fight were identical to the humanoid mobile suits she and Nick had first fought through in the simulation where they'd met. Déjà vu indeed.

Nick was waiting across the room from her. He wore the same mask of impenetrable, unreadable boredom that always colored his features before combat. Her gaze found a line of eye contact. She sketched a salute—only half joking—toward his side of the room.

The mask slipped a little. For a sliver of a moment, the Nick she'd seen on rare occasions—uncertain, soft, oddly warm—emerged, as one corner of his mouth tilted upward. Vi's pulse sped a little. Adrenaline, in all likelihood.

That momentary softness was short-lived. "Cadets." The familiar, clipped tones of Karolyn Winchester crackled over the intercom. "To your mechs, please."

The order schooled Nick's face back to blankness. He sketched a salute back to Vi—a real one this time—and made for the cockpit. Vi suppressed a little sigh and did the same.

The room went dark. Vi breathed out slowly, trying to control her pulse rate as she scanned the room for movement. Sense memory of her last combat sim floated vaguely in the back of her mind. She snatched at it for wisps of wisdom. What had she learned from the first time she and Nick had faced each other in mobile suits? That he favored relentless pressure in his attacks, which were as much defense as offense. She never had room to budge. She had to change that.

But how? What, if anything, had she learned from the first tourney? *He's not immune to fear.* Rosalyn's voice cut back through her mind.

In the same moment, metal moved in the corner of her eye. Vi sprawled just as it shot forward. Her timing wasn't quite right—she landed awkwardly, too far forward over Nick's mech. Powerful metal arms tangled themselves in the legs of her own mech, driving them both over. Vi swore.

Nick wasn't done. His mech's legs hooked themselves under Vi's, trapping her effectively in place. Gritting her teeth, Vi snapped her own mech's arms up to defend its head—where her cockpit sat. If

Nick tore through her defenses and into the head, the whole thing would be over.

He seemed to have realized as much. He drew one unforgiving metal fist back, then brought it down hard. Vi's mech's arms buckled but held. For the moment. Her teeth clenched tighter. If he kept that kind of brawling up, her defense wouldn't hold for much longer. She had to get out from under him.

Nick raised his mech's fists again. For a split second, his weight shifted. Hope niggled in the back of Vi's mind. If he wanted to continue hammering at her head, he'd have to keep risking his balance. It was the tiniest of opportunities, but tiny was better than nothing.

The fists crashed down again. Once more, Vi blocked, but this time she trapped one of the metal arms between her own, clamped one foot over his, and bucked her mech as hard as she could.

Miraculously, it worked. Nick's mech slid sideways. Vi scrambled her mobile suit back to its feet. Her view screen blinked a few times— she hadn't gotten out from under him unscathed, but it was better than being pounded into scrap metal before she even had a chance to fight back. She hit him hard—with a series of quick jab crosses— hopefully before he could figure out that he'd rocked her.

His mech stumbled back a few steps, but it didn't keep him off her for long. He returned the blows in kind. Vi swore. *Damn.* She'd forgotten how fast he was.

One hit cracked her mech right across the chin, scrambling her view screens again. She forced herself to breathe through it. She dodged the next hit and shot in on him again, locking her mech's arms low around the base of his mech's body, right above the legs.

He went down—sloppily, but he went down all the same. No time to waste. She pressed her advantage for what it was. Her mech's metal knees slammed down on either side of her opponent's torso and pinched hard. Her heart raced as she buckled down over his mech's heavy metal frame. If she could hold a control position on the other mech long enough, she might just get the upper hand.

Unsurprisingly, Nick didn't plan on making that easy. Metal creaked beneath her as he moved, aggressive, exploiting every minuscule opening she allowed him.

It took her a moment to notice the floor trembling beneath her knees. When she did, Vi thought at first—nonsensically—that it was his fault. That Nick's mech must have sported some capability she'd been previously unaware of.

Then the floor quaked harder. Vi's belly dropped down to her toes. Sense memory flooded her veins.

Nick's speakers came on. "The hell?"

It wasn't him, then. Vi's belly dropped lower still. She'd been here before. And last time, unattributed floor quaking had brought with it a rain of plasma fire and rogue dragons. Which meant they had to get out of here.

Vi tried to stand. It was a mistake. The next quake shook the floor so hard, it went right out from under her mech's feet. Her shoulder slammed against the wall of the cockpit, her teeth rattling as she tried in vain to get her bearings from inside the mobile suit. She was still struggling for visibility when the view screen blacked out.

Her knees slammed to the floor of the cockpit. Confusion plundered her mind. "What in hell," she began.

Lights flooded the room. Nick and his mech had returned to their side of the room, metal legs braced. For balance, not for an attack. The tourney was over—or it should have been.

Except that the floor was still shaking.

"Park! Lee!" That was the Headmaster, her voice colored with uncharacteristic urgency, blaring over the intercom. "You both need to get out of here now!"

"Why?" Vi yelled back. "What's going on?"

An alarm began to blare. The doors of the examination halls slid aside with a rumble. Shouts echoed across the school grounds, frantic yelling punctuated by shrieks of terror.

"We're under attack," said the Headmaster over the intercom. "Jefferson Lynch, an arms dealer I made the mistake of doing business with back in the day. It seems he's here to collect on an old debt. Take shelter immediately."

Vi didn't think. She just acted. She slammed out of the cockpit and sprinted toward Nick's mech. "Nick!"

He'd already dropped out of his cockpit. "I have to go."

"Don't be stupid!" Vi strode toward him. "You heard the Headmaster. We've got to take cover."

He shook his head. "You don't understand. I've got somewhere to be."

"The hell you do, unless that someplace is a designated emergency shelter!" She grabbed his wrist. "Listen. If we don't get out of here and find shelter, we're both going to get cooked by one very angry arms dealer."

She stopped short of speaking the worst of her suspicions aloud: *Unless, of course, said angry arms dealer is your long-lost evil dad.* The series of expressions that flitted across his features didn't exactly help. Surprise, bitter amusement, and finally, a settled sort of calm. "It's nothing I haven't handled before." His wrist twisted toward her thumb, freeing him in one quick motion. "Seek shelter if you need to. I've got unfinished business."

"Nick!"

He paused, just for a moment. Lifted his eyes toward hers. "If you've still got a working bond with a sentient," he said, "now might be the time to use it."

He didn't have to spell it out for her to understand what he meant. Stormbrewer. She and the dragon had found each other once. They could do it again.

It was one of those moments that would stick with her much later: Nicholas Lee, fire behind his gaze, as he canted his head toward her. He was such a great, strange puzzle of a boy. It had been so easy, all this time, to frame him within her own imagination as an obstacle. A riddle that needed solving, or a door that needed unlocking, or a video game boss that needed defeating. Protecting him was, honestly speaking, likely against her own best interests. For one thing, she'd probably win their match by default if she left him to die in a giant fiery explosion or whatever it was that angry arms dealers did when they attacked mech pilot academies. For another, considering the very real possibility that he was a spy for the angry arms dealer in question, her protection was quite possibly the last thing he deserved.

But protect him she had. That confrontation with Rosalyn—the single act of putting her body between Ros and Nick, and the blood on her hands—had shifted something irrevocable in how Vi looked at the boy she'd meant to beat. Too late to put an end to it now.

Yet when Nick turned to go, this time she didn't try to stop him.

Vi had a decision to make. On one side of things, shelter, as Winchester had ordered. On the other, Nick. Nick, and the proposal implied between the tilt of his head and what remained unsaid between the words he spoke.

In total, it took Vi two minutes to make her choice. As Nick slipped away, his wrist sliding from her grasp, the choice crystalized.

◆

FINDING STORMBREWER WAS, surprisingly, the easy part of the whole affair. That was the thing about a good bond—once established, it was hard to break. All Vi had to do was follow that same song in the back of her mind. Somewhere beneath the floor of the forest where they'd first met, the dragon's AI-fueled consciousness awakened, brushing up against Vi's desperation. She found the thread and followed it, until her world was silver scales coiled, lying in wait beneath the canopy of trees, the promise of lightning crackling between the chinks of chrome.

This time, the cockpit was ready for her. Stormbrewer understood what was necessary, perhaps better yet than Vi herself did.

They weren't the only mech-and-pilot pair who'd gotten it into their heads to prepare for a fight. Behind the lens of the view screen, Vi caught sight of a couple GAN-branded dragons bursting across the sky with a mighty mechanical roar. Peacekeepers, in all likelihood, or ambitiously heroic cadets who'd hijacked their ride. They dove toward the opponents lumbering across the ground: wheeled battle bots, equipped with cannons that Vi was willing to bet were loaded up with plasma fire cartridges.

She didn't stick around to watch the outcome. Instead, Vi kept Stormbrewer under the cover of the same forest where she'd found him. If she were an arms dealer trying to make a point over a grudge, she wouldn't keep to open spaces where battle bots could do her dirty work for her. She'd want two things: one, cover from both friendly fire and counterattacks, and two, a confrontation (not with schoolchildren, and not even with run-of-the-mill GAN pilots).

There was one spot on campus that provided both. If she'd come to collect on an old debt from the Headmaster—whatever it amounted to—she'd head for the Headmaster's well-fortified, tree-canopy-shielded office.

It wasn't a pretty journey over. Jefferson Lynch's ambush had already dealt its share of damage across the campus. Plasma fire scorch marks carved ugly black grooves across the manicured green lawns, as the people down below ran for cover. The lucky ones, anyway. A few lay hauntingly still on the grass. Badly injured, clearly. Or worse. Even from her place in the cockpit, Vi recognized the GAN cadet patches on the flight jackets of the downed.

Bile rose in Vi's gut. With an effort, she forced it down, squeezing her eyes shut. Focus. There was work to be done. She'd commandeered Stormbrewer in the first place hoping to protect who she could. Maybe she'd failed to protect the people who'd already fallen, but she'd protect no one at all if she lost her shit now.

Stormbrewer's audio alert system picked up on the hiss of raised voices before Vi did. Even under the cover of the trees, distinguishing individual voices from the cacophony of panic unfolding across the campus was asking a lot of ordinary human ears. A good sentient mech, though, could isolate certain known quantities, and Vi recognized instantly one of the voices that the dragon had picked up on.

"—out of here," Nick was saying. His voice was distorted by extra noise on the mic. Wind, maybe. Vi squinted through the view screen, looking for the source of that sound.

It didn't take her long to find it. Nick was balanced on the roof of the Headmaster's tower office, glaring up into the eyes of the biggest mech Vi had seen since she'd fought Jellicoe's Giant in simulation.

"I'm not going anywhere." The voice from the mech, a deep baritone, was smooth and controlled. If Vi didn't know better, she'd have wagered the pilot sounded affectionate. "Karolyn has rented you out from me far longer than I would have allowed anyone else to. Honestly, I'm impressed she managed to hang on to you for as long as she did."

"Rent?" Nick's voice carried, pitched over the sounds of destruction beyond the woods, as he looked up at the hulking monstrosity of a mech. "I'm not one of your luxury automaton cars."

The mech bent closer to him. To Nick's credit, he didn't so much as back up a step. "You watch your mouth. My relief at finding you doesn't preclude a need for respect."

Nick barked a laugh. "I made a deal with Winchester," he rasped. He swayed back and forth a little, his arms outstretched to maintain a precarious balance on that rooftop, but the expression on his face, zoomed in through the dragon's view-screen lenses, was utterly calm. "I'm not yours anymore, Dad."

That last word wrapped ice around Vi's heart. So Vi had been right. Nicholas Lee had been Jefferson Lynch's boy all along. She hadn't wanted it to be true. She hadn't realized how badly she wanted it not to be true until this moment.

"Well, that's disappointing. I thought I raised you smarter." Lynch sighed, a harsh breathy sound over his mech's amplified mic. "It's simple, really. You can wear their uniform. You can even pilot those great hulking mechanical beasts they call dragons. But you'll never wash away the place you really came from."

What happened next felt as though it unfolded in slow motion. Nick's gaze skittered toward Vi—no, not her, Stormbrewer. Those near-golden eyes locked on the dragon's for just a moment, but a moment was all they needed. As Nick's father's mech grabbed for him, Vi and Stormbrewer surged forward, serpentine body curling upward from the ground to create a platform. Nick leapt—fell, really—to land bent kneed on the spiraling coils.

"Viola?" A note of surprise crept into Nick's voice. He knocked lightly against Stormbrewer's head. "Is that you piloting Stormbrewer here?"

"Never you mind!" snapped Vi. "Get in so we can get the fuck out of here."

Nick made a noise that Vi suspected was a laugh—or the beginning of some wry retort—but at least he obeyed. A hatch slid aside, and Nick landed in the cockpit beside her. He rubbed a hand over his face. "I suppose I owe you an explanation—"

"Later!" yelled Vi. In the back of her mind, Stormbrewer roared his agreement.

The three of them rounded off, trying to put as much distance as possible between themselves and that monstrosity of a mech. Vi had known, even as they whipped around, that it was a lost cause. Stormbrewer was a hardy creation, well designed for his purpose, but his purpose had been beachside combat. Outpacing a war mech of that size on land hadn't been what his engineers had in mind. Lynch was going to catch up to them, probably sooner rather than later. The best they could hope for was to stall for time. Vi shut her eyes, her willpower syncing up to Stormbrewer's, laced with both their desperation. "Come on," she whispered. "Come on, come on, come—"

A piercing shriek interrupted her mantra. Immediately, it raised the hair on the back of Vi's neck. Her first, wild assumption was that it had to be someone caught in the crossfire in the battle beyond the woods, maybe, probably someone hurt. A second shriek joined the first, which was when Vi's brain finally caught up with her adrenaline-fueled terror. Those weren't human shrieks at all.

Those were the sounds of GAN dragons taking wing overhead.

Relief melted Vi's bones down to jelly. She slumped back against the wall of the cockpit as the pair of dragons she'd seen earlier dove between Stormbrewer and Jefferson Lynch's mech.

The mech, for its part, didn't seem interested in fighting the GAN's airborne reinforcements. Two enormous arms rose in apparent surrender. Yet Lynch's voice still boomed out of the mech's speakers, calmly self-satisfied: "A man who's already won knows when to yield."

Beside Vi, Nick turned chalk white. Vi frowned at him. "Nick? What's he going on about?"

In answer, Nick simply raised his phone. Several alerts were going off on the screen—student message forums, campus alarms, but what rose to the top of his feed was a projection of 3-D video footage, broadcast across the Academy's internal wireless network.

At the center of the hologram, Nick's figure stretched his arms out like a bird buoyed on the wind, swaying back and forth on the rooftop. "I'm not yours anymore, Dad," he informed the war mech hulking over him. The one branded with Jefferson Lynch's business logo.

And his father's voice, damnation and satisfaction all rolled into one, loud and clear over the footage: "Oh, Nicholas. Haven't you figured out how any of this works yet? We all belong to our families in the end."

Jefferson Lynch had attacked the GAN Academy with brazen, terroristic intent. He had solidified himself as the villain of the piece: a man who'd attack cadets—teenage students, most of them—in broad daylight just to lay claim to what he wanted. And then he had broadcast the identity of his chosen prize—his son—to the entire student network.

◆

THE AFTERMATH OF JEFFERSON Lynch's attack on the GAN Academy—and his arrest at the hands of Peacekeepers—rippled through the piloting community in seemingly endless waves.

First came the questions of why he'd done it in the first place: the story everyone got fed about a business deal gone sour; the one everyone actually talked about, the all-but-confirmed rumor of his kid being held within the walls of the Academy as a glorified hostage to the GAN; and of course, the conspiracies—the idea that a GAN insider had set him up, or that he'd just plain lost his mind. At the very least, it seemed to solve the riddle of who'd been picking off Peacekeepers in the first place: Lynch had had means, motive, and opportunities aplenty. He'd wanted his kid back—and probably to stick it to the Peacekeepers for good measure, all told—so he'd launched the attacks to weaken the Alliance's most powerful fighting force and sow chaos. These were the ideal circumstances under which to slip in behind the mighty GAN's walls and simply take what he'd wanted. He'd only screwed up his gambit by getting impatient and transitioning from his straggler pick-off strategy to trying to fight the GAN head-on and attacking their own personal talent storehouse.

"We should have known," some muttered. "He's one of the most notorious black market weapons merchants still running free. He has every reason to hate the GAN, even without his son in play. Who the hell else could it have been?"

Privately, Vi thought that hindsight was twenty-twenty. It was easy enough to declare what may have seemed obvious with the benefit of a bird's-eye view, once all the facts were pulled together just so. Topping things off with a literal murder spree on the grounds of the GAN Academy itself was just icing at this point.

Everyone felt the impact of what had happened. No deaths, but students and teachers alike had been injured in the attack. GAN personnel tasked with cleanup of the damage, both physical and reputational. The fear you could practically smell on campus now, as everyone wondered what came next.

But one person bore the brunt.

As a child, Vi had played a mental game with herself sometimes, which she'd dubbed the Mirror Game. In the game, she imagined everything in her life—the classes she preferred in school, the cousins who either bested or were bested by her in sparring, even the inane routines of her daily life like choosing toothpaste flavors and setting her alarms—flipped to its opposite extreme. A world where she could defeat an undefeated battle mech savant, but lost to the sloppiest and laziest of her cousins during training. A world where she had no Alex or Aunts Anabel and Cat, but still had her parents. A world where enemies were friends and friends were enemies.

For the first few days after Jefferson Lynch attacked the Academy, then revealed Nicholas Lee's true parentage to his schoolmates, Vi wondered if the Mirror Game had invaded her reality. She remembered her first few days on campus, when Nick had seemed like the exception to every rule: the probie who courted respect or fear or desire from the other students, the probie who could beat the snot out of you, the probie who'd won the favor of the Headmaster and the Davies girl alike, the probie who made you forget he was a probie at all.

Now Nick was a focal point. It wasn't disdain he attracted, per se. But in the aftermath of Jefferson Lynch's attack on the school—the aftermath of his father's attack—people saw the badge pinned to his flight suit for the scarlet letter that it was. He could still court fear, but it was tempered with other emotions now: skepticism, mistrust, and an almost-predatory curiosity, as if they waited with bated breath for Nick to show his true colors, colors that would surely match those on the logos of Jefferson Lynch's weapons products. No one could ever overlook or forget Nick's probationary status now, not by a long shot.

Vi thought of the aunties at the family dinner table whispering to one another, "The Academy swallows its students whole," as she watched Nicholas Lee eaten alive, and wanted to throw up.

She knew something was off, the first time Sifu paired them together for a hand-to-hand training exercise after Jefferson Lynch's attack. That in itself didn't surprise her. Even before the Academy, she'd handled her fair share of people who fought because they were trying to externalize their internal demons. The mech-piloting business was a great way to fast-track some seriously messed-up headspaces. And she knew Nick. She still remembered the first match, with the rattan sticks, that had escalated far beyond the normal parameters of a friendly contest. She'd been braced for a reprise.

She hadn't been ready for the way he just dropped all pretense of defense halfway through the bout. They'd been going at their usual pace, and suddenly, she had a takedown he'd stuffed a million times before, and she was on top of him. Far too easily. Her muscles went tight. She forced them to relax. At first, she thought he had to be baiting her—setting her up to knock her down, maybe. But he didn't move. He didn't, in fact, do anything at all. Just stared up at her with a feverish-looking gaze, chest rising and falling, expression blank. "Well?" His hands splayed beneath her. "Go on, then. Finish it."

An unexpected bubble of fury popped inside of Vi. "You really think I'm like that?"

The nasty little laugh he gave vibrated right through her. "Everyone's like that when push comes to shove. They want one of two things. To beat you down, or . . ." He trailed off, expression shifting slightly, lashes low over his eyes.

Vi leaned over him, their faces inches apart, her heart a wild drumbeat against her ribcage. "Or what?"

He surged up beneath her, a sudden, sinuous movement. Her body barely had time to register surprise before his mouth was on hers.

He kissed like he fought, with finely controlled aggression almost uncannily attuned to her body. He had his hands on either side of her face, his fingers a surprisingly gentle contrast to the force of his hips as he bucked up under Vi, or the rasp of his lips against hers. If he'd pushed her with just a little more force, she would have been overwhelmed; instead, the two of them lingered on the knife edge of something that wasn't quite intimacy and wasn't quite violence. Her legs were still splayed on either side of him. It should have lent her some sense of control, maintaining the dominant position. It would have, if this had been a fight.

But it wasn't, even if it felt like one, and when she kissed him back, she wasn't sure she'd ever want to stop, her hands digging into his hair with an angry desperation that tugged a sharp, breathy gasp from him before his teeth caught her lower lip. They'd mangle each other like this, she thought, her pulse a roar in her ears, his body a brand against hers. She'd seen the way he kissed Rosalyn. She knew what going there with Nick meant.

That, more than anything else, knocked her senses back into her.

Her hands closed around his wrists, leveraging herself backward from his grasp. "Stop," she said quietly. "Stop, stop, stop. Hey." She let go of his wrists. Instead, her hands found their way to the sides of his face, cupping his jaw, a bizarre reversal of their earlier position. "Hey," she repeated. "Look at me. Please."

He did, slowly, his shoulders hunched, lashes downcast. He didn't say a word, his mouth still red where it had pressed against hers.

She let go of him abruptly to massage her temples. She'd known he'd be a headache from the first time she'd laid eyes on this boy, this candle flame caught within the sterile walls of an Academy classroom. He'd proven her right, over and over again. Yet she couldn't seem to quit circling back to him. "I don't want to sleep with you," she told him bluntly.

The quickness with which his eyebrows rose shot heat straight to her cheeks. "I mean, that's not to say that I . . . argh!" Her hands covered her eyes, as if that might somehow stanch the mortification flooding gradually into her gut. Good god, this wasn't going at all how she meant it to. Why did nothing involving Nicholas Lee ever go the way it was supposed to?

"I'm not going to pretend to not find you attractive, because you'd see right through that, and I don't want to be one more person who lies to you," she finally managed to amend. "I think we're pretty goddamn past the point of playing coy. But getting into your pants has never been the point of spending time with you."

He looked at her, unblinking, unreadable. "Then what is?" His hands spread, along with a half-hearted smirk, barely even pretense at this point. "Because aside from that, Park, all I've got to offer is a phenomenal knack for violence. The one thing my father instilled in me. But you had that figured out from the start, didn't you?" He gave up on the smirk, the corners of his mouth flattening out at whatever he saw in her expression. "Yeah. You did. It's why I'm so very, very good at hurting people. It runs in the family."

"Okay, number one"—Vi held up a finger—"that is objectively untrue, you enormous drama queen. Take it from someone that you beat up quite magnificently the first time we ever met. You're good at combat tournaments, clearly. But I've been creepily stalking you for the better part of the school year now in an effort to learn your weaknesses, and I've got to say: it does stand out to me that you've never once bloodied someone—in or out of the cockpit—outside of a sanctioned match."

"Because I don't want to," said Nick. Self-loathing curdled his tone. "It doesn't mean I can't."

"Fine, well, that leads me neatly into my point number two." Vi held up a second finger. "Being good at something doesn't mean you enjoy it." She swallowed hard. "Hell. Sometimes, being good at something just makes it easier to hate. You might be great at mauling men and machines, but you sure as hell don't seem to do it for love of the game."

"I don't exactly have much of a choice, though, do I?" Nick shot back. "This is the deal I made, if you haven't figured it out. I've been trying to escape my father's roof since I was thirteen. Karolyn Winchester gave me my best shot at it—for a price."

Vi sucked in a breath. "Piloting for the GAN. Enrolling here as a Peacekeeper-to-be." The pieces clicked back into place. Not a spy, nor a bargaining chip. An indentured servant. No wonder Nick had been marked a probie from the start. As a member of the probationary class, he'd be technically eligible for the Peacekeeper Corps, but the scarlet letter of the probie badge would also satisfy any GAN school board officials who dug a little too deeply into his past. "How did she get Lyn—get your father to agree to that?"

"The same way anyone gets my father to agree to anything," said Nick. "Negotiating the right price." His mouth twisted. "It wasn't supposed to be forever. It would have been like the old mandatory-military-service protocols some countries have—you serve your time for a few years, you get out."

Vi bit her lip on an impulse to point out that he'd also done a pretty good job just then of describing prison sentences.

"I was supposed to get fast-tracked through the Academy," Nick continued. "It was a good deal, all in all, especially considering my checkered past. My dad didn't exactly work alone."

Vi's heart stopped. "You killed people?"

"No." He shook his head. "At least, not directly. But I might as well have. I helped him with his weapon designs. And I used my own affinity for sentients to warn him when GAN dragons were near so he could dodge Peacekeeper patrols. On paper, it doesn't look like much, but it meant more violent AI being more easily dealt into violent hands. At the very least, I'm an accessory. The GAN Council would never let that stand. Hence the Headmaster's deal: two years on probation at the Academy, and then a year of service in the GAN Peacekeeper Corps, in exchange for immunity from my father's war crimes." He swallowed, jaw working hard. "Like I said." His voice was all sharp edges. "It was a good deal. I was happy to take it, at the time—as happy as I could be, anyway."

"What changed?" asked Vi.

Nick huffed a bitter little laugh. "What didn't? I didn't like being here much, but I liked it better than being under my dad's roof, and he hated that. Headmaster Winchester, on the other hand, loved having me here. So the fast-tracking went out the window. She wanted to drag out the allotted time, see what she could get away with. And the entire campus got caught in the crossfire. Literally."

Vi opened her mouth, and closed it again. She'd grown up in a family of power mongers, many of them petty beyond belief, but what Jefferson Lynch had done—for nothing but sheer, spiteful possessiveness—seemed beyond the realm of reasonably human possibility. "You're his son," she said at last. "He—that could have *killed* you."

"Please." Nick shook his head, bitter and rueful. "You think that attack on the Academy was bad? You should see what he's like at home, or in the office playing boardroom politics. And don't be mistaken: he absolutely considers me one of his better-built projects, so you can imagine how pleased he was to have the Headmaster of the GAN Academy snatch one of his prize weapons out from under his nose for a second more than he'd bargained for in the business deal."

"That," said Vi, very carefully, "is not what you are."

"No?" He rounded on her, aggression abrupt in the motion, eyes flashing. "Then what do you think I am?"

Silence, taut as a rubber band pulled to snapping point, stretched between them.

"A person," Vi croaked at last. "No better or worse than any person. And a person is always so much more than a weapon or a prize."

Her hand found his shoulder, gripped it tight, working through tense muscle. She could have shoved him away with that grip, just as easily as she could reel him into an embrace. She did neither, but she met his eyes when she spoke. "You aren't just what your family made you. I've seen how you fight, in and out of the cockpit, yeah. But I've also seen how you are with mechs. How you tried to save those rogue GAN dragons. The way you talk to sentients. Like they are precisely that. Sentient. Living creatures that we might have created, but living creatures deserving of empathy, all the same. The way you are with them, that's not something that can be taught, Nick, not usually—and if it were, I'd bet the entire Park clan bank account that it's not a lesson Jefferson Lynch taught you, because it's the opposite of blood thirst, or violence, or whatever nonsense it is that you're basing all your self-worth on."

His eyes narrowed. "And what is it?"

Vi's mouth went dry. "I don't know," she said honestly. "But for lack of a better word, I think I might call it kindness."

Silence returned to the room, but it carried a different quality this time. Heaviness hung between them, in the big-eyed surprise flashing into vulnerability across Nick's face, the sudden weight of the heart inside Vi's chest, and the scant inches of space separating their bodies. The memory of his mouth on hers, just a few minutes ago.

Very slowly, as if he were a sentient mech that might be startled, Vi leaned toward him again, one hand rising to tangle her fingers through his hair. He released a breath, a sharp little exhale, as his head tilted, canting toward the angle of her mouth.

Their phones went off at the same time. They sprang apart. "News alert?"

Nick nodded, cheeks a little pink, scrolling through his. "Another missing pilot." He frowned. "That doesn't make any sense. My father—"

"Might not have been the one responsible after all," said Vi slowly. She snapped her fingers. Hindsight, hindsight, hindsight. It would be the death of them all. The missing pilots had been arguably the greatest crisis in the GAN's young history. Jefferson Lynch's attack on the Academy—and the revelation of his ties to Nick—had struck precisely when every member of the GAN was desperate to solve the mystery. Jefferson Lynch had presented himself as such a neatly terrible, logical answer to the question that had plagued the Alliance for months. Was it any wonder that everyone—Vi included— automatically conflated the Peacekeeper disappearances with Lynch's taste for destruction?

So Jefferson Lynch had been handily arrested as the leading

suspect, and now sat comfortably in GAN custody. Yet here was another pilot, gone missing just like all the rest.

"Nothing's ever fucking simple," muttered Vi. She ran a palm over her face. "If not Jefferson Lynch, then who really did it?"

Nick remained silent. The color had drained from his face, save the dark shadows lurking beneath his eyes. Evidence of everything he'd been carrying for the past two years. He closed his eyes for a long moment, which only darkened the shadows. When he finally spoke, his voice was quiet, but steady. "I honestly don't know."

"Of course not," said Vi. Maybe a little too quickly, spurred by a complicated guilt. Nick just looked so goddamn tired. "Shit, why would you? I don't expect . . ." She trailed off helplessly. "I just wish we had some other leads."

That seemed to snap Nick back to himself. "We might. They released the pilot's name this time, at least."

The scrap of information—any information—should have left Vi hopeful. Instead, a chill seeped through Vi's veins. "What name?" Even as she asked the question, her thumb found the answer, questing through the alert for precisely what she'd been dreading for weeks:

"Alexandre Santiago Lamarque," said Nick.

When Vi first failed the Academy entrance exam, she'd thought that if she lived through that, she could live through anything. Surely, there would come a point in life where you grew used to your world falling apart around you. Surely, the human heart could adapt to anything, including the loss of solid ground beneath your feet. After all, human minds had once built dragons.

Vi didn't know how to be sure of anything anymore. But she wasn't the girl who'd rewritten the fate of the Battle of Jellicoe's Giant any longer. She wasn't even the girl who'd thought being a probie would be worse than death. She didn't know who she was, exactly, but it was someone who'd learned to navigate a free fall.

And she was going to find Alex.

She'd never really been a social ringleader. It was a skill encouraged in the family, and Aunt Anabel excelled at it perhaps above all other members. Still, it was amazing what the combination of terror and fury could do to motivate you.

The other probies answered Vi's carefully encrypted text message on a moonlit Friday night in the shade of the woods, in the crook of Tai Mo Shan. They could have been a film poster, trickling in:

first the Huang siblings, side by side, looking on the proceedings with identically bright, curious eyes; then Tamara, lounging catlike against one of the trees, all businesslike scrutiny; and finally, Nick, padding quietly into place to round out the rest of the group.

"So," said Elsbeth brightly. "What's this about hijacking some dragons?"

Tamara snorted. "Credit for enlisting the school delinquent population to commit further delinquency, at least. Real case of matching skills to the job."

"It's a half-baked plan at best," said Vi. Her palms were moist with anxiety, but she clenched her hands together all the same. Had Alex been here, he'd have told her to treat it like a recital. And that's what this was, in a way. A truly terrible, possibly violent recital, for which she hadn't practiced a single note of music. "But it's what we've got."

"The sentience mechanism that links dragons to pilots isn't limited to bonding us," said Nick quietly. "They're like organic animals, which means they also form relationships with each other. Like pack animals." He shook his head, mouth curling. "The higher-ups at the GAN aren't always the most comfortable with how much agency their weapons have—they'd rather just point them at the Alliance's enemies and have done with it. Which means they've neglected one of the best chances they have of scouting out the location of their missing Peacekeepers. Karolyn—Headmaster Winchester—keeps a fleet of dragon prototypes in her vault. And I happen to have a key." When the others glanced toward him in surprise, he wiggled his fingers in a sardonic little approximation of jazz hands. "I'm her attack dog, remember? Fancy top secret weapons are kind of part of the deal."

Amadeus coughed lightly. "So you think we should just waltz into this mythical forbidden vault and commit grand theft auto. I must say, as a seasoned thief myself, I enjoy the flair of drama, but I also have to ask the obvious question: What's in it for us?"

"What else?" Vi opened her fists to spread her hands, doing her best salesman impression. "Job security. Sifu said it herself about the conscription tournament. If being drafted to replace missing Peacekeepers guarantees you a livelihood, imagine what solving the mystery of their missing pilots to begin with will do."

Amadeus still looked skeptical. "And you've been spurred suddenly into this remarkably impulsive action by . . . what, exactly? Presumably, the GAN authorities are still on the hunt for the real culprit behind the Peacekeeper disappearances, upon discovering that Nick's secret evil father may have been a red herring after all." He paused, casting a sheepish glance toward Nick. "Er, no offense meant, of course."

"None taken," said Nick dryly.

"In any case," continued Amadeus, "with all due respect, I don't see why we're trying to do the GAN top brass' job for them. Maybe, surprise of surprises, we'll succeed where they've failed. More likely, we won't. Job security and monetary gain are fine bribes, but that doesn't quite cut it here. Why risk such a gambit?"

Several possible answers warred their way through Vi's head. In the end, she opted for a small, selfish piece of honesty: "I lost family."

Silence greeted that revelation.

"The latest pilot who joined the missing." Vi glanced around at the other probies, then abruptly away, trying to ignore the way her throat tightened and her eyes burned. "It was . . . well, we weren't blood. But we were family. I don't have a good answer for why the rest of you should take the risk. But I can't just sit here and do nothing."

The silence from the others stretched on as they processed her words. Vi closed her eyes, mentally recalculating her plans for how to go about mobilizing the dragons. She'd previously envisioned it as a roughly organized scouting mission. She might not have much to work with, but she did still have her little list of last known locations of the recently missing, thanks to her previous research. They could cover more ground with multiple pilots, starting with those spots, then branching out to older mission locations. Leveraging the additional tracking instincts programmed into their dragons. Sharing new information with each other, and developing new mission protocols accordingly.

It would be a lot harder to pull off by herself. But she'd do it if she had to. Maybe that was what this entire stint at the Academy had really been leading up to. She'd survived a scandal. She'd survived probationary status. She'd survive this too.

Then Elsbeth spoke up. "Fair enough. Don't give me that look, Amadeus. You'd do it for me."

"I would," her brother admitted. "But—"

"But nothing," said Elsbeth in decisive tones. She looked at Tamara, then Nick, before her gaze landed at last on Vi. "I think it's reasonably safe to say that pretty much everyone here has someone in their life they'd do the same for. That's what's really in it for us."

A slow clap rang through the clearing. Vi's pulse froze. That hadn't come from any of the five of them. When she turned her head, Rosalyn Davies smiled at her from the edge of the winding campus pathway. Moonlight cast a coppery tint over her hair, like blood on the surface of a lake. "Quite the moving little epiphany," she called.

"And what do you imagine will be in it for me, when I turn every last one of you in to the Headmaster herself?"

Vi froze.

Pivotal moments in her life often felt like the Renaissance paintings she'd seen replicated in her European history modules back at New Columbia Prep. A group of people, all driven to the same place by different circumstances, performing a hundred different reactions. Open fear on Amadeus's face, as he took a step back. Elsbeth, meanwhile, had stepped forward, her dark eyes narrowed, stance wide and aggressively planted. This was a girl who'd killed before, and would have no problem killing again. On the other side of the clearing was Tamara, who refused to telegraph a response in her expression, but had straightened her spine and bent her knees. The smuggler, ready to run.

And finally, Nick, who simply stood there, expression neutral, hands unclenched with his palms open. It was a deliberately vulnerable pose from the boy Vi swore could beat anyone senseless.

The fight-or-flight instincts rising up inside of Vi quelled, just for a moment, as she remembered the weight of Rosalyn telling her, *I think you'll find most friendships are transactional, at the end of the day.*

"There will be more in it for you if you help us," Vi blurted out.

It wasn't what anyone had expected out of her. Amadeus made a sound as if being strangled, and quickly covered it with a cough that cut off the faint noises of protest from the other probies. Only Nick remained silent, his eyes on Vi and Rosalyn, waiting to see what they would do, like an opponent before a mech fight.

Rosalyn hadn't moved. She'd lost the swagger to her gait and stood stock-still, wariness frozen on her face. Vi took a moment to send a quick prayer to every god she'd ever failed to believe in, tried her best to channel a pilot dealing with an ornery sentient, and took a few steps forward. "You're a massive bitch," she said bluntly.

"Maybe not the best way to get her on our side, Park," muttered Tamara out of the corner of her mouth.

Vi ignored her. "But you're a massive bitch who—if everything I've seen you do and heard you say is true to the picture I've got in my head—used to have your heart in the right place."

"Used to?" Ros's voice was dangerously soft, but some of the wariness in her gaze had been replaced by something else. A tentative sense of hope, perhaps.

"Didn't you want to save the world once?" Vi barked an involuntary laugh. "Come on, families like ours? We were practically raised from the cradle to think it was our goddamn birthright to be heroes. Don't tell me you didn't want that once. Not the glory, not the promotions, not the fucking job security of a GAN gig, but doing good for good's sake, cheesiness be damned."

Ros's mouth thinned. "And you're so sure this is the right path?"

"It doesn't matter what she's sure of." That was Nick, striding forward to stand beside Vi. "When push comes to shove, you have to figure this shit out for yourself. What do you think is right? What do you want, Ros?"

"Preferably, figure it out soon," said Elsbeth, glancing at her phone. "We've got a narrow time frame to work with for this incredibly high-risk act of expulsion-worthy crime."

Ros's gaze darted between Nick's face—the resolute belief there—and Vi's, before trailing over the other probies. "You really think you can find the missing Peacekeepers?"

Her voice was small. Almost childlike. Vi thought suddenly,

absurdly, of Rosalyn Davies growing up lonely and ambitious in empty mansions. Rosalyn Davies, dreaming of becoming a hero, who believed in the true values of what the GAN had been built on. It didn't excuse the way she toyed with people, the way she treated Nick like he was just another plaything. But maybe, when push came to shove, she could still find some spark of the child who'd wanted to be a Peacekeeper for all the right reasons.

"I don't know," said Vi honestly. "But I think we should try. Or what the hell else is the point of being at the Academy at all?"

A series of expressions warred across Rosalyn's face. "I can't promise that those dragons will bond me. That's the cost of sentient life. A lack of predictability." Her gaze flickered toward Nick. "In other words: free will."

He shook his head. "Only one way to find out."

Slowly, those green eyes slid back toward Vi. "All right, Park. I'll try. But if that bond doesn't take—"

Vi clapped a hand on the other girl's shoulder. "If that bond doesn't take," she said kindly, "then we're all fucked."

Tamara cleared her throat. "And on that lovely note," she said, popping out her phone. "Well, then, as the most logistics-minded member of this little crime party, I must inform you that we've got thirty-ish minutes to bond those dragons before the Headmaster is scheduled to return from her meeting at the GAN consulate in Australia. So let's make it twenty. Chop-chop."

◆

THE DRAGONS WOKE ALMOST instantly when they arrived in the storage hall. Vi nearly backed up into Nick at the sight: nothing but darkness, then silver eyes glowing to life, pair by pair, flaming stars against the night sky. Gears creaked as they drew closer, sniffing out potential pilots—or prey, depending on how they felt.

Vi recognized the first brush of an AI consciousness against her mind: the familiarity of the personality, and the curiosity of the mech behind it. Her breath hitched. "Stormbrewer?"

It was Stormbrewer. The mech canted his head, surveying the team Vi had assembled. She glanced toward Nick. Inspiration moved Vi. "Nick," she called. "You think you can handle the cockpit this time?"

Nick blinked, clearly surprised. "You bonded him first."

"And I can find a new bond." She was startled to find that she meant it. Even mere weeks ago, she wouldn't have. "You have a knack for this, and the greatest amount of familiarity with new dragon prototypes." She grinned. "Besides, he likes you."

Nick stepped forward, hand outstretched. Stormbrewer curled toward him, long metal coils loosening. Vi turned toward the other dragons, trying to control her oxygen intake. *Inhale. Exhale. Inhale again. Exhale, and—*

A low rumble echoed beneath their feet.

"There's something else in here," Elsbeth interrupted. Her voice was unusually tight for a girl who normally seemed so preternaturally calm. "Nick. You've been here before. Is there another level below this unit?"

Nick's brows knit together. "Yeah. But that's—"

"Where the next import of new-generation sentient models were going to be stored," said Rosalyn. "But they shouldn't have arrived yet. And they certainly shouldn't be live."

A crash echoed beneath them. Something shuffled, stirring below, and didn't stop. The sounds had begun to grow louder. Closer.

"Shit." Amadeus pushed his hands through his hair. "We don't know what kind of shit we're gonna run into. What do we do?"

"The sensible thing," said Vi, forcing down the terror rising in her chest. She turned back toward the dragons. "We face it with backup."

The dragons seemed to pick up on the rise of tension in the room. Metal wings shuffled, and claws stamped in agitation. Vi turned to face them, slowing down her breaths, opening her mind to the shifting meld of AI consciousness permeating the space between them.

One shuffled forward, a low mechanical rumble in its throat, to press a cold snout against Vi's outstretched hand. The bond from this one was a slow, carefully offered thing. The dragons didn't know what to make of the creatures that lay beneath their feet either, but they had picked up on Vi's strategy, and they were in agreement: united, mechs and pilots stood a better chance at facing down the unknown than either did alone.

Vi pulled herself into the cockpit of that first dragon. From the corner of her eye, she saw the others following suit. The red shock of Rosalyn's hair flashed across Vi's field of vision, as the Davies girl hesitantly reached for the scales of the remaining dragon.

Vi didn't have time to see if Ros made it or not. A final crash smashed the back door to the storage facility open. It took Vi a moment to recognize what swarmed in on them. They weren't dragons. They weren't even the wyvern lookalikes that Sifu sometimes threw at her in simulations.

They were the same humanoid mechs that Vi had been equipped with in her first successful sentient simulation—the second-generation prototypes—but they didn't move like the outdated models that had put most humanoid mechs as a whole out of style for combat. These were fast, uncannily so, and attacked with limber, explosive movements that forced Vi immediately onto the defensive. Metal fists crashed hard into the body of the dragon, forcing her backward. Whoever was piloting these things knew how to command the space between combatants, and do it with devastating efficiency. Vi, still struggling to regain her dragon's footing under attack from her own opponent, barely made out the action around the rest of the room, but none of it looked good.

She'd nearly fought off those arms when a familiar voice rang out, loud and clear, over an intercom. "Stop. All of you."

Obediently, the humanoids paused as one. Vi's head fell back against the cockpit seat, as she swallowed gulps of air, riding out the adrenaline rush of the fight. One shaking finger tapped at the speaker function on the dragon's dashboard. "Headmaster Winchester?" she managed. "Please tell me that's you, and not another angry rogue arms dealer trying to ambush the Academy to enact revenge on the GAN."

"It's me." The Headmaster was speaking over the same sort of intercom that most training-simulation rooms were equipped with. It was as out of place as the humanoids.

Vi frowned. "How come you've got training speakers in a storage facility?"

The Headmaster chuckled. "Because, Miss Park, this isn't a storage facility. It's a training room, same as any other."

That couldn't be right. The hair on the back of Vi's neck prickled. For a moment, all she could think of was that shadowed tower where the Headmaster sat, torchlight glinting off her jeweled fingers as she toyed with Vi's destiny. "Is this a test?"

"Of sorts." The intercom clicked off. Footsteps approached through the wreckage of the storage facility—or what Vi had thought was a storage facility. The Headmaster's familiar blond head bobbed into view, rings still glittering over her fingers. "But really, that's an understatement." She raised those glittering hands outward, taking in the humanoids and dragons alike, paused where they were, midflight. "This is the next logical step in the GAN's Peacekeeping mission."

"Breaking and entering?" hazarded Amadeus over his own dragon's speakers.

"Oh, I was hoping you'd try." Winchester smiled. "You are the members of the probationary class, after all. It could have been someone else who'd cotton on to the idea, but I had bet on you. All of you, but especially you, Viola."

"I don't understand," said Vi. "Why would you hope for the exact kind of criminal behavior we've ostensibly spent our time at the Academy being punished for?"

"Why else? To correct it. For good, this time." Winchester gestured lazily at the humanoids, thumbing over one of the gems on her hand. Their visors popped up. Oxygen fled the room.

Vi recognized the face of every single pilot in those cockpits. Every last one of them was a missing Peacekeeper. Her gaze found Alex's last of all.

He stared back at her, impassive. He was alive, but no one was home.

"What's wrong with them?" Vi croaked. "What did you do?"

"Precisely what I just said." Winchester smiled up at her. It was a genuinely pleasant expression. "Correction. Your aunt Cat Park's innovations in sentient mech technology were brilliant—for the needs of the world a decade ago—but technology marches on, and so does the world. Her one mistake was creating mechs designed to partner with human pilots, when human fallibility on the battlefield has been the source of every major tragedy the GAN has ever suffered. The alternative is natural: allowing the mechs to assume full control of a pilot's brain. By replacing pilot-mech imprint bonds with fully automated AI, we will eliminate the element of human fallibility—human wrongdoing. Permanently. That, Viola, is how you build a real global utopia."

Vi sat back in the cockpit, shaking her head. "You're wrong. That's . . . a complete perversion of the bond between Peacekeepers and their dragons. The entire *point* of the bond is the human element. By eliminating it, all you're doing is creating mindless machinery."

"As if that's somehow worse?" demanded the Headmaster. "Where exactly has the human element gotten us? Unchecked arms dealing, soaring crime rates, tragedies in the field that fall hardest on those who try to prevent the inevitable. You should know this better than anyone, Viola, given your parents—"

"Please," hissed Viola. "Please, go ahead and bring my parents into this. I'd love the excuse."

"The excuse?" Winchester blinked those big blue eyes up at her. "To do what, exactly? Attack me? That's what you and your fellow probationary students would like to do, isn't it? You're not known particularly for doing the right thing, much less playing by the rules of polite society."

"And is this doing the right thing? Or playing by the rules?" Vi gestured expansively. "You're literally kidnapping your own Peacekeepers. You're the reason the GAN has been thrown into chaos for the better part of a year. That's, like, the actual definition of wrongdoing. You could be your own fucking dictionary entry."

Winchester's answering expression was full of condescending amusement. "You don't understand at all, do you? Why would you? All of you probies are children, reaping the consequences of acting on impulse and selfishness, unable to understand where you went wrong. This is something entirely different." The blue eyes were cold, bright with passionate intent. "Everything you just said— kidnapping, mind control—was done with purpose. At the end of the day, ridding the GAN Peacekeeper Corps of human error is going to build a better world. It's going to build better *people*."

"Cool motive, still an evil kidnapping mind-control scheme," Vi shot back. She cast a glance toward the dragons, her fingers clenched tight against her palms.

Winchester followed her gaze and barked a laugh. "Oh, I'm sorry. Were you under the impression that you—the delinquents of the school, the ones most in need of the corrective options offered by the full automation of second-generation sentients—that you were going to put a stop to this?" She jerked her head toward the dragons, visibly tickled. "Piloting those?"

Before Vi or any of the others could utter a response, the Headmaster snapped those jeweled fingers again, passing a thumb over one of the rings.

The consciousness inside the mech gave a shudder that rattled Vi's teeth. And then the dragon was moving without her control. She tried to open her mouth, to speak, and found that she couldn't. She couldn't move her limbs either. The mech overwhelmed her utterly with its needs, its programming: to obey, perfectly and mindlessly.

The ring, Vi thought hazily. The Headmaster must have inserted remote programming for those master controls through one of the gemstones decorating her fingers. A simple formula, really: control the dragon, control the pilot through the dragon's bond. Such a small, stupid thing. It was always small, stupid things that fucked you over.

"You see?" The Headmaster waved the dragon over—and Vi, helpless in the cockpit, followed, as the mech lay down beside her, the other dragons and probies following suit. "Isn't this better?"

Maybe this was where Vi was meant to end up all along. Stuck under the thumb of her own mistakes, controlled and reprogrammed until she'd stop making them. Hell, maybe this was where all the probies were meant to end up. Already the lowest of the low. No wonder it had been so natural for the Headmaster to bend them all to her will, just like she'd bent the missing Peacekeepers.

Except for one. A defiant flash of scales glittered at the edge of Vi's view screen, as a single dragon broke free, its head rearing up from the herd. Gears cranked as it struggled to resist the Headmaster's commands.

A painful twist of hope flared to life under Vi's ribcage.

Winchester sighed. "Oh, Rosalyn. I'd have thought better of you."

The mech's speakers cranked on. A labored inhale, followed by a sharp, violent exhale, echoed through the room. "Yeah, well," Rosalyn managed. "I thought better of you too, Headmaster. I guess we're both disappointments."

Plasma fire streamed forth from the dragon's mouth. Winchester's eyes widened as she dove. The blast missed by a hair. "Disappointment indeed." Winchester's fingers snapped again. "Initiate self-destruct protocol."

Rosalyn's dragon lurched forward, once, twice. Plasma fire bubbled along the edges of the chrome scales. "No!" cried Ros, fury and defiance laced through her voice. "No, no, not like this! No, I—" Her scream cut out, like a wireless holovid being snapped off by a phone shutdown, as her dragon shuddered back beneath the control of the Headmaster's compulsion.

Vi tried to cry out, tried to scream too, tried to say something, anything, but her throat refused to work. Her dragon was still in the Headmaster's thrall, still lulled into stony silence, immovable. An eerie, dissonant silence blanketed the room for seconds that felt like hours.

Then Rosalyn's dragon self-destructed, plasma fire enveloping the entire mech—and the girl inside.

Time paused. Vi was caught in that painting once more, one of the moments in her life that would seem, for those few seconds, permanently frozen. The flare of plasma fire, beautiful and terrible and irrevocable, where Rosalyn had existed just seconds before, snuffed out without even a wisp of smoke trailing behind. The other dragons, still trapped in place, along with their pilots, like stone statues offsetting that bright burst of flame.

Her encounters with Ros played like a reel across her mind's eye: A disdainful Rosalyn Davies, stiffly introducing herself to the probationary Park girl upon Vi's first arrival at the Academy. A warmer Ros, offering a clinical, conditional friendship. Ros, destroying the rogue dragon with a flick of her hand, as easily as Karolyn Winchester had destroyed Ros. Ros, attacking Vi in the seconds after their tournament match. Vi's body between Ros and a bleeding Nick, Vi's fist in Ros's face. Ros, half suspicion and half hope, following a pack of probies on an impossible gambit.

Following them to her death.

Vi didn't have time to process. She didn't have room in her heart. All she had going for her was the inch of space lingering between her mind and the awful, alien control of the dragon's consciousness over her actions. She found the bond, seized ahold of it.

"Come on, come on," she whispered, her mental voice desperate as she railed against the thing controlling her dragon. *I don't know your name, but we're two in one, mech and pilot. Two halves of a coin. We can't function correctly without each other. You can take over my mind, control my body, do as you will, but if you erase me completely, you'll only ever be alone.*

The dragon paused. An inch of space. Sometimes, all you needed was an inch of space. Stormbrewer was in her sight line now.

Painstakingly, Vi dove deep into the bond, searching for the thing that linked her dragon with the others. She opened herself to memory: that first meeting with Stormbrewer, the sight of the dragon's coils curled around the boy she'd eventually know as Nicholas Lee, the moment Vi's own link with Stormbrewer had finally clicked.

It wasn't much. But for just a moment, it was enough. Stormbrewer's reptilian head turned toward hers, barely, silver eyes flashing.

Two dragons wasn't much of a fleet, but it was the beginning of something. Slowly—so faint that Vi thought it was wishful thinking at first—the other dragons registered in the mind of her own mech, one by one.

And underneath the dragon minds were human ones.

Amadeus. Elsbeth. Tamara. Nick. Desperately, she cast her consciousness outward, hoping to seize some wisp of one of them. Vi searched for shared history, mining her mind for sense memory:

a glancing blow from Amadeus's fumbling fisticuffs as they sparred; the caress in Elsbeth's voice when she spoke of sentients; Tamara's knee knocking against hers as they sat side by side on one of the beds during study hall; Nick, the weight of him bearing her mech down to the ground the first time they met, so devastatingly real even in a sim; Nick's rattan sticks clattering against hers again and again; Nick, trying so hard to save those rogue dragons even as they rained plasma fire down on campus; Nick, the warmth of him at her side as he murmured, *Ros wasn't always like that.*

And then Nick was in her head. He stirred, struggling to meet her where she stood. What did she need? He wanted to know.

The rings, she thought frantically at him. *It's the rings on her fingers. If we take them out, we end the compulsion entirely. If we take them out, we're home free.*

Their dragons turned toward Winchester. Nick's moved first, loosing a stream of plasma fire.

It had been the wrong move. The bright flash of crackling flame sent a stir rippling through the Peacekeepers—or the creatures who had once been Peacekeepers. In the blink of an eye, they'd swarmed to protect the Headmaster, the powerful chrome bodies of their mechs forming a wall around her.

Nick moved to attack again.

"Don't!" cried Vi aloud.

He hesitated, just in time.

She reached through the mental link between their dragons' bonds: *We don't stand a chance against a pack of fully fledged Peacekeepers under Winchester's thrall. If we try to go through them to get to the rings, we'll get killed.*

His frustration blossomed down the length of the link between them. *What can be done instead, then?*

Vi bit her lip. *I have an idea. It's honestly not much easier, but there might be slightly less of a chance of getting us killed. By like a couple percentage points, if we're lucky.*

And what's that?

At that, Vi gave a silent, savage grin. Her lip, tender where she'd bitten into it too hard, smeared blood across her teeth. *A bit of good old-fashioned Nicholas Lee magic. Maybe you were raised a fighter, but your inclination—where you can—is to seek a bloodless solution. And in this case, it may be the only solution.*

Breathing deep, Vi steadied herself. If Ros could break free of the Headmaster's compulsion—just for a moment, one bright defiant moment, but break free all the same—then Vi could do this much. Fighting a wall of Peacekeepers was a losing proposition. But fighting wasn't the only way to win.

Exhaling, Vi reached for the humanoid mechs of the Peacekeepers before them. Alex first. She flooded her mind with music: Tchaikovsky, Debussy, every obnoxious classical composer he'd ever made her study for a recital. Food next: hot Mexican cocoa and homemade poutine, the recipe straight from Montreal; big fancy multicourse Korean meals with Aunt Anabel and Aunt Cat and the rest of the Parks. Memories of soft woolen sweaters, early mornings, and banter over the piano keys.

Come on, Alex. You know me. Don't lose yourself. Don't lose the man that you are. Not to this. Please, not to this.

Silence filled her ears.

And then, a single voice, crackling over mech speakers, careworn and familiar: "Vi? Viola?"

"Yes." Viola's throat worked, croaking out the word, stiff from being trapped under alien control. It hitched on a sob. "Yeah, Alex. It's me."

A ripple ran through the Peacekeeper mechs as they shifted in place, disoriented. Vi braced herself for an attack. None came. A beat passed, then another. One visor popped up, then another, as Peacekeepers blinked confusedly at one another. The compulsion had broken.

Behind the crumbling wall of her guards, the Headmaster's face had gone white with fury. "Well," she said. "I suppose there's nothing to be done about a failed experiment." Her hand rose, rings glittering. "Save disposal."

Before she could snap again, a blast of plasma fire caught her upside the head. Winchester went down like a stone.

Stormbrewer rose over the prone body. "Don't worry," Nick rasped. "I . . . it was a modified blast. Not the full thing. She's alive." Then, with some wonder, "She'll see justice."

◆

THE GREATEST TROUBLE WITH the headmaster of a major training institution for the world's foremost global peacekeeping organization turning out to be a megalomaniac moral absolutist with a thing for mind control was, ultimately, the logistical nightmare her arrest created.

The weeks after the revelation in that storage unit, chaos descended in the form of meetings and paperwork, as seemingly every member of the GAN Council scrambled to provide viral sound bites over who should replace terrible, disgraced Karolyn Winchester as headmaster at the Academy.

Multiple names were put forward: a handful of decorated Peacekeepers, retired or on the brink of retirement; a couple Council members who had served in the mech-piloting service arms of national militaries for their respective home governments. Even Aunt Anabel's name came up at one point, though she quickly demurred, citing other Council obligations.

Still, one name rose above all others. Prudence Wu—newly returned from the ranks of the missing Peacekeepers—was the universal favorite. It wasn't until Vi showed up at Sifu's office to debrief on the whole mess that she finally understood why.

For one thing, Sifu wasn't alone in there. As Vi entered the room, Sifu's three guests—Aunt Anabel, Aunt Cat, and Alex—all looked up at her.

Vi paused on the threshold. "Is there some kind of 'we're sorry our headmaster turned out to be a child-endangering criminal with a side of mad scientist' parent-teacher conference I wasn't told about?"

Aunt Cat snorted delicately, while Alex covered his smile with a hand.

Aunt Anabel heaved a sigh, rolling her eyes toward Sifu. "You see what I mean when I say she reminds me of you?"

"Please," demurred Sifu, sounding mildly horrified. "All I wanted to do was pass high school. I was never that thirsty for glory or adventure, thank you kindly."

Vi's gaze flitted carefully between all four of the adults in the room. "I'm missing something, aren't I?" Her attention paused on Sifu, her eyes narrowing at that unremarkable face. "Who are you, really?"

Sifu made a soft little sound of resignation, and reached for the underside of her own jaw. "I must say, Cat, your fancy spy gadgets have improved since we were kids, but this was not one of my favorites." Wincing, she peeled a sheer mask of shimmering, holographic material off her face.

The features that remained behind weren't inherently dissimilar from those the mask had provided. The small dark eyes and wide mouth, the snub nose and big round cheeks were all familiar. The only difference was that Vi now recognized exactly whom those features belonged to.

"You're Prudence Wu," she breathed.

Sifu—the first mech pilot ever to bond a sentient, and the reason the GAN Peacekeeper Corps existed—offered a rueful smile. "Got it in one." She waved the translucent mask dangling from her fingers back and forth. "I couldn't have the Headmaster—or really, anyone—cluing in to who the batty old probationers' teacher really was. Not while I was trying to keep an eye on Academy intrigues. So your aunt Cat here developed a mask that would . . . well, not alter my face, exactly. But make it less recognizable to the average viewer."

"So Nick wasn't the spy—you were." Vi frowned. "Did you know what Winchester was up to the whole time?"

"No." Sifu's reply was blunt as ever, which, oddly, made Vi trust it more. "I didn't. I had my suspicions, but no real evidence. Until you and the Lee boy stumbled right into it."

"And you didn't stop us." Vi didn't mean to sound accusatory, but the words tumbled out of her all the same.

Prudence Wu pinched the bridge of her nose. "Lord knows I tried to. What do you think all those private lessons where I paired you off in sparring were all about? You both had so many personal problems messing with your heads, I figured dealing with those alone would keep your busybody little noses out of broader political intrigue."

"Poor strategy there," drawled Aunt Cat. "Personal problems never stopped you or Anabel from making a mess of high-stakes politics when you were her age."

Wu shrugged a shoulder, looking rueful. "I suppose it runs in the family." Wu's attention, mask-free and focused on Vi, pinned her in place with an intensity that batty old Sifu had never quite mustered. "The question is whether you want to continue doing this, Viola."

Vi blinked. "Doing what?"

"Everything," said Wu. "Being a student at the Academy. Piloting. Wreaking inevitable havoc. Because you're good at it. I think you've proven that, and proven it amid a number of setbacks. But do you want to keep doing it?" Her gaze flittered toward Alex. In the space of a few seconds, something intangible passed between Wu and Alex, the weight of shared trauma, perhaps, or the joint survival of it. "Alex didn't."

"Which sparked some pretty legendary shouting matches, as I recall," said Alex. His voice was still a little hoarse—the aftereffects of Karolyn Winchester's mind-control thrall hadn't treated him gently, but the curl of his smile was wryly genuine.

Vi's attention flitted from Alex toward Wu. "You didn't want him to quit?"

"Au contraire," said Wu. "Once I understood why he wanted to, I encouraged it. Quitters get a bad rap, but sometimes it's the right move." Wistfulness flickered briefly across her features. "Even if it did mean losing my copilot."

"You've had other copilots," said Alex without heat. "Good ones, even."

Wu chuckled. "Sure. But none of them have ever quite replaced you, bougie boy."

Vi coughed. "So why the shouting, if your great dragon-piloting breakup was so amicable?"

"Because the GAN brass didn't want to let Alex retire in peace, so Pru-Wu here decided the appropriate response was to ambush multiple council meetings, uninvited, and yell at the top of her lungs at everyone present," said Aunt Anabel dryly.

Wu shrugged, utterly unfazed, every inch the give-no-fucks Sifu of the Academy's probationary class. "It worked, didn't it?"

"Only because the old curmudgeons on the Council got tired of attempting to have you arrested," Alex pointed out.

Wu smirked at him. "You're welcome." For a moment, grinning at each other like that, Alex and Wu looked like the pair of teenagers they'd once been. Watching them now, it was hard to believe they'd been apart for nearly a decade: the greatest hero of the Alliance and the humble music teacher. What must they have been like, in their copiloting days? What scars had they borne together, and how many had persisted through the long years of absence between them?

Wu's hand strayed toward Alex's, as if she intended to twine her fingers through his, then stilled. Loudly, she cleared her throat, focus snapping back toward Vi. "Anyway, the point of all this is: sometimes, quitting is the right call. Sometimes, quitting is how you save your own life. And I want you to know, Viola, that it's okay. It's okay to walk away from ambition, if you want to. It's okay to save yourself, while letting someone else save the world." She held Vi's gaze. "But if you want to keep doing it," she continued, "that's a choice that only you are fit to make. Only you have the right to decide."

Vi swallowed, looking around the room. Aunt Cat, the cybernetic eye bright in her face as she stood to the side, observant as always. Alex, hands returned to his trouser pockets, his smile small but encouraging. And finally, Aunt Anabel, who strode forward to take Vi's hand, and squeeze it tight.

Vi squeezed back, so hard she thought she might break both their hands. "So, uh." She cleared her throat. "I guess the rest of the conscription tournament is canceled, huh?"

Wu barked a laugh. "I'll say. With the missing Peacekeepers recovered and sleeping off the Headmaster's bout of mind control experimentation, the GAN has essentially negated the need to recruit literal children out of the Academy."

"Oh." Why did that weirdly deflate Vi? She should have been relieved. The tournament matches had been an ever-present thorn in her side from the moment she struck that cursed deal with Karolyn Winchester to fight Nick. Winchester, who had only offered Vi that deal at all because she thought probies might make good little mind-controlled soldiers one day, and wanted to bring out their most violent attributes to use for the Headmaster's disposal. The whole game meant nothing when Vi had only ever really been a pawn.

Yet still, a little part of Vi craved another match, another fight, another shot at proving herself. The tournament had woken something in her blood that remained more restless than ever. She wasn't sure she'd ever put it back to bed. "Can I have a few days to decide?" she asked at last.

Aunt Anabel nodded and didn't let go of Vi's hand. "For once? You can have as much time as you need."

♦

VI FOUND NICK ON the same knoll where he'd once talked to her about Rosalyn and the girl she used to be, the fading sunlight dappling across his hair. Rosalyn, who'd died in the cockpit of a dragon after all. Maybe she'd had more Peacekeeper in her than anyone had thought.

"I'm not staying," Nick told her as she wedged herself on the hillside next to him.

"You could, you know," said Vi. "There's . . . things will be different, without the Headmaster here. You won't be beholden to keeping her secrets, or fighting her battles. You could make a place for yourself here."

He shook his head. "Maybe I wouldn't have to fight her battles. But I'd still have to fight. Logically, there's nothing wrong with that. I know there is a time and place for violence. But not at my hands." He looked down at his fingers. Long, pale, elegantly formed. Vi had seen them swinging sticks or wielding the controls of a battle mech so often, she'd rarely ever thought of them as anything but weapons. Now they simply lay in his lap, finally at rest. "I've never known what it's like to be allowed . . . not to fight. Not to beat someone bloody just to preserve your own survival. And now that I do?" He offered a sideways little smile. "It's a little addictive. I won't hurt anyone anymore. Not if I have a choice about it. Which means that when it really comes down to it, there's no place for me in the cockpit of a battle mech, or at the helm of a fighting force. Not even on behalf of the Alliance."

"God, isn't that just irony?" Vi raised a hand of her own, shielding her gaze against the last rays of the sun. "In some ways, you'd make the best Peacekeeper of us all. It's even in the name. Peace. Keeper. And you're a pacifist at heart if ever I knew one."

He laughed. "Maybe so. But the world will never know."

The reality of that sobered Vi. "Where will you go instead?" she asked softly.

He shrugged. "I don't know. Somewhere. Anywhere. Someplace where they need folks who understand sentients. Training camps in Australia, maybe, or even back in the North American Barricade cities."

Her shoulder bumped against his. A sore, tender spot had bloomed somewhere inside her. She blinked back an inexplicable hot prickle behind her eyes and nose. "How does freedom feel?"

Nick turned his head toward hers at last. "Terrifying, if I'm honest. But isn't everything when you've never experienced it before?"

She blinked faster. "I was terrified of the Academy before I came here. Of being a probie. And then I met you, and . . . well, I remained terrified, actually, but watching you, seeing how you seemed to survive everything, it made me think that maybe I could too."

He rested his forehead rested against hers, his eyes shut. "You could come with me, you know. You've always had a choice. You don't have to stay here either."

That ache inside of Vi twinged. It filled the part of her that wanted to change the decision she'd already made. The part of her that wanted to say yes. The part of her that wanted to take his hand, and fly away, and never look back.

Instead, Vi's palm found the side of Nick's face. "I think I do, actually. Have to stay."

He didn't seem surprised, the side of his mouth curling upward. "The Peacekeepers. You still believe in them."

"I think I believe in *me*," said Vi. She thought of her family. She thought of Alex, and the other probies, and even Nick—perhaps Nick most of all—and how badly she'd wanted to keep them all safe. How, in the moments that she bonded Stormbrewer, or went tearing off into the Headmaster's vault, or stepped between Nick and danger, she thought maybe she understood her parents a little better. "People die, and disappoint, and fuck up, over and over and over again." Vi swallowed. "But I think I believe that if I stay here, and fight like hell, maybe I can protect a little piece of what's good in our world. And for me, I think . . . no, I *know* that's enough."

Nick swallowed, Adam's apple bobbing. "Then I'm glad," he said softly. "For you. And for all those little pieces of good in the world that cross your path. I hope they know how lucky they are." His gaze flitted away for a moment, then back to hers with an intensity that nearly stopped her heart. "Will you—"

"Can I—" she began at the same time.

They both stopped. Vi pulled back a little. "Wherever you go," she said at last, "make sure it's someplace dragons can fly to."

They both knew what that meant. What she was really telling him.

Nick's fingers closed around hers. Nicholas Lee, the boy who'd always look like a candle in the dark, pressed her hands to his lips and promised, "There will never be a place we can't."

ACKNOWLEDGMENTS

I had been warned that my sophomore novel would be one of the hardest pieces of writing I'd ever tackle, and boy, *Renegade Flight* did not disappoint in this respect! Throw in a pandemic, a new day job, and the seemingly endless parade of various pseudo-apocalyptic woes both personal and public that generally accompanied everyone's year 2020, and I had myself an uphill climb that I absolutely could not have completed without a phenomenal support network.

First of all, thank you to my incredible publishing team: my agent, Thao Le, for her steady guidance and hand-holding through many a caffeine-fueled race toward deadline, and my editor, Julie Rosenberg, whose brilliance is matched only by her astonishing levels of patience and empathy for her writers. Julie, you took a book whose challenges at one time felt insurmountable, and turned it into work that I am so genuinely proud of—I don't know what bookish witchcraft you employed to make it happen, but I am eternally grateful. I'm also indebted, as ever, to the rest of this remarkable team: my copyeditor, Jackie Dever, whose tweaks made all the difference in the finished text; my publicist, Lizzie Goodell; managing editor Jayne Ziemba; production editors Abigail Powers and Marinda Valenti; proofreader Kate Frentzel; my lovely cover art illustrator, Mike Heath; and of course Alex Sanchez, Casey McIntyre, Kim Ryan, and Jessica Jenkins. To all of you: the things you do for authors and readers alike are truly magical.

To Grace Li, Em Liu, and Gina Chen: thank you for helping me see past my own self-doubt and anxiety long enough to start falling quietly, tentatively back in love with my own work. I could not ask for more thoughtful first readers, or more generous cheerleaders.

Amanda Quain, Anna Bright, and the rest of the One More Page Books team: thank you for doing such an amazing job with my *Rebelwing* book launch—it was the first moment that I remember being really excited about diving back into this wild world of mechanical dragons, political intrigue, and teen angst!

Professor Bethany Schneider of Bryn Mawr College, who in many ways put me on the path to publication in the first place: thank you for being the first person in my life who showed me it was possible. *Renegade Flight* is the conclusion of a debut duology whose scope I'd never have dared tackle without your early encouragement and mentorship when I was your student. Thank you for teaching me to read thoughtfully and write passionately when I was eighteen; thank you for teaching me to chase my dreams with both discipline and heart when I was twenty-one and entering the wild postgraduate world of adulthood; and thank you, perhaps most importantly, for teaching me bravery.

Lisbeth Redfield: you were the first honest-to-goodness publishing-industry professional who really took the time to answer my questions and coach me through my early, fumbling attempts at starting a writing career. Your generosity of spirit, thoughtful guidance, and gentle wisdom set the bar for everyone else I've met in the book world. Thank you for answering every panicked two-a.m. text from some weird, foreign time zone, every hand-wringing question about penning queries and choosing agents. *Rebelwing* and *Renegade Flight* both owe so much to you.

To my wise and patient friends outside of the immediate publishing community: thank you, also, for your staunch belief in me as I waged my wars of attrition with edits and rewrites and more edits and more rewrites still. I owe a particular debt of gratitude to Raphael Baseman and Morgan Tornetta, upon whose living-room floor I wrote, snacked, drank copious amounts of alcohol, wrote some more, possibly cried a little, and yes, continued writing. Thank you so much for your hospitality during all those sweatpant-night weekends, and congratulations on the dubious honor of your old apartment being the literal birthplace of my very first draft of *Renegade Flight*!

To Asher Willner: thank you for being such a generous teacher, stalwart source of support, and general delight to spend time with. Thank you for getting me out of my studio when I needed to be out of my head, and supplying me with a steady diet of encouragement and late-night snacks when I needed to hunker down and write. You and the rest of the wonderful Fighters Garage community (special shoutout to Becca Hurd and Raven!) have been invaluable to both my mental and physical health. I hope the fight scenes I pen don't embarrass you too badly!

And speaking of physical health: special thanks to Kavon Atabaki and Joshua Davis of Functional Fitness VA. We so often think of writing as a solely intellectual pursuit, but training body alongside brain—particularly in the past year—has been integral to helping me push through the creative challenges of a second contracted novel.

Thank you for equipping me with the tools to keep myself healthy, happy, and safe; it's a lifelong gift that I'll treasure.

Finally, to my parents: so much of both *Rebelwing* and *Renegade Flight* have fundamentally been stories about family, and I am daily astounded by how fortunate I am to be part of yours. Thank you for being mine, always and forever.